D0201825

HOME IS WHERE THE HEART IS

CALGARY PUBLIC LIBRARY

JUN - 2018

HOME IS WHERE THE HEART IS

THE DAKOTA SERIES • BOOK 3

LINDA BYLER

New York, New York

The characters and events in this book are the creation of the author, and any resemblance to actual persons or events is coincidental.

HOME IS WHERE THE HEART IS

Copyright © 2018 by Linda Byler

All rights reserved. No part of this book may be reproduced in any manner without the express written consent of the publisher, except in the case of brief excerpts in critical reviews or articles. All inquiries should be addressed to Good Books, 307 West 36th Street, 11th Floor, New York, NY 10018.

Good Books books may be purchased in bulk at special discounts for sales promotion, corporate gifts, fund-raising, or educational purposes. Special editions can also be created to specifications. For details, contact the Special Sales Department, Good Books, 307 West 36th Street, 11th Floor, New York, NY 10018 or info@skyhorsepublishing.com.

Good Books is an imprint of Skyhorse Publishing, Inc.®, a Delaware corporation.

Visit our website at www.goodbooks.com.

10 9 8 7 6 5 4 3 2 1

Library of Congress Cataloging-in-Publication Data is available on file.

ISBN: 978-1-68099-354-7
eBook ISBN: 978-1-68099-365-3

Cover design by Jenny Zemanek

Printed in the United States of America

TABLE OF
CONTENTS

CHAPTER 1

SPRING ARRIVED ON THE NORTH DAKOTA PLAINS LIKE A FLIRTATIOUS young girl that whispered promises of warmth and sunshine, melting icicles and turning snowdrifts into untrustworthy mounts of sodden slush.

The long drought had come to an end thanks to the melting snow and ice that replenished the arid soil, turning the prairie into a quagmire of slick brown mud and crumpled yellow grass.

Hannah stepped off the porch, a woven basket full of wet clothes balanced on one hip and an apron containing wooden clothes pegs tied around her narrow waist. A married woman now, she still resembled the same Hannah Detweiler she'd always been.

Dark-haired, with dark eyes like wet coal, defiant, missing nothing, she strode to the wash line like a soldier, threw down the basket, and proceeded to hang clothes on the line in quick, furtive movements.

Hurrying back to the house, she looked neither right nor left, her mind churning on the best way to accomplish all that needed to be done when spring actually arrived.

The two-year drought had depleted her herd of cows to five head. Jerry said he'd had money put by when they were married in the fall of the year, but lately he'd given no indication of a stash of money or a checkbook. Her mother and siblings had returned to the home of their birth, with all the rest of the Amish folks who'd been bitten by the pioneer spirit but chickened out when it stopped raining. Soft Lancaster County stock that had everything handed to them by their fathers, and their fathers before them.

What did they expect in North Dakota?

Her mother wrote lengthy accounts of their lives back in Pennsylvania. Manasses (Manny) had begun courting Ike Lapp's adopted daughter, Marybelle, who was working as a hired hand for Sammy Stoltzfus, Rufus's Sammy. She lived with her aging father and two brothers on the homestead. Mary and Eli went to school in Leacock Township. Hannah read every letter with interest, but always threw them down as soon as she was done, as if she couldn't bear to think too much about the contents.

Deserters. That's what they were. It still stung about Manny. She never thought he'd leave the ranch. After all they'd been through, he followed his mother back East like the obedient puppy he was.

Well, she had Jerry, who'd married her, which was something. She had told him there would be no love involved. She wanted to stay on the ranch and his money was the only way they could. It was an arrangement that worked well, so far. Jerry was kind, talkative, but kept his distance. Like brother and sister, they lived together in the sprawling ranch house made of lumber that had been shipped from the East, already weathered gray, with a porch along the front, and a barn with a low-pitched roof and a barnyard. The windmill churned about three hundred yards behind the barn. There were five head of Black Angus cattle, four of Jerry's horses, and a few good mousers, wild as cougars, that slunk around the perimeter of the barn.

Beyond, there was only the vast immensity of the North Dakota plains, stretching in all four directions to a level horizon, limp brown grass, dead from the long drought, huddled in clumps of leftover dirty snow.

Hannah loved the land with an unexplainable passion. The emptiness and solitude suited her reclusive nature. She could breathe, expand, fill her lungs with the air no one else breathed, a luxury that was priceless.

People were like clinging vines, parasitic growths that wound their way around your well-being until the life was choked out of you. Most people annoyed Hannah. Especially men. Loud, sure of their own decisions, acting so superior to women, she couldn't stand any of them. Well, maybe Hod Jenkins. He knew more about this prairie, the weather, cattle, everything, than anyone she'd known.

If her mother had not been so devoted to her Amish heritage, she could have married Hod after Abigail died.

Hod loved the land, same as Hannah. She looked out across the wet prairie as she hung up the second basket of clothes, watching for Jerry. He'd ridden to the Jenkinses' without saying why, so she supposed he'd be back before dinner.

That was another thing she hadn't bargained for—marrying Jerry. She cooked three meals a day, but she hated it. Told him so, too. He'd grin good-naturedly, get down the cast-iron skillet, fry a few pieces of beef, and eat it with bread she had baked.

The bread was coarse and hard as a rock. She sawed at it with the bread knife, served it, and never said a word, so Jerry didn't either. The poor man tried to sop up the lumpy ground beef gravy to soften it, but it acted like a metal spoon and shoved all the gravy around on his plate. His mouth twitched, Hannah had seen it, his desperation to keep from laughing. She'd yanked her plate off the table, ran the dishwater, and hid her flaming face. She couldn't help if she couldn't bake a decent loaf of bread. Besides, he'd better count his lucky stars that she baked any-thing at all, with provisions so meager and times so hard.

Jerry didn't say much, ever. There were a thousand questions she wanted to ask him, but would never risk throwing them out into the air heavy with tension. Especially her insatiable wondering about this new winter wheat everyone was talking about.

What if they could raise a profitable crop along with the cows? Acres and acres of soft winter wheat that was sown in the fall, sprouted sturdily in spring, soaking up the cold rains and flourishing in the summer sun.

Other than Hod Jenkins, Jerry was the only person Hannah felt the slightest twinge of respect for. He was tall, wide in the shoulders, his long, dark hair often hiding his expression. A solid jaw, a wide mouth, and eyes as black as her own.

Jerry had loved her, pursued her, even kissed her at every opportune moment a few years ago when he thought he had a chance with her. Which he didn't. Still didn't, in spite of being married to her. She'd made that very clear. Only for his money, the last chance to get this homestead up and running. If they failed now, she saw no reason to keep trying.

She swept the wide, varnished boards of the living room floor, shook a few rag rugs out the door, then took up a soft cloth and began to dust the tops of the furniture.

The playful breezes set a loose board to whirring at the corner of the house, so she made a mental note to tell Jerry. Or, better yet, she'd fix it herself. She finished her cleaning, went to the barn to find the wooden stepladder and a hammer, rooted around on the tool bench until she found a few nails, and carried it all back to the house in quick strides.

She was settling the stepladder, trying to find a level spot so she could climb up to the eaves and fasten the loose board, when she felt hoofbeats vibrating the ground beneath her feet.

A rider appeared, bent low over his plunging horse, galloping in a headlong dash and throwing mud and dead grass, the white lather coating the wet coat of the winded animal.

Hannah stood rooted to the ground, not a muscle moving, as she watched the horse and its rider approach.

Closer he came. She gripped the handle of her hammer. Her breath quickened. A small man, he was wearing a flat-crowned, greasy hat, the brim flapping drunkenly. Soiled clothing, a coat that flapped open, revealing a torn shirt. When the horse slid to a stop, she knew who it was before she actually saw the sizzle of desperation in his eyes.

Lemuel Short! Old, wizened, hardened by another stint in prison, coming back to haunt her. The horse hung his head, his sides heaving, drops of sweat and flecks of foam dropping to the mud below.

"Hide me," Lemuel rasped. "They're after me!"

Hannah gripped her hammer and tossed her head. "I'm not hiding you. You want me to get in trouble with the law, same as you?"

Lemuel Short, small, tough, and wiry. He had terrorized the whole family after they'd shown him all that dumb kindness, nursing him back to health with the Scripture about loving your enemy seared into their consciences.

She looked up into the cold metal barrel of a pistol held by a thin claw that shook violently. Hannah didn't think. Propelled by a fierce disdain for this desperate little liar, she stepped up as fast as midsummer lightning, swung her hammer, and knocked the revolver out of his hand.

It clattered to the ground. Hannah swung the hammer again, hitting the haunches of the sweating horse, frightening him into a swift gallop, Lemuel hanging on to the saddle horn as he fought to insert his feet into the stirrups.

Hannah heard the receding hoofbeats, the unintelligible screams of the escaped prisoner, shrugged, and bent to retrieve the revolver, turning it over and over, noticing its silver gleam, the deadly shape of it. Stolen, too, no doubt, same as the horse.

Well, it might come in handy, so she'd hang on to it. She turned to finish the job of nailing down the loose board, unshaken, her hands steady.

She wasn't afraid of him. Never had been. The sheriff would find him again and stick him back in jail, same as he always had.

She whistled low under her breath as she watched Jerry's arrival, forgetting about the silver revolver lying in the grass until he rode up to the house and stopped his horse, a question in his eyes.

"What?" Hannah asked.

"What yourself. What are you doing up on that stepladder?"

"What does it look like? Fixing a loose board."

"And what is this?" Jerry dismounted in one graceful, fluid movement, bending to lift the pistol in one hand and giving a low whistle. He looked up at Hannah. "I guess this fell from the sky?"

"Not exactly. Remember Lemuel Short?"

Jerry nodded, his heavy eyebrows drawn down.

"He rode in on a lathered horse and asked me to hide him. I told him I wasn't going to do it. He aimed that thing at me, and I knocked it out of his hand with my hammer." She jutted her jaw in the direction of the gun, shrugged her shoulders, and climbed down the stepladder, cool and unruffled.

Jerry watched her fold the hinges of the ladder, his mouth dropping open in amazement. Finally he said, "I hope you're aware of how easily you could have been killed."

Hannah gave her legendary snort. "He's like a harmless little rat. He's afraid of his own shadow. He thinks he can go around scaring people. Puh!"

Jerry looked at Hannah with an undetermined expression, then turned to go into the house. Over his shoulder he said he was hungry. Which meant she was expected to follow him and come up with a tasty dish in less than half an hour.

Instant rebellion! What was it about men, looking at a clock three times a day and thinking about their empty stomachs and a handy wife to cook them a delicious meal? She'd never get used to it. Never. What she felt like doing was telling him to get his own dinner. He knew how to fry mush, or a few strips of beef.

She walked stiffly into the house and began slamming cast-iron pans about on the cook stove top, harder than necessary so Jerry would know she was not pleased with him.

Jerry threw himself on a wooden chair on the porch, removed his straw hat, and raked his hands through his long, dark hair. He listened to the banging in the kitchen, smiled ruefully, and then looked out across the prairie.

What he wanted to do was go to the kitchen, tell her to go ahead and finish whatever she'd been doing outside, and he'd prepare dinner. But after living with her for a winter, he knew this was no ordinary girl who could be won with love and kindness.

He had married a hornet's nest of self-will, single-minded ambition bordering on obsession, the success of the ranch occupying most of her thoughts. Without fear, she was bold, having no respect for men, needing no lady friends as far as he could tell. She was the biggest challenge he had ever undertaken.

He had loved her for years. Ever since the day she drove that open buggy into the forebay of his barn in Lancaster County, soaking wet and irritable as the proverbial wet hen. Did he love her still?

His gaze was soft, filled with a nameless emotion, as he pondered their six months of cohabitation. They lived together but certainly not in peace and harmony. He had never held her hand or slipped an arm about her waist. He'd promised to keep his distance. Their marriage was only one of convenience. She needed his money to keep the ranch going.

What would the Amish in Lancaster County think if they knew? This was certainly not what he had been taught. Or she. Defeat rose its hideous visage and swept through him in a cold chill. It was just much harder than he had imagined. She did everything she could possibly think of to irritate him, to drive him to the edge of patience and understanding. And he had never figured out why.

He was ready to admit that God alone could change her temperament, change the way she looked at the world through her dark, angry eyes. He had always thought that love never failed, love opened doors, broke down barriers, acquired the seemingly impossible.

He wasn't so sure anymore.

Each day was a genuine battle. She needed good old-fashioned discipline but woe to the person who would deliver it. He grinned, listened to the pans banging and the dishes clattering. He'd continue praying, believing there was a reason he had always loved her, and see what God had in store for them both.

Jerry sat down at the table, waiting until she joined him, then bowed his head in silent prayer before lifting his fork to shove the fried meat to the side, helping himself to some green mush that vaguely resembled beans. Applesauce on the side, or was it some kind of preserve?

Grease and blood pooled around the meat. Underdone again. Grimly he cut it with his knife, lifted a forkful to his mouth, and chewed, ignoring the taste of raw meat and blood. Hannah ate very little, choosing the unnamed vegetable and bread and molasses. So Jerry helped himself to another piece of meat, which seemed to be a bit better than the first.

She wanted to ask him what he'd learned at the Jenkinses' but figured if he wanted her to know, he'd tell her.

He finished his food, leaned back in his chair, and told her about Hod and his two boys riding out on the prairie for a cattle check. Mild winter, less snow, but the wolves got too many of the calves. They figured at least ten or twelve of them.

Hannah nodded, her eyes averted as she toyed with her fork. "It's always been that way," she said dryly.

"Why wouldn't we try to raise something else, like sheep or goats or simply forget cattle and raise horses?" Jerry asked.

Hannah considered his question and for once came up empty. She shrugged. Jerry pushed back his plate, tilted his chair on two legs, his shoulders wide, hands in his pockets, his too-long hair falling into his eyes. Hannah looked away.

"I mean, surely there is something we could do to make a living, to keep the ranch going until it's ours, that isn't quite as dependent on the weather, which seems to be the biggest problem so far."

"Smart man," Hannah answered, a touch of mockery in her voice. Jerry chose to ignore the bait for an argument.

"There's this new strain of wheat. Winter wheat. Sow it in the fall, reap it in early summer before the drought hits. Hod talked about it. But you need to till acres and acres and with this soil . . . I don't know. I can only see reasonable profits with gas-powered tractors. Unless we find a tough breed of horses. Belgians? Mules? What do you think?"

A shadow crossed Hannah's face, a slice of dark remembering . . . the dying horse, the heat, the fanatic belief of her father. She clenched her jaw, her eyes hard and glistening. "What makes you think we couldn't use a tractor?" she asked.

"Hannah, we're of the Amish faith, and our bishops don't approve of modern machinery. So, if we're going to consider this winter wheat, I would suggest mules. They're tough and they're easy to keep. So, why not?"

"I won't allow any animal, horse or mule, to plow this

prairie," she said, with so much force that she left her chair in one quick motion. Jerry raised his eyebrows and leaned forward until the front legs of the wooden chair banged against the oak floor.

"I didn't say that was a definite plan."

"Well, it's not."

"Why?"

Hannah turned to face him, her hands on her hips. "You weren't here to see my father kill Dan in the plow. He ran that horse until he fell over. Dan's breathing, the foam and sweat, the way the sun beat down . . ." Her voice trailed off. She turned to grip the edge of the sink and gazed across the brown landscape.

Jerry could tell how agitated she was by the rise and fall of her shoulders. He wanted to go to her, place his hands on her shoulders, and comfort her as best he could. But he didn't have the courage, so he stayed put.

She whirled around. "Of course, what would you know about that? You were safely at home in Lancaster County, shoeing horses and counting money, pitying those half-crazy Mose Detweilers that lit out for North Dakota after they lost everything!"

"That's harsh, Hannah."

"No, it isn't. You can't tell me you didn't hear about my destitute, misguided family. Everybody did. Our reputation was mud. Mud!" she shouted.

Jerry watched her, wondering where all this was coming from.

"You know you remember."

"I'm not going to defend myself about what your family did or didn't do. Of course, I remember hearing about you, but I certainly didn't know you, or worry about it."

"You probably laughed with all your buddies about those pathetic people who had no clue what they were doing."

There was no right or wrong answer to her senseless accusation, so Jerry got up, reached to the wall hook for his straw hat, and strode out the door to the barn. He forked loose hay into a neater pile, swept the forebay, and pondered Hannah's outburst.

Was her past so painful, the shame like a hidden disease? Who could tell what a headstrong daughter had suffered with the public shaming and all? Hadn't he heard something about a homemade distillery and whiskey?

Perhaps Hannah wasn't so hard to figure out after all. People were not all cut from the same pattern, that was sure. Some could live through a traumatic childhood and come out unscathed, turning into loving, normal adults, while others wallowed in thorny nostalgia that served to hurt only themselves. Was her bitterness a product of her past?

He decided to buy mules and asked Hannah to accompany him to a ranch ten miles southeast of Dorchester, close to a small town called Bison.

Hannah was cleaning, her apron front black with the cleaner she was using on the stove top. She kept rubbing vigorously without looking at him.

"Are you riding?"

"No, it's too far. Hod Jenkins is taking us in the truck."

"Us?"

"Oh, come on Hannah. You want to see the mule farm. This guy has other horses, too."

"I told you, I won't stand for farming with horses."

"Well, just a couple of mules for making hay."

She squinted her eyes and looked at him like a stray dog that hadn't decided whether he'd be friendly or take off running.

"I'm not dumb."

"I know."

"Well, then."

"Come on. Change your clothes. Wear a covering. You look extra pretty with a white covering on your dark hair. Better than that men's handkerchief you insist on wearing."

"What do you care?"

"You're my wife."

She almost told him she wasn't his wife, but she was, so there was nothing to say. Plus, she had to admit to herself that she wanted to see the mule farm. She ducked into her bedroom and closed the door firmly behind her.

He looked at the closed door, a small smile playing around his mouth. When she emerged, the snowy white covering was pinned to her sleek, black hair. The deep purple of her dress brought out the heightened color of her cheeks, her large, dark eyes snapping with anticipation.

She took his breath away, so he turned, kicked off his boots, and went to the sink to wash his hands and face. He was drying his face on the roller towel when he caught a glimpse of her watching him with an inscrutable expression, one that baffled him and tormented him for days. What was she thinking? Could he ever win her love?

She'd made it clear from the beginning that this was not a union based on love, and he had agreed, with a young man's audacity that he was invincible. Everything was possible, wasn't it?

In the spring, a young man's fancy turns to thoughts of love. Perhaps that was the ache in his chest, the concealed sadness and lack of hope. He'd thought he could do this, but after the long winter was over, the soft breezes everywhere, she was not responding to his kindness and seemed farther away than ever, an iceberg drifting away in dark, frigid waters, abandoning him.

Well, she was wearing her covering, so that was something.

The pickup truck rattled up to the ranch house, its blue color faded to gray, the fenders laced with rust, dust clinging to everything, mud splatters and bits of yellow grass on top of all the rust. Wooden racks sagged at various angles, flopping and waving precariously, while empty gasoline cans and pieces of rope and barbed wire, paper bags, and feed sacks puddled into corners or slid around to each side, depending on the direction the truck was headed.

Hod's window was down, a greasy coat sleeve slung across the door, his once-white Stetson aged into varying shades of brown, gray, and yellow, his weathered face like fissures in old canyon rock.

His eyes lit up at the sight of them, his tobacco-stained teeth appearing as his face crinkled into a smile like a discarded paper bag. "Ain't you a sight for old eyes there, Hannah? Better looking 'n that husband o' yourn."

Jerry grinned and bumped Hod's arm with his fist. This impressed Hannah more than anything. Jerry's easy relationship with Hod and his boys, Hank and Ken. Clay, the oldest, had married Jennifer, a girl from town who, in Hannah's opinion, wasn't worthy of him. Hannah had almost been persuaded to be his girl and leave her family and the Amish way of life. She wasn't exactly sure what had held her back, other than her mother's prayers, she supposed.

Jerry held the door for her, and she scrambled inside, scooting over beside Hod to allow room for him. She hadn't realized a truck was so narrow. She had to sit sideways to allow Hod to shift gears with that odd-looking stick with a porcelain knob at the end, which meant she was jammed up against Jerry with no room for her feet.

"May as well hold 'er on yer lap, Jerry. This Ford ain't new. Think they're makin' the 1947 models wider, I heard."

"We're fine," Jerry said, smiling at Hannah, who was looking straight ahead with the high clear color in her cheeks that meant she wasn't fine at all.

Hod looked over at her. "Loosen up, honey. My word, we ain't goin' to yer ma's funeral."

Hannah gave him a tight smile, and he shrugged his bony

shoulders and talked nonstop to Jerry. Never could tell about Hannah, pickin' her moods. Worse than an ornery old cow.

Hannah rode along, alternately jostling against Jerry, or trying to slide away from him, which meant she'd interfere with Hod's driving. She was acutely aware of Jerry's nearness, the length of him, the hard strength beneath the sleeve of his denim coat. He smelled of hay and horses and wood shavings and toothpaste.

He'd smelled of mint toothpaste once, long ago, when he kissed her. If he dared to put his arm around her, she'd bite him!

CHAPTER 2

THE TRUCK SLIPPED AND SLID THROUGH RUTS FULL OF MUDDY SLUSH. All around them the prairie lay flat, waiting to be awakened at the first kiss of the sun. Gray skies were woven with patches of white and blue, scudding along as if threatening the land with another blast of winter's fury.

Hannah half-listened to Hod and Jerry's conversation, her eyes roving over every corner of the Ford's windows, taking in the barbed wire and rotting old posts of a derelict ranch, the well-kept buildings of another. But mostly she searched the horizon for cattle, observing the size of herds, their well-being, and which ranchers raised wheat or corn, or simply cut the prairie grass and used it to feed their livestock.

It was good hay, nutritious, that native shortgrass called buffalo grass. Sedges and switch grass, the never-ending, God-given supply that kept all the overhead costs of these ranches to a minimum.

She jabbed her elbow into Jerry's arm, pointing to the right, where a distant herd of antelope streamed over a rise like brown and white liquid, as smooth as the wind. Those antelope sightings filled Hannah's soul the way she imagined Bible reading and prayer filled her mother's.

The untamed freedom of wild creatures—their lack of restrictions and rules and authority—thrilled her innermost being. It was spiritual for her, raising a belief in the God of nature, of a creation that was so huge and vast and awesome, it could only produce a deep humility.

The way the antelope coexisted with wolves and coyotes, prairie dogs and foxes—it was all an endless circle of life. One Hannah understood and wanted to belong to as she raised cattle and cut grass for a winter's supply of hay. She would be strong enough to withstand anything nature threw at her.

Living on the plains was an endless challenge. The future was unpredictable. Seasons came and went, with their surprises and dangers, leaving all the ranchers and farmers scrambling to make ends meet, to face the drought and snow storms and wind and fire, the wolves and lawless men, and to rise above the despair.

Hannah glanced quickly at Jerry's profile and wondered if he felt what she experienced when she sighted the antelope. Nothing in his eyes or the set of his jaw gave away his feelings, so she looked steadily ahead as the truck ground its way through water-filled ruts and potholes.

It would be exciting to see what actually occurred after a drought, as far as the return of vegetation went. Would the wildflowers reseed themselves? Hannah thought of her mother squeezing tomato seeds onto a rag, leaving them to dry for planting in the spring. Leaving pole beans and chili beans to dry, the seeds rattling in the leathery pods like dead bones. But how long could soil be dried out before roots and seeds died? She wanted to ask Hod, but decided to listen instead.

"Yeah, this dry spell's been a doozy. Guess you heard how many people from town's moving to Illinois?"

Hannah shook her head. Jerry said no, he hadn't heard.

"Guess a buncha folks is raisin' turkeys. Cheap land. Rains there, mostly. Sounds as if some folks is thinkin' turkeys is good profit. Ralph went, you know, Ralph at the feed mill. His wife's been bellyachin' as long as I've knowed her to git him to move off these plains. Good ol' Ralph. He'll hate them turkeys. Dumber'n a box o' rocks. A turkey chick will drown in its own water bowl. Abby tried raisin' them dumb chicks every year. Mighta kept one outta a batch o' twelve."

Hod turned the steering wheel sharply to the left, reached down to shift gears, rolled down the window to send a stream of brown tobacco juice out of the opening, then rolled the window back up.

Hannah swallowed and looked straight ahead.

"Owen's been thinkin' on movin', didja hear it?"

"The Klassermans?" Hannah whipped her head around, shock and surprise widening her eyes.

"Sure."

"Why? Why would they consider moving?"

"Wal now, honey, that I couldn't tell you. Guess you'll have to ask 'em the next time you see 'em. I heard he's tired o' the battle. Think he lost a good bit o' cattle. That's the trouble with them fat Angus. They're fine till the goin' gits tough. Now, look at my steers. Them longhorns is uglier than a mud-splattered cat, skinny and mean. But they'll git through jest about anything. They'll travel for miles, exist on scrub and old dead grass if they have to. The Klassermans' is too soft."

Hannah sat up, clutched the dashboard, her mouth compressed to a grim line. Doubt stabbed her chest. She flinched from Hod's words. The Klassermans' ranch, the well-rounded, beautiful Black Angus herd had always been her goal. And here was Hod, the true survivor of the plains, who took every disaster as it came, met it head on with real grit and good humor. As tough as the land itself. Would Jerry be up to the challenge? Or would she always be holding him here without his heart really being in the land?

For one panicked moment, she regretted the desperation that

had driven her to marry him. Her heart pounded in her ears. She chewed her lips as she listened to Jerry's gravelly voice.

"Are you serious? I've been thinking a lot about cattle raising since the rest of our group moved back to Pennsylvania. Whether it's a good idea to attempt it at all in these parts."

A shot of anger coursed through Hannah. These parts. Huh.

Jerry continued, "I finally came up with the conclusion that you have to have something for the land, for the life, living on this wide-open land. It has to be in your blood, the way milking cows or horseshoeing, or anything else gets in your system and stays there. I'm about to agree with you about the Angus, too."

Hannah drew in a sharp intake of breath. "I'm not raising longhorns." Hod looked at her. Jerry didn't. They bumped along in silence.

"Seems to me you don't have much say so in the matter, missy," Hod said. "Yer married to this feller, Hannah. He seems to have a good head on his shoulders."

"You know I don't like longhorns."

"Wal then, you jest might have to move to Illinois and raise turkeys."

Hannah searched Hod's profile for signs of laughter and was shocked to find there was none. He meant it.

The subject was dropped, the cab of the truck filled with uneasy silence. Hannah was relieved when the truck nosed its way to the left, following a path of brown mud and bits of gravel to a set of gray buildings clustered around a stand of cottonwoods. Leafless and wind-blown, they appeared dead from the drought and hot, pulsing winds.

The buildings were well-kept though, fences mended, roofs in good repair, barn doors hung straight. And yes, there was one of Ben Miller's windmills, tall and straight, whirring away, the long steel arm driven by the paddles of the wheel pumping water from underground streams, the only source of water in the years of drought.

The house was long and low, like theirs, Hannah observed. The yard was bare and windswept, without clutter. Two medium-sized dogs came tearing around a corner of the house, barking uproariously, their short, pointed ears alert, their short legs muscular and pumping like pistons.

A curtain was pulled aside from the low windows that faced the driveway. There was no sign of an automobile or truck. The dogs took up their position at the door of Hod's truck, alternately bouncing on their short legs and barking.

"Which one of us wants to get chewed up first?" Jerry asked Hod, laughing amicably.

Hannah stared out the window, thinking that if this was a horse farm, she'd eat someone's hat. There was not a single horse to be seen anywhere.

Hod opened his door, swung to the ground, and was instantly surrounded by the yelping, jumping canines. "All right, all right, that's enough. Calm down. I ain't gonna hurtcha."

The door of the house burst open and a small, thin man appeared, poking his arms into a denim overcoat, a black felt hat with a narrow brim pulled low on his forehead.

"Hey, hey. Knock it off. Here. Shut up! Toby! Tip! Cut it out." The dogs quieted immediately, sat on their haunches, their mouths wide, tongues lolling, pleased to have announced their master's visitors.

"Hod Jenkins! How's it going, old man?"

Hod grinned, stuck out a weathered hand, and gripped the man's hand. "Good. Good. Couldn't be better." He turned to the truck, lifted a hand, and beckoned with his fingers. "Brought you someone interested in mules."

Jerry got out, held the door for Hannah. Introductions were made, with Jerry's easy friendliness and Hod's teasing making short work of feeling accepted and liked, in spite of their Amish clothing.

The man's name was Obadiah Yoder. He looked at Hannah's white covering and said his mother used to wear one of them. He came from a plain background, he said. River Brethren. Used to baptize in rivers. An old, old religion that went way back. They still didn't accept automobiles.

Now he and his wife weren't practicing members anymore. Being the only ones for hundreds of miles, they'd fallen away from some of the old practices. Never had any children, but hard telling what would have happened if they had, being the only River Brethren for miles around.

When Jerry nodded in agreement, Hannah held back a snort. What was he agreeing about? There would be no children for them, so he didn't have to hang on to his Amish ways for them.

"So, you want mules?" Obadiah asked.

"I'd like to look at what you have, see if I can get a team of four."

"Four?"

Jerry nodded yes. "You could kill a horse on this land."

Hannah swallowed, felt the heat creeping into her face. Now, why did Jerry have to say that? She felt as if this Obadiah Yoder could see the fact that her father had done just that, the memory of it like an exposed wound that festered with contempt.

"So, you're planning on tilling the prairie?"

"Well, there's all this talk of winter wheat, so I figured it might balance out the loss of calves and help keep a steady profit going," Jerry said evenly.

"It's gonna hafta rain, sonny," Hod said dryly.

Hannah ground her teeth. What was all this honey and missy and sonny? As if they were mere children. What did Hod Jenkins know about getting ahead, with his ranch in disrepair and the prairie crawling with ugly cattle that were nothing but a set of horns, long hair, and ribs?

Jerry said something about yeah, they'd have to depend on rain. *Oh, just shut up*, Hannah thought, crossing her arms and biting down hard on her back molars.

Obadiah chuckled, a sound like a prairie hen trying to attract a mate. Hannah glared at him through half-closed eyes. "Well, if you want to look at mules, then I guess I'd better send Tip and Toby to get them for me, huh?" he asked, his lean face wrinkling into a full smile.

He looked at the dogs, who watched his face intently. They stood on all fours, shifting positions, whining and begging. When Obadiah said, "Hep, hep," they were off like a shot straight across the prairie, disappearing into vague shapes in less than a few minutes.

Hod whistled. Jerry shook his head. Hannah wanted to stay quiet and aloof, but she couldn't help being intrigued by the dogs' instant knowledge of their master's orders, the eagerness with which they flew to obey.

"What kind of dogs are they?" she blurted before she could catch herself.

"They're Blue Heelers," Obadiah said. "Bred in Australia, also called Australian sheep dogs. They're easily trained. Herding animals is bred into them. I've had them most of my life, although these two are exceptional. Never had better dogs."

Hannah nodded and thought of the many ways they would be valuable on the ranch. Manny had left his dog but it had disappeared like fog in a hot sun the minute he left on the train. She looked at Jerry, who was paying no attention to her, watching the direction the dogs had gone instead. She wouldn't have to answer to him for every little thing she wanted, since their marriage wasn't the way most people's marriages were.

She had no money of her own, that was the thing. She had to

ask him for everything, which included these dogs. Did he even like dogs?

Hannah heard the hoofbeats long before the brown mules trotted into their line of sight, the dogs dodging in and out of the moving hooves, never making a sound, simply pushing the mules in the direction of the barn, steadily working together as a team, guiding them through the wide gate into the wooden corral.

After Obadiah closed the gate, he reached into a pocket of his coat and handed each dog a treat that looked like beef jerky as he praised them for doing so well.

There were eight mules. Hannah climbed onto the second rail of the board fence and looked them over, her hands clutching the top rail, wondering why this fence was so much higher than most corrals she'd seen.

The mules stood facing her, their long, narrow faces like corncobs, their ears the size of a good sail on a boat. One was as ugly as the next. Mud brown. Big hooves, ratty tails that had long hair only on the ends. Her father said man created mules, breeding a donkey and a horse, so God really did not create them, which had rendered them useless to him. He would never own a mule, or use one to plow his fields. A camel was almost better looking than a mule! Hannah had seen pictures of camels in a Bible story book, so she knew their eyes were huge and soft, with sweeping black lashes like little brushes. There was simply not one nice feature about a mule!

Jerry stood apart with Obadiah and Hod, conferring, a man's conversation that excluded her. The wife. She had absolutely no say in the matter. Hannah couldn't believe she was caught in a situation very similar to what her mother's had been. Quiet, taking the back seat, obedient. Every ounce of her rebelled against it. She didn't want these mules. She was not about to make hay to keep these knock-kneed, flop-eared creatures alive. She stiffened when she felt Jerry beside her.

"Hannah."

"What?"

"What do you think?"

"Does it matter what I think?"

"Of course."

"They're mud ugly!"

Jerry laughed long and loud. He reached up to grasp her waist to pull her off the fence, which frightened Hannah so badly that she jumped off backward and almost lost her balance. She stepped back, away from him, refusing to look at him.

"Hannah."

"What?"

"I know they're ugly, but they're God's creatures too."

"No, they're not."

Jerry cleared his throat. "I know what you mean, but these mules are good mules. Top of the line. I mean, look at the power in those long, deep chests."

"They'll be tired after the first hour carrying those ears around!"

Jerry whooped and laughed. Hannah tried not to smile, her face taking on all sorts of strange contortions.

"Hannah, listen. It's our only hope of putting in a crop of wheat."

"We could get a tractor."

"You know what I want."

"Then why do you want my opinion?"

Jerry sighed and looked off across the prairie. "I know you don't want the mules, but you do want to try to raise the wheat. We already discussed this, didn't we?"

Hannah shrugged.

"So, it's mules and wheat or no wheat," Jerry said evenly.

If only she didn't feel as if she was giving in to Jerry, it wouldn't be so bad. Her whole being wanted to refuse him, watch him flounder and wheedle and beg, then refuse him anyway. Guilt welled up in her, like a blot of black ink that she could not ignore. For a fleeting instant, she wondered at the need to control the men in her life, the disdain for her father, her superiority over her brother, Manny. And yet, she was helpless to stop it. She didn't want the mules, it was as simple as that.

"How much money do you have?" she asked, short and blunt.

"Enough."

"To buy two dogs, too?"

"He doesn't have more than these two."

"You get the mules. I get the dogs."

"You can't buy these dogs."

"I know. I want two just like his."

Jerry caught her gaze with his own, hers black and defiant, but with the beginning of a golden light behind the darkness. What passed between them was mysterious, not decipherable to either one, but its evidence was known. Like two opposites that melded for a split second, producing a miniscule spark of recognition, they both knew the first inch of a long journey had begun, here on Obadiah Yoder's farm, west of Dorchester on the North Dakota plains.

The shining, two-bottom plow was drawn through the crumbling soil, still dry after the snows of winter, the brown mules plodding along under the warm spring sun with seemingly no effort at all.

Hitched four abreast, the new leather harnesses gleaming, Hannah was taken straight back to her childhood in Lancaster County, watching her father plow the soil with his Belgians. She loved to hear the mules' hooves hitting the earth, the clanking of the chains hooked to the plow, the creaking of the leather as it moved with the mules' muscles.

Jerry stood on the steel-wheeled cart, balanced seamlessly, driving the mules with one hand, and turned halfway to watch the soil roll away behind him, pulling the lever whenever he came to the end of the space that would be wheat.

The summer had flown by, with haymaking, a new and bigger corral built around the barn, the beginning of the new herd of longhorns grazing around the windmill.

They had sold the Black Angus cattle to Owen Klasserman, who had dispersed of his cattle, his farm equipment, and then sold his ranch to a wealthy cattle baron from Texas.

Sylvia cried great wet tears for Hannah, as well as every neighbor woman for miles around, saying she would never have better neighbors, no matter if they traveled from one end of the world to another.

Hannah swallowed her snort, endured Sylvia's soft, perspiration-soaked hug and felt not the least regret to see the shiny, pink couple ride away, probably never to be seen again. She did write the news to her mother, who responded in a month's time saying she was so happy indeed to hear that Sylvia was able to move out of North Dakota.

So, nothing had changed. Her mother, Manny, and Mary and Eli were settled in, happy to live on the homestead in Lancaster County among a growing population of the Amish faith in an area of Pennsylvania called the Garden Spot by many. Which is certainly what it was. Fertile soil, plenty of moisture, a hub of industry between the capitol city of Harrisburg and the seaports of the East Coast.

Hannah never failed to compare Jerry with her father, Moses. All his steps counted. He never seemed to hurry, yet things were accomplished in record time. Everything was well thought out, reasoned, and bargained for, with Hannah being the sole person he sought out when he needed help.

Rains came in the form of thunderstorms, although sparsely.

The prairie rebounded after the drought, sprang to life as moisture revived every tiny seed that had dried out and lay in the dust, creating a kaleidoscope of unimaginable wildflowers. The south slant of unexpected swells of land were dressed as delicately as a new bride, with the lacy, lavender pasqueflower. The low places harbored chokecherry, buffalo-berry, and gooseberry bushes, which Hannah discovered when she was out training their two dogs.

She had had them for over three months now, and by the way they responded to her commands, she knew they were on to something. They were like hired hands, the way they knew instinctively where to look for cows or horses. They routed out prairie dogs, badgers, foxes, even terrorized deer that outran them, their legs carrying them like wings.

They had named the dogs Nip and Tuck, which suited them perfectly, the way they tucked into a group of cows and nipped at their heels.

Hannah named them, and Jerry thought she was awfully clever. He told her so, and watched the color spread on her cheeks like an unfolding rosebud. He told himself the long wait for her love would someday come to an end. More and more, he realized the difference in her, when she felt she performed a task to his approval, versus when she failed to meet the stringent requirements she set for herself.

Jerry could never tell her his discovery. She would viciously deny it and then stop communicating altogether, pouting for days, punishing him with her silences. It wasn't only the silence that got to him, but the resentment and bald-faced disapproval that was like a slap in the face the minute she was aware of his presence.

He knew now, though, that the harsh judgment she ladled out on those around her, she also ladled out for herself. She didn't like herself, so how could she stand anyone else?

A work in progress, he constantly reminded himself.

Jerry plowed the land with ease, the prairie soil falling away behind his plow, the mules plodding like a cadence, a symphony of sound and wonder. Skylarks wheeled across the hot, azure sky, and dickeybirds called their vibrant chirps. Grasses bent and swayed, rustled and shivered in the constantly teasing wind.

There was a stack of winter wheat seeds bagged in pretty muslin prints sitting against the wall of the forebay. It was their first crop on the prairie, and hopes ran high thinking of next summer's profit, God willing. Almost forty acres of wheat. Jerry calculated, counted low. Even with that amount, they would be able to buy many more longhorns, which was still a sore subject with Hannah.

Jerry figured that Hod Jenkins was the real authority on long-term survival. Not Hannah, nor those German Klassermans, nor any fancy government brochure that touted the merits of life on the high plains.

You had to live it, experience it, and not for only a few years. Jerry didn't know if he had a love for this Western land or not. He knew if he was meant to be here for Hannah's sake, God would provide for them, for sure.

So he insisted on longhorns, or they would not raise cattle at all. Hannah yelled and slammed doors, threatened and shouted, said she wasn't going to lift a finger to help him with those arrow-tipped monstrosities, and when he'd laughed, she got so mad she threw a plate against the wall, then stayed silent for weeks, talking only to the dogs.

That time she outdid herself, refusing to cook, so he made his own salt pork and eggs, ate a can of beans, made toast by holding a long-handled fork inserted into a thick slice of bread over hot coals. Then he applied a slick coat of butter, ate it in two bites, and made another.

The house turned blue with smoke, but neither one acted as if they noticed. Hannah threw her apron over her nose and coughed until she choked the minute he went out the door. She slammed the lid on the cook stove, when it lay crookedly until she nipped it with her finger and heard the skin sizzle before she felt it, then lived in pain for hours afterward. A huge, watery blister formed on the tip of her finger, burst, and an angry red infection set in. She treated it with wood ashes and kerosene, lay wide-eyed in bed at night thinking of blood poisoning and lockjaw, remembering in vivid detail the story her grandmother told of Uncle Harry who died, skin and bones, his jaw locked so tight no one could pry it open, even in death.

She wondered if she would go to hell for being stubborn, then got so scared she tiptoed across the hall and asked Jerry if he thought she might have blood poisoning or might get lockjaw. He said it looked as if it was healing already, that he didn't think she'd need to see a doctor. She looked so genuinely terrified that he reached for her, only to comfort her as he would a child, but she stepped back, slipped into her room, and shut the door with a resounding click.

CHAPTER 3

THE WINDMILL CREAKED AND GROANED AS THE GREAT PADDLES ON the wheel spun in the wind. Cold water gushed into the huge galvanized tank from the cast-iron pike that ran into it.

Brown, speckled, gray, black, or brindled cows with various sizes of horns roamed the plains around it. There were exactly nineteen head. They resembled Hod Jenkins's herd somewhat yet there was a certain sleek roundness to their bodies, the absence of long, coarse hair.

Jerry set out mineral blocks, salt blocks, and wormed his cattle. Hod said once a year was plenty. Jerry nodded his head in agreement and then went ahead and did it more often, which resulted in healthier cows. They'd done it in the spring, when they acquired the herd, and with the forty acres plowed, it was time to herd the cows for their de-wormer, as Jerry called it.

"Why don't we de-horn them, too?" Hannah asked, testy at the thought of all those contrary cows swinging those horns at her.

"I don't think so. Those horns will keep the wolves away this winter."

"Hmph. Hod lost ten calves."

"Out of a herd of a hundred and twenty."

"It's still ten calves." Hannah turned and flounced off, her men's handkerchief bouncing on her head. At times like these, Jerry wished he could shake some sense into her.

They saddled their horses without speaking. Jerry's horse, King, was a brown gelding, magnificent, huge, with a heavy black mane and tail as luxurious as a silk curtain. Hannah's horse was a palomino, the horse Jerry had made many attempts to gift to her, which she accepted now, as his wife, although she never spoke of those past offenses.

Nip and Tuck whined and yelped and tugged at their chains, but Jerry felt they were two young to help with this serious work. What if one of them got hooked by those massive horns? They had better wait until they were older and more experienced, he claimed.

Hannah argued her point. How would they ever gain experience but by being allowed to help? Obstinate now, more than ever, she refused to get on her horse. She stood like a tin soldier, her limbs stiff with resolve.

It was already past the time that Jerry had planned on starting. The black flies were thicker than water, which meant there was a storm brewing somewhere and he was not about to stand there and try to persuade Hannah in a patient manner.

He lost his temper. Stalking over to Hannah, he shoved his perspiring face into hers and said, "Fine. Stand there all day. I'll herd these cows into the corral by myself. You're not going to take those puppies out on the range."

He swatted the pesky little flies out of his eyes, leaped into the saddle, kicked his heels into King's side, and was off across the prairie in a cloud of dust.

Hannah's mouth dropped open, disbelief taking her breath away. She felt the beginning of a sob forming in her throat. The tip of her nose burned as quick tears sprang to her eyes.

Well! He didn't have to get all mad. Goodness. She had the distinct feeling she'd been wadded up like a piece of paper and thrown in the trash.

She blinked. She sniffled. She wiped a hand across her nose, hard.

This was an interesting turn of events. For one thing, she had to save her pride and let him bring in the cows by himself. If he wanted her to stand here all day, that is what she would do. She would stand here by the fence and watch him try to herd those despicable longhorns by himself. He'd never accomplish it.

Jerry disappeared over a rise. That was disappointing. She had hoped to be able to watch him wear himself out on King.

She unsaddled the palomino and put him in the barn, gave him a small forkful of hay to keep him happy, then hooked her elbows on the barn fence, her boot heel on another rung, and looked in the direction Jerry had gone. She swatted at the bothersome flies, then got tired and slid down by the fence into the dusty grass.

Hannah wondered if there was any trace of her father's blood left in the soil after all these years. She was sitting at the spot where the angry old cow had brought him to an untimely death.

Even now, the awful incident brought a feeling of overwhelming despair. She knew her father was in a better place, heaven being his only goal, the many prayers and devout reading of his Bible preceding him in death.

It was the story he lived before his demise, the shame Hannah still carried with her, the sensitivity to the loss of their homestead, the humiliation of the ride to North Dakota. Like tramps. No, like Amish gypsies. Different, weird people that traveled roads and highways with two tired horses, asking ordinary folks to stay a night here, feed their horses there.

"Would you spare a pound of butter for travelers?"

"Would you allow us water for our horses?

"Thank you. God bless you. You'll be blessed." As if they were some ragged apparition sent from heaven to test people's ability to be kind.

There was a disgrace, an indignity attached like a loathsome parasite to all those painful memories, a part of her past she would never shake.

Ordinary folks, English people of class and citizenry, would peer through the opening of the covered wagon to find them seated among their belongings, unwashed, raggedy-haired, poor, stupid misfits. The people would stand there and stare, make clucking noises of banal sympathy.

Hannah felt like an orangutan at the zoo, a strange monkey, an amazing sight. If she allowed herself to think, it was like drowning in wave after wave of embarrassment, impossible to rise above it. She could control the self-loathing as long as no one took advantage of her, or used their authority in a demeaning manner, making her feel as if she was in the back of the wagon again.

Evidently, neither one of her siblings suffered from the same malady. They were all sweet and simple and obedient to this day, same as her mother. Bland as bean soup!

She'd been lost in her own thoughts, wrapped up in the past, which effectively sealed her off from Nip and Tuck's constant yapping, whining, jerking on their leashes, then starting all over again. "Hey! Quiet down there. It's not that bad." She walked over to play with them, scratching the coarse hair between their ears, rolling them over to rub their bellies, but keeping them tied the way Jerry wanted.

She heard the distant chuffing sound of an automobile, lifted a hand to shade her eyes to see if she could catch sight of who was coming to the ranch. A dark car with gold lettering.

She straightened and saw the gold star on the side of the car. The sheriff. Her heart fluttered, then began to pound. Please don't let it be a death message.

The car rolled to a stop, the cloud of dust thinned and was blown away. The passenger door opened first, the dark shirt and trousers, the white Stetson. The door on the driver's side opened with an identically clad sheriff, tall and sober, unfolding out of it.

"Hello."

Hannah nodded, her mouth gone dry. The dogs set up a racket, bouncing on two hind legs as they strained on their leashes.

"We're making the rounds of Elliot County. Have you seen anyone here on the ranch that answers to the name Isaac Short? Older fellow, small and skinny."

"Isaac? Only Short I know is Lemuel. He was here in early spring—April or May. Riding a horse. Wanted me to hide him."

"Lemuel, you say."

"Yes. When my mother still lived here, he stayed with us for months. Gave us a story that was all a lie."

"Mind if we search your house and outbuildings?"

"No."

So Lemuel was still loose. Nothing she was going to worry about, that was for sure. She watched for signs of Jerry, waited until the men completed their search, acknowledging their warnings politely, her hands behind her back, tipping forward then backward from toe to heel.

"You have a man here with you?"

"Yes."

"Well, you make sure you're not alone, unless you have a sizable dog to protect you. I understand you don't use firearms in self-defense. Your faith."

It was only then that she thought of the revolver. Her eyes widened as she put her hand over her mouth.

"What?" Instantly alert, the trained sheriff picked up on her astonished expression.

"I forgot. When Lemuel Short was here, he threatened me with a pistol. I knocked it out of his hand. I swung a hammer quick before he saw I had one. I have the revolver."

That was, of course, a tremendous help in tracking him down, so Hannah received words of praise for her quick-wittedness, her bravery. They thanked her and left.

Well, that was something now, wasn't it? She felt good from the inside out. She watched for Jerry, anxious to tell him, then decided against it. If she told him now, he'd never leave the ranch. He'd stick close like an unwanted burr, and she had absolutely no intention of putting up with that.

Her stomach growled. Time for lunch. She'd skipped breakfast, for some reason she couldn't remember. Oh, Jerry wanted oatmeal, she remembered. She had eaten so many bowls of rolled oats as a child, and again here on the prairie when starvation was very real. So now, when she could choose other foods, she did.

She heated a saucepan, added leftover ham and bean soup she'd made a few days ago. With rivvels. She loved rivvels. Like small lumps of noodles, they were pure energy. All that good flour and egg mixture dropped in tiny chunks into a bubbling pot of soup. She put rivvels in chicken corn soup and vegetable soup, or any other stew she threw together.

She got out the sourdough bread which, as usual, was hard as a rock, but toasted in a pan and spread with lard or butter, it was edible.

Her meal completed, she wiped the tabletop, put her dishes in the sink, then looked around the house with a sense of satisfaction. The afternoon sun slanted through the west-facing windows, bathing the front living room and kitchen in the golden glow of late summer. The deep gleam of the polished oak flooring added a warm luster to the white walls. The brown davenport and wooden rocking chairs both had a scattering of bright pillows and throws. Jerry's rolltop desk stood against the east wall, where the wide door led to the kitchen.

Hannah had been fortunate to be able to keep all the furnishings when her family returned to their home in the East. With

Jerry's belongings, the house was filled up nicely, except for one spare bedroom.

Mam had had no desire to take the furnishings, even if she could have. It was not what she'd brought when her and her beloved Mose had made the trek out West. That had all burned in the fire. The furniture that graced the rooms now had all been generously donated by concerned members of the Amish congregation in Lancaster, and by well-meaning neighbors here on the plains.

The day the gasoline engine threw sparks and ignited the tinder dry grass had been one of the worst days of Hannah's life. But now, so many good things had come out of that fire. The generosity of friends and family had gotten them back on their feet.

Charity or not, Hannah had never looked back.

She walked back to the barn, still searching for Jerry as her eyes scanned the position of the sun, then moved back to the direction he'd gone when he left. He would likely ride in alone, knowing how hard it was to round up cows that had no intention of leaving their buffet of thick broom grass.

A small brown dot appeared on the horizon, turning into a bobbing, weaving mass as it neared the ranch. Hannah shaded her eyes, thrilled at the sight of Jerry on King, driving a tight knot of lowing cattle that seemed to be walking along without being agitated or cranky, as they often were.

Quickly, she moved to the gate, swung it wide, then fastened it with a piece of rawhide before disappearing into the barn. She knew how frustrating it was to drive a herd of cattle successfully for miles, only to have them veer in the wrong direction at the last minute because someone was lounging on the corral fence. She could watch Jerry work now, without being seen.

On they came, led by the largest, oldest cow, the brindle bull behind her, his massive horns swinging, his eyes rolling. As they neared the buildings, Jerry pushed them harder, yelling and swinging his rope, maneuvering expertly from right to left, tightening loose ends and keeping them in a rectangle of movement, never allowing any stragglers.

King took her breath away. It was as if he'd been bred to chase cattle, which Hannah knew he had not been. If he was still back East, he'd likely be pulling a gray-and-black market wagon, in the rain, with a driving harness and blinders on his bridle. He'd only be half the horse he was here.

Jerry wore no hat, saying they were useless in the prairie wind. His thick, dark hair flopped up and down, blowing every which way depending on the direction of the wind. His skin was darkened, fissured by the elements. It suited him. If he lived out here another forty years, he'd look much like Hod. Hannah swallowed, thinking of Hod's tobacco juice.

The cows were coming faster now, bunched together, the lead cow becoming agitated as the ones behind her pushed her forward. She bawled, her eyes rolling, but on she came.

Jerry yelled, "Hey! Hey! Get up there! Hup!"

Hannah gripped the barn windowsill until her knuckles were white. Would the lead cow go through the open gate? So close now, only a hundred yards.

On they came. Hannah held her breath, feeling weak and dizzy. She could smell that bovine odor, the tart, sweet scent of cows. She heard the nineteen noses breathing hard, the hooves milling up the dusty ground around the barn. A cloud of dust and black flies followed the herd, sometimes almost obscuring them for a moment.

And then they were in, smoothly, without one straggler. Hannah was relieved, ecstatic. She ran out of the barn, unfastened the rawhide in one quick movement, swung the gate wide and lifted the wooden bar to place it in the proper notch.

She dusted her hands and looked up at Jerry, ready to receive his praise for her quick work. To her chagrin, he wheeled King around and dismounted, working the girth and throwing the reins before dragging off the saddle and throwing it on the floor of the barn.

Without looking at her, he walked off in the direction of the house. Her first instinct was to catch up to him and tell him about the soup on the stove. But she stayed, watching him go. What was wrong with him now? He'd done an excellent job of bringing the cows in. Why was he acting like this now, when everything had gone well?

She climbed the fence, sat on the top rail, and surveyed her herd of cattle. Still nineteen. Why did it seem as if this herd, these strange-looking cattle, were truly hers, her way to becoming successful now, with Jerry by her side?

Or, rather, she was by his side. Without doubt, Jerry was far superior in everything to any man she had ever known. She couldn't begin to compare him to her poor father, may he rest in peace. Even the Jenkins did not have the skills, the work ethic that Jerry had.

She knew he intrigued her, the way he planned ahead, asked for advice and took it, both priceless attributes when it came to managing the ranch. Those forty acres of plowed ground, done so effortlessly, the four plodding mules doing what they were meant to do, without fuss or fury.

Well, she couldn't tell him these things or he'd think she was starting to like him. Likely he'd try to put his arm around her shoulder or her waist like he was always wanting to do. Those arms were a trap, one she had no intention of being caught in.

When Jerry returned from the house, she stayed on the top rail, but did dare to look down as he approached. He was looking up at her, then climbed up, threw a leg across a post and perched on it.

"How did it go?" she asked, in a small voice.

"How did what go?"

She glanced at him. His face was pale and sick-looking. "What's wrong with you?"

"I got sick. Hannah, I don't want to hurt your feelings, okay? But I absolutely hate rivvels. We, uh . . . you know, eat lots of rivvels. I know you love them, so you go ahead and make them for yourself, but I'll need potatoes or something else instead. Sorry."

Hannah wished she could disappear like a cloud of dust. Her embarrassment turned into anger, and to save herself she retorted, "You can make your own meals from now on, then."

"Hannah, I told you, I'm sorry. I knew this would hurt your feelings. I didn't mean to."

"Yeah, well, you did. So get over it. What do you want me to do as far as worming these ugly brutes?"

"We need them in the chute, one by one."

"I know that much."

"Can you give an injection?"

"I think so. Manny or my . . . my father always did it."

They worked together the remainder of the day sorting cattle and getting them into the narrow chute, lowering the gate behind them like a trap door and shooting the needle into their tough hides, putting pressure on the plunger and forcing the worm medicine into the cows' bodies.

Jerry was quick and vigilant, avoiding the horns as he drove the cattle with a sturdy black whip, one he mostly cracked above their heads, or used the handle to prod them along. He told Hannah that he didn't believe any of them were truly dangerous, or a threat to their lives. You just had to be careful around them, that was all.

Hannah looked at him, trying hard to cover her admiration.

The work was dirty, with dust coating everything. The cows milled about in the soil, throwing up everything under their feet with their ungainly cloven hooves. Hannah's eyelashes, the top of her head, everything seemed painted with the cloying dust. She choked, blinked, swiped at her eyes, then yanked the man's handkerchief from her head and tied it over her nose and mouth the way the Jenkins boys had taught her.

After the last cow had gone through the chute, Jerry walked over and told her she had done a great job. "Another man couldn't have done better.

Hannah looked at her feet and refused to meet his eyes. She didn't say thanks. She didn't smile. She just walked off and told him she was going to make rivvel soup for their evening meal.

That evening, though, things seemed to be changing, if only enough to allow Jerry a miniature ray of hope for the future. Hannah did make a small pot of rivvel soup for herself. But she cooked a pot of potatoes with ham and red beans for him, which was actually an overcooked mush with lumps of gristly ham and beans so hard they would have bounced off the wall if someone had thrown them.

But he was ravenous after losing his lunch so he enjoyed the dubious-looking mess and was grateful. He figured she'd learn as time went on, although he wished she would try and befriend some neighbor women who could teach her a few of the basics.

They sat together on the porch, Jerry on the steps, leaning back against a post, one knee drawn up with an arm slung across it. Hannah sat on a wooden chair, her legs crossed, swinging one foot, her elbows resting on her top knee.

Crickets chirped beneath the wooden floor of the porch, seeking out the only dark moist corners they could find. Grass-hoppers leaped and chewed their noisy way through the grass by the fence, and evening larks called their plaintive call to one another as the sun slid behind the horizon.

A cow lowed from the corral. Another one answered. "How come they're still in the barnyard?" Hannah asked.

"I want to make sure none of them get sick."

"Good idea."

"I'm not looking forward to winter. Out here, everything is just so unpredictable. The blizzards, or no snow at all, or freezing, bitter cold and a wind that never stops."

"I love the prairie winters."

Jerry looked at her sharply. "You're serious?"

"Of course. Every day is a challenge. I love getting up in the morning without knowing what will present itself. It's never dull. Getting enough firewood, for one thing. You know the cottonwoods and oak trees in the creek bottom won't last forever. Will we have to buy coal from town? Or will we travel farther to find enough firewood?"

Jerry looked at Hannah with an unnamed expression. "So this challenge, this day-to-day onslaught of obstacles, the surprises, is what keeps you here?"

Hannah's gaze was riveted on the disappearance of the orange orb of the sun setting in its usual display of grandiosity. She jutted her chin in the general direction of the sunset. "Yes. And that."

Jerry watched the sun disappear, felt the twilight creeping over the plains, shadows of night encroaching, the air turning cooler and carrying a hint of frost, a harbinger of the howling winds of winter. He felt a foreboding, a portent, shivered, then shook his head from side to side. "You are different, Hannah."

"Don't you feel the same way?" she asked.

"I do, at times, yes. But I can't say I look forward to winter. And I miss the social life of Lancaster County, the hymn sings, church, the frolics and hoedowns in the barn. I miss the friends of my youth." The minute the words were out of his mouth, he knew he'd spoken too plainly.

Her foot bobbed faster. She removed her elbows from her knee and sat up straight, glaring at him with baleful eyes. "So you regret out marriage? You wish you could return, exactly like my mother and all the rest of them did?"

"I didn't say that. I just mentioned the fact that I miss the goings-on back East."

"There are churches in Pine. We could go to any church we choose."

"Hannah, we are of the Amish faith. I have no intention of leaving and changing my beliefs, or the way of life we were taught from our youth. I'm very comfortable living under a bishop and ministers who look out for our souls."

Hannah had nothing to say to this. They sat in silence that was fraught with unspoken longings, doubts about the future, about the marriage they both knew was as empty as the prairie itself. Jerry could not have known how difficult the path would be, seeing how Hannah drew into herself with no visible sign of harboring even the beginnings of a natural love for her husband.

His patience was God-given, this he knew. But when he thought of the years stretching before him, one after another, filled with only a swirling mist, a substance devoid of anything real, he felt only doubts and a nameless dread.

"You're always better than I am," Hannah remarked, as shadows deepened around them."

"No. No, I'm not. You know that."

"You don't have to stay."

"I want to stay here with you."

Her foot bobbed faster than ever. "You'll get tired of me. I'm not a very nice person."

"Hannah, I married you for one reason. I love you. It's up to you when you're ready to return my love."

Jerry could only watch as she lowered her face to her knee, and whispered very soft and low, "Thank you."

CHAPTER 4

THE NEXT MORNING, JERRY WHISTLED AS HE BRUSHED HIS MULES, working from the top of their broad backs, down their sides, their haunches, to the tops of their oversized hooves. He threw the black leather harness across their backs, tightened cinches and buckles.

He needed only two of the mules today. The drill used for sowing wheat was not heavy. It was easily pulled by the best two of the four—Max, the largest one, and Mike, the slightly smaller but energetic one. He knew if Mike didn't get worked enough, he'd be frisky.

Four mules—Max, Mike, Mollie, and Mud Mule. It was the naming of the mules that brought their first real laughter together. They could not come up with a fourth reasonable name that started with "M." So, Jerry suggested Muddy and they shortened it to Mud. Hannah forgot herself and snorted in laughter, which encouraged Jerry to carry on about their precious Mud Mule until they both were laughing so hard they had tears in their eyes. The poor mule was no beauty, as mules go, his nose even longer than his teammates', his eyes slanted and bulging like a frog's eyes. His tail was much shorter and had less hair on the end of it.

After that whispered, "Thank you," last evening, Jerry could take anything. It was like a sip of water to a parched throat. She was human after all. She said she appreciated his love. The sky was blue, the sun was golden, the birds singing songs of joy as the wind whispered a rhythm of longing and love.

What could go wrong now? Nothing. He felt as if he knew the right way, the times when she would need a firm refusal, the times when he could win her with kindness.

Jerry poured the sleek kernels of seed wheat into the hopper, the fifty-pound bags weighing almost nothing, the muscles in his arms rippling with strength, a song on his lips and his heart filled with hope. Back and forth the mules plodded steadily, the creaking wheels on the drill releasing the millions of wheat seeds into the well-harrowed soil, waiting for the autumn rains and sunshine.

He was thrilled to see Hannah walking toward the field, Nip and Tuck bouncing and jostling around at her feet, the wind blowing her skirts in all directions, her gray apron flapping unhandily. He loved to watch her walk. Her long-legged stride covered a good distance in a short time, effortless, as graceful as any of God's creation.

Impatience was in her way of moving, her long, slender neck leaning forward just a bit, her jaw elevated, jutting forward slightly, as if her mind was running ahead of her feet.

Now what had she thought up? What was important enough to come all this way with her fast gait? He caught her eye, pulled on the reins, called to the mules. When the squeaking of the drill stopped, the silence around him held nothing but the soft sighing of the wind, a sound like the breath of God or the whisper of angels' wings, as he often imagined the wind to be.

"Hey, Hannah!" he called.

As usual, no greeting. Only the exact reason for her arrival. "I'm going to the new neighbors."

"Why don't you wait until I can go with you?"

"No."

"All right. Are you sure they moved in already?"

"No, but I plan on finding out."

"Be careful."

She had already turned, but flapped a hand over her head to show she'd heard, and then she was gone, out of earshot.

Jerry shrugged, called to the mules. He was almost certain no one had moved in at the Klassermans' place, the way Hod said these Texans were planning on enlarging everything, both the house and the barn. But hey, let her find out for herself.

Jerry watched Hannah lead the palomino out of the barn, run the grooming brush all over, thoroughly, then throw the saddle across his back. He wondered if she'd take Nip and Tuck.

Hannah rode off in a cloud of dust, the sun shining down on her squared shoulders, her men's kerchief blowing in the wind. And then, nothing, as far as he could see. Emptiness all around him, the sky gigantic in its unknowable immensity, the grasses waving like dancers, pirouetting in every direction until he imagined the prairie to be made of water, with waves and eddies and whirlpools hidden in its depths.

Hannah rode hard down the dusty road that led north, away from the ranch, into the prairie where she could feel the freedom of being on a horse's back, feel the power and strength beneath her, thrill to the rush of wind in her face.

She missed the Klassermans already, if she admitted it. It was always nice to know the next ranch over was inhabited by someone she was acquainted with. So now, it seemed strange to be riding along the same road without knowing who, if anyone, she would meet.

Why would someone from Texas move to the plains? Surely they weren't thinking straight. Well, if they thought they were going to move out here and buy up every acre they could, they wouldn't get very far. Folks in these parts didn't take kindly to someone throwing their weight around. They liked things the way they were, and the way they had been for decades, and no upstart from Texas was going to change the way they raised cattle or grew wheat or built long, low houses—or anything.

Hannah smiled, slowed the palomino, gazed around at the swells and dips of the land as she caught sight of a badger slinking away beneath a thick stand of swamp grass. He was fat and clumsy, his bright eyes popping out of his striped face.

She noticed dust rolling on the horizon and kept to her side of the road as a truck approached, the sound of the motor an invasion of her senses. Wheezing and gasping, the truck careened out of a low place, covered in mud, the front fender missing, wooden racks clapping and swaying, as if the whole haphazard mess would let loose and splinter into a thousand pieces on the road.

Wasn't Hod Jenkins. This truck was even worse than his. Inside was a small man, barely visible above the steering wheel. No passenger. Hannah reined in the palomino as the truck wheezed to a stop, acutely aware of being alone with no ranch in sight.

Well, she was on a horse, so she'd be fine.

The window on the driver's side was being cranked down with a painful squeaking noise. She saw an elbow, followed by a small, wizened face with a bill cap pulled low over the eyes. Those ferret eyes. She'd know them anywhere. Hannah drew up her shoulders, straightened her jaw, and said, "What?"

"Sittin' high and mighty, there, aintcha?" Lemuel Short rasped, his words like fingernails on a chalkboard, followed by a series of coughs and throat-clearing, and a splat of phlegm that landed at her horse's feet. The palomino sidestepped, snorted. Hannah reined him in, spoke to him soothingly so he'd settle.

"Can't handle a horse like him, huh?" Red blotches of color suffused the small man's face, pock marks like fissured rock, bristly stubble over everything, the desperate brown eyes glinting like a cornered badger. From his shirt collar, blue veins protruded on his brick-red neck, as scrawny as a pecked chicken.

"I can handle him. Stop spitting on him." She glowered down at the man she had protected, sheltered, even cared about, even after all his lies and half-truths he'd used to gain the Detweiler family's sympathy. Almost, she had come to like him.

"Where's my gun?"

"I have no idea."

"What'd you do with it?"

Hannah shrugged.

"You better tell me. I mean it!"

"I wouldn't give you the gun even if I knew where it was."

Lemuel did not answer. To meet his eyes was like gazing into a volcanic pit, seething and churning with a nameless emotion that jarred her from the disdain she felt for him. A quick wave of shock rippled over her body. Whatever humanity Lemuel had once had in him had disappeared, leaving behind this icy creature who could be capable of anything.

He coughed and spat. Hannah loosened the reins and dug her heels into the palomino's flanks, leaned forward and prepared herself for the surge of power that would come when her horse took off. She didn't look back.

She flew down the dusty road, the wind in her face, the steady *thock-thock* of galloping hooves, the horse's great muscles propelling them forward. She focused only on the amazing sensation of the horse's pure power.

Then she heard it. Low at first, like a whine. The sound of a bumblebee in wood. The whine turned into a roar, then a high, crazed screech.

Hannah turned to look back over her shoulder. The sight that met her eyes was almost comical, if she would not have sensed the danger. Bent low over his steering wheel, both hands gripping it, Lemuel Short had every intention of running her down. The truck careened through dust and low places where the mud flew up in showers.

If the ancient, wheezing piece of junk he was driving went any faster, he'd catch up. Better to veer off to the right, onto the open prairie, even if she had to slow down on unknown territory.

The prairie could be deceiving, appearing as level as a kitchen table, but filled with surprises. Badger or prairie dog holes, rises in the most unexpected places, or hollows that were not visible to the eye.

She slowed her horse, then laid the reins flat against the left side of his neck, steering him to the right. It was called being neck reined and was gentle on a horse's mouth. Obediently, the palomino slowed, then cantered at an easy, rocking pace, his ears flicking forward, then back, alert to his rider's commands.

Hannah turned in the saddle, saw the truck slow, but didn't wait to see if he would pursue her. There was no way he could navigate the prairie in that old truck—certainly not fast enough to overtake her.

She still was not seriously frightened, but it was hard to forget that look in his eyes. He was old, small, and desperate, like a dark wisp of smoke that could be nothing or could be deadly, depending on the size of the fire at its source.

He probably stole that wheezing old bucket he drove. If he came after her on the prairie, he'd break an axle or run out of gas. At least she'd never have to worry about car problems for herself. Not that she wouldn't have loved to drive one of those late models, long and sleek, the kind you occasionally glimpsed in Dorchester. No one in Pine had enough money to purchase a decent car. They all drove around in rusted-out pickup trucks that dated back to the twenties.

Jerry was as Amish as *schnitz und knepp*, that century-old dish of home-cured ham and apples with dumplings. It didn't make a difference that they lived out here on the plains by themselves. He considered himself of the Old Order and fully expected to remain there, honoring the dress code and corresponding with the Lancaster County ministers via mail. No automobiles for them.

She shrugged involuntarily. She'd been desperate enough to keep her homestead that she'd married him, and now she had to follow his rules—or at least try. But it had worked and that's what mattered. She still had her beloved homestead on the plains.

Things were becoming steadily more complicated, though. Take last night. Oh my. What had possessed her to thank him? A burning shame washed over like rain. Now what? She didn't give two hoots if he loved her or not. She certainly did not love him, didn't even really need him except so she could stay on the plains. She would be happier on her own if she could be.

And so, her thoughts kept time to the horse's hoofbeats, until she realized she'd have to turn directly north, to the left, or she'd miss the Klasserman ranch.

No sight of Lemuel Short and his decrepit old junker. Good. She leaned forward in the saddle, eagerly scanned the surrounding land for the neighboring buildings, and wondered who these Texans would turn out to be. Friendly? Wealthy? Hostile? What would they think of her peculiar Amish lifestyle?

She really didn't care. Folks in Pine had been less than welcoming to the Detweiler family at first, but they'd warmed up to them eventually. So would the Texans.

Her calculations had been right. She caught sight of the dull gray galvanized roofing of the large barn their former neighbors had built. They'd raised a large herd of Black Angus cattle with German determination and a work ethic that far surpassed her own father's lackadaisical ways.

She still found it hard to believe they had actually retired and went back to the old country, especially now, the way Germany was still healing from the war. They received no newspapers and had no radio so the images of World War II were strictly hearsay. Sometimes Hod would rant on about the whole mess, in his words, and Hannah had no interest in any of it. They were self-sufficient, or almost, so what went on in the world was of no concern to her.

"Whoa!" She pulled back too hard and too fast on the reins, startling the palomino to a haunch lowering stop that almost unseated her. She grabbed the saddle horn and settled back down in her seat. What was that?

It looked like railroad cars lined up in a circle. Or wagons. The way a wagon train parked in a tight circle for protection from the Indians years ago. She counted eleven white horse trailers and as many trucks. There were men wearing white hats everywhere.

They were building, digging post holds. Horses everywhere. And not one single cow. It was like watching an anthill, or a beehive, only everything seemed to be white. Even the horses!

Hannah gasped. Those horses were white and they were enormous! Or was it only the fact that she was observing all this from a distance? From her slightly elevated standpoint, a rise in the deceptively level prairie, it seemed otherworldly, as if she was in a dream where the scene was devoid of color.

She wasn't aware that she was shaking her head back and forth and murmuring, "No, no, no. I can't go there." She remained rooted to the exact same spot, the only movement the wind flapping at her skirt, the legs of her trousers, the horse's mane, riffling through the autumn grass, and the constant flicking of the sensitive, waiting ears of her mount.

Were there no women? Only men, wearing those widebrimmed white hats. No, she wasn't going there without Jerry. She clicked her tongue, laid the reins to the left, and was on her way back, fleeing now, half-afraid one of those white-hatted men would see her and follow, chasing her off his property. That would be embarrassing. Like she was a common spy, or worse yet, an intruder, a tramp.

She retraced her route, keeping an eye out for Lemuel Short, but there was no sign of him. The sun was still high overhead, although she could tell by the angle of her shadow that it was well past noon. And Jerry would be hungry.

Would all her days from now until her death be punctuated into three separate pieces? Breakfast. Dinner. Supper. Every day. If she lived to be seventy years old, that was a lot of ruptured days.

She'd wake up in a good mood and then realize she had to make him breakfast. A few hours of work and then there was another meal to be reckoned with. Figuring out what to cook was the hardest part. There wasn't much of a variety after two years of drought, and Jerry was as stingy and tight as her Uncle Jonas who'd had a reputation for being the most frugal person anyone had ever heard of.

Well, they hadn't met Jerry Riehl. Every bit of bone and gristle from a piece of meat was given to the dogs. Vegetable peelings went to the hens in the henhouse. All leftover grease that remained in the frying pan was left until the last meal of the day, to reuse again and again. Leftover bachelor philosophy is what it was. One of these days, she'd get tired of his tightfisted ways and tell him so.

Marriage vows didn't necessarily include cooking. You promised to care for them, in sickness and in health, although there was no mention of exactly how. As long as Jerry wasn't losing weight, it meant he had kept his health okay, right? There was nothing saying she had to cook *well*.

As she approached the ranch, Hannah searched the wheat field for the nodding mules and Jerry's straw hat, but found the field empty. The team was standing by the corral fence, so she figured her calculations were right on the dot. Jerry was hungry.

She stabled the horse, carried herself to the house with her long strides.

She smelled the dinner before she saw him standing by the kitchen range, spatula in hand, batter down the front of his white shirt. He turned when he heard the screen door slap closed.

"Hannah!"

No reply, as usual.

"You're back so soon." A smile spread his mouth wide, creased the dark eyes with a glad light. Almost Hannah dropped her guard, but she caught herself in time. Almost, she forgot herself and blurted out the whole story of the strange goings-on at the Klassermans'. She almost mirrored the enthusiasm in his eyes with her own. But she held back.

"It's not too soon," she said gruffly, as she turned and disappeared into the bathroom to wash her hands.

"I'm making pancakes."

No answer, only the running water and hand wringing, the drop of the lava soap into the dish. When she reappeared, her face was dark with an unnamed emotion.

Jerry stood eyeing her, his hands on both hips, the pancake turner sticking out of his curled palm like a growth. "What's wrong with you?"

"Who said there was anything wrong?"

"You look troubled."

"You can't tell."

"Sure I can. Something isn't right at the neighbors'."

Hannah didn't reply. How did he know? She walked over to the stove and peered in the cast-iron frying pan. "You're burning your pancakes."

Quickly he inserted the turner under a bubbling orb of batter, lifted it, and bent his head to examine the color. Straightening, he announced, "Wrong!"

His face, his shoulders, everything was too close. His nearness was too much like a magnet, starting with those crinkling brown eyes that enveloped her with that disturbingly happy light, a glow that was so genuine, so real, a light she had begun to accept, which was a weakness, a letting go of . . . something. He continued to smile at her, the light in his eyes changing to a darker one, with even more magnetic power.

Hannah stepped back, called over her shoulder, "I see you trailed mud into the washroom, like you always do." Harsh, grating words. The tone accusatory.

Jerry flipped the pancakes, felt the rebuttal, was used to it. One step forward, two back.

"No syrup?" he called.

"Molasses."

"Boy, what I would give for a glass jar of maple syrup."

"I hate that stuff."

One eyebrow arched as he stared at her. "Maple syrup? Hannah, come on."

She didn't answer, slammed two plates on the table, added glasses, knives, forks, and spoons. They ate in silence. The clock ticked on the wall, the pendulum clicked, catching the afternoon rays of the sun when it swung left.

Hannah was ravenous and devoured three pancakes with a thick coating of molasses, washed down with milk. Jerry watched her eat, loved the way food disappeared in small, neat bites, efficiently consuming as many pancakes as he did.

"You want coffee?" she asked, when she was finished.

"Is it hot?"

"Did you heat it?"

"No."

"Won't take long."

And so they chipped away at the solid wall between them, like digging mortar from between bricks with a toothpick, leaving all Hannah had seen, all she had experienced, uncovered and untouched.

He didn't need to know about Lemuel Short. As far as those white people at the Klasserman ranch, he could find that out for himself. She didn't know who they were or what they were doing, so there was no use talking about it.

CHAPTER 5

To STAND BESIDE JERRY ON A MILD AUTUMN AFTERNOON, TO ALLOW him to show her the small green shoots of wheat appearing above the tilled prairie soil, to feel the same sense of hope and accomplishment, was something she had not prepared herself for.

Anything that had to do with the prosperity of the homestead struck a deep emotion in Hannah, one that eclipsed every other aspect of her life. It was beyond comprehension, glorious.

The success was coming with almost no anxiety on her part, no staying awake worrying how the poor, worn-out horses would ever pull a plow through this awful soil. It seemed like a luxury no one deserved, least of all, herself.

For the first time in his life, Jerry experienced Hannah's face alight with approval and happiness. She was so beautiful. So unreal. Like an untouchable photograph.

"I can't believe it!" she said.

"You can. It's real! If this warm weather holds, we'll be the proud, new wheat growers of the county. The best winter wheat."

"How high does the new growth need to be to survive the winter, do you think?"

"Oh, a couple more inches. It's well-established. If you look across this whole field, you can already see the drill rows."

Hannah nodded. "The whole field has a green haze, like a veil."

"It's a promise. If all goes well, we'll have a strong stand of rippling, golden wheat by next summer. With rain, of course. And the Lord's blessing."

Hannah chewed her lower lip. "And, no hail, fire, or any other natural disaster."

"You're worrying, Hannah."

"No, just thinking out loud." The wind tugged at the black scarf on her head, tossed her apron away from her dress skirt. "It just makes me sad for my father."

"Why?"

"Oh, he had the same dream we do. The same goal. He just didn't have the resources, the horsepower, nothing. It seemed like all he had was a firm determination, a rock-solid faith that God would help him out. I used to get so mad at him and he knew it."

Jerry grinned. "You know, if you don't stop getting angry with me, I'll have an accident, and you'll regret it."

"Stop saying things like that!"

"You don't need me, only my money."

Hannah felt the furious blush of color rise in her face. She tried to speak, opened her mouth to deny his words, but it would be hollow, false, if she tried to answer him otherwise. The truth was what he had just said. It was exactly the way it really was.

"You married me for better or for worse. So, I'm worse."

Jerry laughed outright, a burst of pure glee, bent over and slapped his knee. "One thing about you, Hannah, you are the most honest person I know."

"Not always."

"When aren't you?"

Hannah shrugged and turned to go. "Time to check the creek bottom for more firewood." Jerry turned to follow, wondering what exactly she had meant.

They had a good supply of firewood and more than enough hay. The longhorns roamed the homestead, growing fat and lazy, contentedly chewing their cuds, luxuriating in the never-ending supply of cold, fresh water pumped into the tank by the whirring windmill. When the wind took on a decided bite and temperatures lowered each week, Hannah's eyes turned to the young blades of green wheat, wondering what, if anything, would keep them from being destroyed by the frequent heavy snowfall, the plummeting temperatures, the wind shrieking and moaning as it blew walls of ice particles around like miniature darts.

How could a whole field of tender new wheat withstand those natural calamities?

There was a mild day, when the wind stilled, strangely, leaving a deep quiet that Hannah felt in her bones, a solitude that took away her calm and shoved her through the house with manic energy.

She cleaned the pantry, a bucket of soapy water by her side, yanking out barrels and bags of flour, salt pork, cornmeal, tins of lard, scrubbing and wiping until her hands burned from the strong soap. She rearranged the containers on the shelves, scrubbed the floor to a deep shine, then stood back to survey what she had accomplished.

Deciding she could not take the strange stillness, she began cleaning the kitchen, yanking everything out of the cupboards, wiping down shelves and doors and the bottom of drawers, washing utensils and dusty pans and bowls her mother had frequently used to make pies and cakes, a duty Hannah refused to do. If her bread was like slices of lumber, how could she hope to bake a decent cake? Pies were completely out of her range, so she may as well not even attempt it.

In the hours before dinnertime, the house took on a strange yellow glow, as if the sun was shining through a veil of smoke. Putting down the cleaning rag she was wielding with so much energy, she straightened, pushed back a lock of dark hair, then stepped out on the porch to cast an anxious eye from one horizon to the other. She tried to recall when she had seen a sky like this. Wasn't it before the blizzard that had kept them all housebound for almost a week, when they used a rope to ensure their safe return when they went to feed the horses in the barn?

She licked her forefinger and held it up to the open air to determine the direction of the wind. As calm as it appeared to be, the right side of her finger felt cooler, so she decided the air was from the north, perhaps a bit to the east. Her brows drew down. October, though. The last week in October was too early for a snowstorm. So, she imagined there was no real danger. She calculated the amount of firewood stacked on the back stoop, the plentiful hay, the leathery resistance of the new breed of cattle, those skinny creatures with long horns that ran a close contest with the mules in a race for ugliness!

She snorted her derisive, dismissing sound from her nostrils. She couldn't believe she'd been such a pushover, allowing Jerry to get rid of those beautiful Black Angus cattle. Here they were, no better than the Jenkinses, with a herd of weird-looking cattle that would bring a poor price at the cattle market in Dorchester. They may be sleek now, but till spring, when they dropped their calves, they'd be nothing but leathery, long-haired hides stretched across bony skeletons. They wouldn't make any profit on them.

She heard the dull sound of hoofbeats, swung her eyes in that direction to find Jerry riding in on King, Nip and Tuck bouncing along by his side.

She turned and went into the house to resume her work, not wanting him to see her standing in the yard as if she was eagerly watching for his return.

When he came into the house, whistling, a spring in his step, his dark eyes alight, she went back to her cleaning, vigorously applying the rag to the cupboard doors, ignoring him.

"Hannah!"

She didn't answer, so he went on.

"It's a great day to ride over to the neighbors'. There's no wind and it's mild. Do you want to ride with me? Just to see if anyone moved in?"

She hadn't told him what she had seen, and he didn't ask, so he wouldn't know that the place was swarming with strange, white-hatted men. She stopped wiping cupboard doors, straightened her back, and looked at him. "I don't like the looks of this weather."

"What's wrong with it, Hannah? It's a gorgeous fall day. Like the Indian summer in Pennsylvania."

"The atmosphere is yellow. It's too still."

"Oh, come on. It's October."

"The last week in October."

"Have you ever seen snow this early?"

Hannah wanted to say yes, but she couldn't say it truthfully, so she went back to her cleaning, shrugging her shoulders.

"Let's eat lunch real quick and then ride over. We can take the dogs."

Hannah said nothing, just picked up her pail of soapy water and disappeared through the washhouse door, flinging the water across the backyard. She set a pot of salted water to boiling, threw in a few handfuls of cornmeal, and went to the bathroom to come her hair and wash her face. She'd go. The lure of the horseback ride and the open plains was too strong to refuse.

To wear a white covering or not? That was the question. She knew Jerry loved to see her dressed in the traditional white head covering. But what if there was a nip in the air later in the day? She'd need her black headscarf, tied securely beneath her chin.

No, she'd wear her head covering. With the green dress, she would look more attractive. Not that she cared what Jerry thought, though. But there were new people to meet, and they may as well know from her first appearance that they were different, saving themselves the explanation that would eventually have to be given.

She tied her good black apron over the green dress, pinned her covering to her head, and made her appearance, going straight to the stove to stir the boiling cornmeal mush.

"You always look so nice in your white covering."

Hannah didn't give him the satisfaction of an answer, simply got down two bowls, the sugar and milk, a few slices of leftover salt pork, and a loaf of bread.

They sat down together, their chairs scraping loudly on the wooden floor. Without looking at her, Jerry bowed his head, and Hannah followed suit, as they prayed silently, or Jerry did anyway. Hannah was thinking about the neighbors being so white and forgot to pray.

She often did that, a habit formed in childhood. She told Manny once that God knew she was thankful for her food, and if she remembered to tell Him once a week or so, that was probably all right with Him.

If she watched Jerry, though, his bowed head, his closed eyes, his lips moving in the most devout manner, she felt guilty, and quickly offered her own thanks. Formal prayer was not always her way, but living with Jerry, for whom she had to carry at least a bit of respect, was different somehow, than her own father, who was given to long and pious prayers, silent or otherwise. He often read the old German prayers from the small black *Gebet* (prayer) book, his words rising and falling in a tearful, emotional cadence that only brought a hardness, a rebellion in Hannah.

He had been so absolute in his devotion to God, and so hopelessly muddled in his way of providing for his family, unable to accept defeat, without a clear vision for the future, expecting a miracle from the God he felt would accept him as superior, special.

And He may have, Hannah thought. Who was she to judge? She just knew there was a difference in her own father and Jerry. (She never thought of him as her husband; it was too personal.) Their marriage was a partnership for the saving of the homestead. Nothing more.

They rode out, deciding at the last minute to leave the dogs at home. They'd had plenty of exercise, running with Jerry when he was checking the cattle. They set up an awful, pitiful whining and yelping, clawing at the wire fence that enclosed them, their brown eyes begging, pleading with all the power of children not wanting to be left alone.

Hannah looked at Jerry. Their eyes met. Hannah watched the crinkles appear on his face, watched the slow smile spread his lips, and she knew he felt the same empathy for their dogs, and opened the gate.

They tumbled out, falling over each other, wriggling and giving short, ecstatic yelps of happiness, then ran circles around Jerry, Hannah, and the horses. Hannah laughed outright, that short, deep burst of sound that came from deep within, a sound heard so seldom that it never failed to shock Jerry.

They mounted their horses, still smiling as the dogs catapulted themselves ahead of them, streaks of brown, black, and speckled gray, their legs almost invisible, they pumped them so fast.

Hannah laughed again. "Those stupid little dogs. They'll wear themselves out," she said.

Jerry was busy holding King back from running with the dogs. His head was up, his neck arched, his haunches lowered as he danced, stepped sideways, fought the bit. He shook his head and snorted, then came up, his front legs leaving the ground. Jerry leaned forward, kept his seat, and told him to settle down.

Hannah kept her own horse in check, scanning the sky with anxious eyes. She did not like the feel of the atmosphere, the yellow light, the sun a hazy blob of illumination, like a bobbing lantern in the distance, or the headlight of a car. It wasn't normal, the stillness, the complete lack of even the faintest breeze.

She kept her worries to herself, knowing Jerry would think she was being too cautious, which she supposed she was.

Where had this come from, now? This lack of speaking her mind. Surely, she wasn't changing that much. She used to tell Jerry anything she wanted, she didn't care what he thought. Why didn't she do that now?

She watched his back, the way he rode his horse, that certain skill that always amazed her when she saw it in the Jenkins boys. When had Jerry acquired that same skill? It was unsettling, this grudging admiration she felt. She had to do something about it, but how?

She trained her eyes on her surroundings, choosing to watch the emptiness, that vast expanse of nothingness where you could not see anyone or anything, yet you often had the uncanny feeling of being watched.

God's eyes, she reckoned. God was everywhere, a fact she'd accepted from her birth, one of her earliest memories. Hearing her mother speak of *da Goot Mon* (the Good Man) was as natural as breathing, so whenever Hannah had the impression of being watched, it was all right with her.

The dogs had chased up a prairie hen, the poor fowl running in zigzags like a rabbit before finally having enough sense to take wing. Of all the creatures of the plains, those prairie hens had to be the dumbest.

She watched the chicken's awkward flight, flapping its wings furiously, squawking in wild-eyed alarm. The dogs' faces lifted, tongues lolling from wide mouths, before giving up the chase and finding another scent to follow.

A flurry of dickcissels rose from the swell of grass to the right like a burst of thrown wheat seeds, their shrill cries telling of their alarm. A larkspur sang its plaintive song from a hiding place, probably somewhere on an extra-large tuft of grass, the bird blending into its native background in much the same color.

They arrived at the corner where the dirt road led off to the right, a row of aging fence posts held up by their hidden length in the dry prairie soil, rows of sagging, rusted barbed wire strung between them.

No one seemed to know anything about this short length of useless fence, or cared about it, so Hannah always used it as a road sign, the right turn to the Klassermans'. It seemed strange to think of them being gone, having put all the hard work into the homestead and then deserting it.

They were no longer young, and certainly not the tough, sinewy type like the Jenkinses, the Moores, and dozens of other natives that dotted this land. Descendants of the pioneers, proud, unflappable, despising change, suspicious of strangers, harboring entire textbooks of knowledge in their brains, their hearts filled with a deep and abiding love of the land, a fierce loyalty to the plains and the elements.

Hannah was proud to be one of them. She believed she carried the same spirit of optimism within, the way the Jenkinses rode with the ebb and flow of the seasons, the extreme weather, the loneliness of being on the prairie for days on end.

The wind, though. She knew well that sometimes the wind was hardest to take. It blew hard for days and nights, on and on without ceasing, moaning around the corners of buildings like unhappy ghosts, ruffling grasses, blowing dust only days after a miniscule amount of rain, drying out any small amount of moisture that fell from the skimpy clouds.

And so she rode behind Jerry, never beside him, to avoid conversation. She liked it this way, her thoughts her own, the solitude a gift, not having to answer to anyone, only the horse beneath her and nature around her.

The road went to the left, then curved right and the sight of the ranch was immediate. No horse trailers. A few cars parked by the house. No activity. Everything strangely quiet. What had happened to them all?

Jerry rode on, never imagining that Hannah had ever been here before or knew anything about these people. She kept her distance, observed without saying a word.

They rode up to the familiar barn, stopped at the corral, dismounted, and looked around. Nip and Tuck were told to stay while they tied the horses to the hitching rack beside the closed barn doors.

Hannah thought that seemed odd, on a balmy, quiet day, to have all those doors closed. There were no white horses to be seen anywhere. No cattle or dogs.

Jerry looked at the parked vehicles, long, low, gleaming in the dull, yellowish light of the semi-dreary day. He gave a low whistle, admiring the teal green color of the Oldsmobile, the brilliant, earth-shaking opulence of the red Ford.

"Obviously, there are no people of poverty here!"

Hannah nodded. "Should we go to the house?"

"I guess. No one seems to be out here."

Together they walked to the house, the dear ranch structure that had housed Sylvia Klasserman and all her eccentric German ways, her florid pink face and enormous girth, the baklava and croissants, cinnamon rolls and raisin bread. Hannah swallowed an unexpected lump in her throat, realized she was blinking furiously to keep back unwanted tears.

No one came to the door, so Jerry knocked again. Hannah felt terribly ill at ease, when the door was pulled open from inside by a man who seemed to be about their own age and size.

From behind the screen door, his face broke into a grin of friendliness as he shoved open the door and spoke in a quiet, well-modulated voice. "Come in. Come in. I'm assuming you're neighbors?" The sentence rose at the end, making it a question. His way of speaking was completely foreign to their own, although the words were spoken in English.

Jerry stepped back to allow Hannah entry before him, a hand laid lightly on the small of her back. She went ahead quickly, so he'd drop his hand.

It was still the Klassermans' house, only it smelled different, the furniture was different, the rugs and pictures changing the living room into something more structured, neater. Gone were the crocheted doilies, the figurines and artificial pink roses, replaced by wooden chests, serviceable trays, green ferns in ceramic pots, throw pillows and blankets in neutral colors, all done tastefully and expensively.

The young man introduced himself. "My name is Timothy Weber. I'm from Salt Lake City, Utah."

Jerry proffered a hand. They shook firmly, met each other's gaze directly. "I'm Jeremiah Riehl and this is my wife Hannah." Hannah nodded, shook hands, and asked, "How do you do?"

"I'm doing well, thank you, Hannah. And you?"

"Good."

Timothy Weber stood back to survey them with curious eyes, taking in Jerry's straw hat with the strip of rawhide circling the crown, his denim coat without pockets, his broadfall trousers, as well as Hannah's skirts and head covering. "So you're . . .?

"Amish. From Pennsylvania."

Timothy whistled softly. "Never heard of them. A religious sect?"

"Yes."

"Well, this is interesting. Very interesting. We'll have to talk. But first, let me seat you. Here, Jeremiah, is it?"

"Call me Jerry. Everybody does."

Timothy grinned an infectious grin. "Tim. Call me Tim."

He really was a nice-looking young man. Brown hair, cut short in the manner of the English, a thin brown moustache above a wide mouth, a prominent nose and expressive blue eyes, hooded by a wealth of brown eyebrows.

Tim seated them on the sofa, a large, deep davenport upholstered in gray. Expensive, Hannah thought, as she reached back to arrange pillows behind her back. Tim seated himself in an oak rocking chair and stretched his denim-clad legs out before him. Hannah looked around, wondering if he had a wife, children, or parents? Who were all those men, with the white trailers and white horses?

"So," Tim began. "The reason it is interesting to me that you are of a religious sect is because we are too. Oh, I meant to tell you. My wife is taking a much-needed nap. I told you we're from Salt Lake City. You probably have heard of the Mormons? The Church of the Latter-day Saints?"

"Yes." Jerry nodded.

"We are of that religious order." His voice turned quiet, and his eyes became averted. He lifted both hands to examine his fingernails, as if mentioning his church made him nervous, self-conscious.

There was an awkward silence. Then Tim sighed. "We moved here to begin a new life after leaving our way of life among the . . . the brethren of the Mormon Church."

Jerry raised his eyebrows, watched Tim's face, but said nothing. Tim took a deep breath, a smile appeared on his face, one that showed his white teeth but did not spread to his eyes. "So, here we are. Pioneers on the prairie. North Dakota. Bought this ranch. I raise horses."

White horses, Hannah thought. She wanted to know what the breed was called but of course, she couldn't say that in Jerry's presence.

"Tell me about your . . . way of life."

So Jerry outlined the Amish faith briefly, the *ordnung*, the way of obedience, the journey from Lancaster County, Hannah's family homesteading the 320 acres, and that now they were the only Amish remaining.

"Why did your brethren return home?" Tim asked.

Hannah spoke up. "The two-year drought."

"You mean . . ." Tim looked from Jerry to Hannah and back again.

"It didn't rain for two years."

"Oh, come on! I have a hard time believing that." Tim laughed, slapping his knee at the joke he'd just heard.

"No, I'm serious." Hannah felt a stab of anger. Boy, did he have a lot to learn.

"You can't sit there and tell me you had not one drop of rain in two years!" Incredulous, Tim leaned forward, an intensity stabbing the room's muted yellowish glow.

"Close to it." Hannah glanced at Jerry, saw his pinched look.

Tim chuckled, a derisive sound that bordered on mockery. The moment was saved by a fluttering sound, a door closing quietly, light footsteps crossing the hallway, followed by the appearance of a vision dressed in white. Almost, Hannah recoiled, thinking a heavenly being was in their midst.

Her hair was blond, an unnatural white blond, unlike anything Hannah had ever seen, surrounding her head like a halo, purely angelic. Her eyes were large, almond-shaped, and blue, her face small and pointed, like porcelain. Doll-like, she appeared to be made of wax.

"I heard visitors," she trilled, in an unnatural child's voice.

Hannah drew back, aghast. How old was this wife of Tim's?

She walked over to Hannah and sat next to her, extending a small, white hand, exclaiming in short sentences how happy she was to see them, and how they would be close friends, how charming her head covering was, and . . . how had they arrived?

Hannah looked out the window toward the corral and noticed the fading light, the restless horses. She spoke a few words of acknowledgment to the girl's overtures, listened to Tim's introduction of his wife, Lila, then rose and said they must be on their way, she believed there would be a change in the weather, but not before Lila mentioned the fact that she was sixteen years old.

CHAPTER 6

THEY WERE SORRY TO SEE THEM LEAVE SO SOON AND URGED THEM TO stay for tea and cakes. But Hannah remained adamant. Jerry told Tim they'd be back as soon as they could, but he'd better follow his wife because she was well-versed in the ways of the weather on the plains.

As soon as they were able to get away from their pleading hosts, Hannah hissed a warning to Jerry. "We have to ride hard." That was all she said, but Jerry heard the warning in her voice. They weren't at the first bend in the road before the yellowish cast turned much darker, changed to a leaden, grayish sheen that held no promise of anything gentle or good.

The dogs were flat out, running to the best of their ability, but could not keep up with the horses' galloping pace. When they fell behind, Hannah slowed the palomino and yelled to Jerry, who turned, and slowed King as well.

Hannah dismounted, pointing a shaking finger to the northeast. "See that?"

Jerry shaded his eyes, his palm turned down, squinting, then shook his head. "What? I don't see anything."

"That gray line. It looks like a wall."

Jerry still didn't see it.

"We're in for it. That's snow. If we ride hard enough, we'll make it. If not, there's a real chance we could get lost."

"Come on, Hannah. Not in October!"

"The dogs can't keep up. You carry one. I'll take the other."

"We can't, Hannah."

"We have to."

"They'll find their way home."

Hannah shrugged and got back in the saddle—there wasn't time to waste arguing. Kicking the stirrups in the palomino's sides, she rode leaning low across the saddle, listening for King's hoofbeats behind her.

The wind picked up immediately, followed by the first gritty snowflake. Hannah became wild-eyed, watching as King flashed by, Jerry low on his neck.

She put the end of the leather reins on her horse's sides, screaming and goading him on. They had not yet reached the crossroads where the barbed wire fence sagged on the right, which meant they had a long way to go after they turned. At least four or five miles.

The dogs were no longer behind them. Hannah twisted her body in the saddle and called their names, but she knew it was futile. They'd find their way home, he'd said. Did he even know how bad snowstorms could be on the plains?

A few hard flakes of snow, and then there were thousands, biting into her face like fierce, sharp teeth. She lowered her head even farther. The horses slowed of their own accord, turned left and increased their speed until Hannah thought she must be rocketing through the air. She gasped for breath and gritted her teeth against the stinging, icy bits of snow that were assaulting her face.

King was still visible, the flying hooves and charging body with Jerry's dark head so low it appeared to be part of the flowing black mane. Hannah was gasping for breath, wiping her nose on the shoulder of her coat, nose and eyes streaming. Her ears felt as if they were being torched.

Oh for a black, woolen kerchief to tie around her head. The flying bits of snow thickened. Ahead of her, King was turning from a brown horse with a flying black mane and tail to a blob of gray, an undulating blob of non-color with invisible hooves.

Panic rose in her chest. She screamed, trying to get Jerry to slow down. The possibility of being lost in a blizzard on the plains loomed before her, the stark reality a slap in the face, a painful blow that took her breath away. She didn't realize she was muttering and sobbing, "No no, no. Please God, no."

Not this way. She didn't want to die, frozen, on the prairie, blatant evidence of her own dumb choice, unlearned greenhorns without a lick of common sense.

It's only October. It's only a squall. Over and over, she told herself this, to keep the terror at bay.

Then, she couldn't see King at all. The wind blasted through her thin coat, the snow like knifepoints. The world turned into a gray void with no top or bottom, no left or right, and she had no idea where she was headed.

Give a horse its head, it'll always find its way home. The thought was a comfort, for a short time at least. When the palomino slowed to a trot, Hannah knew there was no use pushing him faster; he'd set his own pace.

Her teeth chattering, eyes streaming, black hair plastered to her head like a rubber swimming cap, Hannah held on with her knees, shivering so hard her arms raised and lowered of their own accord like a chicken after its head is severed on the chopping block. Grimly, she reminded herself to stay calm, stay reasonable.

Her world was a whiteout now. Everything was obliterated except for the orb of whirling snow and the icy, driving wind.

"He'll get me home," Hannah whispered. Over and over. "Home. Home. He'll get me home."

A hard bump. A lurch. Hannah grabbed for the saddle horn. Too late! The palomino went down, falling with a grunt, the air expelled from his nostrils as Hannah flew off the saddle, down over the horse's bent neck, hitting the ground with a crunch on her left shoulder.

A knife edge of pain shot all the way from her fingertips to her neck. A ripping, tearing monster of agony that took away every sensation, the whirling whiteness of the storm, the downed horse, and the cold. Everything.

She slid blissfully into unconsciousness.

Jerry let King have his head, knowing Hannah was on his heels. He didn't become too concerned until the snow became so thick he had trouble keeping the side of the road in his sight. After that, it was up to King. Trusting his horse was the only way. He had never been so cold in all his life. He turned in the saddle, repeatedly calling Hannah's name, but the wind tore his words out of his mouth and flung them away. He imagined the wind laughing at him, a hysterical, evil cackle that robbed him of the small amount of confidence he had.

He prayed for God's deliverance from the grip of this awful storm. He prayed for deliverance if it was God's will, though, always putting his life in God's hands.

Whether we live or whether we die, we are the Lord's. Over and over, this verse coursed through his mind. The pain of his cold hands was almost unbearable. He envisioned black, useless fingers. Hanging the reins across King's neck, he sat up to tuck his numbed hands under his armpits, but felt only more cold and ice.

He sucked in a lungful of air, blew it out, then shivered uncontrollably. Calm. Calm. Stay with it. He talked to himself repeatedly. King slowed, picked up his head to trot, then slowed again. Each time he slowed, Jerry turned, his eyes boring through the whirling whiteness, hoping for a glimpse of Hannah on the palomino.

He was becoming sleepy, while shivering like a wind-blown leaf on a tree branch. He released his hands from beneath his armpits, slapped them against his chest, kicked his feet out of the stirrups and pumped them up and down, whacking his knees against the sides of the saddle.

King plodded on, his faithful ears still turning back, then forward, pricking through the whirling, spitting, hissing gray world being flung in Jerry's face, a cruel reminder that he was a mere mortal who had made a stupid decision, a miscalculation. Why hadn't he taken Hannah's warnings more seriously?

Not that she'd ever take his warnings. He winced when something hit his left knee, then shouted weakly, the sound like a mewling kitten.

The corral. Thank God! He stopped, waiting for Hannah.

The realization that she was not directly behind him arrived slowly. Finally, to stave off his rising panic, he dismounted on legs that seemed to be made of liquid. He fell, his bare hands scrabbling in the deepening snow as he righted himself, wobbled to the barn, his stiffened fingers fumbling with the latch like a young child.

Surely Hannah would be here soon. He unsaddled King, rubbed him down, fed him, gave him a small amount of water, his ears tuned for the sound of Hannah's arrival. *Please, please.* Over and over he begged. *Keep her safe, Lord. Keep her safe.*

He made his way to the house by unspooling a long length of hemp rope, missing the house several times by a good one hundred feet each time. First to the right, then to the left, before bumping solidly into the side of the house, cracking his nose until tears ran down his cheeks.

Somehow, he kept enough of his senses to start a fire in the cook stove, open the draught until a roaring fire turned the stove top cherry red. Repeatedly, he went to the window, fighting down the dragon's fiery panic, the imagined monster that took away his sense of hope, his ability to pray and believe that God would look down with mercy.

Please. Please.

Hannah struggled as if she was under water, bravely fighting to open her mouth and fill her lungs with life-saving air.

She was so cold. So terribly cold. *She was a child, playing in the snow, her crocheted mittens soaked, her hands red and wet and freezing. There was Manny. She'd get his mittens. She ran after him, calling, calling, but he seemed never to hear her at all.*

She was crying when she regained consciousness. The palomino was down and, by the looks of it, had either broken or otherwise injured his foot. He made no attempt to regain his footing, merely huddled in a heap of golden hide and cream-colored mane and tail, his eyes closed against the whipping wind and snow.

Hannah's first logical reasoning was to stay where she was. She knew that to wallow about on level land in zero visibility was courting death, and she had no intention of dying this way. She took stock of her situation.

One downed horse. No one to rescue her this time. A saddle and yes, a saddle blanket. Both impossible to remove. If she could somehow loosen the girth strap, she'd be able to use both to try and keep from freezing. Then she'd have to wait out the storm and hope for the best.

She moved, which sent an electric shock through her shoulder. She felt like she might lose consciousness again, which really made her mad.

She took her right hand and grasped her left shoulder, pushing and prodding, squeezing her eyes shut against the pain. Nothing broken, just bumped and bruised.

Hannah got to her feet, crying now, the pain almost unbearable. She slipped a hand beneath the wide girth strap, and pulled. She pushed, working the girth up over the belly of the horse, shaking her numb, red hands over and over, alternately muttering and crying.

When the girth strap would not let loose, she fell on her backside, hard, then went back to tugging the saddle and blanket loose from the horse's body. She realized the importance of these two items, the difference between life and death. Gritting her teeth, she squeezed her eyes shut and kept pulling, over and over, yanking, urging the palomino to roll just a bit. Just a bit.

Only when the tears froze on her numb cheeks did she realize she was begging, crying, pushing on the horse's stomach with one hand, yanking on the wide girth strap with the other.

She lifted numb hands to cup her flaming ears and the side of her head. How long could a person expect to survive in these harsh conditions?

She freed the saddle with a mighty heave, then the blanket. Quickly she found the lee side of the horse, away from the driving snow.

She tucked herself in, pulled the fibrous, itching saddle blanket over her body, rolling up in a tight fetal position, then reaching out with one hand to draw the saddle over her head and shoulders. A blessed reprieve, if only for a short time. She felt the absence of the wind's fury, the stinging of the icy snow. Exhausted, she reveled in the still, dark cocoon of the horse's body, the blanket, and the saddle.

Thank God for the trousers and boots, the woolen socks on her feet. She was still shaking with the cold, miserable with goose bumps going up and down her spine and across her shoulders, her ears and hands burning with the extreme cold and moisture of the melting snow.

Her teeth clacked together. She put her hands between her knees, rolling and grimacing with the pain. Well, she was here, now. In the biggest mess she'd ever been in. She guessed it was up to her to figure something out, with Jerry on his own and the dogs having gone their way. She hoped he wouldn't be dumb enough to start out on his own in this storm. Many more people than she cared to admit had died on the plains in a blizzard.

Had they discussed this together? She couldn't remember. She had no choice, no other option but to stay where she was and hope the storm would soon blow itself out and she could attempt to find her way back home. She would freeze to death if she tried to get to their homestead, if the storm continued through the night.

The horse afforded some heat. Why did he lay here? If his leg was broken, Jerry would have to shoot him. There was no repairing a horse's leg bone. She regretted not having taken him as a gift. The horse with no name, as she recognized him. If she would have accepted the gift of the beautiful palomino, she would have felt beholden to him, like she owed him the favor of being his friend, which she resisted.

And now she'd gone and married him, to save the homestead, and was in the same unsteady boat in the same swamp of her own will.

Perhaps it would just be easier to die out here on the prairie that she loved. Frozen stiff.

A fierce resistance to her own demise roared through her, leaving her shaken and unable to understand her intense, overwhelming fervor for life.

She would not die. She had this makeshift cave of sorts, the heat from the horse's body, if he lived through the night.

The sound of the blowing snow scouring the blanket told her the storm was still roaring across the prairie. Like a freight train, this wind. There was no stopping it, no directing it where you wanted it to go, or when you wanted it to cease.

She felt as if God was above the storm, mad at her, teaching her a lesson, like a child being punished. He certainly was not showing any mercy, no matter how much she cried and begged.

Well then, if this was what He thought she needed, then she'd take her punishment, and take it right, without complaint.

Her father had spanked her many times as a child so she figured this was the grown-up version of a "paddling" in the woodshed, where her gentle father would get down on one knee, grasp her shoulders tenderly, and explain to her in great and lengthy detail how she had disobeyed and, in order to correct her for doing wrong, she needed to feel the pain of the thin, flat piece of wood. To disobey made the Lord sad. Children who were left to their own devices, who never learned to submit to their parents, would find it hard to submit to God in later years.

Hannah stoically endured the few whacks of the board, which hurt, but not much. She never cried. Her father cried, which she thought was awfully strange. Why would you spank someone if it was that heartbreaking? What was so bad about chasing the cows into the pond? They liked the cool water. They just looked funny when they ran! Hannah never really felt bad about chasing cows. She never understood all this sorry and repent and all that. He could have tried to see it her way.

As she lay shivering beneath her makeshift tent, many incidences from her childhood roamed through her mind, like a herd of memories that found no comfortable way to disappear, so they just wandered around, bits and pieces, snatches of mischief, episodes of anger and disobedience.

Repeatedly, she had been chastised, talked to about sin and repentance and the eyes of God. About Jesus, who died on the cross. Countless times, she'd heard different ministers speak of these things, in many different sermons, and had always been completely and thoroughly bored.

Nothing ever stuck to her heart or mind it seemed. She could listen to the most fervent sermon, and remember only the bristles on the speaker's cheeks, or his too-long, greasy hair, or the way he unfolded his severely ironed handkerchief. Three hours of sitting on a hard, wooden bench was much too long, so she found ways to amuse herself, usually whispering, playing with straight pins, or watching flies or, if she was fortunate, looking out a nearby window.

Her father had patiently explained the new birth, but that never made much sense, either. She understood the basics of the Christian life—to do good, stay away from evil, and accept Jesus Christ as your personal Savior. Actually, she wasn't sure if she had ever done exactly that, in a deep, meaningful, spiritual way. She wasn't normal, maybe. Formal worship, like prayers and Bible reading, simply didn't interest her.

But so many times, beneath the enormous sky on the emptiness of the prairie, she felt as if she was a small dot, a worm, the pinhead of every human being, so small, so unimportant. And yet, God being as big as the sky and as tremendous as the wind, He *knew* her, every ounce of her. He knew her thoughts and her actions and how rebellious she was and how ignorant to other people.

But He had given her that nature, hadn't He? Well then, He would be able to change her heart when it was time.

Lying in the increasing discomfort of dripping snow, where the heat from the horse's body caused a melting stream to constantly trickle along her back, sent wave after wave of cold through her spine. She inched away, only to allow a fresh wave of cold to enter beneath the elevated blanket.

Oh, misery! She writhed with pain, allowing herself only inches to relieve stiff joints and aching fingers and toes.

How long? How long would the storm blow? She tried to will away nighttime, the encompassing blackness with no stars and no moon. Once night came, it might not leave before the horse, the saddle, and the blanket with her beneath were completely obscured in snow. Drifts on the plains were often two, three feet high, which would shroud their dead bodies until the spring thaw.

Who would find her? Jerry? The Jenkinses? A whole pile of rescue workers from the town?

She wasn't ready to die. She wanted to stay right here in North Dakota and keep the homestead. She loved her life on the prairie, the cows, the wildflowers, the animals and birds, the ranch house and barn, the mules and Jerry's horses.

Him? Jerry? Did she want to stay here in the world for Jerry? If only she could understand God and love and all the good things other people understood then perhaps she'd have a chance at loving her husband. But what exactly was love? Who could explain it to you? Help you find it?

And now she was getting sleepy. So terribly tired. The thought of closing her eyes and succumbing to a blissful cloud of sleep was the single most enticing emotion she had ever felt.

She'd heard somewhere, though, about the danger of falling asleep when a person is freezing cold. But she had to sleep. Had to. She couldn't stay awake. It was not possible.

Her eyelids fell. She drifted off into a place where the wet smell of the snow on the horse's body, the shivering goose bumps and pain, the knives of ice and frozen snow, disappeared to be replaced by an unimaginable place of softness and comfort, warmth and light.

Jerry paced. His hands knotted behind his back, he walked from room to room, his neck thrust forward, his dark hair falling in his eyes, a black stubble of whiskers growing across his ashen cheeks. That it should come to this.

He loved her. That was the pain of his existence, his single reason for staying with her in this ranch house, so far away from family, from his friend, Jake, from any human being who could make this vigil bearable.

When he heard the dogs barking, he ran to the door and flung it open, ushering them in to the warmth. Icicles hung from their thick fur and clumps of snow stuck in their paws. He hurried to get towels to wrap them in and brought them fresh bowls of water, thanking God that they had found their way.

Grateful for the dogs' company, he kneeled on the floor between them and prayed to the One he knew intimately. He begged his Lord and Savior to spare Hannah's life, but always had to add, "If it is Thy will." God's blessed will, which was to be honored above all else, even the treasure of his love for Hannah.

There were times of peace, when he felt his soul yielding to God, pliable, soft, accepting of his fate. Then came a desperate need to see her face, hear her voice, to apologize for letting her drop behind on their mad dash through the storm that grabbed him in a grip like a vise, until he thought he would surely lose his mind.

The storm battered the house, the wind and snow like flung pellets of stone against the windows. When darkness came, he began to shiver. His limbs turned to water, his breath came in short, hard gasps of agony.

Oh, Hannah. Hannah. Your suffering is more than I can bear. He would have gladly laid in the snow himself if it meant he could save her.

Please stop. Stop. Stop the snow and the wind.

His thoughts were becoming maudlin. If only he had gone back, if only he hadn't assumed she was behind him all the time.

He flung himself down on the davenport and cried hard, painful sobs of anguish and despair.

Had he been too selfish in his single-minded pursuit of her? He had to have Hannah at all cost. He'd given up the security of his Amish community, the horse-shoeing business, a bright and enterprising future, to live her with her—and for what? Oh dear God, for what?

His breathing slowed and became even as he fell to his knees, his face buried in his hands, groaning softly, begging God without words.

He sat up, drained and exhausted, cold and shivering. He lit a kerosene lamp with shaking fingers, had to blow at the match flame three times before it would die.

The fire in the cook stove had gone out, not an ember remained. Dully, he threw in a handful of kindling, held another match to it, opened the draft to watch it burn.

He added larger pieces of wood from the wood box behind the stove, noticed the few pieces remaining, but could not bring himself to go to the back stoop to collect more wood. He'd have to know, then, how deep the accumulation of snow had become.

He felt guilty as he spread his hands to the warmth, knowing that Hannah would have nothing to warm her freezing body.

And still the storm raged on.

Jerry resumed his pacing. He went to the windows, touched the glass with his fingers, as if he had power to stop the onslaught of deadly snow and ice. He put more wood on the fire.

I love you, Hannah, with all of my heart and soul. If it's not God's will that we live together in love, then I pray you will know perfect peace in Heaven.

He felt calm now, accepting his destiny, abandoning his own will to God's. What was his selfish, paltry, little love compared to God, who had sent His only Son so that we may live?

He stood still. Was the storm lessening? Was there only a slight change in the wind? Or was it all his own hope that made it seem so?

He sat down, weakly. He listened, holding his breath, hardly daring to exhale, for fear it was like a mirage, a cruel hallucination.

Decidedly now, there was a weakening of the storm. He whipped his body around to look at the clock. Almost eleven o'clock at night.

He couldn't wait until morning. He simply could not. He'd take a lantern and the dogs. His only hope was a lack of wind. All he needed were starlit skies, a moon, and a bit of calm.

He was on his feet, running to his bedroom for warm clothing, an extra pair of socks, tears running unchecked down his face.

CHAPTER 7

It was common knowledge on the plains that a blizzard brought to a halt all outside activity. It was dangerous, foolhardy, to attempt a rescue or to search for lost cattle or horses if a storm of this velocity swept through the area.

If only they had never ventured out. Jerry stepped off the porch, alarmed to discover the depth of the snow. It was a good two feet in some places; other places were windswept, and fell to less than a foot.

The barn loomed dark through the snow that was now falling more slowly and thinly, as the storm gave its last gasp, giving Jerry a burst of elation. If he could only get to her before the inevitable wind unleashed its power on the unprotected prairie.

With fumbling, frantic movements, he saddled King, mounted, and held the lantern out from the eager, bouncing horse. With a whispered prayer, he gave King his head, bowing his own head to the spitting snow, the tail end of the storm.

How far would she have come? He tried to concentrate and stay on the road, though the road and the prairie were all one solid blanket of white now. If only there were trees, embankments, fences, neighbors, the way the countryside appeared in Lancaster County. He'd need a keen sense of direction, and the skill to search beyond the small circle of yellow lamplight.

The cold had not worsened, thank God. King was tiring already, so he slowed him to a walk. The snow was up to his chest in some of the lower areas. Jerry could only lean forward, his eyes straining above the glow of the lantern, piercing the darkness with a desperate gaze. The thought of this being foolish, being out at night alone directly after a storm, crossed his mind and left him with a rising sense of despair.

Should he have waited until daybreak? King charged on, plowing through the deep places, increasing his speed where the power of the wind had swept the ground almost bare. If only Hannah could be on a rise of ground and visible. He guessed the palomino would have wandered home, found his way, if he had remained upright. He knew the power of these storms, the mind-sucking confusion that robbed even seasoned Westerners of all sense of direction and level-headedness.

All the gopher holes, the prairie dog and badger homes that dotted the grasslands like set traps, meant that the palomino could have gone down. He likely did. All Jerry could hope for was Hannah's safety, that she had remained by her horse and stayed conscious. The saddle and blanket were her only hope of even a bit of shelter.

He pulled on the reins and stopped King. He had to get his bearings. Lowering the lantern, his intense gaze swept the level land as far as he could see. He calculated he'd come more than a mile, which meant he had about three more to go until the turn to the Texan's ranch. If the barbed wire and sagging posts were visible, he'd know he was on the right track.

But who knew how far off the road the palomino might have drifted? The sense of futility settled in and left him slumped in the saddle, his arms draped across the saddle horn, the lantern too close to his horse.

Should he return to the ranch, keeping his own safety in mind? He knew well the astounding fury of the wind after a winter storm, sending walls of thick snow scudding across the prairie without mercy on man or beast. A shiver went up his spine. He prayed, asking the Lord to guide him.

He sat motionless, the vast darkness around him, the great white void of the treeless plain suddenly becoming a menacing pit that had swallowed Hannah, never to surrender her frozen corpse.

He shook his head to clear it. After praying, why did such thoughts wedge their way in to his mind? He needed a stronger, better faith.

A sense of his own weak humanity encompassed him. *Miserable creature that I am*, he thought, *chasing my own will and desire.* Chasing Hannah and living out here in this tough, unforgiving land, his only reason being to obtain her love, something that seemed to be as elusive as a thin wisp of fog, a mirage in the desert.

He groaned within himself, could not accept her demise. *How can I sit here crying Lord, Lord, when perhaps all this is a lesson, a hard-earned lesson in self-denial?* He knew there were countless young women dotting the hills and valleys of Pennsylvania, young women of worth. Respectful, well-brought-up girls who never asked for more than a reasonable husband, a roof over their heads, food, and children to raise, filling their husband's quiver with offspring who adorned his table. Young women who were taught submission and the blessing of a meek and quiet spirit, who understood God's will for a woman, and strived obediently to be a helpmeet, a friend, lover, nurturer, using all of the gifts God bestowed on women.

But they weren't Hannah. This knowledge unfolded in his chest and bloomed to fill his heart with its essence. He bowed before it.

As if on cue, the moon slid silently from behind silver-white clouds, throwing the snow-covered landscape into waves of blue-white and shadows of dark gray. Every rise and hollow was visible, the impotent yellow light of the lantern a pitiful mockery. He threw it into a snow drift, where it hissed and died. He'd find it in the spring.

A wild elation rose up, a sense of clear direction now. He goaded King, his head swiveled from side to side, his eyes burning from the cold and his intense, piercing gaze. He knew if he found the fence, he'd have gone too far. She had been riding behind him at least halfway from the Texan's ranch.

This merciful calm. Surely God was on his side. But how long until the wind began to howl, burying them both in its strength?

The moon's white light on the snow proved to be even better than the limited yellow glow of the coal oil lantern. One by one, stars appeared, lending their merry dots of illumination, shoring up Jerry's flagging confidence, allowing him a few minutes of courage. He rode on, scanning the snow for any mound that could be Hannah buried in the snow.

And there it was.

A bump, a protrusion that was much bigger than a clump of grass, too small to be a rise, a swell or an unexpected hillock on the otherwise level, snow-encrusted land.

He turned King in the proper direction and slowed him to a walk. His heart leaped as the mound of snow gave way, the light color of a horse's head and neck appearing, followed by a resounding whinny, the low, urgent sound of a horse in pain.

Ah, so that was it. Her horse had fallen. He threw himself off King and waded to the palomino's head, reassuring him, then dug frantically, scraping snow off the upended saddle, the frozen blanket, heaving it off the inert form curled beside the horse.

"Hannah?" he called, unable to comprehend her stillness. He fell on his knees and touched her cold, white face. "Hannah."

Louder now, he grasped her shoulder and shook with all his strength. A low moan escaped her lips but her eyes stayed closed. Thank God, she was alive!

He called her name again and again but was unable to revive her. He straightened and took stock of their dilemma.

A downed horse. His unconscious wife. Likely hypothermia had set in. Gtting her to the house was his first concern. He'd have to get her up on King, somehow, before he would be able to get himself into the saddle.

If only she'd wake up. "Hannah! Hannah!"

Another low moan, but no reason for him to think she would regain consciousness. Well, there was only one way, and that was to heave her up onto the horse's back.

With herculean strength, he picked her up and tried repeatedly to drape her across the saddle, afraid of hurting her already frozen body, knowing he could not leave her here while he went to summon help.

Finally, he was able to position her across the front of the saddle before placing a foot in the stirrup and leaping up himself.

He had to call to King repeatedly and grab the reins to stop him from leaping into action. He carefully cradled Hannah in his arms like a child before allowing King to walk away from the pitiful form of the palomino. The injured horse's eyes were wild, his neck outstretched as he tried repeatedly to gather his legs beneath him and stand, only to topple over in the deep, light snow, sending up a cloud of white powder as he sank onto his side.

Jerry well knew the palomino would never walk again, but Hannah had to be his first priority. He'd have to be put down, but he'd left his gun at home. He couldn't bring himself to think about it now.

The cold stabbed through his coat. The breeze raked a cold, ominous hand across his face, sent a shiver of alarm through him. He figured he had four miles to go, maybe more. He adjusted Hannah's weight, cradling her shoulders firmly before leaning forward and calling to King to go.

He released the reins and felt the surge of power beneath him, but knew it would be short-lived the minute King's legs hit a deep drift. Snow was flung into his face, the wind picking up by the minute. *All right, God. The rest is up to You. I'm done. I've done all I can do. If it is Thy will that we survive this, then guide my horse. Give me strength to hold on.*

The reins flopped loosely in Jerry's hands. It was up to King. The horse was powerful, a magnificent specimen of his breed, but to arrive safely to the ranch in the face of these obstacles would take every ounce of his strength. It would be the ultimate marathon of his life.

The moon faded and disappeared as a prevailing blackness surrounded them. One by one, the stars were erased from the cold, menacing sky. The breeze became stronger, playing with King's mane, slapping against Jerry's face like a punishment, grabbing his courage and flinging it away.

King was smart, Jerry knew, but would he find his way? Hope rose in his chest as King leaped to increase his speed when the snow lay thinly on the high spots. He raced across these areas, then plowed through the drifts with unbelievable strength.

The snow, the prairie, the sky, everything became one, then, as the wind began to wail and howl, the song of the elements. It battered Jerry's face with stinging ice, flung his woolen stocking cap into the vast, blowing vortex of the onslaught that followed every blizzard, sending tremendous clouds of snow racing across the miles and miles of prairie. There were no mountains, no tree lines, nothing to slow the great blitz of the North Dakota wind.

And still King lunged, gathering his muscular, rippling haunches beneath him, his breath coming in powerful exhalations, his nostrils distended as he sucked in the oxygen he needed for the pumping of his great heart, the expansion of his vigorous lungs. His head was lowered, his thick neck distended, as he used every muscle in his resplendent body, sensing the danger, knowing he was pleasing his beloved master.

He never stumbled and he slowed only when it was absolutely impossible to keep up his pace, his ears flicking back, waiting for a voice, a command. Jerry urged King, spoke softly to him, but the power of the wind tore his words away from his mouth and sent them uselessly away.

But King knew. He knew Jerry was urging him. He sensed the danger, and so he stayed on course, faithful to his training, obedient to the one master he adored.

Pain crept up under Jerry's eyelids and his ears were on fire with the cold. His right arm was cramped, sending dull throbs of pain into his shoulder. King slowed to a walk, snow up to his wide chest. When it thinned and lessened, he lunged forward.

On and on. Jerry placed complete trust in his horse. He had no idea where the buildings were situated, had no idea how far they had come or how much distance they were required to travel before there was any shelter. All he knew was that as long as King stayed on his feet and kept moving forward, if he could keep Hannah and himself in the saddle, they still had hope of survival.

Over and over he repeated, *It's up to You. It's up to You.* And it was. It was simply whether God chose to save them both. *Whether we live or whether we die, we are the Lord's.* The verse brought calm and a renewed spirit.

And then King stopped. Jerry lifted his head and saw the looming gray wall of the barn and yelled a harsh, maudlin sound he wasn't aware of making. He lifted Hannah's form and held her against his chest with superhuman effort as he swung a stiff leg across the front of the saddle and let himself fall, still holding Hannah as best he could. As he sprawled awkwardly in the deep drift by the barn wall, he let her limp body roll into the snow.

He yanked the barn door open, led the heaving King inside, then returned for Hannah. Staggering under her weight, he laid her in the loose hay by the horse stalls. Without a lantern, he worked quickly and efficiently. He rubbed the horse all over with a feed sack as he talked, crooning and praising King, alarmed at the amount of sweat and lather. He stroked his wet neck, cupped a hand to the still muzzle and laid his forehead against King's. Then, he led him to the watering trough, but took him away after a few sips. He fed him well, without sparing the hay or grain, then lowered the bar on the gate to his stall.

Jerry checked the length of rope to the house. Still there.

He bent to pick up the inert form of his wife, grasped the rope firmly in one gloved hand, and struggled to open the door and close it again before embarking on the long, arduous trek to the safety of the ranch house.

He told himself to stay calm, to take one step, one moment at a time. Visibility was almost nothing, except for an occasional glimpse of the rope he grasped with a desperate grip. He had come this far, but what if he lost the rope, missed the house by inches, and they both froze on the prairie, the fate of many hardy pioneers who lived on this harsh land before them?

His shoulders ached. His arms burned with the strain of his cold muscles called to perform this heroic effort.

The porch loomed in the whirling darkness, sending a surge of adrenaline through his bursting veins. He staggered up the steps, let go of the rope, lurched across the floor of the porch and fell against the door.

Then there was a blessed calm. A dark stillness. He realized the roaring in his ears was merely a remnant of his time in the wind.

Gently now, he laid Hannah on the sofa, alarmed at the stiffness of her limbs. Quickly, he lit a kerosene lamp, stoked the fire, opened the draft, and was rewarded by an instant crackling as the wood began to burn. He held his hands to the warmth, felt the tingle of pain in his frozen fingertips.

He shed his coat, vest, and one flannel shirt, then turned to Hannah, carrying the lamp to place it on the oak table beside the sofa. A doctor was needed, that was one thing he knew for sure. He crossed off that possibility immediately.

Hypothermia. Did people die from this condition? Why was she still unconscious? Helpless in the face of her still form, Jerry stood gazing down at her as she lay still, barely breathing, her face a waxen, ivory pearl . . . unreal.

"Hannah?"

No response. Gently, he touched her face, her ears. He opened the buttons on her coat and lifted her limp arms to pull the garment off. He didn't know what to do about the frozen skirt of her dress, the trousers that were caked with ice. The smell coming from her clothing was offensive, like an unwashed horse. Perspiration from the horse's body, he guessed.

He should rid her of those frozen clothes but, if he did, and she woke up? Well, he. . . . It was unthinkable.

He got two towels, dried off her skirt and trousers and pulled the boots from her feet, thankful to see the layers of woolen socks.

The stove turned red hot, roared, the draft beneath the burning wood causing it to go wild. Quickly, Jerry shut off the draft, then resumed his duties.

He rolled Hannah into a sheep's wool comforter, then another. He pulled the couch across the oak floor, kicking rugs from his path, until he was satisfied that the heat was close enough to begin the warming process.

He touched her face. "Hannah?" Nothing.

Soon enough, when the heat penetrated her frozen limbs, her ears, she would have to be brought back to consciousness. The pain would wake her, he knew. He applied cold washcloths to her ears, until he saw a bit of color returning. He would likely need to put her hands in cold water, too, to thaw them. Hot water would be unbearable.

The wind howled and whined, threw grains of snow and ice against the window panes. An overwhelming gratitude rose in Jerry, for the heat from the stove, the good solid walls and roof, and their deliverance from this awful storm.

He stopped applying the washcloths. He felt her fingers on both hands. So cold, almost as if there was no life.

He laid his head on her chest, heard the quiet flicker, the weak beat of her heart. He caressed her cold face. "I love you Hannah. Please wake up."

He kissed her cheek and smoothed her hair. He knew without a smidgen of doubt that he could wait as long as the Lord saw fit for her love. God had brought them through this for a reason. He traced the contours of her cheekbones, memorized the way her lashes fell like delicate feathers on her perfect face.

She drew in a sharp breath. Jerry stepped back. She coughed, softly, drew in a ragged breath, then choked. She kept choking, gasping for breath.

Jerry laid her on her left side, propped up her shoulders and supported her head. Her eyes flew open, dark pools of terror and pain. She whimpered, drew up a hand to drag it across her right ear. Her fingers flopped like helpless strips of cloth.

She blinked, squinted, struggled to swallow. She tried to form words, straining to use her tongue, but no sound emerged. He thought she said dirty, dirty, and began to apologize for her wet, frozen clothes. But she was thirsty. So thirsty, there was a desperation. He brought a tumbler of cold water, raised her shoulders, and held it to her lips.

"Just a few sips, Hannah, or you'll get sick." He knew she was conscious when she glared at him, grasped the glass in both hands and drained it, then leaned over the side of the couch and threw it all up. He held her head, wiped her mouth with a washcloth, then cleaned up the floor with rags and soapy water.

She drew in a sharp breath. A resounding "Ow!" came from her mouth, followed by howls of protest. She yelled and hollered and whimpered. She grasped her fingers with the near helpless fingers of her other hand, squinted her eyes, and rocked from side to side, loosening the comforters in her struggle.

"Do something!" she wailed.

Jerry lowered his face to hers. "You need to drink only a little at a time. Cold water for your fingers and toes. No heat. It will only make it worse. I'll make you hot tea."

She turned her face away and told him to shut up. He hid his grin. Definitely awake! So, he put the teakettle on the stove and shook a few tea leaves into a sturdy, white mug, adding sugar. He filled an agate basin with water from the faucet.

"Put both hands in this water."

"I can't," she yelled, louder than ever.

"You have to, Hannah. Listen to me. It will only get worse if you don't."

It was a long night. She refused the basin of cold water, cried and begged for mercy. She wouldn't allow him to remove her socks, said she could do it herself, which she obviously could not, so he didn't make any further attempts to ease her pain.

She did sip the hot tea, though, which was something, he supposed. The odor coming from those comforters was a nauseating smell that filled the room. How she could be unaware of this was beyond him, but he said nothing.

He must have dozed off shortly before daybreak. He awoke to morning's white light across his face. He sat up from his blanket on the floor and quickly realized that Hannah was missing; there was only the heap of smelly comforters on the sofa. He sat up, rubbed his eyes and saw the bathroom door was closed.

Oh. She must have found her way to the bathroom then, which meant she had been able to walk. He listened. Complete quiet.

He rapped softly on the bathroom door, placing an ear on the wooden panel. "Hannah?"

"Go away."

"I'm just checking if you're okay."

"I'm not okay. I'm frozen stiff!" she screeched.

Jerry turned away and felt a deep release of laughter. She was going to be okay.

When Hannah emerged, her dark hair wet, her face pale and thin but, mercifully, clean, a woolen blanket around her body like a giant shawl, she walked painfully to the sofa and sat down carefully. She pushed aside the comforters and asked him to take them out on the porch.

She was shivering uncontrollably. Her hands shook as if she had a palsy. Tears slid from beneath her lowered lashes, until Jerry asked her gently if there was anything he could do for her. He tried to take her hands, but she yanked them away and glared at him.

"Hannah, it's hard for me to see you suffer."

"It hurts so bad," she whispered.

"Do you want to try cold water?"

"I already had a bath. I could hardly do it."

"I believe it. You're strong, Hannah." He thought, strong-willed and determined, but didn't say it.

"I smelled horrible."

"Just horse, is all."

She didn't want to talk after that. She simply sat on the couch and suffered in silence, her stinging fingers repeatedly going to her ears, the tip of her nose. She watched in baleful silence as he fried steak in the big cast-iron pan, sliced bread, and soft-boiled four eggs for himself and two for her.

Hannah almost fainted from the delicious aroma of the frying steak. She was so terribly hungry, but there was no way she could hold a spoon.

He quietly filled two plates and brought them both to the couch and sat down beside her. He set her plate between them, then bowed his head in silent prayer before lifting his fork to his mouth with a bite of piping hot steak.

Hannah swallowed. She glanced sideways at the soft, gelatinous egg, the buttered toast. She swallowed again. As if it was the most natural thing in the world, Jerry cut a bite-size piece of toast, loaded a spoon with the soft-boiled egg and held it out to Hannah's mouth, a question in his soft, brown eyes.

Her hunger overrode her pride, and she opened her mouth like a fledgling. And so they ate breakfast together quietly, without speaking. She met his eyes once, and they held their gazes exchanging questions and answers.

He wiped away a bit of egg from the corner of her mouth. She looked at her helpless fingers. "They hurt so bad."

In answer, Jerry lifted them both to his mouth and kissed the tips of each finger. Drawing her hands away, she put them back in her lap, hurriedly, with averted eyes.

"You could have died, Hannah," Jerry said tenderly, his voice raspy with emotion.

"So I owe you a big thank you," she said, with only a trace of sarcasm.

They both listened to the wailing of the wind, turning their faces to watch clouds of roiling snow being hurled across the prairie, and they knew. They recognized the stark reality of what might have been, and what God had wrought. The perfect lull in the storm's aftermath, the timing that had been so critical, and the fact that they were here, together, warm and safe.

CHAPTER 8

Aʟʟ ᴛʜᴀᴛ ᴅᴀʏ, ʜᴀɴɴᴀʜ ᴅɪᴅ ɴᴏᴛʜɪɴɢ. ꜱʜᴇ ꜱᴀᴛ ᴏɴ ᴛʜᴇ ᴡᴏᴏᴅᴇɴ rocking chair, wrapped in the woolen blanket, her dark hair tied into a ponytail, her eyes swollen and red, alternately clutching her fingers as she grimaced in pain, or holding a warmed washcloth to her ears.

Jerry kept busy feeding the livestock, tending the two stoves, stacking up wood in neat rows from the pile by the back stoop, repairing broken gates inside the barn, coming in every few hours to see how she was faring.

She could not sleep. The pain kept her awake, so she sat, bearing it stoically, refusing any remedy Jerry suggested. He cooked bean soup in the afternoon and offered to share it with her but she shook her head. "Tea would be nice," she said, flatly.

Jerry could barely make the tea fast enough. What a sweet request. Oh my.

He sat with her, eating his bean soup as she sipped her tea. He decided to say nothing but to allow her time to ask questions, if there was anything she wanted to know.

She whispered so soft and low that he could barely decipher her words. "It was awful."

He nodded.

"He fell. The horse."

"I know."

"Where is he now?"

"He's down. About four, maybe five miles from here."

"Is that where you found us?"

"Yes."

She said nothing more. He waited for her to ask more questions, but she didn't. In fact, she never asked any questions after that, not once.

The wind died down, as all prairie winds eventually do. The sun shone and melted the snow, but only partially, where the wind had swept it clean. Patches of winter wheat showed green—limp and bedraggled, but green.

Hannah's frostbitten fingers and ears healed, but she seemed changed somehow. Her eyes were large and dark in her pale, thin face, and they seemed to have dimmed. The fire that used to flicker in them so often seemed to have been snuffed out. Jerry wished he could read her better, understand her thoughts, what was causing the lethargy, the deflation of the static energy that normally propelled her from morning till evening.

One day, when another dark bank of clouds rode in from the northwest, another blizzard in the seething black mass, Hannah stood at the window with her arms crossed like a vice around her waist, her shoulders jutting with tension. "I don't know if I can stand another blizzard again," she said through tight lips.

Jerry was repairing a saddle with an awl and strips of rawhide. He looked up from his work, a question in his eyes. "The cows will be all right," he said slowly.

"I'm not thinking about the cows," she snapped. "I think once you've nearly lost your life, the weather takes on a different kind of menace. I can't really explain it the way I would like to, but it's almost as if you're not sure you have it in you to sit here and just . . . well . . . you know, take it. Take the wind and the

lashing of the snow and the cold and the loneliness . . . and the
. . ." Her sentence dangled between them, unfinished, mysterious.

Now was not the time to point out that she was the one who
had chosen to stay here, to fight through the miserable winters
and dry summers.

"This one might not be so bad," Jerry said, bending his head
to his work.

She said sharply, "You need a haircut."

"Why don't you cut it?"

"I never cut my own hair," he replied matter of factly.

"Who's going to cut it?"

"I guess you'll have to."

"No. I don't know how. I can't. Go to town or something."

Jerry laughed.

Hannah scowled.

"You could do it," he said, almost teasingly.

"I never cut anyone's hair and I'm not planning to start,
either."

"Good. I'll just let it grow, then. Eventually, I'll put it in a
braid, the way a lot of the pioneers did."

Hannah almost smiled. "I miss my mother."

This was so unexpected that it took Jerry a few seconds to
absorb her words. He busied himself shoving the awl through a
soft piece of stirrup, his hair falling over his eyes.

"I miss my mother, and Manny. Eli and Mary are probably
going to the same school in Leacock Township that I went to." A
wistful note crept into her voice so Jerry looked up from his work.

"Would you like to go to Lancaster for a visit?"

Much too quickly, there was a sharp refusal, a vehement shaking of her head. Then, "You never talked about the palomino."

"What is there to say?" Jerry asked gruffly.

"Was he still alive?"

"Yes."

"And then?"

"Hannah, listen. There is nothing harder in the world than putting a bullet into a horse you love. The only reason I could do it at all was to relieve the pitiful creature of its suffering.

"So you had to put him down?"

"Of course." He hadn't meant for his words to come out quite so sharply.

"I guess now you think it was my fault."

"Of course not. It was a blizzard. There was nothing you could have done differently."

Hannah was silent for a while, standing at the window and watching the storm approach. Then suddenly, without turning she said, "You probably wish the palomino was still alive and I was dead."

"Stop it, Hannah." This was spoken sternly.

"Would it have mattered to you if I'd have died?" she asked, almost coyly, but not quite.

"Yes, Hannah, a great deal."

"You would have headed back East so fast it wouldn't be funny. You'd marry again. Have a nice life. One without all this sacrifice."

Jerry stuck the awl back into the stirrup, got to his feet, and went to the window. He grasped Hannah's elbows from behind, and turned her to face him.

"What are you saying? What is wrong with you?"

"Well, you would have. You know you'd go back East if you didn't have to stay here on the homestead to keep up your end of the deal."

He could not deny it. Yes, he would. But he didn't say it.

Hannah twisted from his touch and flounced to the kitchen, banging pans on the countertop.

She baked a cake while he continued his work fixing the stirrup. Jerry couldn't tell what was going on in her head, but a comfortable silence settled throughout the house like the pleasant aroma coming from the cook stove—a companionable calm that brought a hum of contentment to Jerry's lips.

She had never before confided any of her feelings to him. And here, in one afternoon, she'd said all that—her mother, her fear, and the palomino. Suddenly, without thinking, he asked, "Why did you never name the palomino?"

"I did."

"You never called him by any name."

She lowered her face and blushed furiously. "That would mean I accepted your gift, and I never did. If I accepted the horse, I'd have to accept you."

"I see." Then, "You have accepted me."

Clearly rattled, Hannah lifted a flaming face, her eyes dark, miserable pools of embarrassment.

"Well," she said.

"Can't you do better than that?" When he looked at Hannah's face, his eyes traveled to her eyes, which now held a mysterious, warm light that threw his world off its steady axis.

"Someday." She let her eyes hold his, with only a hint of sparkle in their translucent depths, followed by the merest hint of a soft smile.

It was only a hint of acceptance, but it was as much as he'd ever hoped to receive. He sank to the low stool where he had been working, his breathing ragged and uneven. Whoa. Steady there.

He left the house, carrying the repaired saddle, then simply sat on a pile of hay with any empty expression in his eyes. If he lived to be a hundred years old, he'd never figure her out.

Someday, she had said.

He wavered between sobs of frustration and wild shrieks of glee. Did that soft light in her eyes mean her fierce resolve was crumbling? Was there the slightest crack in her rigid armor of bitterness and self-will? Too soon to tell. Perhaps that was most of his fascination with Hannah. She was so complex, so hard to comprehend. You never knew which way her mood would take her. He wondered, though, if that night on the prairie had not dispersed some of the worst of her rebellion.

He shook his head to clear it, jumped up, and began to clean stalls as if he had only one afternoon to do it.

The mules' gigantic ears pricked forward. Mollie yawned, stretched her mouth wide, bared her immense yellow teeth and then closed them with a clack. Then she bent her head and went back to nosing around for a forgotten wisp of hay.

True to Hannah's words, each storm that drove in from the northwest seemed to be a test of endurance. She found herself pensive, brittle, pacing the kitchen when Jerry was not around, wishing he'd go outside and leave her alone when he was in the house. He always tried to ease her unhappiness with cheerful words which, she decided, was like running your fingernails down the blackboard at school.

She didn't sew, wouldn't read, and hated to write letters. She refused to get on horseback if there was an inch of snow on the ground. She argued endlessly about Black Angus versus longhorns, and was simply a burden both to herself and to Jerry.

She wanted to go to town. She wanted to visit the Texas folks but, no, she would not go. For one thing, she didn't trust Bobby, the quarter horse. He was sorrel and chunky and cranky. She'd never seen a sorrel horse she liked. Even Nip and Tuck failed to pull her out of her slump.

Jerry told her the first thing they'd do in the spring would be make a trip to Pennsylvania to see her mother. Hannah averted her eyes and closed them off with lids like little feather-lined window curtains and didn't say anything.

Jerry's hair grew down to his shoulders, so Hannah told him one evening that if he didn't cut his hair, she would.

"Go right ahead," he answered, unconcerned. He didn't think she would do it.

Armed with a towel, a scissors, and a brush and comb, Hannah approached Jerry. "Sit up straight," she commanded.

He obeyed.

Instantly, the comb was dragged through his long dark hair, tearing at the snags until his nose burned and tears sprang to his eyes.

"Let me do that." He reached for the brush and comb, but she pulled them away. He sat down and bent his head, resigned.

"Take it easy."

Hannah said nothing, just proceeded to rake the comb through his long, tangled hair until he thought half the hair on his head had been pulled out by the roots. He gritted his teeth, bearing the pain.

She leveled her face with his, sighting along his floppy bangs, estimating, and then slowly drawing the blades of the scissors precisely where she wanted them.

Her confidence increased as the curtains of hair fell away from the scissors and she formed the traditional bowl cut of the Amish, leaving his hair longer over his ears than the bangs on his forehead.

Jerry thought he'd been shot when her scissors crunched into his ear, snapping a deep cut along the top where his skin was thickest. Making some sort of involuntary grimace and a whoosh of disgust, he leapt to his feet, a hand going to his ear that was already spurting blood.

Hannah moved back, a hand to her mouth, her eyes wide with fright, too embarrassed to utter a word of justification for her actions. He went to the bathroom and held a cold washcloth to his throbbing ear, trying to staunch the spurting blood.

When he returned, the scissors, comb, and brush lay on the table, the towel in a heap on the floor, with no sign of Hannah. Her bedroom door was closed, and remained that way until the following morning.

At breakfast, she burned the toast. Not just burned it, but completely blackened it until it was as black as soot, smoking and shrunk to about half its size. She burned her fingers as she retrieved it from the oven and had to hold them beneath the gush of cold water from the faucet at the sink.

"I'll make more toast," Jerry offered.

Hannah didn't look up from her cold water therapy. She didn't let him know she'd heard him. She looked at his hair from the back and it looked all right. He must have finished cutting it by himself. There was a large, angry cut in his ear, about three-quarters of the way up. She decided he'd get over it, but wouldn't talk to him all day, so he gave up trying and kept to himself.

When Jerry came in from the barn late that evening, Hannah was sitting in the oak rocking chair, perfectly still, her hands folded in her lap. As he hung up his coat, she turned to look at him. "I think I'll go crazy if I don't have anything to do," she said.

Her words were spoken in short, hard jerks, as if she didn't have enough breath to complete the sentence. Her face was thin, her eyes huge, a frightened look on her features, as if she had seen a ghost lurking in the house while he was at the barn.

"Well, Hannah. I don't know what to tell you. We're pretty much snowed in. We have no telephone, no mail, no neighbors. You've lived here longer than I have, so surely you knew what the winters were like, didn't you?"

"I did, but it was different when my family was here. And the Jenkinses would come."

"We can ride over there."

"No." Her answer was decidedly emphatic and forceful. She would no longer venture out on horseback in the snow, saying it was foolish. If you were caught on the prairie once, you'd have no one to blame but yourself if it happened again. She had no desire to check on the cattle or watch for the herds of flowing antelope. Nothing.

"Hannah, you've changed."

"I don't want to die. It was close enough, that time."

"I mean, your sense of adventure is gone."

"It has nothing to do with adventure. It's foolish, is all. I'll ride again when spring comes, and not one day before that."

That night, after Jerry had gone to bed, she sat alone on her rocking chair and thought of Abigail Jenkins's diaries, those recordings of times like these, when the long, tedious days of winter drove her to questioning her own sanity, her fear of being pushed over the edge by the power of isolation. To be alone, day after day, in an endless expanse of white, while knowing one storm would eventually be followed by another, the time crawling by like snails.

Suddenly, without warning, Hannah began to cry. Her nose burned, her mouth wobbled, and quiet heaves of her chest ended in silent hiccoughs of distress. She let the tears and the overwhelming need to be sad rock her in its grip. She didn't try to hold back or prevent it.

She wanted her mother. She was so homesick for the sight of her kindly face, the soft etchings that would eventually turn into wrinkles. She wanted to eat her mother's food and listen to her words, knowing that she was there for her, no matter what. She wanted to put her fist into Manny's arm, to see him grab the spot where she'd clubbed him good and proper, grimace and sway, bent double, and then come after her, yelling his revenge.

Sweet Mary, so innocent and loving. A child. And Eli. She groaned within herself and let the tears come, welling from her eyes in soft trickles down her cheeks.

They were her family. She'd spent every day, every week, every month and year of her life with them. How could she be expected to live without them?

Jerry had said she was changing. What did he know?

She just knew that, suddenly, in the dead of this North Dakota winter, the homestead was no longer quite as important. It had lost some of its shining luster like a tarnished silver teapot. The Klassermans were gone, with the sleek black cattle she had envied, planning to fashion the homestead after their example. Now here she was, her land containing these raw-boned, hairy old longhorns that she could as soon shoot as look at.

The homestead was not the real homestead without her family. There! She'd admitted to herself what she'd tried to stuff away without her head knowing what her heart had tried to reveal.

Perhaps if she loved Jerry the way other women loved their husbands, she would feel as if he was her family.

She didn't know. All she did for Jerry was cut his ear, burn his toast, and kill, yes, kill his best palomino. That poor horse! So faithful, left on the prairie for the eagles, ravens, and wolves. She felt as if it should have been her left out there. For the first time in her life, she wasn't absolutely sure of what she wanted, what she knew, or if she had ever known anything.

If only that incident had never happened. Lying out there on the prairie without knowing if she'd live or die had taken away all her confidence. It was like she'd been bucked off a horse and wasn't quite able to summon the courage to get back on.

Well, she'd have to do better. She couldn't sit in this house and weep around like a starving barn cat, that was one thing sure. Sniveling, whining, complaining. That simply was not her.

She dried her tears, blew her nose, and went to the window to look out at the stars, feeling the same sense of despair she had felt when she began to weep. She sat back in the rocking chair and began all over again.

Which is where Jerry found her. Unable to sleep and knowing that Hannah had not gone to bed, he got up, dressed in clean clothes, and walked softly on stocking feet to her side.

"Hannah." The gentleness of his voice only brought another barrage of tears. He handed her a clean handkerchief. She honked long and loud, swiped viciously at her streaming eyes, and told him to go back to bed.

She sent an elbow into his side. "Go away."

"Just tell me what's wrong, Hannah. I'll do anything, anything to make you stop crying. I've never known you to be like this."

"Go away. Just go!"

"No."

Almost she got away from him. She rose halfway, turned, but his hands caught her waist and brought her to him, close enough that she could smell the soap from his washing, the baking soda clean of his teeth.

"Tell me, Hannah." His words were spoken against her hair, so soft and dark and silky, they seemed to be liquid.

Almost she stayed in his arms, breathing in the smell of him, putting her arms around him, and sinking against his solid strength.

Then her pride reared its face, the alpha force of her existence, and she extracted herself, but not without a sense of loss, unacknowledged even to herself.

"I'm all right. Go back to bed. It's just been a long winter."

A lesser man than Jerry might have lost his patience and tried desperately to reclaim the moment, thinking selfishly of his own desire. But he let her go, stepped back, and recognized what had occurred. For the space of a few heartbeats, she had been his.

He knew time and patience were on his side.

Hannah's spirits were a constant worry now. She roamed the house, her eyes vacant with an unnamed hopelessness, a look that drove fear into him. He tried to draw her out by suggesting different things, but what could be accomplished on the prairie in the winter was limited.

He had heard of pioneer women who were unable to hold onto their sanity, some of them losing their reason and never getting it back, turning into mentally ill patients that had to be "put away," that awful phrase that meant they were incarcerated in an institution, a mental hospital.

This was a whole new challenge, and a fearful one. Jerry knew she was trying to beat the dark moments, but she seemed unable to rise above the clouds of darkness that came down on her head like a heavy fog.

Then she refused to eat. For one whole day, she drank only bitter black tea and sat staring straight ahead, her dark eyes boring holes into the wall of the house, her arms hanging by her sides, the rocker squeaking as she rocked. Her eyes remained dry. She didn't cook and she didn't wash dishes. The floor remained unswept and the laundry piled up in the washhouse.

Jerry knew it was time to do something, anything. He had no clear path, but he had to make an effort. To ride through the snow would take a huge effort. The closest telephone was at the Klasserman ranch, now the Timothy Weber home.

He didn't relish going there. The couple left him with an unsettled sense of questioning, a strange atmosphere he couldn't define.

He had to get help for Hannah. He knelt at her side, without touching her. "Hannah." Dull eyes shifted to his, then fell away.

"Listen, I'm going away. I'm riding to the Klasserman place to use the telephone, to get help for you. You need to see a doctor."

"I don't need a doctor."

"Yes, you do. You're going from bad to worse. You're not feeling well at all. This is so unlike you, to sit like this. You're not eating."

"I will when I'm hungry."

"You keep the fire going, Hannah. Please. I have to go."

"Don't leave me here alone."

"Then you'll have to come with me."

She shook her head. "It's too cold. Too far. A storm could come up."

"Then you'll have to stay here. We have no choice."

Hannah stared into space and resumed her rocking. Her eyes clouded over with a startling veil of despondency.

Jerry rode hard, without sparing King. He struggled to keep the fear at bay, kept assuring himself that Hannah would be all right, that it was only the midwinter blues.

It was hard going, but they had ridden through plenty of drifts, been on the open range in snow up to King's underside. As they neared the turnoff, Jerry sniffed, drew his eyebrows down in bewilderment. There was a definite smell, an odor hovering in the air, a smell like . . . burnt something. It smelled like wood smoke. The Webers must be burning their stoves very hot. He rode on, noticing the dense sheen in the atmosphere.

As he drew closer, up over the rise of land and around the curve where the clump of cottonwoods huddled together like ancient refugees, the smell became overpowering, a thick, cloying smell of burnt wood and . . .

He gasped! What had been the Klassermans' house was a pile of charred timbers and twisted metal roofing, the snow around the dwelling melted away by the inferno that it must have been. All that remained were the black, twisted pieces of metal roofing, with smoke reaching to the endless sky, a pall of gray whisked away by the everlasting prairie winds.

The expensive automobiles stood blackened and charred in the front, a testimony of mystery, the truth of Timothy and Lila's inability to escape.

King snorted with distaste. Jerry reined him in and dismounted with numb extremities, his mind unable to comprehend what his eyes were seeing before him.

CHAPTER 9

JERRY STOOD BEFORE THE REMAINS OF THE HOUSE, HIS HEAD BOWED, his hat in his hands, as he prayed for guidance and for the souls of the departed. He sensed his own mortality, the limits of his ability to change the horror of what had occurred, felt the power of an all-seeing, all-encompassing God who allowed calamities of this magnitude.

Why, Lord, why? He turned to the barn, where he heard the restless banging of horses, the frightened rattling of halters pulling on the chains that kept them in their stalls.

Jerry dropped King's reins, which dangled to the ground, a sign for the horse to stay on that spot, an obedience he had learned well. Quickly, Jerry ran to the door, lifted the metal latch, and let himself into the dim interior of the large structure.

The overpowering stench of ammonia made him cough. He drew a gloved hand across his face and coughed again. The horses rose on their hind legs and whinnied, their nostrils quivering. As he drew closer, they reached out with their noses, begging, clearly needing water, anything to reassure them that help was on the way. The manure was piled around them. They were without bedding of any kind, their wooden troughs torn and chewed.

He turned to find the watering trough dry. Sparrows flitted from the rafters, twittering anxiously. Mice scurried across the top boards of the stalls, all signs that no one had been in the barn for some time.

Jerry shivered unexpectedly, a sense of horror washing over him. When he heard a thin, wailing cry, he turned toward the sound immediately to find a small child sitting in a corner of the forebay, a quilt that had been white with a design of pink and blue sequins, a crib blanket, laying in an untidy heap beneath him. Or her.

Jerry went to the child, bent to lift him, noticed the filth, the thin, trembling body, the coat that had been worn for too long. The child smelled of its soiled diaper, the face dirty, streaked with dust and tears.

"*Ach.*" It was all Jerry could think to say, an expression of profound dismay. He reached for the child and held him up, resisting the urge to gag. The child clung to Jerry, laid his head on his shoulder, his body molded to him as if he would never allow himself to be pulled away. He cried great, dry, wracking sobs, then became still, breathing faintly.

Clearly, one dilemma marched in right after another, but Jerry wasn't sure if this one would not prove to be his undoing. Such a mystery. What had happened? Why was the child here, without any sign of its parents? How could he get this child to safety in the cold?

First, the horses needed water. Then he'd have to get the child home. He tried to loosen his grip, crooning, telling the child he'd be all right, he needed to see to the horses. But he soon realized the folly of that thought.

He tucked the child by his side, then began filling the watering trough with water that gushed from the hydrant. One by one, he loosened the horses, who almost ran over him in their need for water.

He saw now that the horses were white Percherons. They were work horses, a common breed among the Amish with their substantial height and wide, deep chests like Belgians. Their muscles were heavy and they had massive legs with a spray of thick hair surrounding their hooves. Their necks were arched and they had well-molded faces and large brown eyes. These horses were of a fine breed, well taken care of until now.

As best he could, he forked hay with one hand, the child gripping his body like a little monkey. Jerry shook his head as he watched the starved horses tearing at the hay. There were eleven of them. Some were tied in stalls, others were milling around in what he thought must have formerly been an enclosure for the dry cows.

He stood surveying the barn. He'd done what he could, so now he must see to this child. He could not get help for Hannah. The telephone was unavailable, so there was nothing to do but ride home to her, carrying the bedraggled child that needed a bath, a change of clothing, and food of some kind.

He wrapped him in the soiled quilt as best he could, with the child straining to stay against him, screaming hysterically if he felt himself being pulled away. Working fast, Jerry wrapped him up, bits of hay and dirt clinging to the blanket. Then he hurried out of the barn, shuddering at the harsh scene of the smoking remains of the Klasserman house.

He shook his head to rid himself of mental images of what might have occurred. Riding home without help for Hannah was not the worst of this day that seemed shrouded in unreality. The air was cold, but the surrounding white of the pristine plains seemed almost surreal after the appalling sight he had left behind.

Jerry clutched the child to his chest with one hand as he held the reins in the other, allowing King to find his way home, as he had done when he rescued Hannah.

When he opened the door of the ranch house, he saw Hannah sitting in the same rocking chair and staring dully out the north window, precisely the way he had left her. She did not turn her head at his approach. The house was cold.

"Hannah." She didn't respond, wouldn't acknowledge his presence.

He held out the child wrapped in its filthy quilt.

She turned, halfway.

"The Klassermans' house burned to the ground. I found this child in the barn." Hannah blinked, sat up, and turned toward him. She rose to her feet, clawing at the edges of the quilt. Her lips moved and a whisper emerged. "*Siss unfaschtendich.*" *There is no sense.*

"I don't know how long he was out there."

She took him out of Jerry's arms, carried him to the sofa, and unwrapped the poor, filthy child, her face grim. "Put the kettle on," she ordered.

Quickly, Jerry set about building a fire as the child began his breathless wailing. Hannah carried him to the bathroom. The water pipes pinged and bumped in the wall as she turned on the hot water in the clawfoot bathtub. He heard her talking in soft, muted tones. The soiled clothing and quilt were hurled out through the bathroom door, followed by a clipped, "Burn these."

Then, "Oh, Jerry!"

Quickly, he went to the bathroom door. "What is it, Hannah?"

"It's . . . she's a girl!"

There was nothing to say, so Jerry just nodded.

"Go get the baking soda. Quick!"

Jerry obeyed.

The little girl screamed in pain as she was lowered into the warm, soapy water, her bottom raw with her own waste, and no one to change the poor child's diaper.

Hannah reached for the proffered baking soda, tears running down her face unchecked, her nose running, her lips trembling. "Bring those muslin sheets from the closet in my bedroom. Cut them into six or eight pieces, it doesn't matter. We need diapers. And oh, Jerry, bring me one of your tee shirts, the nicest one you have. Oh, and the talcum powder on my dresser."

Jerry felt very much like a husband as he collected the items, although he hesitated as he approached Hannah's bedroom. He felt like an intruder. He had no idea what talcum powder looked like, but picked up an oval, pink container with roses on the front that he guessed must hold powder. He handed it to her, and she reached for it without looking at him, her one hand cradling the child's head as she lay in the soothing bath.

"Poor, poor baby girl. Jerry, put about half a cup of oatmeal in a dish and pour some of the water from the teakettle over it."

Again, Jerry did as he was told, vaguely aware of the rumbling from his own stomach. He spread the muslin sheet on the table, found a scissors in the sewing machine cabinet, and began to cut diapers.

Hannah appeared, the child wrapped in a large towel, her face glowing from the heat in the bathroom, two safety pins clutched in one hand. She toweled the little girl dry, then leaned back and surveyed the face with the mop of brown hair, wet and curling, that lay against the clean scalp, the large, frightened eyes in her small oval face.

"Who is she, Jerry? Where did you find her?"

Jerry related the whole story as Hannah dried the small body. She beckoned for a square of muslin and turned her back to diaper the child, then sat back down to draw the much too large tee shirt over her, securing it at the neck with another safety pin.

Jerry couldn't help noticing what a capable mother she was. But then, she had been the oldest in her family which, he presumed, would have given her some skills in caring for children.

"I'm going to the kitchen to feed her some oatmeal." It was an open invitation for him to join her at the kitchen table so he did just that, settling himself in a chair and watching the way she balanced the child on one hip, stirring milk and molasses into the oatmeal with the other. She brought it to the table before sitting down, sliding the child expertly into her lap, a move so motherly, so fascinating that it conjured up moments of his own childhood, a time in his life he'd as soon forget.

Hannah bent her dark head, coaxing the little girl to try what was on the spoor. Timidly at first, then with more courage, the child ate small bites of the sweet, milky porridge.

"Tell me more," Hannah said. So he told her in detail about the grim specter of smoking debris, the heat-damaged cars, the thirsty horses, the poor child.

"But what happened? We can't just sit here with the child without trying to contact her family. We know their names. Surely the deed to the property is recorded somewhere here in North Dakota. The sale's transaction. Something. How did the child end up in the barn if both the parents were trapped in the house? Or were they kidnapped, robbed, their house set fire to by thieves? Horse thieves? No, I guess not. You said the horses were still in the barn. My word, Jerry, we have to do something!"

While Hannah was speaking she was eating the leftover oatmeal the child was unable to consume. Still talking in fast, clipped tones, she made a larger pot of oatmeal and left it to set up while she returned to the table.

"She looks a bit like Timothy. Do you suppose it is their child? Did he even speak of having had a child?" Her questions were hurled so fast that Jerry felt as if he had to dodge some of them, while they zinged overhead like a volley of shots fired from a rifle. Sometimes he shrugged. Other times he shook his head. But most of the time he admitted he did not know.

"But we can't keep her," Hannah concluded.

"Likely not, in the end."

"Oh, but we have her now, sweet, innocent angel that she is. Who would put a helpless baby in a barn in the dead of winter? I can't begin to imagine the trauma, the fear. What kept her from freezing?"

"There are a lot of horses in that barn. Percherons. Huge, white ones."

Hannah opened her eyes wide. "Is that what they are?" she asked.

Jerry nodded.

"This is too much. I can't handle any of this. All I know is the fact that this sweet baby is safe. Oh, Jerry, I never saw such a pitiful bottom. Blistered. So fiery red. It will take days and days to heal." She blushed, having spoken on a high note of emotion.

Hannah bent her head over the sleepy-eyed child, drew her head against her chest, and rocked back and forth, another move that made Jerry's heart ache with memories of his own mother.

"She's sleeping," Hannah said, awed by the drooping eyelids, the relaxed expression of bliss. "Get down a few of the sheep's wool comforters from the high shelf in the closet of the guest room."

Jerry hastened down the hallway, smiling and thinking what a good husband he was turning out to be. He found the comforters and met Hannah in the hallway as she whispered, "Spread them in my room in the corner, beside my bed. Get a clean sheet from the chest of drawers in the bathroom."

Again, he did as he was commanded, trying to spread everything straight, the corners tucked in, then stood back, allowing Hannah to pass him and gently lower the sleeping child. She nestled down contentedly, giving a soft little moan.

Hannah shooed Jerry out of the way before retrieving a blanket at the foot of her bed, covering the small, weary body with the folded warmth of the heavy coverlet. She stood back, crossed her arms, and sighed with contentment. "Oh my. All winter I'll have her to look after." And then she did the most unexpected thing. She felt for Jerry's right hand with her left and grasped it, held it.

Afraid to breathe, Jerry stood still, silently praying that she wouldn't let go.

"It's just so unreal. I was at the end of my rope. I'm sorry. I don't know why I let everything get to me so horribly. It must have been the . . . you know. That night." And she still held his hand.

"Let's go. She's sleeping so good." She pulled gently, drew her hand away from his, but stayed by his side until they reached the kitchen.

"I'm hungry. Do you want a dish of oatmeal?"

Too flummoxed to say anything, he spoke with his eyes, nodding his head. Still asking questions, Hannah put the kettle on, making plans, what she would sew, the good thick flannel for diapers, the flowered print mattered not a snitch, the cotton fabric in the lowest drawer of the bureau that her father had been given when he left home. They had brought it the whole way out here to the Dakota prairie, can you imagine?

She'd need socks, though, and shoes, eventually. Hannah wondered if she could walk or crawl. How old was she? Was she really the Webers' child? Who else could she be?

Jerry could only sit and listen as he tried to make sense of Hannah's complete transformation, going from a vacant, immobile figure in a chair, to this animated, bright-eyed, talkative woman.

He had been convinced she was desperately depressed, sick with some mysterious ailment of the mind. And now, the sight of this soiled, derelict child had plucked her out of her despondency and placed her into a whirlwind of planning and curiosity.

Had she been aware of holding his hand? Probably not. He thought for the thousandth time, he'd never understand women, and most certainly not Hannah.

They ate in comfortable silence until Hannah scraped the last of the oatmeal from her bowl, a flush already appearing in her pale face, and looked at him squarely, her eyes boring into his with an intensity that bordered on panic.

"But, Jerry. Eventually we'll have to give her back, right? We have to do the right thing and find her family and all, right?"

"Yes."

"How will we do it?"

"I'll ride into Pine and see if there was mail at the post office, check the sheriff's office for documents from the sale. Anything. There must be family who needs to be notified."

Hannah crossed her arms, rubbing her palms up and down her forearms. "It gives me the shivers," she said. "It's just so awful."

"I agree. It's too confusing to let your mind dwell on what could have happened."

The fire in the cook stove snapped and popped. A stick of wood fell. Outside, the wind howled in the dark of night, sending sprays of snow skimming against the windows, skittering across the wood siding to the north.

Hannah felt the smallness of the homestead, little black dots on a vast, expansive land that seemed to have no beginning and no end, a sea of cold, white, frozen snow. How easily they could be erased from marring this unspoiled land. Was it good that they were here, her and Jerry, and now this child? For the first time in her life, she felt a drawing back, almost like an infidelity, a thing gone wrong. To barge ahead without a doubt had always been her way. But, somehow, here tonight, there was a growing sense of trembling and wavering under a power that seemed out of her control.

Was she deserting ship? Forsaking her true courage and fortitude the way a loose woman left her husband on a whim? An infidelity, yes. In one sense, her god had been the homestead. Or its success, whichever way you looked at it.

Hannah was unaware of her own dark brooding, unaware of the way Jerry was intently watching the softening of her face, the myriad emotions that crisscrossed it like invisible pathways.

Suddenly, she shivered. "Sometimes I wonder how long we'll be able to stay here."

Jerry started. "Why do you say that?"

"I'm not sure. All that's happened, this string of calamities, it just . . . I don't know, sort of takes the wind from my sails or something. I feel as if the strength is gone from my ranching legs."

"You'll feel better once summer comes. Spring, I mean. You just have an extraordinary case of the winter blues."

"No, it's more than that."

Jerry waited.

"I read Abigail Jenkins's diary once . . ."

She did not continue. He watched her face, the heavy lids drooping, the sweep of dark lashes on her pale cheeks, the tense line of her full lips. One hand crept across the table, found a teacup, her forefinger and thumb tracing the handle over and over.

She got up and went to the cook stove to put the kettle on. She measured tea leaves into two heavy ironstone mugs. When the tea was ready, she brought both mugs to the table and set one down at his elbow. She took her seat across from him, stirred sugar into her tea, and sighed.

"I read Abigail Jenkins's diary once," she repeated.

He raised his eyebrows. "And?"

"Well, she was as tough and wiry as shoe leather, you know."

"I never knew her."

"No, I guess you wouldn't have. She died of pneumonia. Hod has never been the same. Anyway, she was brought out here as a young bride and barely survived the winters. It was the wind. The loneliness. She suffered. I never would have imagined that of her. She seemed as if she was made for the prairie, tough and resilient. Nothing fazed her. I always imagined I was exactly like her. Designed for solitude, for wide-open spaces. Laughing at the elements. Now, I'm not so sure. And yet, I'm afraid this feeling of not being sure is somehow wrong."

She suddenly burst out, clearly exasperated. "How do we know what is right and what is wrong?"

Jerry sipped his tea, picked a bit of tea leaf off his tongue. "We don't always know. We pray for guidance, then God allows us choices, and if they're the wrong ones, we keep going in that direction until we learn."

"How do you know that?"

"I don't. It's just something I heard a preacher say one time. We're human beings so we make mistakes. The biggest thing is that we care whether we do the right thing."

"That's important?"

"I think it is, yes."

Hannah held her mug in both hands, her fingers curled around it for comfort. "You think being here is the right thing?"

Before Jerry could answer, a thin wail from Hannah's bedroom shocked them both into action.

"She's crying!" Hannah said breathlessly, already on her way with Jerry close behind her.

Then Hannah was on her knees, asking what was wrong, touching the baby's forehead, checking her diaper, examining the safety pins. The thin cry turned into a wail, so Hannah scooped her up, blanket and all, and took her to the low, armless rocker where she rocked steadily, her head bent over the child, talking to her in a low voice. As the cries quieted, Jerry asked if perhaps she was used to having a bottle of milk at night.

The rocking stopped. "You know, she just might be. And I bet you anything there's still one of Eli's bottles . . . Oh no, our house burned down. I forgot. We don't have a baby bottle of any kind."

"Could we feed her more porridge?" Jerry asked.

"She's sleeping again. She might wake up repeatedly, with all she's been through."

And that was how they spent that first night with the child. Almost every hour, she awoke, crying out, cold and frightened. Hannah was always there for her, so Jerry went back to sleep, knowing she would tend to the little girl's needs.

He awoke with a start, the sound of clattering from the kitchen yanking him out of a deep sleep. Thinking he'd overslept, he pulled his trousers on, buttoned his shirt sleepily, and wobbled bleary-eyed out to the kitchen.

"Sorry, Hannah. I overslept. I'll get the fire."

She stood poking at a piece of firewood that didn't want to settle between the grates, her black hair in a long braid down her back, a white flannel nightgown that was about three sizes too big trailing on the floor.

She thrust a forefinger toward the clock. Jerry saw the time, 3:15 a.m. "Oh, sorry," he said. "I'll go back to bed."

"No, you won't. The little one is hungry, the house is cold, and I need you to fix this fire so I can heat some water for her oatmeal. I haven't slept more than an hour at the most."

So, once again Jerry obeyed and felt so much like a good husband that he whistled low, his breath coming in happy little waves of song.

Who could have predicted this? Life was, indeed, the strangest thing. Lifted from the pit of gloom and helplessness to this newly restored, softer Hannah, was a blessing far beyond anything he deserved.

He whistled as he got the fire stirred up and going, put the kettle on, and took the canister of rolled oats from the pantry. Hannah brought the child to the table. The soft light of the kerosene lamp surrounded them, the kettle hummed, and the fire crackled as the wind moaned in the eaves.

Jerry watched as Hannah spooned the oatmeal into the child's mouth. She ate and ate, opening her little mouth to receive another spoonful, and another, on and on, until they both laughed, unsure if they should be feeding her so much. But they found out that hunger was her main problem, and after she ate a large portion, they tucked her in and dragged themselves wearily back to their own beds and feel into deep sleep until the morning light awakened both of them.

Jerry rode off the following morning, alerted the Jenkinses, and made the necessary telephone calls. He accompanied the sheriff to the scene of the fire, then returned on horseback with Hod and the boys, just before dark. Hannah had begun to worry.

They came stamping up on the porch, all big wet boots, heavy coats, and caps pulled low over their ears, ruddy faces sporting uneven stubble like corn fodder, their beards unkempt where they hadn't bothered to shave.

Hannah scolded and said Abigail would be having a fit. They laughed and teased Hannah good-naturedly, said she was a sight for sore eyes. Ken and Hank both accepted coffee, their faces chapped and red from the cold, teeth stained brown from the plug of tobacco that very seldom left the side of their mouths.

They gawked at the little girl, shook their heads, their eyes wide as Jerry gave his account of the day he'd ridden over to use the neighbors' telephone. Hod pursed his lips and squinted at the fading light in the west window.

"If the cars were gone, it would make more sense. But there's no explanation for findin' the kid in the barn. Where are her parents? Did they do it? You jest can't wrap yore head around it, seems like."

Hank said the sheriff and the fire company would figure it out. "That still don't say we'll find a home for the kid," Hod argued.

Hannah held her tightly, her arms wrapped around her possessively, her eyes dark with the challenge already forming in her mind. *Let them try to come take her away. Jerry had found her. She'd have died if he hadn't. She's mine.*

"Best not get too attached," Hod said, watching Hannah.

"I already have," Hannah answered.

Hod shook his head. "I'se afraid o' that. My Abby never got over the loss of her baby girl. Not right. She mourned that child to her last breath."

"How long does it usually take to find the next of kin?" Jerry asked.

"Depends. They'll make phone calls. Write letters. Iffn' they got a decent address that is. Where'd you say them folks was fron?"

"They said they were from Texas."

"Not if they was Mormon they wasn't. They's a whole cluster of 'em in an' around Salt Lake City. No, I don't reckon they was Mormon. Somepin' ain't right."

Hank said them horses looked like they come from the circus. Never saw such clodhoppers in his life. What would a horse like that be? May as well turn 'em loose.

Jerry laughed, his teeth white in his tanned face. Hannah noticed and thought of mint toothpaste and baking soda and cleanliness and the times he'd kissed her. She compared his clean teeth to the Jenkins boys, and remembered Clay. Almost, she had loved him.

She vaguely listened to the men, but was thinking of a name for her child. No child should be without a name. Sarah? Anna? Rachel? All fine old Amish names from the Bible. But this was her child, and she was a special one, found in a cold barn. Fate, or God, probably mostly God, had directed Jerry to that barn.

She would call her Jane. Jane. To match Jerry, both starting with a J. Jane Riehl. Now there was a nice name. Not too fancy, not too pretentious. Hannah held her close and planted a soft kiss on the curly brown hair, then laid her cheek against the spot she had kissed.

CHAPTER 10

THE LAST OF THE SNOW FELL FROM THE ROOF IN MUTED THUDS against the ground. A warm wind melted the icicles that hung from the porch roof like jagged teeth. The drifts of snow became smaller, lost their pure bluish-white shine, took on a dusty yellow and gray appearance as they melted into the wet, cold soil, mingling with the limp, brown grass.

Geese honked overhead, flying in perfect V formations, their calls plaintive, beckoning, the call of changing seasons, on their way to the shores of the big lakes to the north. Whistling swans flew higher, their high, piercing cries shattering the early morning stillness.

Hannah stopped on the porch step, laundry basket balanced on her hip, pausing to listen to the cries of the swans. She lifted her face to the beauty of their faraway, white forms, their outstretched necks propelled by the magnificent power of their huge, muscular wings.

She couldn't stand there too long. Janie would be waking soon. Since she had come into their house, life revolved around her. The washing was done while she slept. Floor scrubbing was hopeless with little feet dashing across the freshly scrubbed linoleum. Hannah would leave her pail and rag to crawl after her, catching her in a corner of the kitchen and showering her with kisses.

And now winter was sliding into spring, bringing warm weather. Hannah would be able to take Janie outdoors and allow her to run and absorb the sun's rays as she grew strong and healthy and happy.

The only dark cloud was the inevitability of the child's relatives coming to claim her. Every day Hannah told herself she would have to give up, to accept the appearance of a grandparent, an aunt, someone who would travel to North Dakota for the horses, and Jane.

The Jenkinses had taken the horses home. They kept them in a makeshift enclosure in their rusted sprawling shed. Hank threatened to turn them loose every day, but Hod exercised his common sense, saying what if the owners did return? Then what?

Hannah taught herself to sew small dresses, thick diapers, little undergarments, hunkered over the treadle sewing machine with knitted brows, her back aching with tension. She was determined to learn.

Letters from her mother began to arrive with regularity now that spring was on its way, informing her about life back on the Stoltzfuses' homestead. Hannah wished she wouldn't call the farm a homestead. *This* was their homestead. Her doubts about whether they belonged on the prairie had melted away with the snowdrifts.

The longhorns had come through the winter unscathed, only thinner and uglier than ever, dropping calves with the same unhurried belligerence that they did everything else, swinging their massive horns at anyone or anything that came close.

Nip and Tuck loved to antagonize the mothers with calves, bounding and yipping just out of reach of those menacing horns, till Jerry put a stop to it. He made them stay in their pen where they cried and begged until they learned their lesson, before they were hooked by an extraordinarily agile cow.

There was never an extra minute in the day for Hannah. She threw open windows, washed walls and furniture and bedding. She tore the beds apart and washed the frames, the rails, and the wooden slats that supported the mattresses. She polished mirrors, emptied drawers and wiped them with strong-scented pine soap that had been left behind from Rocher's hardware where she used to work.

She could never use the soap without thinking of the unhappy couple and their merchandise in a store that was called a hardware store, but had almost anything you could ever need. And now, they had moved back East to Baltimore, Maryland.

She wondered vaguely whether poor Harry was surviving the city. He had not wanted to return, but with a wife as miserably unhappy as Doris had been, he didn't have much choice. He did the right thing, giving his life for his wife, giving up what he loved most and taking her home where he knew she would be happy. Hannah hoped he was blessed every day. He was a good man and Lord knows, there weren't many of them.

Janie sat beside a drawer, pulling out handkerchiefs, scarves, anything colorful, putting them carefully on a pile and patting them with her soft little hands, saying, "Now, now."

She spoke quite a few words, so Hannah guessed she might be nearing 18 months old. Older than a year, but less than two.

Hannah was on the porch emptying a bucket of water when she spied the dark vehicle plowing through the mud, water, and slush, veering sharply in the back as the driver struggled to keep the car on the road, such as it was in spring.

Her heart beat once, flopped over, then rushed on. Blood pounded in her ears. They had come. Her first instinct was to run inside and grab Janie, hide her, tell a lie. She couldn't do this. Nausea rose, a hot bile in her throat, as the color drained from her face. Her mouth went dry and her nostrils dilated as her heart thumped.

She struggled for control, to regain a sense of composure. Janie was still playing happily in the bedroom. She checked her appearance, plucked a few stray hairs, adjusted the navy blue *dichly* on her head, then watched as the car slid to a stop in front of the house.

She drew in a long, steadying breath as the passenger door opened, and a white-haired lady dressed in a fashionable coat and hat stepped gracefully from the car. The driver emerged at the same time, a tall, older gentleman dressed in brown tweed, a hat on his head.

It had to be them. The grandparents.

She hoped Jerry was in the barn. She badly needed him to greet them. There were no other passengers in the car, which was shocking. These two aging people had come all this way on these back roads, driving a car that required skill on roads that were barely passable in some places.

They stood, looking uncertainly at the house. Hannah forced herself to go to the door, open it, and call out a greeting. Immediately, the couple's gazes relaxed, a smile appeared on the woman's face, and they made their way up the muddy path to the door.

Where was Jerry? Well, nothing to do but face this thing head on. She had known it was coming. She stood by the door, waiting until they were both on the porch, and then extended her hand. "How do you do?"

"We are both well, thank you." They shook Hannah's hand, the gentleman's grip firm, his blue eyes inquisitive but kind. His wife had a soft handshake, her round face showing no emotion, only a calm curiosity from colorless eyes behind a pair of gold-rimmed spectacles, as round as her face.

"You must be Hannah Riehl."

"Yes, I am."

Visibly relieved, the gentleman sighed, shook his head, and gave a small laugh. Before he could say more, Hannah stepped aside and ushered them in, closing the door behind them. The prairie wind still had a bite to it, as Hod would say.

"Please, sit down. Make yourselves comfortable."

They sat side by side, stiffly, their feet tucked in beneath them, their gloved hands in their laps. Tension hummed between them.

"We are Thomas and Evelyn Richards. We have journeyed here from Utah. Have you heard of Salt Lake City?"

Hannah's heart dropped as if it was falling into her stomach. The room spun as she struggled to breathe normally. She licked her dry lips and answered, "Yes."

Soft footsteps came down the hallway as Janie made a shy appearance, her thumb thrust securely in her mouth, her eyes large with fright.

Hannah leaned down and extended her hands. "Come."

The couple watched Janie intensely. "We are Lila's parents."

"I see."

"And this is . . .?"

Hannah was clinging to Janie, holding her too tightly. She wriggled, wanting down, but Hannah only pulled her closer. "We call her Janie. Do you know the story?"

Mr. Richards nodded. "Some of it. I don't know if we'll ever be able to sort out the truth from the lies."

Hannah nodded.

"Lila ran off with Timothy Weber when she was fourteen years old. They disappeared one night, and we heard nothing for close to six months. By then they were in Texas." He stopped, struggling to control his emotions.

His wife continued for him. "They were taken in by a wealthy rancher by the name of Caldwell. I have no idea why or how they ended up here in this . . ." She spread her hands.

Hannah smiled. "Most people find the prairie unattractive," she commented.

"I don't mean to say that, but it is isolated. We knew they had had a child and that they lived in North Dakota. And then, we were notified about the fire, the child, and their presumed deaths."

Mr. Richards took over. "They are believed to have perished in the fire. The chief of the fire company said there was a gold wedding band in the ashes. A ring. Why only one, was my question. Later, they found the other one.

"So, I suppose, no matter how hard we try and tell ourselves they could still be alive, we know they are not. Why the child was in the barn is a searing question to which we may never know the answer. We may have to live with this for the rest of our lives."

"She is our granddaughter," Evelyn Richards said softly.

"She doesn't look like Lila, does she?" Thomas whispered.

Hannah replied matter-of-factly, "We actually only met them once and had a nice visit. Lila had gone to lay down for a nap, so we only talked with her briefly. She was so young."

"Yes. Sixteen. So you see, we're heartbroken. Grief is a terrible thing. Especially in circumstances that are beyond our understanding. The whole thing is a mystery, a nightmare we have to live with. If only we could wake up and it would all be a bad dream." Thomas Richards would carry the mark of this tragedy to his death. Hannah bit her lip and pushed back the sympathy that welled up.

"Lila was disobedient. Madly in love with the much older Timothy Weber. We hope she had time to repent. She was always such a sweet, loving daughter, never caused us a moment's trouble, until she met Timothy."

Thomas Richards's piercing gaze fastened on Hannah. "You say you met them once. You were in their house? You sat and had a nice visit? Nothing strange?"

Hannah thought back to the day of the storm. She shook her head. "He seemed a bit arrogant, maybe. Over optimistic. We saw no child and he said his wife was napping, so perhaps she was putting the child to sleep."

"Why would he not have mentioned the child?"

"I have no idea."

Evelyn Richards began to weep, delicately bringing a lace handkerchief to her face. "Lila may have suffered at the hands of this man."

Thomas patted his wife to console her, his face gray with pain. "We have the child, dear," he said. Evelyn nodded.

So, it was final then. Hannah felt as if there was a stone in her chest instead of a beating heart. She told herself to have courage, to be strong enough not to break down visibly.

"So you do realize, Mrs. Riehl, that we are her legal guardians."

"Yes." Hannah's voice was a whisper.

"Your husband? Is he about?"

Hannah sat up to look out the window. "He was here earlier but I believe he rode out to check on the cows. It's calving season."

"Yes, of course."

"May I offer you a cup of tea?"

"No. No. We have a long drive ahead of us. We may as well not linger here."

Hannah sighed. She looked into Janie's face, clasping her shoulders, and saw the question in her eyes. "Do you want to go to your grandmother, Janie?" A sob in her voice. Quickly, she swallowed.

As long as Hannah lived, she would remember the look of absolute trust in Janie's round eyes before she slid off her lap and walked to her grandmother. She stood at her grandmother's knee like a little princess. So much grace, so much trust, Hannah thought.

Evelyn reached for her, and Janie went into her arms willingly. The lady's tears flowed, but a smile appeared through them like sunshine breaking through on a rainy day. She touched Janie's hair, her nose, her pert mouth. She murmured and stroked as

Janie sat staring at her intently. Thomas reached over to touch the brown curls, tears in his own eyes.

How strange, Hannah thought, that Janie accepts them both immediately. Perhaps God was in all of it, and, in her mother's words, it was simply "meant to be."

"I'll get her things," Hannah said quietly.

She cried while she packed the flannel diapers, the home-made dresses, and the little stockings. She had no shoes. Her coat was a stitched-together, made-over affair from one of Hannah's own, made without a pattern. She felt ashamed, then, of Janie's meager belongings, and her own inability to sew.

She heard the door open and close, voices. Jerry had come in. Viciously, she swiped at her tears, set her mouth in a determined line. She would not allow him to see how devastating this was. She had her pride to uphold. He'd seen her down too many times already.

She brought the cardboard box out of her bedroom, her face expressionless. Jerry was deep in conversation with the Richardses, so she set the box on the table beside the rocking chair and stood politely, her face a mask of self-control.

Jerry could supply no more information than Hannah had been able to, but Janie's grandparents were more than satisfied to be able to claim the child, a consolation they would have as they lived out their days.

They would find the birth certificate and call her by her given name. Janie would live in a Christian family with a group of caring adults around her and therefore, would never know of the tragedy in her past. Jerry and Hannah would never be known by her, never remembered, never longed for. Mercifully, she was too young to know.

And then, Hannah desperately wanted this to be over. She wanted them gone, with Janie, so she could begin to live her days without her and to see if she would be able to survive.

She handed Janie's coat to Evelyn, who began to insert the

little hands into the sleeves. That was when she reached for Hannah, a puzzled expression giving way to howls of protest.

Quickly Jerry picked her up, finished putting on her coat and scarf while Thomas and Evelyn stood there.

"Just go," Hannah said, tightly.

Her last memory of Janie was seeing her over Jerry's shoulder, both arms outstretched to Hannah, crying, "Mama. Mama!" until Hannah closed the door with more force than was absolutely necessary. She ran into her bedroom and threw herself on her bed, the pain eventually melting into heaving sobs and rivers of tears that soaked the quilt.

She heard Jerry return. Her bedroom door was firmly closed so he'd leave her alone. She listened for the sound of the car engine and thought there was always a chance they'd changed their minds, take pity on her and on Janie.

She knew they'd be good to Janie, knew she'd have a nice life. Knew too that this had all been inevitable, but all that was of small comfort.

Hannah had never realized the joy of caring for a child. She had not known she would ever feel this way. She had loved her siblings, but not the way she had loved Janie. It was all a mystery, this bond between a mother and her child.

She thought of children of her own and knew she wanted them now. It was a settling of her mind, the sure knowledge of motherhood. Well, one day at a time.

Spring was coming, so she'd stay busy. She'd bury herself in work, ride with Jerry when he rode out to deal with the longhorns, and eventually, time would heal, as it always does.

But first, she'd have to learn to control her emotions.

Supper that evening was a strained affair. Jerry tried to talk about Janie and her grandparents, but Hannah cut him off with a harsh word of rebuke.

And yet, he saw and understood Hannah's anger. She had never been angrier and more ill-mannered than she was now, living in the quiet house, a bleak space surrounded by four walls, devoid of Janie's happy chatter, the little feet that were like a musical cadence.

Where most women would have cried and spoken of their loss, allowing their husband's comforting arms to surround them, Hannah built a complex, efficient wall by the force of her own belligerence.

Nothing suited her. She made fun of the winter-toughened cows, despised the mules, said the wheat looked sparse, yelled at him for walking into the house with mud on his boots.

And never once did she mention Janie, the tragedy at the Webers', nothing. The final straw came a few weeks later when she blamed Jerry for the palomino's loss, saying it wouldn't have happened if he'd known anything about how the weather works on the prairie.

He listened to her senseless tirade, his back turned and his shoulders squared as he held very still. When he turned, Hannah recognized the fact that she had pushed him too far.

He stalked to her on swift, furious feet, grasped her shoulders with claw-like fingers, and shoved his face close to hers, so close she could see the small red veins that stood out on his nose.

"Stop it, Hannah! There is absolutely no truth in what you're saying. You were the one who wanted to go. That, Hannah, is your whole problem. Whatever happens in your life is always someone else's fault. Your father, your mother, and now me. It's time you grow up and take responsibility. If things continue like this, I'm going back to Lancaster County. I'm serious." He released her roughly enough that she had to take two steps back to keep her balance.

Her mouth opened in disbelief as she watched him yank open the door with much more force than was necessary, and disappear. It pleased her to know he wasn't quite a saint. He was a normal man, but at the same time she felt the most uncomfortable sensation she'd ever experienced. A deep sense of shame stung her cheeks. He may as well have slapped her.

What if what he said was true? That part about going back to Lancaster. So he did want to go back. Return to his homeland like the rest of them. Like whipped puppies. Well, she had news for him. He'd have to go alone.

She thought of Harry Rocher going back East to Baltimore, Maryland, a stifling seaport that teemed with people, heat, and humidity. Would he find peace and happiness there? She pictured him standing on the dock, watching the barges, feeding seagulls, returning to a home with a happy wife, visiting relatives.

Harry had done the right thing. Hannah knew his personal struggle and how difficult it had been for him to lay down his life for his wife, to love her the way Christ loved the church.

Her own father, pious and self-righteous, secure in his plain Amish way of life, could not do what Harry had done, and he a man of the world. There was the sticker. Being Amish was all right and good, a fact she could appreciate the longer she lived with Jerry. But you had to be careful. To take the title of being Amish as a passport to righteousness was a falsehood. "By their works ye shall know them."

But then, her mother had submitted, truly submitted in the way the Bible taught married women to do. No one would ever know the cost of her submission. But that had been right as well.

Jerry didn't know everything. He had no idea what her father had done. Her anger was her father's fault. How could she ever say that it wasn't? He had done wrong, not her. This thought, that had played over and over throughout her life, firmly embedded in the groove of her mind, spurred her into action. She lifted dishes and slammed them into the sink, breaking the handle off a cup, running water so hot she burned her fingers, adding far too much soap as she mumbled justifications to herself.

Jerry did not apologize. He merely went on his way, plowed the garden, spoke of the weather, the calves, the need for rain, as if that incident had never occurred. But it had! For Hannah, Jerry's temper and his threat stayed in her consciousness like a prickly burr, uncomfortable and sometimes making her miserable. It caused her to lower her eyes, unable to meet the forgiveness in his, as she clung to her sense of having been wronged.

The wheat grew, the roots absorbing the moisture the snows of winter had put into the prairie soil. The grass grew strong. The warm winds blew like a hushed promise of hope for the homesteaders that dotted the vast land, these clutches of buildings that housed the hardy souls of the Western prairie.

A month passed, then two. Every day the sun rose, a fiery orange ball of heat that promised a day exactly like the previous one. Heated winds blew, a drying, hope-sucking swoop from the west. There was an orange cast to the land, a yellow fog in the atmosphere, that wore down Hannah's resolve, working away at her determination like sandpaper on a rough piece of wood.

Surely not again. A drought this year would mean failure. An incomplete wheat crop, thin, bawling cattle, calves who trotted after their mothers as they roamed in larger and larger circles, tearing at the withered grass that gave way to a brittle lack of moisture.

The great metal fins on the windmill whirred and creaked, the bolts straining against the indestructible frame, the pump working feverishly to draw water from the stream far below the surface.

The moaning, hot wind clattered against the eaves, tore at the tin roof and the wooden siding, sent porch chairs skittering across the floor, dumping them off into the dust of the yard.

Open windows afforded comfort, the air moving through the stifling house but carrying a fine silt of gray dust that lay over everything.

Dishes in cupboards had to be wiped clean with the corner of Hannah's apron, a swift dab for every tumbler or cup before it could be set on the table. Even then, they had to be placed upside down before they sat down to a meal.

They never spoke of the weather. There was nothing to say as long as Hannah clung tenaciously to her hope of rain.

All the washing Hannah hung on the line dried within the hour. She had to wrestle it all in as soon as possible or it would be torn from the clothes pins and hurled away by the wind.

Jerry and Hannah rode into the town of Pine for supplies, windblown and sunburned, King and the unruly quarter horse hitched to the spring wagon. Entering the town, Hannah asked Jerry to tie the horses. She was ashamed to drive down the main street with the exhausted team covered in white foam from the chafing harness on their wet bodies.

Rocher's Hardware had been bought by a man named Amos Henry, a hardworking man from Illinois. Rumors floated around the countryside. Supposedly, his wife had left with a cattle dealer and lived in luxury in California, leaving all the children behind with Amos. There were ten of them, all blond-haired and blue-eyed, devoted to their father and the success of the store.

Hod Jenkins said the man was a wonder. Never complained, never spoke of his wife. You could see his devotion to them kids, in Hod's words.

He'd added a room, filled it with tools and plowshares, harnesses and saddles, tractor parts, nails, screws, lariats, halters, everything a rancher might need.

The dry goods were all stacked neatly, bolts of cloth upright, sorted by color, the plaids and patterned fabric separate. Spools of thread, packets of needles, scissors and elastic, buttons and snaps, all of it was sorted in convenient bins within easy reach.

Hannah walked among the many items she would have liked to purchase, but she had no idea whether Jerry could afford them. The shining teakettle, the new soup ladle. She held both of them, rubbed her palms over each item and wondered at the shine. Like a mirror. She became aware of a presence at her elbow.

"Pretty, isn't it?"

Hannah turned and found a girl, shorter than she, with beautiful eyes like cornflowers, hair like new straw.

"It's called stainless steel," she informed Hannah.

CHAPTER 11

HER NAME WAS MARGARET HENRY, AND HANNAH LEARNED SHE WAS the oldest daughter. She was a mother to her nine siblings, a sweet-natured girl of eighteen, eager to help Hannah with anything she might need.

"Call me Margie; everyone else does," she said, smiling happily, her eyes alight with curiosity and interest.

Hannah was aloof at first, which was her nature. She did not need friends, certainly not strangers, and she wished Margaret would go away and leave her alone. She answered Margaret's inquires with short nods or clipped words, which did nothing to deter the young woman's friendliness.

Hannah chose a packet of needles and a few black buttons to repair some articles of clothing. Then she ran a hand down the blue fabric that resembled the sky. She'd never buy it. She couldn't ask Jerry for money, and she certainly didn't have any of her own.

Margaret reached up to touch her white organdy covering. "That's nice," she said. Then, "Why do you wear it?"

Hannah desperately wanted her to leave, had no inclination to explain the Bible verse the Amish adopted to explain the reason for a woman's head being covered. "I don't know," she mumbled, her face flaming as she turned away to examine a packet of steel hairpins.

Margaret laughed, a high, sweet sound of delight. "You don't have to tell me," she said agreeably.

Hannah didn't reply, so Margaret offered nothing more, simply turned and left, leaving Hannah to herself, thankful for this moment without her presence.

Hannah knew she wasn't friend material. Girls and their blathering, their senseless tittering, stupid secrets, and howls of accompanying laughter, weren't anything she wanted or needed.

Jerry walked over to find her. "Get what you needed?" he asked. She nodded and they walked to the grocery section, where she purchased cornmeal, rolled oats, tea, coffee, brown sugar, salt, flour, baking soda, baking powder, and then asked Jerry if he wanted anything else.

He picked up a package of chocolate and some tin cans of fruit for making pies. "I'm hungry for chocolate cake," he said. Hannah avoided his eyes, nodding curtly.

Margaret watched and thought he was the most handsome man she'd ever seen. Putting up a hand to adjust her blond waves, she ran a hand over her hips to smooth the pleats in her skirt. His wife was a piece of lemon, now wasn't she?

When all of their purchases were grouped by the register, she began her curious interrogations again, a high pink color in her cheeks, those cornflower eyes darting repeatedly to Jerry's face while he kept up a lively banter with her. Well, let him, Hannah thought sourly. She was married to him.

"Yeah, Ma left," she was saying. "No heartache for us kids. She hated the West. Hated the town, all of it. Life was no fun with her around. To live with an unhappy person corrodes your own spirit. Like rust. Don't miss her at all. I did all the work anyhow, so I did. Now, is there anything else I can get you?"

She was looking straight at Jerry, her eyes bright with interest, her white teeth flashing in her face. He answered with a too-wide grin of his own, enjoying this exchange immensely.

A shot of unaccustomed jealousy liquidated quickly into ill manners. Hannah's eyes shot daggers of deep brown fury in Jerry's direction. "If you can tear yourself away, it's time to load up these groceries." Her words held all the warmth of an icicle during a blizzard.

Flustered, Jerry scrambled to retrieve the brown paper bags, picking one up too quickly. He broke his hold as a large piece of bag tore off.

"Oh. Here, I'll get you another one," Margaret said breathlessly. "It happens all the time."

Hannah's dark eyes bored into Margaret's blue eyes. "I'll bet," she said, followed by a derogatory snort.

But at the feed mill, she sat spellbound, her hands folded loosely in her lap, held captive by the men's talk. Lounging against the high wooden counter, one leg crossed over the other, their old Stetsons stained with perspiration, tall, short, round in the stomach, or stick thin, these men were all cut from the same cloth, their parents and grandparents staying on their homesteads, eking out the meager existence they seemed to love.

Nothing dampened these grizzled men's spirits. They thrived on difficulty. Monetary success was a concept they didn't understand. They measured with a different yard stick than the rest of the world. The prairie was their life. "Got into Grandpap's blood, and his pap before him. Ain't no other place to live, far's I'm concerned."

Hannah felt a deep respect and awe for these battered Stetsons. Their sunburned faces were like prunes, deep lines and crevices etched from brow to chin, a map of their lives. They lived on the land, gleaned from it what they could, raised a few scrawny longhorns. Success was an evening spent on the porch, a barn cat rubbing along the creaking hickory rocker, a dog at their feet, and the spectacular sunset their entertainment.

"If the wife became unhappy, wal, then, she'd have to go back East cause they shore weren't gonna leave the prairie nohow."

Today, the subject was the drought. Wasn't it always?

"Ain't rainin' this summer." Stated bluntly, with absolute conviction.

"Who said?"

"Aw, come on. We'll have us a few good soakin' thunderstorms. What're you talkin' about?"

Wads of tobacco shifted, streams of dark brown juice were aimed expertly at the copper spittoon in the corner. By the looks of the dried dribbles on the outside, plenty of misses had taken place.

Hannah swallowed.

"Nope." The first speaker leaned forward, removed his elbows from the high counter, uncrossed his legs, and went to thump a feed sack of grain to form a perch for himself. "No sir, I'm tellin' you. We had that yaller look about us, come spring. You get that, it's gonna be dry as Abraham's desert."

Jerry stood off to the side, taking in every word, but seldom speaking himself, listening to learn the knowledge of the plains.

"Any o' you ever hear more about that house fire out there where them Germans usta live?"

Most faces turned to Jerry. He nodded. "The grandparents of the young wife came to collect the little girl. They're from Utah, where Timothy Weber said he was from, so we know that part is true, but not much else."

"Them young people died though, for sure? In thet there fire?"

Jerry shrugged. "They think so. Found their wedding rings."

"They shoulda found more'n that. No body turns completely to ashes when they burn." Heads nodded in agreement.

"I still think there's somethin' afoot."

Bill Hawkins, an old bachelor that ran the biggest herd of longhorns, cleared his throat, spit a long stream of molasses-colored liquid from his mouth, wiping his mouth on the cuff of his sleeve before commencing with his point of view.

"What kinda people would leave their kid in a barn in the dead of winter? They were a normal couple, weren't they? Come out here, bought that property fair and square, with good intentions. Nobody burns up that fast."

Hannah recognized again the common sense of these prairie dwellers. She had thought the same thing, often. Did a person turn completely to ashes in a house fire? Or did someone place those wedding rings on the floor to throw everyone off?

As if he read her thoughts, Bill continued. "Them fire company big shots don't know nothin'. They make a good calculation and guess the rest. Whatever suits 'em, is what they go by. We got enough horse and cattle thieves around. Them white Percherons was in somebody's sights, I'd say."

"They was all in the barn, though."

Hannah felt a jolt of excitement. There had been more than eleven horses the day she'd been there. All those white horse trailers. She sat up straight, opened her mouth to speak, and was cut off by a short, stocky fellow who tipped his hat back on his head, scratched his thatch of orange hair, replaced his hat and lined up his four fingers to examine the wealth of dandruff he'd scraped loose.

Rubbing his nails down the side of his oil-stained jeans, he hacked loudly, cleared his throat and said that nobody knew how many o' them oversized chunks o' horseflesh had been there ta begin with.

"More than eleven." Hannah spoke without thinking. Jerry turned his head sharply and looked at her. Hannah didn't look back; she looked out to the general circle of men and went on, her eyes like dark sapphires.

"It was a few months ago, early in the spring, when I rode over to see if the people from Texas had moved in . . ."

"They wasn't from Texas," Bill Hawkins said.

Jerry corrected him. "The young couple was."

"Anyway," Hannah continued, "the place was crawling with white horse trailers. I didn't count them but there were definitely more than five. If there were two horses in each one, I'd say there were more than twenty horses."

"Thet barn ain't thet big."

"It wasn't. It isn't. They weren't all in the barn," Hannah said quickly.

"Hm. Ain't that somepin' to think about?" Bill Hawkins asked.

"Ah, you know how it goes. Don't matter what we think. Them there horse thieves is slicker'n greased pigs. How you ever gonna ketch 'em? One sheriff in two hunnert miles and they don't give a . . ."

Bob Daley glanced at Hannah, cleared his throat, and said, "Don't care." Hannah grinned good-naturedly and said he was right. She wanted to tell them about Lemuel Short but Jerry didn't know about that episode and she had no intention of telling him, either.

"Any high falutin' caravan o' white trailers movin' into the area like that is like the wasps to a cake o' honey. Them horse thieves probably had them pegged way back in Missouri, if they came from those parts."

Heads nodded. "That's fer shore."

"Yer right."

"Yeah, but to light that house. That's just goin' too far."

The conversation changed directions, turning to the growing of wheat, half a dozen different opinions crisscrossing the hot, dusty feed mill.

Jerry and Hannah stopped at the butcher shop for lard. A five-gallon tin would hold them over for a while.

Seated on the high wooden seat, Hannah felt rich, endowed

with great wealth. Such a large amount of supplies was something. The ability to ride into town and purchase even more than was necessary was an indulgence that she could not have imagined for many years. She hoped she would never take it for granted and forget to realize the gift of provisions.

Hannah gazed at the land with unseeing eyes, her thoughts churning faster and faster. Was this the secret to the true homesteader then? What separated the greenhorns from the true pioneers? The ones who stayed. It was possible. Over and over, the folks who stayed lived through drought and hail and all kinds of calamities. They kept their homesteads, adapting their views and values to suit the environment and not someone else's version of success.

Worry did not fall into their vocabulary, posed no threat. If it didn't rain, they pulled their belts tighter and ate cornmeal mush and prairie hens. Here, success might be measured by the ability to weather whatever the Almighty handed you.

She didn't want to reveal her thoughts now, while Jerry was busy controlling the cranky quarter horse, reining in King, who wanted to run full out, which was the way he always ran when he was hitched to a spring wagon.

She might just keep the whole thing to herself. She wanted to ask Jerry how much money he still had in his bank account, but was too proud to ask. How did one ask for sky-blue dress fabric without giving him the notion that she was buying it to be attractive to him?

Which she definitely wasn't.

The wheat had turned from the brilliant, earth-toned green of spring to a drab, olive-hued, windblown mess, probably half the height it should have been. Hannah turned her head to keep from looking at it more than was absolutely necessary.

"Here we are," Jerry called out, his usual good humor

evident. She didn't answer, just stepped off the spring wagon and began the trek to the house, carrying armloads of provisions. She couldn't tell him, but the solid weight of the food was a joy, a feeling of luxury, a cared-for and appreciated gift of sustainability in the face of another drought. The surge of happiness she felt gave her strength.

She knew she should thank him that evening as they rested on the porch after carrying buckets of water in an effort to save their potatoes and pole beans.

"What do you think, Hannah? Is it worth lugging water?" Jerry asked.

"Long as it doesn't rain," she answered.

"But the potatoes look half-dead."

"They always do. You can't compare Western potatoes with what we were used to back East."

"Do you get any potatoes to dig?"

"Sometimes."

They fell silent as they listened to the sounds of the evening. When the wind slowed for the night, the sounds of birds and insects became easier to distinguish, the crickets and grasshoppers, the little dickeybirds and the evening whistles of the larks. Hannah loved this time of day. The serenity of pure, empty skies in several shades of lavender and pink, the blue fading to gray before twilight followed the setting of the sun, that effortless disappearance of amazing light and heat.

She thought of all the crow's-feet etched along the side of these ranchers' eyes, imagined they squinted all day long from beneath their filthy hat brims. Tentatively, she reached up to run the tips of her fingers along her own eyes, the outer edges still smooth. She lowered her hands quickly when Jerry looked her way.

"So, what do you think, Hannah?" he asked.

"About what?"

"We are having another drought, whether we admit it or not. I don't know if we can expect any wheat at all. Which means the calves are our only source of income, and they're not too great either."

"You heard the men."

Jerry looked at her. She was sitting on the porch floor, her knees drawn up, her skirts pulled taut down to her brown feet. Her arms rested on her knees, her neck long and graceful like a swan. Her hair had come loose from the heavy coil that lay on her neck and strands of it were blowing lightly in the evening breeze.

As black as midnight. Black as coal. His mind wandered, thinking of a different time, a different place, another girl with black hair. What had kept him from marrying her? Why had he walked away from Ruth Ebersol?

God's ways were far above his own, but sometimes the thought of being successful in business at home in Lancaster County, with a girl . . . no, a wife like Ruth, seemed like a bright beacon of rest, one he had missed entirely.

He wanted to go back home and resume a normal life.

"I heard them, yes."

"Well, what did you get out of what they were saying?"

"One thing's for sure. They don't look on droughts or . . ."

Jerry laughed ruefully. "Or anything at all with too much concern," he finished for her.

Hannah met his gaze, her eyes flashing. "Exactly! You do understand." In the depths of her eyes there was a spark or recognition that kept his eyes riveted on hers.

"Oh, Jerry. Don't you see? Today at the feed mill I found the reason why some people stay here in North Dakota and all the lands west of here, and others don't. It's so plain to me now, especially why our Amish neighbors went home. These people out here measure their time on earth in a completely different way than we do. They don't care about what we call success. They are happy, Jerry, happy with food on the table and a roof over their heads, enough wages to keep their clunker automobiles or trucks going. In other words, getting ahead, our version of it, with a large herd of cows and money in the bank, simply isn't important."

Jerry narrowed his eyes. "So you're saying to be a successful homesteader, you need to adopt a different attitude."

"Yes."

"You mean, a drought isn't so awful, as long as you're content with what you have."

"Right."

Jerry said nothing for a long while. Then he asked, "Would you be content here, like this, if we never had more than we have now? No church, no fellow Amish, no parents or relatives, simply this seclusion day in and day out?"

"Yes."

His heart sank. He didn't speak again. He simply rose, let himself in the house, and let the screen door flop behind him. Decidedly, the conversation had taken a new and different turn, and he needed time to think.

Hannah remained on the porch, her chin resting on her arms, now a bit miffed. That was unnecessary, Jerry cutting off the conversation like that. He just couldn't bear to think of staying here. He figured she'd break down yet. Well, she almost had.

But after today, she wasn't so sure. These old ranchers had something, an element of satisfaction, of peace, no matter what happened. They took it, made the best of it, enjoyed themselves with simple pleasures. Oh, the list went on and on.

She thought of her father, the manic fasting and praying, believing that God would come on his terms and bless him because he was a righteous man. Wasn't he misguided? Which one was God's way?

The ranchers gathered in a feed mill with total kinship, saying what they thought, accepting and accepted, easily doing the same with whatever life handed them, paragons of patience and contentment.

Her father had left Lancaster County because of the argumentative brethren who aired their highly esteemed opinions, took offense and held grudges, all in the name of Christ and his written word. Her father would not have wasted the time telling her these men were all unsaved heathens, and perhaps they were. But that part was up to God.

Hannah knew her own mind. These *ausrichy* (outsiders) displayed plenty of the fruits of the Spirit, in her view. They demanded nothing from God, appreciated plenty, and lived in peace and harmony, helping anyone who needed it. They would have starved, the whole Mose Detweiler family, if Hod and Abby had not given and kept on giving.

And so Hannah remained on the porch watching the pinpricks of white stars appear, one by one, then in clusters, then in numbers far beyond her ability to count. Nip and Tuck came from the barn, surprised to find her, shoving their wet noses in her face, then flopping down beside her.

"Phew! You smell. Have you been unearthing your treasures? Get away from me!" She shoved them aside with her foot. Killing prairie dogs and other rodents was play for these swift-moving dogs. They buried the excess, then retrieved it after it became putrid.

And still she lingered, her thoughts racing from one subject to another, questions left unanswered, new ideas like cartwheels cavorting through her mind. She couldn't expect Jerry to stay if he simply did not see things her way. Neither could she keep up her expectations of living together for the sake of enough money to keep the homestead.

Clearly, she was in over her head. To move to Lancaster now

was simply not possible. He'd have to take her by force, kicking and biting like a wild horse!

As for that other. . . . She felt so tired so quickly, her thoughts dragging along like a hundred-pound weight, trying to reason her way out of it. Regret was suddenly very real. Why had she married Jerry on a whim? For money of course, when money was still important. After today, she'd have to be honest and somehow have the courage to tell him she would never return to Lancaster County and give him the option of leaving to go back by himself.

Jerry lay in his own bedroom with his own thoughts, trying to be reasonable. Mentally, he made a list. Number one: he was married to her, the girl of his dreams, who obviously had no normal love or desire for him. Number two: her goal in life was to stay on the prairie, especially after today. His goal was to leave this endless prairie, the dust and wind that shaved away at his goodwill and patience. Number three: today, she had come up with a whole new philosophy.

He was weary, bone-weary, in mind, body, and soul. Regret for the marriage became an insistent whine, which he tried to slap down like a mosquito, but he had to face it. He wished he'd never met her. That marriage certificate was binding by God and by man. Holy Matrimony. He turned his face to the wall.

He felt old, bitter, and hostile toward Hannah, a whole new, uneasy accumulation of thoughts and feelings. He couldn't pray in this state of mind. But he did tell God that he was in too deep and couldn't find a way out. So, he'd allow God to lead and go where He thought best, and if it was His will, he would stay. He would sacrifice his life for Hannah's love. But he did require Hannah's love, if it was meant to be.

The summer ended without rain. The wheat stayed short and never grew to a head. The dust blew between the limp plants and lay like volcanic ash. They worked together to put up enough hay to last through the winter before the worst of the drought. They never talked about the failed wheat crop, or the endless dust.

Just when Jerry thought things could not get worse, Hod Jenkins came by in his rusted, blue pickup truck in a cloud of dust, almost setting it on its nose, he hit the brakes so hard.

Hod strode up to the porch, brought his fist up, and banged on the screen door. He said they'd had a telephone call from Abby's sister that lived down Ventura way.

Hannah moved quickly from the table, opening the door to let him in, her eyes wide with dark apprehension.

Their food turned cold as Hod told them what Tessa had said. "There are horse thieves around. Seriously dangerous ones. Men who won't think twice about knockin' you off to git at yer horses. That King o' yourn . . ." Hod shook his head. "They's workin' at night. Hittin' every ranch from Ventura to Calvin. Gittin' closer by the day. She says even the sheriffs is afraid of 'em. Callin' in a buncha cops from the capital. Alls I'm sayin' is to keep watch at night. I dunno how yer gonna keep 'em from takin' yer horses, though. Iffen they do show up, uer better off lettin' 'em take 'em, I guess."

Hannah set down a mug of coffee in front of Hod with shaking hands, her face gone pale. Jerry's face looked grim, but he said nothing, allowing Hod to have his say.

"They'll ketch 'em, eventually. The thing is, will they git 'em fore they git this far? Hannah, now if they show up, don't you go doin' anything stupid. Stay in the house. Act like there ain't nobody around." He slurped his coffee and grimaced.

"An' they say there's a green tint to the east. Old timers used to say the grasshoppers is walkin'. Like the plagues of Egypt, mind you. Time'll tell, I guess."

CHAPTER 12

AFTER HOD LEFT IN A CLOUD OF DUST, JERRY SAT IN A KITCHEN chair dazed, as if all the vigor had gone out of him. He couldn't bring himself to look at Hannah. He didn't want her opinion just yet. He needed space to think. He drained the last of his coffee, stood, and walked out.

He was halfway to the barn when he heard his name being called in strident tones laced with the old belligerence. He stopped, turned.

"Come back in here!" Hannah shouted. It was about the last thing he wanted to do, but he knew ignoring her would only make things worse. He returned to the kitchen and sat down without meeting her gaze.

"You know you're acting like a coward. Like an ostrich! Or whichever animal it is that sticks its head in the sand when trouble comes along."

As irritating as a burr in his sock. "An ostrich is a bird."

"We have to talk," Hannah said, ignoring his correction.

"Go ahead."

"Don't *you* have anything to say?"

"No. Go ahead. Tell me what's on your mind."

Hannah sighed. "I wish you would go first, okay? You won't like what I have to say."

"Well, keep going. I want to hear it," Jerry urged, trying to sound like he meant it.

"All right. I know you want to go back to Lancaster. I don't. I want to stay here, away from all the people who know everything about everybody. After our afternoon at the feed mill, I feel like I finally have a grasp on what it takes to make it out here. And I love it so much."

"I know you do, Hannah. And if it means so much to you, we'll stay, for a while anyhow. But didn't you want to talk about the horse thieves? And the grasshoppers?"

"Oh, you can't listen to that Hod. He's always making this stuff up. I don't believe all his horse thief talk either."

Jerry's eyebrows shot up.

"Don't look at me like that!"

He shook his head. "It's good to have confidence, Hannah, but to be too confident after a warning like that can be extremely foolish."

Hannah snorted, that grating sound that said everyone was foolish except her. There were few things he actually disliked about her but that was definitely one of them. He wanted to bring up the subject of how long they would still be living in this manner, but he figured that wouldn't do him any good at this point, either.

Was he a coward? Quite likely. He preferred to think he was patient and understanding.

At first, they thought a hailstorm was brewing. The greenish cast to an otherwise cloudless day seemed the harbinger of a mighty storm.

Hannah was watering the garden while keeping an eye on the approaching strange weather, whatever it was. She dumped water from a tin bucket, watched the parched earth soak it up greedily, and noticed the healthy green of the plants, especially the beans. All the hard work had paid off. The bean runners climbed to the top of the poles. The beans were hanging thick and healthy. The cabbage heads were firm, if small, which meant they'd have sauerkraut this winter.

If the storm kept coming toward them, they would be able to quickly harvest an amazing amount of vegetables before it hit. Jerry would certainly be impressed. She'd show him that with a bit of hard work and good management they could beat the odds.

But, what was that odor? She straightened and sniffed the air. She turned her face in every direction, taking deep breaths through her nose. Strange, that smell.

Well, likely it was a dead animal somewhere. Nip and Tuck were always dragging some putrid carcass from their burying places. Thinking no more about it, she refilled the bucket and finished her watering. She went to the house to finish the breakfast dishes.

The hens were laying well, plenty of eggs every morning, a treat she appreciated as she cooked eggs to perfection, serving them with fried mush made from the newly purchased cornmeal. She thought of the ear corn they used to buy, roast in the cook stove oven, shell and grind for their cornmeal, thus saving a dollar or so, when her mother and Manny were still here. Every penny had meant the difference between hunger and eating a meal, even if it was just cornmeal mush eaten with a pinch of salt.

The strange smell permeated the house now. Hannah tried to ignore it, finishing the dishes with a puzzled expression before stepping out on the porch to sniff the air again.

Jerry came in from the barn, his eyes questioning. Hannah met his eyes, shrugged, and shook her head.

They sat together on the porch steps, side by side, pondering the stench and the green atmosphere, as if the air contained green dust. Jerry rose uneasily, searching the sky, the waving drought-sickened grass. He paced from one end of the porch to the other.

"Sit down!" Hannah growled. "You're making it worse than it is."

"I've just never seen anything like this. Something is so weird. Strange. I don't like the dust or the smell."

Suddenly, he turned sharply. "Hannah, you . . . could it be the grasshoppers?"

She gasped, sprang to her feet, shading the strong forenoon light with the downturned palm of her hand.

Oh, please no, she thought. She'd heard tales of millions of gnawing creatures walking, plague-like, through the land and destroying everything in their path. But that was years ago. This was now the 1930s, modern times. Somehow, the automobiles, tractors, all the newer inventions did not seem like they could coexist with the grasshoppers of old.

Jerry pointed a shaking finger. "What is it?"

Hannah stood staring in disbelief. A wall of greenish-brown, yellow, and black. A moving front of writhing, gnawing insects. Spellbound, they watched their approach, a descending cloud of unreality, like a bad dream holding them captive.

"We need to close windows," Jerry said, quietly, too calmly, as if he would be punished if he raised his voice.

"What about the barn?"

"We can't help that. Cracks in the eaves, under the door," Jerry replied.

"The hens? Nip and Tuck?"

Jerry leaped off the porch, raced to the barn to corral the flapping chickens. Hannah dashed after him. They shooed and yelled, Hannah screeching and flapping her apron, maudlin with fear, as the wall of grasshoppers advanced steadily.

Nip and Tuck were stuffed into their doghouse, the rubber

flap closed securely with nails, before Hannah and Jerry turned and fled to the house, panting, slamming windows and doors, stuffing rags in every noticeable crack.

They heard a grinding, buzzing sound. The sound of countless jaws chewing grass, briars, weeds, each other. The dead insects rolled over and over until a sticky mass of body parts quickly putrefied in the sweltering, dust-infused sun.

Hannah felt a rising panic. She put both hands to her cheeks, her eyes wide. On they came, across the driveway, over the barn, scaling the walls like a million prehistoric creatures with oversized jaws, half flying, half leaping, grasping any available vegetation and completely mutilating it.

Hannah screamed, a long, hoarse, primal yell of fear and loathing. She screamed and screamed, stamped her feet and flapped her apron, as if her actions could put a stop to this disgusting onslaught of horrible creatures.

Quickly Jerry was at her side. "Come, Hannah. Don't watch." She was crying now, shaking like a leaf, begging Jerry to do something or they'd crawl in the house and over both of them. He pulled her away from the window, begging her not to watch. But she seemed powerless, mesmerized, her fingers spreading across her face, still peeping through them, wild-eyed with fear.

"Do something, Jerry. Please help me!" she screamed.

Jerry realized she was in danger of losing her sound reasoning, so completely was she consumed by her loathing of these large insects. It was a situation that was so out of her control that she felt powerless. And because she was such a fiercely determined person, he felt afraid for her.

He sat on the sofa, pulling her down, turning her face to his. He made her look at him until her eyes focused.

"Listen. Hannah, look at me. They can't get in. We're safe. Did you hear me? They'll walk over the house, but they can't get in. Hannah, look at me."

She was wild with revulsion. She clawed at his shoulders, broke free and ran to the door, tried to yank it open. He caught her just in time, hauled her back and held her.

Finally, when the grasshoppers reached the house and began their ascent up the north side, she shuddered and fell against him, sobbing, a desperate heaving of her body, choking, begging him to hold her.

The whole house was consumed by a grinding, sawing noise, the sound of millions of raspy legs and gossamer wings and devouring, ravenous mouths. Up from the ground they walked, up the wooden side, across the roof and down the other side, through the garden, leaving not even a tendril of green.

Jerry held Hannah, her face buried in his shirt, the stifling air inside the house causing them both to perspire freely. He could see the undersides of the insects, their bulging eyes, their high, crooked green legs and oversized jaws as they tried repeatedly to scale the slippery glass of the windows, falling back to be walked on or eaten by the grasshoppers who came behind them.

They fell down the chimney into the low embers of the cook stove, dropping by the hundreds and sizzling to their death. The chimney became clogged with grasshoppers. The stove began to send out a scent of burned insects, puffing out a sickening stench.

Hannah trembled, clung to him with all her strength. Putting his handkerchief over her face, he turned her head against his chest to hold her ears shut. It was like being in a vacuum, knowing the chewing insects were like a second skin, finding any crevice available and crawling through. They sat together, hardly breathing in the unbearable stench coming from the cook stove.

Jerry wiped the sweat from his forehead, felt it sliding down his back. He took an arm away to swipe at the soaked hair on his forehead, but quickly put it back around Hannah when she cried out in distress. "I can't. I can't," she kept saying over and over.

"Listen, Hannah. It'll be over soon. They'll stop coming eventually." He was seriously afraid for her. So impetuous, so angry, so sure of herself. Her breakdown after spending the night in the blizzard. And now this. He was afraid this was far worse.

She had been through so much, too much. An overwhelming need to protect her, to keep her safe from more disastrous situations, rose in him. If only he could take her back to safety, to the normal weather patterns, the hills and dales of the fertile valleys he loved so much. To keep her safe among friends and relatives. To take her to church and social events.

He chasteneth whom He loveth.

Deliberately, he drew her closer, his hand stroking her trembling back. Ah yes, he well knew the ways God chastened His children. He must love Hannah to put her through so much.

For the Lord looketh on the heart.

He saw in Hannah something worth redeeming or He would not allow all of this. Is this why I love her, then?

The grinding clatter of insects continued as they huddled together in the overheated, noxious house. The fumes from the stove were overpowering. Scratching, clawing, falling back, climbing over each other, killing one another—the march of the dreaded insects moved on.

Jerry sat up straight, listened as the rasping sounds lessened, then clearly faded. No grasshoppers out the north window, which meant the end had come and was on its way out.

"Hannah."

Her only response was a distinct tightening of her arms, her face burrowing deeper into his chest. "No, no, no, no."

He tried to release her arms, prying with all the strength he could muster, but her grip was like a vise, a panicked death grip.

"Hannah. Hannah. Let go. It's almost impossible to breathe in here."

"No, no, no."

He had to open windows, had to get away from the fumes coming from the cook stove. He wrestled her away from him with a strength born of desperation, shoving her onto the sofa where she collapsed, crying hysterically.

He tore open windows, gagged at the smell of dead grasshoppers strewn over everything, hanging body parts from window ledges, edges of siding, drooping from roof edges like cooked noodles. It was a grisly scene and there was a horrible, slimy stink where dead insects had been half-eaten by their peers.

He left Hannah and walked across the bare yard, stripped of any and all vegetation, a dry desert, a land cursed with the plague of Egypt come to visit them. He crunched across dead grasshoppers. Kicking them away, he gagged and swallowed the saliva that welled in his mouth, then gave into the nausea, leaned over, and threw up his half-digested breakfast.

First, unclog the chimney. He grabbed the wooden ladder from the tool shed and hurried to the house, setting it against the wall, climbing onto the porch roof, and from there onto the roof of the house.

Clogged, black with insects. It was a good chimney, made of creek stones and mortar. He'd simply burn them out, which is what he did, with paper and kerosene. Lighting a match on his thumbnail, he threw it in the cook stove. He was rewarded with a mighty whoosh, a roaring, crackling sound with clouds of smoke rolling out from under the stove lids.

Nothing to do about that. He'd have to help Hannah wash walls later. He swept the porch and steps, flicking his broom along the siding to rid the house of dead grasshoppers that clung to cracks in the walls.

The smoke in the kitchen was a better aroma than the sizzling insects. He heard the satisfying roar of the burning chimney, then searched for any stray insects before he went to urge

Hannah to sit up and notice her surroundings, to calm down and think of it as a bad dream.

Looking back, Jerry could remember the moment when Hannah's courage overrode her fear. Her disbelief and revulsion faded and normalcy returned. She followed him to the barn, to the creek, across the land to check on the cattle. She refused to stay alone. She asked him to stay in the house till the dishes were washed and she had tidied the house.

Often, her eyes would return to the horizon, searching for another wall of insects, her hands clenched into fists. There was no fight in her eyes, though.

Something had changed, but exactly what it was, Jerry couldn't say. She didn't sleep at night, but paced the floor, locked and re-locked the doors, until she passed into a stupor toward the morning hours. She begged him to stay with her, her pride and anger hidden away, erased by the memory of the crawling grasshoppers.

Finally, Jerry could not take the sleepless nights. He walked around the homestead in a fog of bewilderment, numb from lack of sleep, watching Hannah become even thinner, with a haunted look in her dark eyes.

He confronted her and told her simply that this could not continue. She lifted frightened eyes to his, like a child who knows they've done wrong, waiting for punishment.

"Hannah." His voice was kind and extremely gentle. "We're a married couple. If you don't want to be alone at night, why don't you sleep with me?"

"I don't sleep. I never sleep."

"We both hardly get our rest."

Hannah twisted her hands in her lap, chewed on her lower lip. "I have nightmares. The minute I close my eyes I see thousands of bulging eyes. . . . Jerry, I never saw grasshoppers that big. They were like monsters!"

"I know, Hannah, I know. It surprises me, though. You're so strong in the face of most things. Angry, charging through."

Hannah picked at a loose thread on her apron, her eyes downcast. "It was Janie." Jerry watched her face closely. "It was being lost in the storm, then Janie. It seems as if God must really have it in for me. As if He just can't think of more bad things to send my way. I know I'm a horrible person."

"No, you're not."

"You know I am. It's my father's fault. He brought me out here."

"Your father is dead, Hannah."

"So?"

"Your father did the best he could."

"No, he didn't. He was crazy."

"Forgiveness never comes easy. I know. And yes, he did put his family through more than most men would deem right. But it's done now, it's over. Your past is like water under a bridge. It's gone. Irretrievable. You'll never be able to change one moment of all that has happened. But you can change your remembering and the way you choose to cling to past wrongs. Let it go, Hannah."

For one second he thought she would soften, her eyes turning liquid with the thought of taking his advice. To try.

And then she sniffed, straightened her back, sat ramrod straight, and turned her head to gaze out of the window, her eyes seeing nothing. "I hate Lancaster County, you know."

"No, you don't. You are deeply ashamed of your past, to this day. Folks forget. They likely barely remember exactly what occurred, and if they do remember, it's bathed in the rosy light of forgiveness, which, you know, fixes a lot of bad memories."

Unconvinced, Hannah pouted.

At bedtime, she spent a long time in the bathroom, running water at regular intervals, opening and closing drawers.

He heard her brush her teeth until she surely must have nearly brushed all the enamel off! He waited.

Finally, she emerged, a long flannel nightgown draped to the floor and covering her body like a heavy curtain. Her arms were crossed and one hand went to hold onto the button at her throat, scraping it nervously as if to reassure herself that it was still there and closed firmly.

"I'll sleep with you."

Jerry blinked. His mouth went dry. Was this all there was to it, then? Those four words, stating her necessity, spoken in her exhausted, gravelly voice, surrounded by the ravaged, destroyed land.

She turned, like a tired ghost of herself, and walked into his bedroom.

Soundlessly, Jerry lifted himself from the bed, careful, quiet. In the light of dawn, she lay on her side, her dark hair spread across the white pillow, her heavy lashes like crescents on her pale cheeks, her breath coming in soft, slow puffs, a hand tucked beneath her cheek. He could have watched her all day.

He gathered up his clothes, tiptoed out, and silently entered the bathroom, checking his face in the mirror to see if his appearance had changed overnight. He blinked. Quick tears sprang to his eyes.

Overcome by emotion, he braced himself with the palms of his hands on the edge of the sink as his head sank to his chest. He squeezed his eyes shut, trying to keep the tears at bay. But in the end, he gave up and sobbed, praising God in a language that came from his heart, a reward for his patience, his bitter cup of self-denial.

So, God was right all along. His love for Hannah was real and not just infatuation or lust, not just a challenge, the winning of her a triumph, a victory. His heart sang praises as his spirits soared. He could live in this harsh land for the rest of his days with Hannah by his side, in spite of having so many misgivings. He would truly give his life for her, give up his own idea of how and where they should make a home. He would love her to the end of his days.

After the barn chores were finished, Jerry entered the house by the back door, removed his shoes, and washed up carefully. The house was strangely quiet, so he made very little noise.

The kitchen was empty, the cook stove cold. He tiptoed to the bedroom door but didn't have the heart to tap on it as he heard soft snores, like those of a sleeping child. Smiling to himself, he decided to forego breakfast rather than wake her. He knew he'd clatter around with the cook stove top and the frying pan, so he let himself out into the washhouse, put on his shoes, and went to the barn and sat.

He simply sat on a sawhorse, his legs stretched out in front of him, his arms crossed, and grinned. He didn't think of anything, and yet he thought of everything. His mind was filled with the wonder of Hannah. His wife.

Their future was in her hands. He was willing to stay. He could sacrifice everything, the companionship of friends and relatives, the ability to become financially successful, the privilege of attending his beloved church services with the brethren, all of it. He could be happy wherever Hannah was.

He went to the door, leaned an elbow on the doorjamb, and gazed at the devastated land. He shook his head in disbelief. Like a desert it was. Nothing remained. Not a stub of grass. Nothing. The garden was visible only by indentations where plants and rows had been. He thought of the potatoes.

They'd need rain before any form of vegetation would grow. The swarm of grasshoppers had been a few miles wide, roughly estimated, so the Jenkinses likely knew nothing of it yet.

The water tank had been choked with grasshoppers, turning the entire metal container into a slimy, tepid heap of stinking bodies. He'd merely kicked the whole thing over and turned away, unable to tolerate the smell of the half-dead, drowned, mutilated bodies of these oversized creatures.

They'd dried in the hot sun and crunched underfoot like cornflakes. He swallowed and shuddered. One of the worst experiences of his life, most certainly. Jerry wondered at the bullheadedness of that King Pharaoh in the Old Testament. That guy sure was stubborn. So many plagues, one right after another, and still he clung to his own way and kept God's children captive. He tried to imagine a sea of frogs coming hopping across the prairie, followed by a spell of darkness unlike anything anyone had ever seen. And even that wasn't the end of it. Jerry could not imagine what the children of Israel had endured before they could enter the Promised Land, and even then, things had never been perfect.

As they would not be with Hannah. He smiled, remembering. The way she described people, the narrow-minded suspicion with which she viewed every person she was not acquainted with. He laughed outright, thinking of the time they met Simon and Drucilla Rutgers in town. Simon was a good fellow, amiable, friendly to a fault. He ran a successful (for that area) cattle operation west of Pine. Simon was a short, wiry guy with a face like a good bulldog, sporting the unusual habit of spitting when he spoke.

Hannah hadn't been in his presence longer than a few seconds before she started glaring at him. She'd stepped back, crossed her arms, and watched in fascination as he sprayed spittle enthusiastically. Later, seated beside Jerry on the spring wagon, she'd started in immediately.

"What's wrong with him? He needs to wear a bib. Or carry a towel in his belt. Honestly, that face. He looks like he ran full tilt into the side of his barn."

Jerry's shoulders began to shake, even now. His nose burned and tears rose to the surface, again. He could never scold her.

It was simply too funny. Hannah did not like people, which, of course, was the biggest reason she loved the plains so. *Ach, my Hannah.*

It was all part of who she was, and he loved even that about her, no matter if it was a fault, a shortcoming. He loved her for being herself, for hiding nothing in the exalted name of pride, the way most folks did. His Hannah didn't care one little bit what people thought of her. She said and did what suited her at the time.

The sun rose higher in the sky and the bare land glared like the balding head of an old, old man.

CHAPTER 13

SARAH SAT IN THE KITCHEN OF THE STONE FARMHOUSE IN LANCAS-
ter County. She was alone, the old clock ticking rapidly from the
high shelf above her, the spigot dripping slowly into the white,
porcelain sink. She'd have to get her father to look at it.

She read and re-read Hannah's letter. It was a long one,
which was unusual. Her letters normally consisted of a few para-
graphs, mostly about the weather and nothing much of interest.
She read it slowly, for the third time. She folded it carefully, put
it back in the envelope, and held it to her heart.

The blizzard. Janie. The grasshoppers. *Ach, my Hannah*.

So much like Pharaoh of old. How long would God continue to chasten? She didn't mention Jerry once. Sarah shook her
head, hoped for the best. She knew why she'd married him, and
it certainly wasn't love. Mothers knew.

She wasn't convinced that Hannah was capable of staying in
North Dakota too much longer now, but neither could she imagine a homecoming. *Oh my Hannah, my Hannah*. The source
of worry, of constant prayer and longing, her heart tethered to
Hannah's by the bond of motherhood, never able to fully sever
it.

She folded her hands, bent her head, her lips moving in silent
prayer.

When the dry late summer air took on the biting cold of autumn, Hannah and Jerry dug the potatoes from an unrelenting, heat-baked garden. Water from the house had been dumped on the potatoes by the bucketful and still it produced only a half-bushel of small, wrinkled potatoes with green tops where the searing sun had discolored them through the thin soil.

Hannah stood in the wind, her scarf tied securely around her head, looking at the potato harvest. She snorted. Picking up her bucket, she flounced off to the house, leaving Jerry to follow, lugging the half-bushel of potatoes.

She slammed plates on the table, scattered knives and forks, thumped down empty water glasses, and sliced bread with a rapid, sawing motion. She heated milk and threw in a couple of eggs. Then she sat, her arms crossed, staring at the floor.

Jerry knew this was not a time for questions. She looked at him, a frank, dark, incomprehensible stare. "What's the use?" she asked.

"The use?" he answered, dumbly.

"You know what I'm talking about."

"You mean the potatoes?"

"Of course." She kept looking at him, fixing him with her dark gaze. The kitchen darkened with her mood, expanding and contracting with unspoken words. The air became heavy with their breathing, the two of them alone with their own thoughts and feelings, unable to break through a barrier of pride.

Finally, Hannah spoke. "I don't know if I can manage another winter."

Jerry said nothing.

"I guess you know I've changed. The grasshoppers. I can't even . . ." Her voice faded, then stilled. "I mean, how many more calamities have to happen before I give up? I can't take another winter. You'll ride out to check the cattle and I'll never know if you'll return."

She stopped, her face reddening. "And, I want children. I've known since Janie left. I want a whole pile. And I . . . well, I remember Abby's impending birth too well. I'm not going to put myself through what my mother went through. I don't have that kind of faith to believe that God will see me through in this isolated place. With me, you never know what God's going to unleash. So, I figure, I'm about done."

"But, I thought you had it all figured out," Jerry said, so kindly.

"I'm not talking about money, success, or financial security. I'm letting go because I have to. How long does God have to let you know something isn't right before you finally get it?"

Jerry blinked, shrugging his shoulders. Everything was happening too fast. But then, this was Hannah, so surprises cropped up with no warning.

"I want to go home." The words were spoken in a flat monotone, as if she was telling herself, first. There was no question at the end, no self-pity. Only her blunt statement.

Bewildered, Jerry raised his shoulders, palms upturned from his outstretched hands. "Home? But what do you consider home?"

"Lancaster County."

"But . . ." Jerry was sputtering now, trying to wrap his head around the possibility she had just presented. "You just said recently . . ."

She cut him off. "I know what I said. I don't like Lancaster County. But it's the best alternative. I've weighed the options, and the scales are definitely tipping toward Lancaster, for one reason. With all I've experienced, I'm afraid to keep on trying. I don't have the courage. The determination, maybe, but not the courage. I can't take the winters with you gone. It's different now since I . . . uh . . . you know. Love you, or whatever."

Jerry watched her face. Her eyes found his and held. Slowly

he rose, his eyes fastened on hers. He reached for her, lifted her
from her chair, and held her, his eyes drinking in the light in hers.

"You do love me, then?" he asked.

She stilled his words with her lips.

Much later, they sat around the supper table, dishes strewn
everywhere, the cook stove turning cold, half-scraped pots and
pans thrown in the sink, the fading light of evening settling
across the house.

They talked, speaking freely with a new intimacy. Jerry felt
reverent with this new and undeserved gift, everything he'd
always longed for presented to him on a platter, almost more
than he had ever prayed for. He told Hannah that he was willing
to stay, willing to try again. Perhaps another year would be the
opposite of this one.

She reminded him that the year after that could be exactly
like this one. It was foolish, this glue-like adherence to the
homestead.

"We've come so far, Hannah," Jerry protested.

"You have no heart for this place, so stop being false. You
know you'd be happy to return." Spoken in the way only Hannah could convey feelings. He grimaced. She was looking right
through him, her eyes like darts. He got away with nothing.

"All right. All right." He threw up his hands in mock
surrender.

She laughed, that short, sharp bark he seldom heard.

Sobering, she told him what had helped her make this choice.
"I could probably live here if it wasn't for our heritage. Our way
of living, our lives entwined with people like ourselves. We have
no one who truly understands us. I've come to the conclusion
that family is important. So is community. Relatives, extended
family. I don't miss people. I just miss my mother and Manny. I
don't want to . . ." Here she faltered, then her eyes found his and

stayed. "I want to be close to my mother when . . . you know, we have babies."

Jerry nodded and breathed deeply. "So, it seems as if we have plans to make and more work than we'll get done if we want to leave before the snow flies."

Her eyes shone. "Oh, Jerry," she breathed. "Now that we're going, I feel as if I can't stay in this house another day. I want to go now. This instant!"

"Not too long ago, you had it all figured out. What it would take to stay here. Remember?"

"I do. And I would turn into a real plains-woman if I had been born and raised here with the rest of these tough, old characters. Perhaps I've grown up. Who knows? I will always love North Dakota, the wide open spaces, grass, cattle, riding horseback, the isolation. But I want a whole houseful of children like Janie. That toddle around and fill the house with their funny words and well. . . . You know, Jerry. Janie was sent into my life to direct my path. It's strange, but she was. I'll never get over losing her."

She paused. A distasteful expression crossed her face. "I'll never get over the grasshoppers, either."

"No, you won't. But you know what I think? I think they may have finished what Janie started."

"Now don't you get all prophetic and spiritual," she said, eyeing him with a look that still held the old rebellion.

"*Hoi schrecka.*"

"Hoi what?" Hannah asked.

"*Hoi schrecka.* Grasshoppers."

"*Hoi schrecka* is German for grasshoppers? Literally, that's hay scarers."

Jerry's eyes turned gleeful, teasing. "Scared you straight into my arms. I love it. I pitied you, but it was extremely nice."

Hannah blushed, a beautiful infusion of color, the soft stroke of delicate pink. No one would be able to produce anything close, not even the most gifted artist, Jerry thought.

"I hope we won't always need a million grasshoppers to lead us," he said, laughing.

They got down to business then. Hannah produced a tablet with lined paper and wrote: mules, King, saddles, harnesses. She looked at Jerry, chewed the end of the pencil, and said that this didn't make sense.

"We can't send all these animals to Lancaster County if we don't know where we're going."

"This list is not our shipping list."

"Well, what else is it?"

"We're going to have to have a public auction if we want to go back before winter."

"You mean . . . ?" Hannah was incredulous. The thought of selling everything was staggering. For one moment, anxiety overtook her. The animals, the beloved land they had worked so hard to keep. What, exactly, was "making it" anyway? How did one go about measuring whether you were successful?

She hated that word suddenly. They had had a lot of small successes, and large ones, too. If their success was measured in dollars, then no, they weren't exactly well to do or anything even close to profitable. The house and barn had been built from the charitable contributions of the brethren in Lancaster, as well as the surrounding community of non-Amish. They had all proved to be caring far beyond anything Hannah or Sarah had ever expected.

So, there was that. They definitely would not have made it without help. They would have been forced to go back East. But how could one measure anything in the face of all they had been through? The list went on and on, a bitter tower built with incidents, layer after layer of hard, natural disasters, each one a monument of suffering, blocks that added to the whole shaping and forming of the past years.

Were they better for all of it, or worse?

"Hannah, you're not listening." Hannah started, blinked, and said she heard every word, but of course, she hadn't.

"It would cost too much, for one thing."

Hannah had no idea what he was talking about, but kept nodding and feigning agreement.

"Should we sell everything? House stuff? Furniture?" he asked.

Hannah considered. To part with these things was something she believed she could do. The heirlooms of the past, what they'd brought from Lancaster in the covered wagon, had burned in the fire. The rest of it? All replacements. Nothing Hannah had ever become attached to. But to return empty-handed, like immigrants from another country, was not something she relished. But would anyone have to know? It's not like everyone would be standing at her grandfather's farm waiting for them to arrive. Maybe they could slide back into Lancaster life without a lot of fuss.

"What do you think?" Jerry's question brought her back to the immediate problem. "If we sell everything, we had better get the public auction done as soon as possible. I don't want to be on a train in the middle of winter," Jerry said.

And so they sat, debating, making plans, batting problems back and forth, finding solutions in a sensible way. Hannah knew that her opinions mattered to Jerry, that she would never be like her spineless mother who had been hoodwinked into making that senseless journey, that ill-thought-out venture into the unknown, propelled by a man who seemed far inferior to her own husband.

Husband. That is what he was. He was a good man. He rose to any overriding problem, faced it squarely, and found a reasonable solution, with her help. He considered her advice. She was suddenly humbled, a sensation she didn't like, so she said loudly, "Nobody is going to want those mules."

"Oh, now, come on, Hannah. They're good mules. The best. You'd be surprised how many of these ranchers still own a good pair of mules."

"Maybe. But no one has any money."

"Times will get better. We may not make much, but we'll be all right."

The day of the auction arrived, a biting wind and a steely sun bringing folks in heavy coats, hats flattened over red ears, women dressed in heavy socks and sensible boots, scarves and woolen overcoats.

Jerry had hired the florid auctioneer from the cattle sale in Pine, who arrived in a new truck, washed and gleaming like a wet bathtub, a silver bucking bronco mounted on the hood, a senseless ornament that raised Hannah's ire.

Fat little man. He could never get on a horse, let alone one that bucked. Why would you have something like that on your truck? She watched him strutting around like an undersized bully, throwing his arms around and shouting orders. She decided he wouldn't get any tip from her. If Jerry wanted to give him extra money for his work, then that was up to him.

Many of the women came up to Hannah, their kind, wrinkled faces curious and alight with interest. One middle-aged woman, as tall as Hannah and almost as thin, met her face-to-face, her dark eyes boring into Hannah's with unabashed questioning.

"So, what gives?"

Hannah was on guard immediately. That was no way to greet anyone. Her eyes narrowed as her mouth stretched into a grim line that didn't contain a shadow of a smile. Coldly, she sniffed and said, "What do you mean?"

The woman waved an arm, taking in the homestead, the furniture in neat rows, the bedding and dishes, everything they had worked so hard to set in an orderly display so that the auctioneer could move up and down the rows in an efficient manner.

"Why? Why the auction?" the woman asked, her voice gravelly like a man's, her face lean and long with cheeks that resembled a burnt pumpkin pie, the kind that was pocked on top.

An intense dislike for this ill-mannered upstart rose in Hannah, but she squelched the fiery retort with all the effort she could muster. "We're going back home."

"Where's that at?"

"Pennsylvania."

Putting one fist to her hip, she cocked her head and squinted, giving a short, nasty guffaw. "Chickens! Turned chicken, didya? Grasshoppers gitya?"

Hannah's heart pounded furiously. She stood her ground, her eyes boring into the other woman's. "It's none of your business," she ground out, turning and walking away, her face cooled by the prairie wind.

There were other women who spoke in a kinder fashion, but mostly, Hannah was reminded over and over that to leave a homestead was a sign of weakness. These women had mostly been born and raised here. The prairie was in their blood. Their suffering and hardship was all a part of life.

As the day wore on, Hannah felt worse and worse, sinking into a darkness that threatened to overturn her resolve. According to these folks, she was a loser. Running home to her mother, waving the white flag of defeat and crying "Uncle! Uncle!"

Then, quite suddenly, a fierce gladness welled in her. No matter what they thought, she was looking forward to seeing her mother, her face like a beacon of light that beckoned and guided her home. And that was all right.

She went to stand beside Jerry. She needed the reassurance

of touching his sleeve with hers. He looked over and gave her a small smile of recognition. "Everything all right?" he asked.

She nodded. His look affirmed his love in the midst of this crowd of weathered prairie dwellers.

Hannah watched the auctioneer on his block, fascinated by the amount of spittle that sprayed into the wind. He must have an endless source of hydration somewhere in that crimson face.

Jerry whispered, "We're getting fair prices."

"That's good," Hannah whispered back.

The auctioneer's voice was like wagon wheels rumbling across a wooden bridge. He spoke so fast that Hannah wasn't aware that an item had been sold until the gavel was smacked against the wooden partition in front of him.

After the trucks had been loaded and most items hauled away, Hod Jenkins came to stand with Hannah. Hank and Ken sidled up soon after, their eyes alight with a new interest.

"So, this is it then?"

Jerry nodded. "This is it."

"Must be hard for you, Hannah."

Hannah lowered her eyes, the toe of her shoe scuffing the dust at her feet. "It is."

"I imagine so."

"Hank here was wonderin', since you can't sell the homestead, we'll jest go to the courthouse or wherever, whatever it takes to take on the land and the buildings. He'll likely have to put in another ten years, but he's good with that. Right, Hank?"

Hank turned his head and directed a jet of dark brown tobacco juice into the dust with a wet smack. Hannah swallowed the nausea that welled up in her throat. "Yeah," he said, shifting the wad of soaked tobacco.

"Reckon he'll find hisself a woman, ifn' he ain't already done that, and this here ranch is better'n ours. He'll be well off afore he even starts."

"Yeah," Hank agreed. "Hannah got married to this guy, so I gotta start all over." He jerked a thumb in Jerry's direction, his wide grin revealing a row of yellow, tobacco-stained teeth like rotten corn. Hannah thought the mule's mouth looked better, even when it brayed! Hay was cleaner than that disgusting wad of tobacco.

Hod laughed. "You coulda had all my boys, Hannah. Every one of 'em was so sweet on you they thought up every reason they could fer ridin' over here. Like bees to honey, they was."

Hannah smiled, but didn't blush. She'd always known. And might have gone ahead and married Clay if it hadn't been for her mother. Hod prodded her with his elbow. "Yer not sayin' nothin."

Hannah smiled. Yes, she might have married Clay but she couldn't think of the disaster that would have amounted to. Young, headstrong, unable to put up with the "aw shucks" of the Jenkinses. They lived out their days with an ambling easiness, nothing riling them too much. If the roof leaked, there was always a bucket to catch the drips. If the fence was broken, it stayed that way. Mud, dust, manure. It was all tracked into the house. Weeds and tin cans and pecking chickens, mangy dogs and skulking cats . . . that was just their way of life.

The divide between the two cultures would have proved her undoing. Would she have been able to love anyone, back then? All the raw misfortune that had presented itself, over and over, had shaped her into who she was today.

Jerry liked to remind her that God puts us through the fire so all our impurities are melted away. We become a golden, shining vessel for His use. Well, she had plenty of dross left over but she guessed it must be true, if you looked at it the way Jerry did.

Hod looked at her. "Now that remark put ya to thinkin."

Hannah nodded, but had no words, no smart retort.

"Ah, likely jest as good this way. Clay an' Jen's happy. They couldn't be here today. Went to visit Jen's gramma over'n Montana somewheres."

"I was wondering where they were," Hannah remarked.

Hod smiled at her. "Wal, I'll tell ya right now. I've been pleased to have you folks fer neighbors all these years. Too bad about yer pa, Hannah. He was a good man, just a mite determined to do things his way. Out here in God's country, ya gotta listen to the old timers. They know what they's talkin' about. Seems as if yer pa had his own ideas, doin' things the way he did back East. But, like I said, he was a good man. Now yer ma, there's the salt o' the earth. Never knew a better woman. I'd a asked her to marry me, but I ain't near good enough. Besides, there's that religion thing. Don't hold with all them rules.

"But jest want to let you know, it's been a pleasure knowin' you folks. Hopefully, we'll do their place proud. Ya'll kin come back 'n visit, and likely Hank 'n his wife'll be livin' in the house, runnin' livestock of their own."

"It seems right that one of you will be living here," Hannah said. "I'm so glad the house won't be setting empty."

And she meant it.

After everyone had gone, the auctioneer went over the results of his day's work and Jerry paid him, along with a too-generous tip, in Hannah's opinion.

Hannah wouldn't talk to him for some time, simply sweeping the house in angry jerks, slamming things around until Jerry got the message that he'd done something wrong.

"All right, what is it? What did I do?" he asked, blocking her way to the near-empty pantry.

She wouldn't answer him then, but later she decided to clear the air and tell him about the auctioneer. She concluded her rant with a firm, "He didn't need a tip!"

"I disagree," Jerry said. "You can't look in someone's face and decide then and there that you don't like them. He's one of the best auctioneers I've ever seen. We were paid well for all our possessions. We have enough for a down payment on a small house when we return to Lancaster County."

Hannah was effectively silenced.

For one last time, she walked across the prairie, felt the absence of Nip and Tuck acutely. How many times had she thrown a stick and watched them rocket after it, dropping it at her feet, eyes shooting sparks, mouths wide, panting? Over and over. Hank and Ken had taken them home. She refused to even say goodbye. It was easier that way.

Her scarf was tied snugly beneath her chin, so she loosened it, held it by a corner, and swung her arms wide, feeling the rush of pure wind in her ears, the headscarf billowing out like the sail on a boat. She twirled on one foot, turning to all four directions, tried to inscribe on her heart the isolation, the wonder of being alone in this vast land. She wanted to capture the wind and the scent of the soil, remember the sight and sound of the undulating sea of grass, forever.

And then she was crying, sobbing with abandon, until her eyes felt swollen and her cheeks chafed with the cold and the runnels of tears. She knew her face was purple, discolored, ugly, but nothing mattered. She was who she was, and nothing would change that.

She whispered her goodbye, and her thanks to this great land that had, indeed, clasped her heart and held it with its awesome, indescribable power.

CHAPTER 14

CLUTCHING THEIR SATCHELS, SUITCASES AT THEIR FEET, JERRY AND Hannah stood by the old railroad station, the cold wind biting their faces with the first icy blast of winter's arrival. Many times in recent days Hannah had nearly changed her mind, nearly begged Jerry to return to the homestead. But that wind reminded her of all the reasons they were leaving and gave her the courage to face the unknown ahead of her.

Displaced, unanchored, a wanderer. Hannah acutely understood the true meaning of losing a home, of striking out in uncertainty, in spite of the fact that she was returning to her roots.

They heard the train, saw the billowing black smoke, long before it rattled and hissed into the station in a cloud of steam and charcoal-gray smoke.

A few bedraggled passengers stepped down. Men wheeled clattering carts of boxes, burlap bags, trunks, luggage of every description. They shouted directions to one another, lifted heavy containers on capable backs, and disappeared into the rail cars. They reappeared, issuing more commands.

Not much different from an anthill, Hannah thought sourly. And then, the conductor appeared on the lower step of the passenger car to their right. Jerry stooped to pick up the largest of their suitcases, nudged Hannah, and said softly, "Here we go."

She followed him, feeling utterly empty. Is this all it would be, then? Board this monstrous thing that smelled of coal gas and tar and rained sparks like the biblical brimstone, then sit in a miserable seat and gaze out a soot-streaked window, all the while crying inside until your heart felt as if it was melting away into nothing?

She arranged her face into a cold mask of indifference, sat as close to the window and as far away from him as possible, piercing the window glass with her hard, polished eyes that held back the torrent of regret, the sadness that rolled over her in waves of pain.

She had known leaving would not be easy. But she was ill-prepared for the onslaught of varied emotions that built up in her throat until she was unable to breathe properly.

Jerry knew to leave her alone. The joy of returning beat strongly in his chest. He knew no regrets. He had made the promise to stay, and would have done it, had Hannah not chosen otherwise.

The whistle sounded, that earsplitting scream Jerry loved. He leaned forward, past Hannah, watched the prairie begin to move, sliding away as the train picked up speed. His eyes shone with the challenge of returning, looking for a home, a small farm. They would find a place that was at a healthy distance from neighbors, away from prying eyes. He looked forward to this new chapter in his life with Hannah.

For miles, Hannah feigned sleep, sagged into a corner, and pouted like a disobedient schoolgirl. Jerry watched the landscape rolling past, and reached under the seat for the packet of cold meat sandwiches Hannah had prepared that morning.

She had refused to make breakfast, saying the cook stove was gone, so how could she? Bread and butter would have been fine, but he drank the last of the milk, wiped his mouth, and said nothing.

He knew the leaving would be hard, but this? Oh well, he was sure it wouldn't be the last time he'd have to face her stone-cold eyes and the disapproval of all he said and did. Especially the things he did. Her unhappiness was like two strong arms she used to pull him in, trying to drag him down with her. He had recognized this early on, so he knew the best way to handle it was to cheerfully ignore her until she got past the dark cloud hanging over her head.

Now, the sight of the sandwiches being unwrapped irked her. "It's not lunchtime," she hissed, her eyes sliding past him to the travelers in the seat beside her who were eyeing Jerry curiously.

"I'm hungry, so I'm going to eat."

She was hungry, too, but swallowed the saliva that rose in her mouth at the sight and smell of food.

"Want some?" He offered half of his sandwich to her, but she shrugged away from him. Hours later she still refused to eat, simply sagging in the corner of her seat and gazing out the window with dull eyes.

They were observed curiously by the passengers across the aisle, but Jerry had his back turned much of the time, his eyes barely leaving the window as he took in every sight, drinking in the scenery in spite of its sameness.

The train stopped at so many stations that Hannah lost track. People gathered belongings, spoke urgently, then hustled off the train, shoving children and crying babies ahead of them, begging pardon for the disruption.

Hannah glared at all of them, fat mothers that smelled like sour milk and howling red-faced babies, sticky-faced children that needed a good wash and a firm reprimand. When an overly friendly farmer leaned in to ask their destination, Jerry opened his mouth to answer but Hannah spoke quickly, telling him it was none of his business and he had food in his moustache.

He walked on but turned to look at her with a baleful,

whipped puppy expression before he exited the car. Hannah held his stare with her cold eyes until he disappeared.

She told Jerry they could have brought Nip and Tuck. Other folks brought animals. Why couldn't they? Jerry explained, patient as always. The journey was only part of it. They had no home yet and to expect her grandfather to take them in along with two rowdy dogs was too much.

Hannah harrumphed plenty about that. Who did he care about after all? Her or her grandfather? Finally, Jerry spoke firmly and told her she was being impossible. He knew this was not easy for her, and he felt her pain. But, come on!

If she was ashamed after that, she gave no indication. Jerry knew that giving up was an ordeal, a genuine misery for her. Most times he found it humorous, or at worst, tolerable. But even he had his limits.

They slept fitfully, cramped in uncomfortable positions, a cold draft seeping through the windows and sending shivers down their spines. Hannah's mood steadily worsened, until Jerry decided it was best just to ignore her completely.

Then trees appeared on the horizon. Vast forests of dark pine and bare-branched trees, miles and miles of them. Hannah reflected on all the firewood, the dwindling cottonwoods in the creek bottom. What would they have done when the last of them were chopped up and burned in the cook stove?

When the first mountain appeared in Northern Pennsylvania, a steep, gray, cold-looking monument covered with trees, rocks, shrubs, and brambles, Hannah sat up and turned to watch as the hills slid by, her eyes now open wide and alight with interest.

Suddenly, she said sharply, "We could live in the mountains." Jerry said nothing, knowing full well there were no mountains like this in Lancaster County. Hannah couldn't explain the overwhelming plenty of trees. On and on, everywhere, there were trees. Firewood to burn. Lumber for houses and barns and chicken sheds. Those trees represented warmth and shelter and safety. Her mind whirred.

So, why couldn't they buy acres and acres of this mountain land and set up a sawmill? They could sell lumber for anything anyone would need. They should have kept the mules. Nip and Tuck would have loved these mountains.

The train wound its way between the mountain ledges and along a cold, gray river flowing to who knew where. If mules were too light, they could always buy Belgians. Those heavy workhorses were what loggers used to drag out the wealth of these forests.

Her mind churned, making plans.

Their arrival at the Lancaster train station was like all other stops, without fanfare, the train gliding smoothly into the station. The city outside the window was a frozen, gray landscape of towers and bulky buildings set beside each other, brick and stone, concrete and painted lumber with windows like spying eyes. The air was gray, heavy with smoke and steam, gritty with soot.

When Hannah stepped off the train, there was an absence of oxygen, a suffocating stillness containing malice and suspicion. Her eyes searched the crowd of people herded together like cattle, but found no one she recognized.

Jerry prodded her elbow with his hand. "Keep moving, Hannah. There are other folks who want off the train." She jerked her arm away from his touch and glared at the conductor who ushered them into the milling crowd.

Her feet were swollen, stuffed into her old, stiff leather shoes. Her face felt greasy and filthy. Her shoulders ached with the weight of her satchels. She wished for wings—huge, flapping, capable bird wings—to lift her above the sordid gray roiling mess of humans, across the mountains, across rivers and plains, depositing her straight back to the lonesomeness of the homestead.

What had they done? What had possessed her to tell Jerry she couldn't survive another winter? She couldn't survive this, either.

They moved along with the crowd, propelled into the high-ceilinged, monstrous railroad station, alive with voices, calls, people shoving, never stopping their constant chatter. Her chest tightened, her breath came in short, heavy puffs.

Then she heard her name. Quickly, she turned her head to find her brother Manny wading through the sea of jostling, straining people. When he reached her, his dark eyes shone into hers. He clasped her extended hand with a teeth-jarring grip and said, "Hannah!"

He wrung Jerry's hand as warmly, saying his name as well. Then he surveyed them both, said marriage suited them, and grabbed a suitcase, pointing to the north entrance. "We'll talk later," he mouthed.

Hannah's mood lightened as she followed the black, broad-brimmed hat and wide shoulders of her brother's black coat. When they emerged from the station, there were still more than enough pedestrians, cars moving, and trucks blatting their horns at incompetent drivers squeezing their vehicles past them.

"Where's Mam?" The question had hovered on Hannah's lips the moment she spied Manny. He laughed. "Oh, you know our mother. She won't step into an automobile unless it's absolutely necessary. I think the train ride to return home aged her ten years. She just doesn't like speed."

"So, she's at home?"

"Yes. With enough food prepared to feed twenty people!"

Hannah laughed, that short, raucous burst of sound, then turned to smile at Jerry, who returned her smile wholeheartedly. So, there was joy in Hannah's return.

The drive from Lancaster was too long for Hannah. She felt

herself pushing her feet against the back of the front seat, willing the driver to drive faster.

The fields and woods were brown, or a drab, olive green. Corn fodder lay like colorless paper, yellowed and torn. Holsteins, sheep, goats, mules, horses of every description roamed pastures, pulled carriages, or plodded in standing fields of brown corn, drawing wooden wagons with rattling sides. Black-coated, straw-hatted men and scarved women were ripping off the dangling ears of corn with a swift movement of their wrists, before hurling the ears on the wagon.

Hannah watched, kept watching, turning sideways in her seat to keep an eye on people husking corn, an expression in her dark eyes that Jerry couldn't begin to decipher.

"Remember?" he asked, gently. She nodded.

In truth, she could feel the cold, the biting, wet air that stung her cheeks and tingled her nose. The satisfying whump of an ear of corn hitting the wagon bed and rattling off into the corner. The gentle Belgians standing in the rows, snacking on corn, moving forward obediently, stopping when necessary, the smell of harness leather, the dusty, drying fields, the exhilaration of being outside in the fields with someone you loved. Her father. In memory, that's who she was with. And he'd sing. He sang German songs on the slow *veiss* (tune) from the Ausbund, the hymnbook they used in church. He practiced over and over, then led singing in services the following Sunday. He had a strong voice, a good baritone to lead the congregation.

Hannah blinked and felt an unwanted lump in her throat. Once, her father had been someone. An honest, esteemed member of the Old Order Amish church, working the farm that had been his father's before him.

The old shame returned, the feeling of inadequacy, of not being enough. Well, she was married now. A woman in her own right. Had taken the name of Riehl. Was no longer a Detweiler.

Her thoughts churned like a spring creek swollen by torrents of rain. Could a name change her past, though?

When they arrived at her grandfather's farm, everything came rushing back, the unhappy time when her mother had given up in North Dakota and her subsequent return to Lancaster County. All a blur of misery.

The house was built of gray limestone, serviceable, sturdy, a monument of hard work and foresight. The trees flanking the house on either side were like sentinels, shading the structure from the heat of summer, heightening the spring glory with their tender red buds that lay scattered across the green lawn like nature's carpeting.

Hannah noticed the bulging corn crib, the corn husking already finished. That was Elam and Ben, likely. She wondered if their work ethic would rub off on Manny, who had learned the ways of the plains before moving back home among his German ancestors who lived to work hard, making every hour count.

The door was flung open and there was her mother. Hannah fumbled for the door handle, then flew to the porch, her feet barely touching the uneven cement sidewalks.

They clasped hands, looked long into each other's eyes, one as dark as the other. There was no hug, no outward display of emotion. That was the way of it. A sincere handclasp coupled with a long searching look, a checkpoint to gauge whether all was well.

Mother to daughter, and daughter to mother, strengthening the bond that would never be severed, no matter what life handed them. Hundreds of miles, trials almost more than could be borne, differences of opinion, verbal arguments, hurts and animosity—all of it only increased the mysterious bonds that held them.

"Hannah! *Ach*, Hannah. *Vie bisht?*"

Nodding, soft-eyed, Hannah replied, "*Goot. Goot.*"

What a mother wanted to hear. Everything was good. Good. Her daughter had married a nice man who would keep her happy and love her to the end of their days. Nothing would change that. A mother's hope is kept alive in the face of tumultuous adversity, always searching, longing to hear the good news, the love, in her daughter's union.

A clatter of men, handshaking, satchels and suitcases, the squeal from Eli and Mary, so tall, so grown-up. Her grandfather was bent and wizened, his dark eyes shedding tears. His hands were like tree branches, bent and gnarled, calloused, veins like tributaries of the strong river flowing from his heart. He still husked corn and could hitch up a mule with the best of them.

Sarah, her cheeks flushed, eyes bright with excitement, bent and swayed, moved from icebox to gas stove. A wonder, this gas stove, she said, between questions and exclamations, barely listening to what Hannah had to say.

She dished up mountains of mashed potatoes, shook the small saucepan with the browning butter till it hissed just right, then poured it over the creamy mound, watching to make sure it did not run over the sides of the service dishes.

She brought out a blue agate roaster and lifted the lid to produce a wealth of browned, steaming *roasht*, one of Hannah's favorite meals. One chicken went a long way if it was roasted, the gizzard, liver, and skin ground in a cast-iron meat grinder, the meat cut into bite-size pieces and mixed with cubed bread, celery, eggs, salt and pepper.

The smell was heavenly. Hannah bent over the steaming roaster and breathed deeply, then pinched a corner of the savory filling with thumb and forefinger and popped it into her mouth. She closed her eyes, savoring the wonderful flavor. "Nobody makes *roasht* like you, Mam," she sighed, reaching for more. Sarah slapped her hand playfully. "Fork, Hannah!"

There was thick, yellow gravy. Homemade dinner rolls, their

tops golden and gleaming with butter. Lima beans. Canned green beans with *schpeck* (bacon). Chowchow, sweet pickles, and applesauce. Homemade noodles, rich and heavy, swimming in browned butter and parsley.

They all pulled up chairs, while Eli and Mary slid along the bench. Without spoken direction, they bowed their heads as one. The grandfather's lips moved in silent prayer, his eyes gleaming with unshed tears as he lifted his head and told everyone to help themselves.

Elam and Ben watched Hannah, each curious to see if she'd come to accept Jerry as more than a business partner. She was something, that Hannah. It had been hard to believe she'd married anyone. Both were convinced that Jerry couldn't be too smart. Or had Hannah seen the light, repented, and changed her selfish ways?

Hannah passed dishes, laughed, talked, and appeared happy, even glowing. But she never spoke to Jerry. As far as her uncles could tell, Jerry wasn't present at all.

When the cakes and pies, the cornstarch pudding, and canned pears and peaches were served, Jerry held his stomach and groaned. "I'll have to let this settle first."

Sarah, always eager to serve, immediately began pouring coffee, telling everyone to sit back and relax, let their food settle because, my goodness, they had all day.

The conversation turned to the plentiful food on the table. "In these hard years," Jerry said, shaking his head in bewilderment.

"Oh, I know," Sarah said. "I hope we never forget to give thanks.

The grandfather nodded, shook his spoon in the general direction. "You have to think about it, though. Everything on this table so far has been raised or grown on this farm. Potatoes, vegetables, eggs, chicken, butter. We farmers have had to tighten our belts some, with money not being worth what it once was. But, the times are changing with President Roosevelt at the helm. He'll get us out of this."

Elam and Ben nodded. "Farms are cheap. Interest is low at the banks. Now's your time, Jerry," Ben said.

Jerry looked at Hannah and shook his head. "Oh, I don't know for sure yet what we have in mind."

Ben thought, *You mean, what your wife has in mind.* But he didn't say it aloud.

Elam narrowed his eyes and looked at Hannah with a knowing wink. "She'll be ready for North Dakota in about a month," he predicted.

"You think?" Jerry's eyes twinkled. "Ask her."

"What do you say, Hannah?"

To Elam's surprise, Hannah faced him soberly and said, "I don't believe I'll ever go back."

Feigning surprise, Elam acted as if he would fall out of his chair. Calmly, Hannah said, "Stop it, Elam. I'm not joking."

"What gives?"

Jerry spoke for Hannah, giving a detailed account of the grasshoppers' march across their homestead, the burning of the Klassermans' house, Janie, the blizzards, everything. His arm stole along the back of Hannah's chair.

Elam listened, openmouthed. Ben detected the shifting of Hannah's weight, the almost imperceptible movement to lay her hand on Jerry's leg, the dropping of his arm to her shoulders.

Sarah shuddered, breathed, "Why didn't you tell us?"

Eli piped up, "What are locusts? I thought only King Pharaoh had locusts." Everyone laughed, but without mirth.

"The grasshoppers were the most horrible," Hannah said quietly. "I never had the heart, the real courage to stay after that. You know what the prairie looks like during a two-year drought? Well, this was much worse. Imagine not a blade of dead grass, not a shrub or a weed. And the smell was unbelievable."

Sarah shuddered. Mary twisted her face in disgust. Jerry said he'd left the final decision up to Hannah.

Her eyes alight, leaning forward, Hannah spread her hands to state her case. "In the end, does it really make sense? Just before the end, I had come to the conclusion that if you really want to be homesteader you have to lower your standards of what we consider success. Out there, success is measured in many more ways than simply how much money you make.

"If you lose too many calves, well, next year will be better. If it doesn't rain, it's a victory just to be able to 'git by.' They're not bothered by small hindrances because they're so easygoing. The biggest thing those ranchers have is settin' at the feed mill, measuring one natural calamity after another, seeing who weathered the longest drought, the worst storm, or whatever. There's a fierce loyalty to the prairie, a determination to live like their fathers before them. They can't imagine anything different.

"But us? Well, we know another way of life. This is in our blood. Although, I know it won't always be easy. In fact, until I saw Mam on the porch, I wasn't sure if I could be happy here again."

"Oh Hannah! Really?" Sarah's smile grew as she did her best to keep the tears from spilling over.

"I missed you terribly, Mam," Hannah said.

Sarah flung both hands over her face and left the table, ashamed to let her family see how much Hannah's words affected her.

After all she and Hannah had been through, every harsh word and rebellious shrug, the storming out of the house leaving Sarah to wrestle with her own bravado, her own fear of mishandling her wayward daughter who, by all appearances had simply hated her. Leaving Hannah in North Dakota had been as painful as losing one of her own limbs.

Sarah was a servant, someone whose own happiness sprang from bringing happiness to others. Her children, her husband, the acquaintances around her, all benefited from her deep inner kindness. She had been so afraid for Hannah. For Jerry. She knew full well Hannah didn't love Jerry. She knew, too, the reason for Hannah marrying him. But here they were, alive and well, with the kind of intimacy between them that only a mother could discern.

Surely God had heard all her begging, her prayers on their behalf. How often had she fallen on her knees in the middle of the night to pray for them? Times when sleep slipped out of her grasp, the terrors of the plains crashing and screaming around in her head until she thought she'd surely go mad. Leaving Hannah in North Dakota had been a torment, a punishment, the blame-taking wreaking havoc with her faith.

She was grateful to Hannah for keeping the blizzard, Janie, the scourge of insects from her, and so allowing her to live in peace, not knowing of their suffering.

Composed now, Sarah dished out more dessert, smiled, and refilled coffee cups, glad to hear the conversation had drifted to other topics.

"So Jerry, what do you have in mind as far as where you'll live and what you'll do to support your wife?" Elam asked, spooning an alarming amount of vanilla cornstarch pudding over a huge square of black walnut cake.

Jerry's eyes widened. He jutted his chin in the direction of Elam's pudding and cake. "Are you planning on eating all that by yourself?" he asked.

"You just be nice and mind your own business," Elam countered, lifting a spoon piled high with the sweet concoction.

Hannah smiled as she cut a large slice of peach pie. The sense of belonging that pervaded the kitchen was like a haven for her battered spirit. Here was the companionship of family, a knot tied with so many intricacies, impossible to be fully separated. Loosened, perhaps, frayed edges whipped by storms and every mischief of the mortal mind, but tied, inexplicably bound and reaching into the future.

CHAPTER 15

ALL THAT NEXT DAY, HANNAH RELATED STORY AFTER STORY, HER mother listening spellbound, intermittently shaking her head, making soft, clucking noises of disbelief. Occasionally, Sarah would try to interject a thought, but words poured from her daughter like an overturned tumbler of water that ran dripping down over the tablecloth and onto the floor.

Finally, Hannah stopped, took her teacup to the white, porcelain sink, and asked if they shouldn't be doing a job, making dinner or something.

"No, not yet. We'll have bean soup and cheese for lunch. But, did you say this little Janie's parents both died in that fire?"

"They say so, but no one really knows. I think they did. The grandparents seem like really nice people. And Janie will never remember her own parents. She's too young, so that's a comfort I still have."

"Right." Then, "Oh, Hannah. I can't imagine all you've been through. You say the worst was the grasshoppers?"

"Yes. Without a doubt. But the winters! After being lost in a blizzard . . ." Hannah's voice drifted off. "Being lost in a blizzard is beyond suffering. The cold is only a small part of it. It's the feeling of being cut off from all you know. Every single thing we take for granted every day is removed and there you are, at the mercy of the howling, driving wind, the snow and ice and brutal cold. I almost lost my toes. Probably would have if Jerry hadn't known what to do."

"So, you and Jerry are in love?" Sarah asked her, emboldened by the conversation that had flowed so easily between them for hours now.

When there was no answer, Sarah knew she had struck the wrong chord. She slid a glance sideways at her daughter, whose eyes were lowered, her teeth worrying her lower lip.

"I guess. I don't know. How do you know if you love someone?"

"Oh, well, you just do."

"I'm not always a nice person."

Sarah laughed. "Nicer than you used to be."

"I would say he loves me, but he hasn't always been nice, either."

Sarah knew this was dangerous territory, so she said nothing. With Hannah, always being nice was an impossibility. She could only imagine the patience it required to live with her.

"But you are . . . I mean . . . you know . . ." Sarah reddened, then blushed so furiously that tears sprang to her eyes.

"Yes," Hannah mumbled, then quickly got up and disappeared behind the bathroom door.

They never spoke about Sarah's marriage after that. It was the way Sarah's mother had taught her; in some matters, things were best left unsaid.

A few weeks later, Jerry and Hannah had found a house. Hannah wanted to live in the mountains, a good distance from other Amish folks, and everyone else, for that matter. She had their whole logging operation already planned out. But after listening to Ben and Elam, Jerry decided that farming and milking cows was probably the best thing to do, especially since he had a good down payment ready for a nice farm.

He listened patiently, considered Hannah's opinion about logging, but knew that cutting trees and dragging logs was not his future. He had no interest in wrecking forests. Not now, and he doubted if he ever would.

They were lying in bed in the blue painted guest room with the high plastered ceiling, deep windowsills, and the ever-present smell of mothballs and cedar that infiltrated the room like a giant's breath. It was their only time for communicating with each other away from the rest of the family, so they often lay there murmuring together about their plans for the future. But this thing about logging and living in the mountains was starting to annoy Jerry; it was like a whining mosquito hovering in his ear whenever Hannah had a chance to be alone with him.

Patiently, he explained his view. Horses would not always be competitive, in logging. Caterpillars, those big yellow machines on tracks, could go where it was difficult for horses and drag out ten times the number of logs. But, if they wanted to stay Amish, then she'd have to think about what was reasonable.

"But I don't want to live on a flat farm surrounded by flat Amish neighbors and all their flat children," she hissed.

Jerry shook with the force of his silent laughter. "We can buy a hilly, rocky farm then."

"No. I don't want to milk cows. I hate cows." Hannah rolled onto her side, punched the feather pillow, huffed a few times, bounced up and down to settle herself, and refused to talk any more about it that night.

Jerry lay on his back, hands propped behind his head, and sighed. He watched the rectangles of gray light that marked both windows, traced the pattern of black branches across the window panes, listened to the sounds of traffic stopping and starting on Route 30, and thought about farming when his wife detested the mere thought of milking cows.

What kind of life would that be? Well, he'd wait. She was still a bit sore about losing the homestead in the West, so perhaps after she had the opportunity to listen to what members of her family had to say, she'd change her mind.

"I hate this smell!" Hannah said out loud.

"Shh. Someone will hear you."

"No one's going to hear," Hannah said, louder.

To keep her from knowing he was laughing, Jerry rolled on his side, as close to the edge as possible. When she found resistance, and had to give up, her rebellion knew no limits. It simply boiled out of her like an overfilled pot of rolled oats, hissing and foaming.

"I don't like the smell of mothballs, either," he said, quietly. Then, "Good night, Hannah."

He was wavering between consciousness and sleep when Hannah said, "Horses aren't going to be competitive with tractors, either."

When he didn't answer, she muttered, "You know that, too." He let her think he was sound asleep. It was easier than thinking of a soothing reply.

The woman was headstrong, self-willed, more determined than anyone he'd known. His thoughts drifted into prayer, not a plea of desperation, but only that God would bless their union. And he was thankful. Thankful for Hannah, thankful for her willingness to return, thankful for Lancaster County.

It snowed, but the storms were gentle, in spite of folks talking about the cold and the large drifts piled by the roadside. The absence of harsh winds and driving blizzards were an immense relief to Hannah, though she didn't mention it. No use letting anyone know she was glad to be here.

On Sunday morning, they rode to church with Ben. They had no carriage of their own, no horse, nothing. Everything had been sold.

Hannah sat in the back seat of the buggy dressed warmly in a heavy winter coat, a woolen shawl, scarf, and bonnet—all black. She had dressed with care, painfully aware of the scrutiny she would be under. A purple dress and cape, the cape pinned neatly to her dress, two pleats down the back, pinned to a V in front, her black apron pinned around her waist. She hoped she'd pass the inspection of curious eyes. She had no idea if anything had changed since she had traveled out West with her parents.

In spite of the austere way of dressing—modest, homemade, the same pattern used for every individual—she had been old enough to know there were ways of pinning a cape and choosing the sleeve length and the length of skirt and apron that set one apart from another.

The girls who were more concerned about fashion than obedience wore shorter dresses, combed and arranged their hair in attractive waves, and set their coverings back on their heads just far enough to set them apart, appearing stylish to their peers.

Vilt. See harriched net. How often had she heard her father say with frustration that she was wild, that she'd never listen? Her mother would nod solemnly, her mouth puckered into a self-righteous petunia. Her parents had always been strict, obeying the *ordnung* to the letter. Hannah had always had a distaste for her mother's severe wetting, *schtrāling*, the way she combed her hair and put it back. Her long, black tresses were always rolled like two worms and then pinned into a bun at the back of her head, each hairpin a single agony of its own.

Her covering had always been larger than most of her friends', the strings wide and tied below her chin in a *gehorsam* bow. Some of the older *rumschpring* girls had narrow covering strings tied loosely and laying on their chests.

The whole idea of fashion was frowned upon, but it was there nevertheless. Hannah figured as long as people were people doing the things they did, some of them more concerned about looking attractive than others, that was simply the way of it.

Well, she had no intention of walking into church services with an appearance that suited a pathetic Western hick. She knew her dress was not one of the most conservative, which suited her just fine.

To shake hands with a kitchen full of women she barely remembered, to have all those eyes following her, was the worst form of punishment she could think of. She held her head high and refused to give the ministers' wives the holy kiss that was expected. She wasn't about to touch anyone's lips, she didn't care if it was a requirement or not. That, of course, did not go unnoticed. Eyebrows were lifted or lowered, depending on the individual, but as a whole, Hannah had set herself apart, refusing to submit.

Tongues wagged. "*Vos iss lets mit sie? Hals schtark. Vie ihr Dat.* What's wrong with her? She's headstrong, just like her father."

Undeterred, Hannah took her place among the women, staring ahead, her large dark eyes hard. Bold.

"*Hott sie ken schema?* Has she no shame?"

She sat among the women, her back straight, showing no emotion. When babies cried and apologetic mothers pushed past her, she held her knees slightly aside to let them pass without lifting her head to meet curious eyes or smile.

After the three-hour service, she stood apart and refused to help prepare the long, low tables for lunch, telling herself it was unnecessary. That was the single girls' job, not hers. If they wanted to stay true to tradition, well, they could.

Jerry was obviously in his element. Hands tucked in his pockets, he greeted old friends, uncles, cousins, a genuine love shining from his eyes. To be among those acquaintances of his past was a blessing, an undeserved joy the Lord had provided, and his heart swelled with gratitude.

His eyes searched the room for Hannah but found no trace of his wife, which left him uneasy. When he took his place at the table, spread a slice of homemade bread with the soft *smear kase* (cup cheese) he loved so much, his eyes were still searching the room for a glimpse of her.

They were invited to Uncle Ezra Stoltzfus's for supper. Jerry accepted gladly. He knew Ezra was one of the more successful dairymen even in times such as these, with depressed milk prices and cows that brought next to nothing at auction or at private sale. He wanted advice from a person of Ezra's experience.

He found Hannah standing alone against the rinse tubs in the washhouse, her arms crossed tightly, her expression keeping everyone at bay. He saw her dark, belligerent gaze, raised his eyebrows in question, and asked if she was ready to go.

She nodded quickly.

"Uncle Ezra invited us for supper," he said, just before she went to gather her things.

Without turning, her head moved from side to side. "No."

"Hannah. Please? I would love to visit with him."

"Then go visit with him. I won't go. I don't know them."

A smiling mother came into the washhouse surrounded by a group of small children and holding a crying baby. Jerry had no wish to press his argument with the woman present, so he turned, let himself out the door, and went to the barn to find his horse.

Hannah dressed herself in the thick black coat and woolen shawl, pulled her black scarf and bonnet severely over her head, thrust her hands into knitted mittens, and stood at the end of the sidewalk by the wire gate, waiting for Jerry.

She waited for a long time, her eyes scanning the parked

buggies, the men hurrying to lead their horses to their own car-
riages, their thick *ivva reck* flapping in the cold, winter wind.

A voice beside her asked, "*Iss eya net an bei kumma?* Is
he not appearing?" Hannah turned her face to meet the kind,
watery eyes of an aging grandmother, stooped and bent, one
gloved hand clasping the smooth handle of a cane. Behind her,
an elderly husband smiled as he kept watch, protecting his wife
from hidden spots of snow and ice.

Hannah smiled, a small quick spreading of her lips, to be
courteous. "Doesn't look that way," she answered. She stepped
aside to let them pass, her rubber boots sinking into the piled
snow along the sidewalk. She watched as a middle-aged man
brought a large, plodding horse hitched to a creaking, ancient
carriage. The horse stood, its neck outstretched, waiting until
the elderly man helped his wife into the buggy, tugging a bit,
pushing at the right moment, years of practice making a smooth
transition from the ground to the cast-iron step, and from there
to the safety of the upholstered seat.

From the depth of her wide-brimmed bonnet, the old woman's eyes twinkled at Hannah. "You can't imagine this now, my
dear, but this is how it goes when you're old." She chuckled,
lifted the heavy lap robe and spread it across her legs. Her husband heaved himself into the buggy beside her, grunting with
the effort, then took a long time to tuck the lap robe around his
wife, while the middle-aged man stood patiently at the horse's
head.

He looked a lot like Yoni Beiler, but Hannah wasn't sure, and
had no intention of asking, either. She had no idea if the aging
couple had lived in this church district so many years ago. That
time seemed like another life, a dim, blurry memory viewed as
if under water.

Hannah watched as the middle-aged man handed the reins
to the driver and stepped back saying, "*Machets goot, Dat.* Stay

well, Dad." The elderly man lifted the reins and clucked to his horse who leaned tiredly into his collar and moved off.

Hannah was seriously perturbed by now. She stamped her feet to warm her toes, clutched her shawl tightly around her chilled body, and glared at the barn. Someone should paint that thing. It looked scaly, like the loose skin on a diseased dog with mange. Maybe Reuben Detweiler couldn't afford to paint it. Hannah guessed that nobody painted their barn during the Depression. Well, times were getting better; she'd heard it on the train.

She sniffed with impatience. If Jerry didn't show up soon, she was going back into the washhouse. He could come looking for her.

She became aware that there was a ruckus from somewhere inside the barn. A horse must be acting up. Suddenly, men ran from the implement shed to the barn. She heard loud voices.

Never once did she imagine that Jerry would be in that barn, so she was not alarmed, only cold and impatient. But when her uncle Ben appeared, his face like a pale, waxen mask, his lips colorless, she knew something bad had happened.

His stricken eyes found her questioning eyes. "Hannah!" His voice sent shock waves through her body like sizzling, painful lightening.

"Han . . . Hannah. You have to be strong. Jer . . . Jer . . . Jerry was kicked in the . . . the chest by a horse."

Hannah reacted with disbelief, then a powerful urge rose in her to hit Ben, to pound him with her fists, hurt him and make him stop his childish stuttering. She felt the color draining from her face, her breathing becoming shallow, as if there was not enough oxygen in Lancaster County to keep her heart beating.

"Is he dead?" Incredulous now. He couldn't be dead. She had refused to visit his uncle. She'd told him no.

Wild-eyed boys raced past her to spread the news to the women. Hannah suppressed the urge to grab them and stop them from spreading gossip, untrue things.

"Take me to him," she ground out, between teeth that began chattering of their own accord.

She entered the barn, the poorly lit interior a harbinger of darkness and pain. Men stepped aside. Someone reached out to her. She slapped the hand away. She smelled hay, manure, leather, the rancid, sweetish odor of cows. Pigs snuffled. "*Bisht die Hannah?* Are you Hannah?" Kind words from constricted throats. Men kneeling over the prostrate form of her husband. His eyes were open, deep and dark. His face was ashen, so pale she thought he was already gone.

His breath was a painful gasping for air. A gurgling. Another gasp. Hannah fell to her knees, tore at the buttons of his white shirt. Someone had opened his coat, loosened the hooks and eyes of his vest, peeled away the *ivva reck*.

Hannah called his name in a strangled voice. "Jerry. Jerry." Her eyes were dry, her throat rasping.

He struggled to breathe. She opened his shirt with trembling fingers and lifted his undershirt. In the poor lighting, she could see the shape of a hoof in deep blood color, the skin around it already black, blue, purple. There wasn't much blood. No more than from an insignificant nick with a scissors. She told herself he'd be all right. She replaced his tee shirt and straightened.

"Did someone use the telephone?"

"Yes."

Her mother was there, then. Her grandfather. Ben and Elam. Jerry's brother David and his wife.

Sarah reached for her daughter but Hannah pushed her away. "Move! Everyone get away from him so he can breathe," she ordered.

From the back of the crowd, a head taller than any of the others, Dave King watched Hannah, saw her refusal to weep or accept her mother's comfort.

He knew whose horse had lashed out. He'd warned Jerry that morning not to tie his horse with Samuel Esh's stallion.

The ambulance from the Gordonville Fire Company arrived. Hannah stood aside, her large, dark eyes burning with bitter, unshed tears, her hands clutching the fringes of her black shawl.

Jerry's strangled scream of pain when they lifted him onto the stretcher was almost more than Hannah could bear, but she knew there was nothing they could do to prevent it.

She rode in the back of the wailing, careening vehicle. She took in every contour of Jerry's face. She memorized the heavy black bangs, the longish sweep of hair sweeping over his pale forehead, his lashes perfect.

She turned away when his struggle to breathe became too hard. She reached out a hand as if to help him, begged the attendant to do something, anything.

Wasn't there anything the medical professionals could do? White beds in rooms painted a sickly green color. Nurses hovering, doctors coming and going. Silence. Whispered conversations. So many questions. And, what was that giant, busy-haired Amish man doing in here? He was no relative.

Hannah crossed her arms and glared at him. He glared back, his colorless eyes cold and calculating, sizing her up. He stepped forward.

"I know you don't want me here but I saw it happen, so I'll need to answer some questions."

"Go to the police station then," Hannah said, coldly.

"I was there. The doctors need me."

Hannah turned away.

Jerry lingered for less than three days. In that time, Hannah never left his bedside, only sleeping fitfully a few minutes at a time. She refused to eat or drink until a nurse told her that if she wanted to stay strong, she'd have to at least start consuming something.

Sarah came and went, as did many other relatives, half of whom Hannah did not know. Stony-faced, pale, her large dark eyes as hard as polished coal, Hannah spoke curtly, repelled sympathy, and efficiently constructed a brick wall about herself, impenetrable, even to her own mother.

Alone at night, she spoke to Jerry. She smoothed his hair, ran her hands along the contours of his face. She told him she loved him. His eyes opened and closed. He strained to breathe. Sometimes his breathing stopped, then resumed in powerful hiccups, hard and fast.

Hannah knew he was in terrible pain, unbearable discomfort, hanging between life and death. Suspended on waves of pain, his heart struggled valiantly. The doctors said there was nothing they could do.

Hannah glared at helpful, well-meaning nurses, listened to concerned doctors, waving both nurses and doctors away with flaps of her hand or curt nods and short words. She wanted them to just be quiet and go away. Shut up. What does all this talking help? He was kicked in his heart and he's not going to make it. If you can't help him, leave me alone.

And they did.

She was alone with Jerry when he inhaled one last shuddering breath, then exhaled in a slow, faint rhythm. The rising and falling of his chest ceased. Complete and total silence.

Hannah sat like a stone, cold and immovable. Slowly she reached out to place one hand, then the other, on his chest. She bowed her head as a great obstruction rose in her throat, followed by a rasping, wrenching sob.

She had told him over and over she was sorry. Now she would spend the rest of her life unsure, wondering if he had heard her words. So many times she had said no to him, refused to budge even on trivial matters. Why?

No one understood Hannah's refusal to shed tears, at least in front of anyone. They called her cold, calculating, abnormal. Older women shook their heads, said it wasn't good. She'd have to be "put away" if she wasn't careful.

The homestead swarmed with well-meaning friends and neighbors descending on the house and barn with cakes and pies, buckets and mops, the men bringing teams of horses hitched to manure spreaders, shovels, and pitchforks. They cleaned and scoured, emptied the downstairs bedroom and cleaned it to a shine. The body arrived from the undertaker in town.

This was the ultimate test for Hannah. To remain dry-eyed while they clothed Jerry in white funeral garb and laid him in the plain, handmade casket, took superhuman effort.

She willed herself not to give way to the sobs in her throat. Over and over she steeled herself under the watchful eyes of her mother. After his hair had been combed and adjusted to Hannah's satisfaction, she stepped back, turned, and walked out of the room, her hands at her sides, her shoulders squared, her eyes brimming but not spilling over.

What had she done? She could have been loving and kind and submissive. Blindly, she walked through the washhouse door, the ache in her throat like a fiery boulder that threatened to steal her breath.

She ran into a hulking figure clothed in wool, rock solid, slamming the toe of her shoe against the leather toe of his shoe. She would have lost her balance had it not been for two paws that stopped her fall. Hannah was tall, but he was taller. His arms were like cables.

She tried to glare, but her eyes were glazed with tears. Defiance made her tears run over, leaving her gaze a mixture of pain and frustration, hurt and remorse, a look that would haunt Dave King for months. He uttered a useless apology.

She swung through the door and out into the wintry yard wearing only her black widow's dress and apron.

CHAPTER 16

As the long funeral procession wound its way along the road to the cemetery in Gordonville, the sun slid behind an increasing bank of clouds, casting gray shadows along wooden fences and sides of buildings. Black branches of trees huddled together in the still, cold air, as if waiting for the snow that would soon cover them.

The sound of steel-rimmed wheels on gravel roads melded with the dull *clop clop* of horses' hooves, the jingle of buckles and snaps, the creaking of leather. White puffs of steam came and went from the horses' nostrils as they tugged at restraining reins, held back to a slow trot to stay in an orderly procession.

Hannah sat in the back seat of the first buggy following the horse-drawn hearse. Her grandfather drove the team. Her mother sat beside her with Abigail. Manny followed, with Eli and Mary.

Hannah said nothing, her ironed, white handkerchief folded in her pocket. Her face was pale, lined with deep fatigue. Repeatedly, her mother tried to draw her out, to express herself, consolation flowing through her words. Sarah had been here in Hannah's place. She had mourned the loss of her husband. She had grieved to the point of ruining her health. A tragedy, they called it. But that didn't begin to describe the pain.

Sarah wanted to make this easier for Hannah somehow, but she had no way of knowing her senseless prattle was much the same as a burr in one's shoe.

Finally, Hannah grated hoarsely, "That's enough, Mam. Your grieving was different from mine."

Bewildered, Sarah set her mouth in a straight line and watched the horse's flapping neck rein the rest of the way. How could grieving be different, she wondered? Grief was grief, wasn't it? But Hannah knew the difference. Her mother grieved for the loss of one she loved more than her own life. She had loved deeply, dependent on her husband to flavor her days with his love.

Hannah's grief was saturated with remorse. That awful unspooling of unkind words, her unwillingness to obey, her defiance and anger, deeds of the flesh that she could never take back. There had been times that were okay, but too many times when things were not all right. Everything, just everything was complicated. She should never have gotten married.

With these thoughts buzzing in her head like angry wasps, Hannah's breathing became fast and shallow. Her head was bowed as she stepped from the buggy, and remained that way. Not once did Hannah lift her face or speak to anyone. Tears ran down Sarah's cheeks as the minister spoke. The young men shoveled chunks of frozen soil on top of Jerry's coffin as the voice of the second preacher droned on. After the German *lied* (song) was read in a quiet monotone, heads bowed in unison for a last silent prayer.

The crowd turned and dispersed. The horses and carriages were loosened and brought to the gate.

Back at the house, the funeral dinner was being prepared by appointed workers. Men straddled benches to mash vats of steaming cooked potatoes with handheld mashers, their wives hovering over them with salt and butter.

Roasts of beef that had simmered in the *eisa kessle*, the iron kettle, were taken up on wooden cutting boards and sliced. In a corner of the kitchen, workers rubbed quartered heads of cabbage across graters to create immense bowls of pepper slaw. Fresh sliced bread and apple butter was ready to be distributed across the tables.

A respectful, quiet hum of conversation rose and fell. The women who seasoned the grated cabbage rolled their eyes in the general direction of workers, then bowed their heads and shielded their lips with the protection of a palm held sideways.

"They say no one has seen her cry yet," Esther Zook hissed.

"Who?"

"Oh, that Hannah. You know."

"Oh, you mean his wife. Oh, I know. She's so cold. They say she didn't love him. Not right."

A forkful of pepper slaw was shoved under the speaker's nose. "Here. Taste this. What do you think? Vinegar? Sugar?"

Mary Miller made an awful face, puckering her mouth like the drawstring on a cloth purse. "No more vinegar. There's enough vinegar in there to pickle a pig!"

"Nah, Mary. Don't be so odd."

"Here, Suvilla. You taste it." Suvilla took a hearty chomp, waving a hand across her mouth as tears rose to the surface. "Too much vinegar! Who put it in?"

"More cabbage. The only thing to do."

"Hurry up. You'd think they'd be back from the *begräbniss* by now."

"Not if Eph Lapp has it."

"*Ach, ya*. He's so long-winded. They say Henner King's wedding, you know, he married Eva, didn't leave out till almost one o'clock."

A very heavy woman sailed over. "Shh! Quiet. They're back. Use a little respect now. Hush!" Noses wrinkled in the disappearing woman's wake, but there was a general air of respectful silence.

Hannah forced herself to eat a small amount of mashed potatoes and gravy, but all she could think of was how much Jerry would have enjoyed them. He'd often made them himself when she'd refused to do it.

A deep sense of shame turned her mouthful of creamy mashed potatoes to rancid slop. She laid down her fork and took out her handkerchief to wipe her mouth. A perfectly ironed square of white linen. Never used once, all day. A sense of accomplishment made her feel better.

She received kind words and handshakes stoically, nodding, murmuring *"denke,"* over and over without shedding tears, devoid of outward feeling.

She was achingly weary. Her knees buckled, her shoulders drooped. She watched the men and women clearing off the tables and carrying out the benches. She noticed the giant man, Dave King, carry benches like they were toothpicks. He grew a beard, which meant he was married. A young woman touched his arm. He bent his head to listen, then nodded. He disappeared. That must be his wife.

Later, when she thought she would collapse on a heap like melted butter, she saw him carry a chair over the row of remaining benches. When he reached her side, he placed the chair on the floor and left without saying anything. Gratefully, she slid onto the chair and sat with her hands folded in her lap.

Strange, the way that simple act of kindness immediately brought stinging tears to her eyes.

Hannah did not sleep at all that night. Over and over, scenes that brought a sickening remorse flashed before her eyes. Jerry had not kissed her good-night. He would have, but he knew she wasn't happy. How gladly would she milk cows with him now.

Her night was raw with regret, bitter with unshed tears. The loss of the homestead, all she had ever known all those years, blurred with the loss of Janie and the palomino, King, and now, Jerry, her husband of a little over a year.

Was that really all the time they'd had together? If she looked back, her sadness was like a jumble of impenetrable rocks, sharp and dangerous, useless to try to navigate. Boulders of mistakes and anger, bitterness and pride. A harsh landscape without mercy.

God did not have mercy on her. He showed her no love.

An empty calendar without numbers. A blank future that likely held nothing at all. An existence where she breathed, ate, slept, and tried to avoid questions and invitations from rude, nosy people she didn't like.

Wasn't there a verse somewhere in the Bible about wings of an eagle and waiting? *Okay, Lord, I'm sorry. I was not a nice person. If You'll forgive me, I'll do better. I need Your mercy. Badly.*

With that short and startling prayer, Hannah got out of bed, dressed, went down to the kitchen, and made three soft-boiled eggs and two pieces of toast with butter. She ate every mouthful. Then she got down the box of cornflakes, poured some in a bowl, and sugared them liberally, dumping milk over them. She ate every last bit. She felt fortified, courageous, and ready to face the future now that she knew God had forgiven her.

She coughed, blew her nose, adjusted her apron, filled a bucket with water, and proceeded to wash the living room floor on her hands and knees. That was where her mother found her at 6:00 a.m., her usual time to appear in her kitchen to prepare breakfast.

"Hannah?" A surprised question.

"Couldn't sleep," Hannah said over her shoulder, her right arm with the scrub cloth making rhythmic motions, great arcs of scrubbing across an already clean floor.

Sarah sank down onto a chair. "*Ach*, I was afraid of it. I

heard you turning. But I must admit, I fell asleep in spite of your suffering. I was so exhausted."

"It's all right."

"Is it?"

"Yes. It is."

Sarah considered trying again to draw Hannah out of her shell of suffering, but thought better of it. She'd talk when she was ready, and not a moment before.

The stodgy lawyer with the vest stretched across his stomach like the skin of a sausage harrumphed and twirled his moustache with the tips of his fat fingers (which also looked like sausages).

"What we have here is a fine example of forward thinking. Mr. Jeremiah Riehl has bequeathed all his possessions and worldly goods to his dear and beloved wife, Hannah Riehl. Which had all been sold at auction, is that correct?" More hacking and throat clearing.

"Yes," Hannah said levelly, swallowing and wondering what the poor man's breakfast had been to create all that phlegm.

He pinched the tip of his moustache and twirled, rolling the coarse gray hair into a twist, then releasing it, whereupon it quickly twirled back to its former waxen spiral. "So, we have an amount of ten thousand, nine hundred and eighty-four dollars to be bequeathed to Hannah Riehl on the date of, let me see . . ." More moustache twirling and attempted phlegm removal.

"Pardon me, ma'am. Pardon me. It's the bacon. Bacon at . . . well, you don't normally make a habit of dining at the eating establishments in the city. You plain folk live frugal lives. I respect that. Deeply admire that." Hannah nodded and willed him to bring this endless meeting to a close.

On the streets of Lancaster, she walked slowly beneath flourishing maple trees and read copper plaques. "Smith, Rembrandt and Heron." Another read "Dougherty" and still another, "Leek and Leek." All lawyers in this part of town. Brick sidewalks and ornate buildings with deep, wide windows.

Hannah was fascinated as she strolled along, drinking in the sights. She was awed at what men could accomplish with wood, brick, stone, and mortar. There were heaps of sooty slush, snow the color of chimney smoke, automobiles in gleaming shades of red, blue, or silver navigating the streets like beautiful brides-maids sailing down an aisle in all their finery.

There were mud-splattered trucks, horse-drawn delivery car-riages with names of businesses embossed in gold calligraphy on their sides. There was milk delivery and freshly baked bread from Emmaus Bakers.

She came to a swinging sign suspended from a horizontal pole fastened to the top of a window frame. ZIMMERMAN'S she read. Just that. Zimmerman's. She knew many Mennonites named Zimmerman. Then she spied the words, F INE DINING.

Now, what if she went inside and paid to have a full-course meal brought to her table? Would that be so awful? She shook her head. Jerry had been buried less than eight weeks, spring was on its way, and there was work to be done. So why should she loiter here, spending her money on unnecessary luxuries? She walked on, but not without a mounting sense of loss.

Hannah walked behind the drugstore to the hitching post where Manny waited in the carriage. She smiled to herself to find him draped across the seat, his straw hat over his face to shield his eyes, sound asleep. The horse looked as if he'd been taking a good snooze as well, standing on three legs with his nose almost touching the ground.

Hannah reached the buggy and shook it with all her strength. Manny's head wobbled on his shoulders, his straw hat sliding off his face. His eyes popped open, clouded with sleep and confu-sion, before he caught sight of her. "Hannah! Stop it!" he yelled in a hoarse voice, his throat constricted with sleep.

"Lazy, Manny. That's what you are!"

"It took you an awfully long time."

"Lawyers." Hannah untied old Dobs, got in the buggy, pulled steadily on the reins to back up, then turned right and began their trip out of the city to return home.

"I got my money. Or rather, our money. Mine and Jerry's," she said. Manny gave her a sharp look.

"What do you mean, Jerry's?"

"A part of me will always belong to the memory of our time together."

Manny nodded, understanding.

"How is it going with Marybelle?"

"I asked her to marry me on Sunday evening."

Hannah turned to look at him, sharply. "She agreed? She said yes?"

"Of course. We love each other very much."

Hannah bit her lip. She had been married but she could not fully comprehend the meaning of his words. What was love? How exactly did you know when you loved someone? And how did you measure love? Who knew the moment they changed from liking someone to loving them enough to want to marry them? It was Hannah's shameful secret. Could she ever ask her brother? She desperately wanted to ask him but a deep sense of embarrassment kept her from it. All she said was, "I'm happy for you, Manny."

"I'm sorry to tell you, after all you've been through."

"No, no. It's all right. You deserve to be happy, Manny. You do."

"Thanks."

There was nothing more to say, Hannah thought. Not now. *Perhaps someday I can ask someone the questions that tag along behind me like unwanted baggage. Someday.* Though what did it matter now? She had had her chance at marriage and love and now that part of her life was over. Besides, she had loved Jerry, she really had. Even if it didn't look or feel like the way other people experienced love.

"What will you do with your money?" Manny asked, slapping his grandfather's horse lightly with the reins he had taken over from Hannah. The only sign old Dobs had felt the slap of the leather reins was a flicking of his large ears, a few quickened steps, before returning to his usual plodding.

"I don't know yet. I don't want to stay at Doddy's."

"Why not?"

"I don't know."

But she did know. Their last night together ending in an argument, Jerry's searching good-night that met with her frigid silence. She hated the blue guest room, could barely tolerate sleeping there, in spite of falling into bed exhausted after a day of washing, ironing, housecleaning, and baking bread.

"You could clean houses for English ladies."

"Uh-uh. No."

"Why not?"

"Because."

Manny shrugged his shoulders, knowing that was the only reason he'd ever receive. So, he turned his head to the right, whistled softly, switched to humming, and back again.

Suddenly, Hannah asked if he liked it here in Lancaster County, her words without kindness. There was an accusatory note in her voice.

Instantly on the defensive, Manny said, "Sometimes."

"Why do you live here then?"

"Well, it's the sensible thing to do. I loved the West, like you, but it's a tough way to raise a family. The hardships . . ." His voice drifted off.

"Yes, but that hardship kept life interesting. Here, we sit in the middle of all this verdant growth, the tropical jungle of vegetation and lots of people, where it always rains when it should and everyone leads normal, secure, measured, ordinary lives, making money and having kids like rabbits. You do and say what is expected of you. You're put in a slot, like a cow in her stanchion. There are never any surprises or anything to appease your sense of adventure."

"Jerry's accident was a surprise . . . and a shock, Hannah."

"Well, that, yes." Ashamed, Hannah fell silent.

Manny did this to her. Always had. He made her feel humble and childish when he spoke the truth.

She watched the countryside, the white farmhouses and white barns, the green already appearing in low places, the pussy willows shooting green growth.

A promising spring, another season to plant, another summer to hoe and harrow, pull weeds and nurture with compost and manure. Another fall to harvest and another winter to start the process all over again.

She wouldn't do it. She would not conform to everyone's expectations. A fierce rebellion welled up within her, like a wild, growing algae in a clear pond, destroying common sense as it grew.

She'd return. Ask Hank to allow her to continue. He'd let her. She ached for the prairie in spring. The colors of the purple and lavender columbine. The patches of white daisies with hidden nests of prairie hen eggs. The crested wheat grass like swaying hula dancers from her geography book. She yearned to hear the myriad songs of the little brown dickeybirds, a flock of them like a spray of buckshot exploding across the waving grass.

She could smell the wet undergrowth, that sharp, pungent odor of moist soil decaying old growth, and bursts of brilliant new shoots appearing like magic.

How could she ever live without it? How could she manage life in Lancaster County without Jerry to keep her there?

At the supper table Hannah was pale and subdued. She pushed a chicken leg around on her plate, nibbled the canned corn on her spoon, took too many agitated sips of water from her tumbler, repeatedly clearing her throat. Her grandfather watched her closely, his kind eyes welling with moisture. He saw Sarah casting bewildered glances in Hannah's direction.

"Hannah, how did things go today?" Doddy asked.

She nodded too soon and too fast. "*Gute.*"

"So, your money is deposited in the First National Bank?"

"Yes."

"That's good, Hannah. I trust you will pray about God's will for your future, now that you have entered widowhood. What is the common saying? 'Take a year. Don't do anything rash. Take your time to see what unfolds.' When a person is grieving, they don't always make the best decisions."

Her face like a ceramic bowl, smooth, with no expression, Hannah looked at her grandfather. He recoiled inwardly. Her eyes were cold and hard.

"Do you have any plans made?" he asked.

"I want to go back!"

Sarah gasped audibly, speaking out of turn, completely unnerved as Hannah's words settled around the table. "But, Hannah, you can't!" her mother gasped.

The grandfather raised a hand, palm outward, to bring calm and quiet. The clock on the kitchen wall behind the table kept up its fierce ticking until it reached six o'clock, adding to the elevated tension that had wound its way into the room. Sarah's face registered wide-eyed panic. Manny's mouth hung open in unabashed disbelief. Mary leveled a look of disgust at Hannah, as only young girls can. Eli went on humming, chasing noodles around his dinner plate with the tip of his fork, thinking of the salamanders that lived in the stone spring house down by the creek.

Doddy Stoltzfus weighed each word before he spoke. When he finally aired his response, there was a bewildered hope in Hannah's eyes. "Hannah, you say you want to go back. I presume you are referring to returning to North Dakota. What makes you want to return?"

"The prairie in spring. The freedom of wide open spaces. Away from . . ." Hannah spread her hands, waving them in arcs in the air. "This. This claustrophobic county crawling with people."

To Hannah's great surprise, a smile spread across her grandfather's face, followed by a wide grin, then a loud guffaw of mirth. Sarah slanted an annoyed look at her aging father. For the first time in her life she thought he was becoming senile, unfit to hand out advice to her wayward daughter.

"Well, then, I imagine if you can't live in a county crawling with people, as you put it, we'll have to let you go. If this is what you truly want, then we'll put you back on the train with our blessing. *Herr saya.*"

Incredulous, Sarah sputtered words of rebuke. "*Dat, doo kannsht net.* You can't. We can't, any of us, go through this horrid ordeal one more time." A hard edge of hysteria crept into her voice. "Hannah, the prairie in springtime is a mirage. You know reality follows. Drought, fire, shriveled garden produce, the endless insanity-inducing winds." Sarah's eyes were wide with remembered agonies. She clutched one arm with the fingers of her opposite hand. She visibly trembled.

Hannah lifted her chin. "I love those winds."

Sarah rose halfway from her chair. She pointed a shaking finger in Hannah's direction. "If you go back out to North Dakota, you will do so completely against my will. I say, 'No,' and I mean no!"

Manny nodded in agreement with his mother. He placed a hand on Hannah's arm. "You are grieving, Hannah. You are missing Jerry more each day. That's what you're trying to escape. Your sorrow."

Hannah's eyes blazed with a black rebellion. She got up from her chair in one swift movement, the chair toppling over and hitting the floor with a crash. "Don't tell me what I can do and what I can't! None of you have the slightest idea what's wrong with me!"

She hurled her harsh words of accusation, her face crumpling like a child's, as grating sobs rose in her throat. Her eyes squeezed shut as the deep spring of her grief opened, the cache of denial she had allowed to fester and grow.

Hannah fled out of the room, away from her family. She threw herself on the bed in the blue guest room, her face crumpled, her eyes squeezed shut, as she cried heaving sobs and groans, emitting the deepest form of grief. She had no thoughts, only a sadness so profound it felt as if she was hurtling into a bottomless pit, a void completely empty of light.

Finally, she stilled. Thoughts entered her head, marching through in quick succession, like soldiers. She filtered truth from thoughts she knew were only an imitation of the real thing. Did she truly want to return to the homestead alone? In spring, yes. But not for any other reason. Not for blizzards or drought or, oh mercy, grasshoppers!

Without Jerry? No. Even with Jerry, if he were alive, probably not. It was living here in Lancaster County, always feeling like the odd person out and now the object of sympathy. The poor widow. The poor thing.

What no one knew was the fact that she had a substantial amount of money. And that she planned to use it to establish herself as a good, solid Amish frau with a business. She wasn't sure what kind of business, yet, but she'd figure it out.

Yes, Manny, I do miss Jerry. I miss him so much that I did want to escape. I thought I could flee, get away from my sorrow, my regret for all the times he was so loving and I was so mean. The flowers he brought. The limp bouquet of columbines. She shrank within herself remembering her snort and her words— "They're wilted." His hurt expression as he arranged them in a mason jar.

Jerry never pouted, never showed his hurt feelings. The man didn't have a selfish bone in his body. Jerry had been the best. Her tears began to flow again, a torrent of regret.

"Jerry, whatever it's worth to you now, wherever you are, I'm sorry. I loved you as much as one mean, selfish, hardhearted person could."

CHAPTER 17

THAT SPRING, THE FRESH DEW LAY ON THE LANCASTER COUNTY countryside, the air was still chill and bracing, and the first peas and onions were shooting from the depth of the rich, brown soil. Hannah was up and dressed, watching the road for the black station wagon.

She could have hitched up her grandfather's horse to the buggy, but she figured with all the miles she had to cover, it was worth hiring a driver. She told no one of her day's plans, giving her mother some offhand answer about going shopping.

She actually was going shopping, but not for groceries or fabric or anything of that sort. She had dreamt of Rocher's Hardware, a dream so vivid she could smell the fabric, the spools of thread, the dusty trays of buttons, and the paper sacks she handed to the women who came to buy necessities. She awoke that morning with her head full of plans, staring at the ceiling, her heart pounding with excitement.

She would be the first plain woman to have a dry goods store. She had plenty of experience with Harold and Doris Rocher in the town of Pine, North Dakota. Paid in flour, cornmeal, salt, and coffee, it was the single thing that had kept their family from starvation. That, and the prairie hens they cooked, salted, and gravied.

First, she needed her own place, which was what she was doing today. House shopping. The palms of her hands were wet with perspiration, her face felt flushed, and she chewed her thumbnails to the quick.

The driver's name was Jim Raudabaugh. He was a retired gentleman, short and portly, stuffed behind the black steering wheel like a sack of horse feed. His white hair stuck out from under his small gray fedora like porcupine quills, but his face was shaved and smooth, his eyes quick and bright. He viewed the world through rose-tinted spectacles, literally, perched on the end of his nose.

The minute she was seated in the car, he introduced himself, reaching across his ample stomach to shake her hand with his own.

"I'm Hannah. Hannah Riehl."

"Yes. Yes. The young widow. Please accept my deepest sympathy, Hannah. A tragedy. Tragedy. A man dying in his youth. Are there children?"

Hannah shook her head.

"That is good." He looked at her with so much watery-eyed sympathy that Hannah felt a burning in her nostrils, the beginning of tears in her eyes. *Bless this kindly man*, she thought.

"Now, where are we off to?" he asked, all business.

"Actually, I don't really know. I'm house hunting. I want to find a small place of my own."

He didn't need any more information. Hannah knew only too well that Amish drivers were the best source of carried news, and often gossip. Which, she supposed, was the Amish folks' fault, the way they rode along with their drivers, offering all sorts of interesting tidbits.

"Well, then, there's a place east of New Holland, on Route 23. But that would be a bit out of the way. Well, tell you what we'll do. We'll drive to Route 340 and follow it a ways. How's that?"

Hannah nodded.

The fields and forests were bursting with color, like a quilt pieced in a myriad of greens, with brown strips of plowed earth, white seagulls flapping behind plodding horses, the lavender and purple of the lilacs, the red and yellow of tulips bordering houses like fancy collars and cuffs.

Clematis climbed wooden arbors, waiting to burst into color. Hedges of forsythia sent forth brilliant green leaves after their yellow blossoms had dropped to the ground. Yes, there was beauty here—a cramped, cultivated sort of beauty, like the women in clothing catalogs with their faces painted and patted with powders and oils.

But the blue sky was above them, the clouds like puffs of cotton balls, pure and white and unfettered. The sun was as bright yellow here as it was in North Dakota, so that was something, wasn't it?

From that same sky and those clouds the rain would fall in spring and summer. In the autumn of the year the creeks would be running full. And winter would bring nitrogen in the form of snow, piling up on the fields with fresh cow and horse manure spread underneath. Here was a land that would blossom like a field of wildflowers. The climate, the soil, the work ethic of the many plain peoples who adhered to their farming practices, bringing trade and a constant influx of enterprising, hardworking folks who would live in prosperity their whole life long, and their children after them.

Hannah planned to be one of the prosperous entrepreneurs.

"So, you're searching for a small home on an acre of ground? Or maybe more than one acre?" the driver inquired politely as he broke in on Hannah's wandering thoughts.

"Well, what I have in mind is a small house, but I do need an addition, or a small garage for what I have in mind," she replied.

Jim was intensely curious, but something kept him from asking more questions.

The house along Route 23, just east of New Holland, was a small house built of cement blocks with a deep porch, immense posts holding up the wide roof, and a garage that was set at the end of the gravel driveway.

Hannah had a bad feeling about the house. Cement blocks were not warm or inviting, no matter if someone had slapped a coat of thick, white paint on the exterior. So, she shook her head no, and Jim backed obediently out of the driveway, turned right, and continued on his way.

The next house with a F OR SALE sign was along Hollander Road. The roof had a fairly steep pitch, with two of the cutest dormer windows she had ever seen sprouting from the shingles. It reminded her of a gingerbread house or a cabin in the woods—homey, cozy. It brought to mind evenings sitting in a comfortable chair with a gas lamp hissing softly above her, a coal fire in a small black stove, a braided rug, and a bowl of popcorn.

The wind could howl around that sturdy house and it would never budge. It was built of brick. The porch was deep and wide, with three windows facing the road. The front door was oak— wooden, solid, and homey.

Hannah's mouth went dry as her heart sped up. This was her house. There were boxwoods planted along the front, sheltering the porch like a green privacy fence. The yard was in need of a good cutting.

"Can we go inside?" she breathed.

Jim suspected this was a house that suited her as he observed her wide eyes. "Well, we'll have to see."

He grunted as he heaved himself from behind the steering wheel and again as he pulled himself to his feet. Hannah stayed in the car, thinking he might be acquainted with the occupants.

She held her breath as he went to the side door that was set lower against the house than the front porch. *Please, please, let someone be at home.* She was not aware that she was chewing down on her thumbnail until she tasted blood. Quickly, she lowered it and wrapped her apron around it.

Yes! The door was opened by an elderly lady in a flowered house dress. They spoke too long, then Jim turned toward the vehicle and motioned to Hannah with his hand.

Hannah fumbled for the door latch and stumbled out of the car, walking too fast, too eager, she knew, but there was no stopping. She extended a hand. "Hello. I'm Hannah Riehl."

The elderly woman peered up at her through round, gold-rimmed spectacles, her small blue eyes set in deep folds. Her nose looked like a tulip bulb, a veritable tributary of purple veins crossing it. Her mouth was small and puckered with the biggest mole Hannah had ever seen sprouting a growth of stiff hairs, like a tiny toothbrush.

"Good morning, my dear. A beautiful one it is, wouldn't you say?" she warbled, in a high, quivery voice.

"Yes. Yes it is."

"So, the man tells me you've come to see my house?"

Hannah nodded, her smile reaching too wide, her eyes going to the adorable little V-shaped roof above their heads. Just enough of a roof to keep the rain off someone who came calling.

"Well, then, I suppose I'll have to invite you in, right?" she chortled, stepping aside to allow them both to enter.

Hannah felt a stir of irritation as Jim, the driver, entered too. He really had no business accompanying them through these rooms, following her around like a nosy pig. Too curious. Did she have a choice, though, without displaying bad manners?

It was two steps up to the kitchen on the left. There were hooks to hang outerwear on the stoop just inside the door. The kitchen had white cupboards, a darling window above the sink with no panes on the lower ones, only two vertical panes on the top. It was bordered by a limp, flowered curtain, yellowed with age and faded by the sun.

The linoleum was black-and-white squares, waxed to a high gloss. The woodwork was sturdy, with routed lines and squares at the top corners with fancy circular grooves, all painted white. Good plaster walls and hardwood floors that were varnished like a mirror.

Hannah gasped audibly when she saw the open stairway with its elaborate bannister, the spindles carved into a complicated pattern that presented a line of perfect symmetry as they marched up the stairs. It was like a dollhouse, except large enough for real people!

A brick fireplace in the living room had a real fire crackling. There were two small bedrooms up under the eaves, with slanted ceilings and more hardwood floors. A bathroom at the top of the stairs had a white claw-foot bathtub, a small sink, a metal medicine cabinet with a mirror, a commode, gleaming stainless-steel toothbrush holder, towel racks—everything she could possibly need or want. A clever little linen closet was built into the hallway.

The thought that she might not be able to afford this house flitted through her mind suddenly, bringing with it a sharp blow of reality.

There was a bedroom downstairs and another small bathroom with only a sink and a commode, the fixtures in green. By this time, Hannah harbored a sinking feeling that she would never be able to purchase this sweet, homey dwelling. For one thing, she didn't deserve it. God knew she was not a nice person, so He only handed her one blow after another. Or let the devil do it. She was never quite sure.

She turned to go down the stairs to the basement, and almost pushed the driver, Jim, down ahead of her as she bumped squarely into him. The old irritation welled up. She couldn't stop herself from wishing he'd either move out of her way or fall down the steps. He'd bounce like a rubber ball, the fat thing.

The basement had gray cement block walls and a smooth concrete floor. Imagine, Hannah thought, being able to clean the basement with buckets of soapy water and a mop. Every farmhouse she had ever lived in had a dirt basement floor, packed down and slimy with moisture. She hated having to go to the cellar for a jar of applesauce or peaches, imagining snakes and lizards and all sorts of wet creatures with beady eyes.

By the time Hannah reached the kitchen, she was filled with deep despair, wearing her self-doubt like a black mantle, all her anticipation squelched.

"I don't want to move, but the daughters won't allow me to live by myself. So they're packing me up to live with my Shirley. Not that she isn't a nice person, but I'll certainly miss my house." Her blue eyes became liquid with emotion. Dabbing at them with a wrinkled handkerchief she fished out of her apron pocked, she sniffed bravely, then stuffed it back.

"I don't need the money, but the girls do, so they told me not to take less than seven thousand. I'm not supposed to be showing this house to you, or telling you the price, but I'm still on my own two feet, breathing through my nose!"

She chortled and tapped her nose. "Or my mouth, when my sinuses act up. Unpredictable as the weather they are."

Jim giggled with appreciation, then cut it short when Hannah gave him a hard look that said, clear as day, *She's not talking to* you.

Seven thousand dollars. Her mind whirred like Harold Rocher's cash register. Could she build an addition for another thousand? Pay for fabric and sewing notions? There would be lawyer's fees for the sale of the house, hidden costs like taxes and so many other things, like shelves for her merchandise, and

a counter. Well, first things first. She'd have to find a good carpenter. She could do without much furniture and she could borrow the basic household supplies from her mother.

Hannah clenched and unclenched her hands, wishing for
Jerry and his sound advice, his knowledge of business transac-
tions. She hadn't known she depended on him, had always made
him believe she was perfectly capable on her own.

Should she make a lesser offer? Return home and ask her
grandfather? No. She wanted this house. The old lady's daughters wouldn't take less and she had more than ten thousand dollars. She was going to go ahead and take it.

"I'll take it," she said firmly, hiding her doubts.

"You will? For seven thousand?"

"Yes."

"But, you likely need to go to the bank. You'll need to be
approved. Where's your husband?" Distrustful now, calculating.

"My husband was buried a few months ago. I'm a widow,
and no, I don't need to make arrangements with the bank. I have
the money."

"Oh, I'm sorry," the old lady said, her voice quivering. "I
didn't mean to be rude. So you lost your husband so young? Oh,
God have mercy. It's a horrible thing to have happened. And you
so young. So young." She went to Hannah and clasped both of
Hannah's hands in hers. Holding them, she looked up at Hannah with absolute sympathy.

"Call me Thelma. Thelma Johns. My husband was Richard,
may he rest in peace."

Under normal circumstances, Hannah would have pulled her
hands away from the old woman, but her mind was elsewhere,
already considering when she'd move in, how she'd arrange her
sparse belongings, what she'd absolutely need to purchase to get
the store up and running.

Her grandfather, her mother, Manny, everyone had to see the house. They hitched up old Fred to the spring wagon and drove over to see it the following Thursday.

It was a perfect spring day. The sun shone like liquid gold, bathing everything in its glistening light. The trees burst with fluorescent green, new leaves unfolding with their newborn colors. Daffodils hung their spent, withered heads like deceased little men. Tulips drooped in faded colors, having spent their finery. But the roses were coming into bloom with the purple irises like bearded kings, showing off their intricate splendor.

New petunia plantings showed bits of pink. Geraniums transplanted from tin coffee cans pushed red blossoms. Yellow and orange dots of marigold heads surrounded symmetrical borders.

Hannah thought all of this was rather artificial beauty, but she supposed if she bought a house, she'd best get used to it and forget about wide open spaces dotted with lacy wildflowers, all dancing in one direction as if in concert, the untamable wind the conductor of the amazing concert.

As they turned onto Hollander Road, Hannah's stomach flipped a bit. She was nervous now, afraid of what her grandfather might say.

Surrounded by woods, down a low rise and around a bend, and there it was, even more charming than she had remembered.

The perfect little house.

An indescribable feeling of joy welled up in Hannah, leaving her breathless, her eyes shining with anticipation.

"Doddy," she called from the second seat. "Turn here. This is it."

He slowed Fred, turned expertly, and brought the horse to a stop. "*Vell*," he said.

"Why Hannah, it's a very nice house, like you said," her mother said, always kind, always supportive.

Manny smiled and nodded his approval. "I think it's worth what you paid for it."

"Thank you. Oh, I'm so glad you approve."

"Can we see the inside?" her mother asked.

"I'm sure we can, if Mrs. Johns is at home."

And so the tour began, led by Thelma, of course, who commenced a lengthy discussion of the house's origin, the happy times spent there with Richard and the girls, until Hannah thought she would fly to pieces with impatience.

"So, how do you plan on providing for yourself?" her grandfather asked once they were back in the spring wagon, Fred clopping clumsily down the road.

"I will be looking for someone to build an addition to the house where I plan to have a dry goods store," Hannah explained.

Her grandfather stared straight ahead without comment. Her mother turned in her seat, her elbow dangling over the back. "But, Hannah . . ."

"What?" Instantly defensive, Hannah brought her eyebrows down, a pinched look to her mouth.

"I don't know. Amish people don't have their own stores. Especially not, uh . . . women."

"So? I can be the first."

Doddy Stoltzfus wagged his head, his wide-brimmed straw hat lifting enough so he had to reach for the brim and tug it into place. "I wouldn't try it, Hannah. I'm sorry, but I doubt if old Ezra would approve of something like that."

"What does he have to do with it?"

Shocked, Sarah turned and said, "He's our bishop!" As if that finished it. She knew she was expected to submit. Total *gehorsamkeit*, unquestioning obedience.

It riled Hannah, this unswaying vigilance, this immediate stop to her plans. She wasn't giving up that easily. She had given up too much already. The homestead, Jerry, oh, just on and on.

It wasn't fair. She had her heart set on her little venture. So what if she was the first one?

"You don't know what he'll say," Hannah said, thrusting her petulance like a wedge.

"I think I do," her grandfather said, shaking his head up and down, dislodging his straw hat again.

"I won't know for sure if I don't ask."

Sarah turned back to Hannah again. She spoke quietly. "Hannah, I wouldn't ask. You know what our *ordnung* is."

A slow burn began somewhere deep in Hannah's chest. This was precisely why she dreaded living back in Lancaster County. Everyone knew your business and handed out advice so freely and easily, taking for granted that you would bow down and live according to another man's wisdom.

She had no intention of giving up her dry goods store. Amish women sewed constantly. Through the worst of the Depression, clothes had worn thin, held together by patch upon patch as families made do with what they had. Or they used feed sacks, the cotton fabric dyed, washed, and sewn into clothing.

Now, with the money market lifting bit by bit and Teddy Roosevelt giving his famous speeches about not being fearful, folks would start buying more.

It was an opportunity. She would be supplying essentials to the community. The Amish women would not need to go to the city of Lancaster to purchase basic necessities. It was discouraged to be among the worldly, so what was worldlier than walking the streets of the city, past the bars, houses of ill repute, cars honking their horns, and men of the world calling out their insults?

No! She was not backing down. She wanted her own business. So she said nothing. And, riding in the back seat beside Manny, letting everyone believe she'd swallowed their refusal to allow her to continue with her plans, she went right on making her plans, choosing to ignore their words.

She didn't ask anyone for help in contacting an experienced carpenter to build the addition to her house, either. She merely talked to the neighbors down the road and asked to use their telephone. She called Jim Raudabaugh, the driver, and asked him a direct question. Who was the most trustworthy man to build the addition, she wanted to know? After many strange sounds coming from his mouth, hisses and clicks like a cornered snapping turtle, he finally came up with a name. Dave King. "He lives over along 340 below Leola," he told her.

Hannah had no idea who he was talking about, much less where he lived. When Jim offered to drive her to his house, she was short with him, saying it would be much cheaper to drive her grandfather's horse. Besides, she had to go speak with old Ezra King first.

So she said goodbye to Jim without thanking him or hiring him to take her in his car, leaving him to hang up the phone receiver and comforting himself with a sausage and ketchup sandwich. He admitted grudgingly that Hannah Riehl was not a very nice person, widowed or not.

Manny told her where the bishop lived, so one evening after supper, she told her mother she was going visiting, which she was. She knew Sarah would be gratified by the thought of Hannah becoming more social, which would keep her from asking questions.

Hannah goaded Fred to a fast trot, scaring him with a nip of the whip on his flapping old haunches. He was losing his winter coat, reddish brown hair flying through the air like snow. She spit them from her lips, snorted through her nose, wiped her eyes, and arrived at the bishop's farm covered in horse hair.

Nothing to do about it. She guessed if the bishop was old, he'd have seen many springs and more horses shedding their winter coats.

She tied Fred to the hitching rack by the wall of the white

barn, brushed herself off as best she could, her black cape and apron patterned with stiff horse hair.

She turned to the house, evaluating its size and layout. Often the aging parents lived in an apartment built onto the original farmhouse with interior doors connecting the two, a perfect arrangement that allowed privacy but also handy access if one or the other family group was needed. She wondered if her life would have been much like this one had Jerry lived to be her husband to an old age.

Ah, Jerry. My husband. A shudder of grief. For the hundredth time she vowed never to marry again. Never. This time, she meant it. Firmly, staunchly. Written in stone. She simply did not need a man. She had loved Jerry. In her own selfish way, perhaps, but she had loved him as much as she knew how. And here she was, awash in missing him, as helpless as one of those hickory nut shells they used to set in the water at the creek's edge, watching the current take it, whirling it away, tumbling past rocks and eddies.

She hated having no control over her grief. It raised its head and looked her in the eye at the worst moments, without mercy. It pounded her with its fists, roughed her up and left her lying there, brutally accosted, beaten down and grasping the air for deliverance.

She blinked, straightened, shrugged off the melancholy cloud of sorrow, and decided to try the door at the end of the gleaming floor of the front porch. Since the younger folks were the farmers and the gable end of the house was turned toward the yard gate, she assumed the main part of the house was the first door. So, she'd go to the second door.

The evening sun slanted across the glossy gray paint of the porch floor, illuminating the freshly planted red geraniums, the tender green lawn in the background, the brown trunk of an oak tree. A bluebird was sitting on the clothes line, a portrait of peace and contentment.

CHAPTER 18

THE DOOR OPENED SOON AFTER HER SOFT TAPPING. A ROUND, BALD-ing head appeared, encircled with wisps of snow-white hair, a sparse white beard, and two small brown eyes as bright as a sparrow's, almost hidden in folds of loose facial skin.

"*Kum yusht rei*. Come on in." The voice was surprisingly light. His height was disconcerting. He was so tiny. Hannah felt like an ox or a giraffe towering over this feathery wisp of a man, who stepped gingerly aside to allow her entry.

"*Vy*, hello." This from the undersized, crooked little woman who must be his wife. There were only a few wisps of white hair visible from beneath the huge white covering. Her eyes were bright with curiosity from behind small, gold-rimmed spectacles.

Hannah tugged self-consciously at her own smaller, more fashionable covering, and introduced herself.

"I thought so." Ezra King nodded his head in recognition. "You are Jeremiah Riehl's widow."

"Yes, I am."

"*An shauty soch*. Such a shame."

"Yes."

"What brings you here?"

Hannah sat in the chair indicated by the petite, elderly wife, took a deep breath, and began, her hands clenched tightly in her lap. "I have purchased a house."

The white-haired old patriarch listened, his eyebrows elevated with kindness, a half smile playing around his mouth.

"I would like to build an addition to own and operate a fabric store."

There! It was out in the open, swimming in plain view in the lamp light. To ease the transition from hidden plan to open scrutiny, Hannah found herself babbling, explaining.

"My grandfather doesn't think I should do it. That's why I'm here. What is the difference? An Amish woman having her own business or having to walk the streets of Lancaster with all its *freuheita*? Would it not be better that the women stay among their own to purchase goods?"

The elderly bishop held two fingers to his lips, contemplating Hannah's argument. Nervously, Hannah twisted the hem of her apron. Finally, he spoke.

"Yes, I can see your point of view. But—and this is the thing—you would be introducing something new. The Amish have always been slow to change. We strive to keep things in a *demütich* way, humble. Would it represent a woman's meek and quiet spirit to be the owner of a store?"

"But . . ." Hannah began, devastated.

He held up a hand to quiet her. "I am not finished. I don't believe there is an Amish store run by a frau here in Lancaster County, and I would discourage such an undertaking. I would be glad to see you accept a no, based on the wife being a keeper at home, quiet, meek, subject to her husband.

"However, you have no husband, and you are expected to allow the church to pay for expenses in all *demut*."

"But, I don't want to do that," Hannah said, with all the force of her powerful nature. "Everyone would watch me, to see what I spend, where I go, what I wear. No, I won't do that."

The old bishop's eyes watched Hannah's face, but he gave no comment. Here was one who knew what she wanted, and didn't like anyone to stand in her way. He weighed with the scales of justice and fairness. If he firmly forbade it, he might not be making the best decision, owing to this woman's strong will. Determined as she appeared to be, to operate a store with that headstrong nature. . . . He wasn't sure.

"Why don't you let us sleep on this one?" he asked, still kindly.

"But I want to know."

"You will not be able to know this evening. I think it is a case that should be presented to the other ministers. We will take into account the fact that you are a widow intent on making her own way, and I will present your argument about Amish women on the streets of Lancaster.

"I hope you are aware, though, just how unusual your request is. Most women would be happy to bake pies or raise butchering hens, sell eggs, or work in a truck patch."

"I am not most women," Hannah replied.

Did she hear a soft, suppressed giggle from the bishop's tiny wife? Stooped over with her black cape falling over her shoulders, her angelic demeanor framed by the halo of her large white covering, she had squeaked out a bit of laughter.

The bishop smiled broadly, then laughed outright. He shook his head in disbelief. "No, you know, Anna . . ."

"Hannah."

"Oh, yes, you did say Hannah. I should say no to this thing. But I will present it to wise counsel, and we will come to a conclusion. Surely, you understand my concern. It simply is not always the best to allow a new thing, although I do appreciate your ambition. It could be a good thing if it stayed within reason and did not become a store filled with frivolous items the household could do without."

Hannah's words tumbled from her mouth in her haste to assure him of her utmost respect for his wishes.

They spoke, then, of the fine spring weather. He asked questions about North Dakota, and Hannah found herself portraying it in the truthful framework of her own suffering. She shared her intense desire to keep the homestead in the face of fierce adversity.

"Yes, yes," he said, his eyes bright with interest. "Your story is interesting. Often in this life we are so certain something is the will of God, and everything goes against us, until we see the truth of His will. For some, it is easily discerned. For others, sometimes never. When we suffer, it is because of God's love. He sees our wayward path and pulls us back, bit by bit. There is much happiness to be found in humbling ourselves under the mighty hand of God."

Hannah nodded.

"The grasshoppers were a mighty blessing, then," Hannah said, a trace of sarcasm adding a bite to her tone. The bishop laughed and Hannah snorted, a spark of understanding between them, igniting into a small flame of friendship.

Hannah rose to go, struggling to accept the outcome of her visit. She wanted to beg him to say yes, but knew it was beneath her dignity. So, she accepted his blessing and the warm handshake and let herself out the door.

She ground her teeth in disappointment, leaned forward to see the crossroad better in the waning light of evening, and went home and to bed. Unable to sleep, she lay on her back staring at the ceiling, the smell of mothballs as unendurable as always.

The thing was, you couldn't always be careful. Worrying constantly whether you were doing the will of God was exhausting. Did God really care that much about every little thing like having a store or getting a job, or butchering chickens to sell, or gathering eggs, or raising pigs?

He allows us to make our own choices, she thought firmly. Well, she was going to go ahead and see this Dave King about the addition. Perhaps he'd be busy and couldn't do it for a few months.

If Jerry was here, he would have soon had it completed. But Jerry wasn't here.

That deep sense of being separated from him, completely cut off, never again to touch him or hear him speak, pressed down on her heart until it became a physical ache, altering her normal pattern of breathing. She willed herself to remain calm, thankful for every good thing she did have. She had safety, a solid structure that housed her, more than enough food to eat, her mother, her siblings, weather that was like a glimpse of heaven. She'd survive all right. She had come through worse than most folks endured in a lifetime.

Mr. Jim Raudabaugh took her to the Dave King residence which, to Hannah's surprise, was not the usual white painted farm. A long driveway that turned into cornfields on either side, a plain white house with an L-shaped porch along the north and east sides, a yard that needed cutting, and no flowers. Not one flower bed. A small barn that was barely big enough to house two horses and a carriage.

Everything was in a perfect state of repair and it was clean enough. But . . . Hannah couldn't find the proper word to describe the place. Was it lonely? Neglected? Poor?

She didn't know, so she shrugged it off, stepped up on the peeling floorboards of the porch, and knocked.

"Just a minute," a male voice belted out.

Hannah waited. She waited so long she was becoming irritated and had actually turned to walk back down the steps, when the door was almost jerked off its hinges and a voice like a thunderclap bellowed, "What do you want?"

Taken aback, Hannah turned. His frame filled the doorway,

his curly head of hair reaching almost to the top of the door frame. For a moment, she lost her voice.

She'd seen this man somewhere before. "Uh . . . I . . . heard you're a carpenter." When he didn't reply, she cleared her throat and rushed on. "I . . . uh . . . bought a house on Hollander Road and I need an addition built."

The smell of burning meat was overpowering. Hannah blinked as blue smoke wafted through the screen door. "Step inside. I gotta turn my meat," he said.

She hesitated, unsure if she should pull open the wooden screen door, or if he wanted her to remain on the porch. "Come on in!" he yelled.

Hannah jumped. He was so loud. So huge and noisy. She did not like this Dave King at all, she decided.

She went in. The kitchen was sunny, with golden sunlight slanting through the window above the sink, dust mites spiraling above mountains of dirty dishes. The whole room was bathed in the blue light of smoke pouring out of the enormous cast-iron frying pan. His back was turned, his shoulders hunched, as he pried at a piece of beef that was vastly overheated.

He was almost as wide as his cook stove. The top of the stove seemed to be somewhere in the vicinity of his knees.

Finally, he turned.

"Push the pan away from the heat," Hannah said, without thinking.

"No. I'm hungry."

"Suit yourself."

They looked at each other. He towered above her, a hulk of a man with unkempt hair, strange yellow eyes, and a grim slash of a mouth.

He reminded Hannah of a moose.

"What do you want?"

"I told you."

"Yeah, guess you did. I'm busy. Can't do it."

"Why not?" Hannah asked.

"I just said."

"You don't have to yell at me. I'm not standing on the porch."

"Aren't you that widow? Anna or something?"

"Hannah."

"Yeah. I saw you before. You're the widow of Jeremiah Riehl. You lived out West. Let me get this meat. It's done. You want some?"

"No."

"You sure? I'll tell you what. If you wait a month or so, I'll see what you want done."

"I want an addition built onto my house."

"Oh yeah. You did say." He searched the cupboard for a clean plate but couldn't seem to find one. Then he turned to the sink, rattled around in the stack of dishes until he excavated a plate, held it under the cold water faucet, wiped it on his shirt, and speared the biggest steak Hannah had ever seen, flopping it on his plate.

She swallowed, thinking of that plate.

He waved in the general direction of the remaining chair. "Sit."

Hannah sat. She turned her head, her eyes taking in her surroundings. An old davenport with blankets and a pillow. His coat and hat thrown in a corner. The rug was mainly mud.

"Where's your wife and children?" Hannah blurted, never one to let good manners hold precedence over blatant curiosity.

"Don't you know?" His look was incredulous. His eyes turned dark, a greenish color like brackish water below tree roots in a drought. A bitter light illuminated his eyes, his mouth set in a hard line of control. "They all died."

"All? How many were there?"

"Just her. And two unborn babies. Twins. Her name was

Leah." His voice grated now as it dragged over remembered pain. He blinked, his eyes focused as on a faraway scene, as if pictures played over in his mind. He shrugged and said it was the way of it. What're you gonna do?

For once, Hannah was speechless. Her throat constricted with jammed-up words that threatened to choke her. Suddenly, her eyes burned with unshed tears of shared pain. When she finally did find her voice, she said, "Right. Well, I'll be on my way. You'll let me know?"

He nodded, a forkful of half-cooked beefsteak on its way to his mouth.

Thelma Johns moved to her daughter Shirley's house about three weeks later. Hannah had ridden with them to a lawyer's office in the city of Lancaster to settle for the property. She fell thoroughly out of the good graces of the lawyer with her impertinence but was soothed by the gentle Shirley and deposited back at the Stoltzfus farm in a huff.

Hannah's family descended on her newly acquired house armed with brooms and pails, rags and soap, vinegar and baking soda and lemon juice.

Manny pushed the reel mower, Eli and Mary raked piles of sweet, succulent grass, running and bouncing and shouting in the early summer sunshine. Hannah washed windows upstairs, leaning out over the windowsill to tell the kids they were worse than wild calves.

Mary stopped, looked up at Hannah. Eli turned an expert cartwheel, righted himself, shook the grass from his hair, and grinned.

"Jump down on this pile of grass, Hannah!" he shouted.

"I guess not! You know you're both old enough to behave yourselves."

"We are behaving!" Mary shouted back.

The woods surrounding the little brick house resounded with the happy cries of the children. Doddy Stoltzfus smiled and smiled. His eyes twinkled at the children's antics as he applied a screwdriver to a loose hinge, and tapped a nail into a broken windowsill. He told Hannah he thought she had chosen wisely. The house was well-built.

Hannah shone with a new happiness at her grandfather's words. She felt validated, lifted above the sense of many failures that dogged her steps.

"Well done, Hannah," he'd said. But he did not approve of the dry goods store. That was only in the planning stages, so there was no sense in sniffing out other people's opinions. The bishop, bless the dear little man, held the ultimate decision.

Or did he? Hannah wasn't ready with an alternative plan if he batted down the whole idea. She knew she wasn't about to disobey openly, but she also wasn't planning on giving up. She would find a solution.

Her determination had served her well on the Dakota prairie, and it would serve her well here in Lancaster County, too.

What was wrong with a woman owning a dry goods store? In Proverbs, the husband praised his wife for her crafting skills, the selling of her wares in the marketplace. She even purchased an acre of land.

So, there you go. A woman had the right to some form of entrepreneurship, as long as it was decent, necessary items she was selling. And what was more sensible than plain broadcloth and cotton and denim for men's work trousers, buttons and snaps, and so on?

Thelma had left the overstuffed sofa, a brown monstrosity that Hannah eyed with a critical sniff. Shrugging her shoulders, she said she didn't know what else to put in the living room. She certainly wasn't going to buy a new sofa.

Sarah suggested covering it with one of her everyday quilts.

But Hannah shook her head. "Quilts slide every which way. I hate a quilt on a couch." So, that was the end of that idea.

Sarah gave her the armless rocking chair, the table in the sunporch, and an extra chest of drawers. But the house looked barren. Unclothed. Cleaned and polished to a high shine, the floors glowed and the windows sparkled. The bathroom fixtures and mirrors shone. Yet there was no coziness, no warmth.

"It's the curtains," Mary trilled, after standing in the doorway of the living room to survey the clean, nearly empty room.

"Mam, do I have to hang green, roll-down window blinds?" Hannah asked.

"Yes, of course. That's our *ordnung*. You know that."

"If you want me to hang them from my window frames, you're going to have to buy them."

"No, that's your responsibility, Hannah. You're capable enough to take care of such matters."

So, she did. She obeyed her mother by going to the hardware store in the town of Intercourse with measurements carefully written on the back of a calendar page.

Manny helped her install them, which made the house look Amish, but did nothing for an aura of hominess.

The family helped her move in, with her meager belongings put in place in an hour or so. Sarah turned to Hannah, shook hands with her, and wished her the best in her *forehaltiss*. Her grandfather told her gravely to keep her door locked. Manny promised to bring Marybelle as soon as he could. Then they all climbed into the spring wagon and were gone down the road before Hannah had a chance to feel emotional.

So, here she was. All alone in the house of her dreams.

Silence reigned everywhere. The floors echoed when she walked. A faucet dripped. Windows creaked. The green blinds flapped in the open windows. She needed so many things. She had no refrigerator. And she had no idea where to go to use the telephone, or the number to call the Ice and Cold Storage Company for ice delivery. She needed a gas stove and a propane company. She needed a horse, a buggy, a harness, and a pen built into the small shed at the end of the drive. She needed more dishes, pots and pans, bedding, towels—just about everything.

Well, one day at a time.

She sat in the armless rocking chair, her hands clasped loosely in her lap. She felt that the rooms around her were enfolding her with a certain safety. The golden sunlight, the variety of green colors, the blue sky and the breezes that were gentle, the hidden trust that it would rain whenever they needed it, one season following another in order and sameness.

She had nothing to fear. That was something, wasn't it? Now, if the bishop would only hurry up with his answer, and if that Dave King wasn't too busy, she'd soon be on her way. Her first priority was getting a refrigerator. She'd have to find the nearest telephone.

She began her search by walking down the road until she came to a house similar to her own. There were children in the yard and a small, brown dog. When she walked up to them, they stopped playing and stood and stared at her with frightened eyes. The dog jumped up and down with the force of its high, yipping bark.

"Is your mother at home? May I speak to her?"

"No!"

Yip. Yip. Yip, yip, yip from the dog.

Hannah looked around, not quite knowing what she should do.

The screen door on the porch was flung open. A thin, pretty woman with blond hair to her shoulders appeared, calling out to Hannah. "Hello! You must be the new neighbor that moved into the Johns house."

"Yes. I am."

"It's nice to meet you. Come on up on the porch."

Hannah met her on the steps and noticed the friendliness that shone from her eyes. Their faces were level, with the blond-haired woman on the top step.

"I'm Diane Jones. My husband, Tom, is at work at Myers Refrigeration. The two children are . . ." she rolled her eyes, "Diane and Tommy Jr."

Hannah laughed. "We Amish often name kids after their parents, too."

"Well, my husband is a stickler for tradition."

They sat in the metal porch chairs, sizing each other up with practiced eyes. Hannah thought Diane was lovely, which caught her off guard. She almost never liked someone right off the bat. Diane thought Hannah could be a model, so tall and with that striking face. But there was something hidden in the depth of those black eyes that was unsettling.

The children clambered up onto the porch—blond, blue-eyed, perfect replicas of their mother. The dog sniffed Hannah's legs. She pulled them back behind the seat of the chair, as far as they would go, and resisted the impulse to push him away. She despised small, yappy dogs. This one was a terrier of some kind. The worst. She eyed him with a baleful look. He eyed her back. Why did small dogs do this to her? Hannah had no idea, but she had a premonition that he'd love to sink his sharp, little teeth into her ankle. She'd bet anything that the minute he saw her arriving with no children to control him, he'd growl, make a beeline for her, and yes, take a chomp out of her ankle.

"What's his name?" she asked, pulling her mouth into the semblance of a smile.

"He's Toto," the small boy lisped, picking the dog up to let him nuzzle his face. Hannah watched and swallowed, thinking the dog would probably give the small boy parasites.

"I came to use the telephone to call a refrigeration company. But I see you might be able to help me if your husband works at Myers."

"He does. Isn't that great?" Diane asked, clearly pleased to be of service to her new neighbor.

That problem was soon solved with Tom Jones delivering a used ice box, ice, and a second-hand stove. Before the week was up, she was equipped with a useful kitchen, all for the price of sixty-five dollars.

One evening, a horse and carriage slowed, then turned into her driveway. Hannah peered through the living room window and saw two somber-faced ministers wearing grave expressions.

She smoothed her hair, yanked her covering forward, and pinned it securely, hoping to convey a sense of *demut* (humbleness) and *gehorsamkeit* (obedience).

"*An schöena ovat,*" one of them said, "such a pleasant evening."

"*Ya,*" Hannah nodded, her shoulders hunched in an attempt to appear sorrowful. A bereft widow, in need of sympathy and approval.

She was told kindly that they had conferred among themselves about her proposal. Hannah's heart beat rapidly. Her head felt as if it might explode. She bit her lower lip and watched those serious faces with a sense of doom.

"It would be best if you gave up the idea," one minister began. "But, Ezra thought that if you promised to stay small and sell only the kind of fabric our women could use, and if you would be frugal in all of your dealings, we could allow it and see if you are capable of such a venture. However, you should have your grandfather, who is an esteemed elder with a good sense of business, to oversee your accounts on a regular basis, as women tend to become sidetracked where sums of money are concerned."

Gratefulness warred with irritation, but her face remained passive. She didn't ask about the addition and they didn't mention it, so she thanked them in the most humble manner she could manage. They made a few minutes of small talk about the weather, wished her the best in her new undertaking, and then left.

When the carriage had disappeared, Hannah's elation knew no bounds. She smiled, whirled across the polished floor, lifting her hands in thanksgiving. She was on her way!

A list started to form in her head. She needed that addition to her house, then she could stock the fabric, and she'd need to get a horse and buggy. She'd also need to have a stall built in the garage. Could she really afford it all?

Well, one step at a time.

CHAPTER 19

DAVE KING HAD HIS OWN OPINION OF WHERE AND HOW THE ADDI-
tion should be built. He stood in the hot morning sun with his
faded straw hat pulled low over his forehead, his white shirt
stained with perspiration and about two sizes too small for his
hulking shoulders.

"You don't want the addition on that side of the house. If you
put it there, you'll never be able to enter your kitchen through
the side door without going through the store. You won't like
that."

A searing flame of rebellion shot through Hannah. "I guess I
know what I'd like and what I won't."

He had the nerve to laugh at her. "You want to lock and
unlock the door every time you go in and out?" he asked.

"I'll use the front door."

Their eyes met. The challenge sizzled between them like the
angry buzzing of bees.

"Well, I guess that's it, then. I'm not building anything until
you use some common sense."

With that, he strode to the car, spoke to the driver, and took
off, leaving Hannah standing there with her mouth hanging
open in disbelief. She was so angry she kicked the doorstep and
banged her big toe. It hurt, but she didn't care.

She'd get Elam and Ben to help her. That big lummox wasn't going to set foot on her property, ever again.

She began to think about the side entrance, the row of hooks on the wall. The more she thought about it, the more the truth dawned on her. Dave King was right. Well, one thing for sure, he'd never have the opportunity to find out he was right. What did he care about? It was her own business. If she paid him, he was supposed to supply a building according to her wishes, not his.

A poor excuse of a carpenter, she decided. He should be farming like the rest of the Amish men his age.

Dave King showed up about a week later, standing in the rain on the stoop at the side entrance, his bulk shutting out the gray morning light. "Did you decide?" he asked by way of a greeting.

"No."

"Well, I thought of a solution. Why not put the store on the opposite end of the house?"

"No! That's not going to work. I won't go through my bedroom every time a customer shows up."

"You can sleep upstairs."

"Look, I don't need your services. My brothers can build what I need."

"What do you want?"

"Oh, come in out of the rain," she said, irritated at him standing there as if he wasn't aware that he was getting wet. She stepped back to allow him entry and watched to see if he'd take his shoes off. Of course, he didn't.

"Your shoes are wet," she said pointedly.

No answer. Of all the nerve! Rude. Ill-mannered. At least he could give her some sort of reply.

It seemed like he filled up the entire kitchen. Her house was very small with him standing there. She watched him as he turned his head from side to side, assessing, measuring, calculating.

He was actually not bad looking with those amber eyes and

rounded nose. Actually, Hannah thought, with a good shave and a toothbrush, he might be attractive. But his size! And his curly hair. Like untamed wool.

"Your feet are wet."

He bent to look at his feet. "Not my feet. My shoes."

She felt scolded. She wasn't sure but she felt a blush creeping into her face. She sincerely hoped not.

"Why don't you go out the back with your store?" he asked suddenly.

"There's no door."

He shoved his face forward, much too close to hers. "That's what carpenters do. They cut doors where they want them."

She stepped back, feeling like a blushing school girl. Which infuriated her. "Is that right," she shot back, her dark eyes blazing.

He laughed, then. He had the gall to stand there and laugh at her!

"Come here," he said. He extended an arm, and looked out the window by the sink. She walked over as one hypnotized.

"Look. Here is where we will put your door, okay?"

Unbelievable! She felt that massive arm come up and his great, heavy hand came to rest on her shoulder. She was aware of his size, his nearness, his warmth. The scent of his shirt did not repulse her. Spicy. Some oddly comforting mix of lumber and summer and leather and fresh mown hay.

Hannah swayed, quickly righted herself. Her breathing all but stopped. She resisted the urge to turn and lay her head on that powerful chest and tell him she didn't want a store. She just wanted to go home with him and wash that pile of dirty dishes, sweep the mud out the door, and sleep in his bed.

All of this rushed through her head like a strong summer thunderstorm, leaving her deeply ashamed and berating herself internally with firm words of self-loathing.

Jerry was barely gone. With Jerry firmly in her mind replacing her thoughts, she crossed her arms and thought of stepping away, but didn't. Couldn't.

She'd never felt like this before. She was lonely, grieving, in sorrow. That was the only explanation that made any sense to her.

"See this window?" Dave was asking. "I'd put a door in here and a few steps down to the lower level and there's your store! Inexpensive. Easy. You'll want windows, though. Women need to see what they're buying." He grinned down at her.

Hannah almost wept with the depth of her feelings. When he stepped away from her, she felt disoriented, leaning against the countertop for support. When he let himself out, she found herself reaching out her hand to stop him. Why was he going home now?

She watched him as he stood in the backyard, his eyes taking in the length and the distance to the clothesline. Without thinking, she let herself out of the door and joined him, her arms crossed as if to protect her heart from galloping off without her permission.

"Shingles or metal roofing?" he asked.

"Which is cheaper?"

"Metal goes on quicker. Less labor. But shingles look nicer."

"How much ch . . . cheaper?" Oh, now she was stuttering. Ch . . . ch . . . like a baby chick!

"I'd say a hundred dollars, maybe more."

"That's a lot."

"I know. But you have shingles on this roof, so it won't look right if you use metal on the new section."

Hannah nodded. He was probably right. But, where was her irritation? She felt as if she had been cast into a whirlpool, spun around, over and under, and spewed out on dry land. Disoriented, dizzy, as if she needed a map to guide her, to tell her which road to take and how many miles there were to her destination.

What was her destination anyway?

Her eyes narrowed as she watched Dave King pace off the length and width, his boots coming down like thunderclaps. Pulling out a tablet, he scribbled notes with a yellow pencil, gazed across the backyard, and thought out loud, like she wasn't even there.

She wanted to jump up and down, wave her arms, let him know she was there standing on the lawn, in the rain. She felt a sob rise in her throat. The rain was falling so softly and gently, leaving grass and flower beds smelling so sweet. She had never known rain to have an odor. It was like liquid ambrosia, nectar from flowers.

Water dripped off his straw hat. He looked up and smiled at her. "Better get in out of the rain," he said.

Hannah turned to go. Yes, better get out of the rain.

Dave King followed her but stopped on the stoop, poked his head in the door and said, "I'll get a rough estimate for you sometime this week." Then he was gone.

Hannah watched the truck back up, turn around, and chug off through the rain. She began to cry, soft little whimpers and a runnel of tears that sprang from her eyes and dripped off her chin. She swiped at them, furiously, trying to make sense of her sudden and overwhelming change of feelings.

She was lonely. Too many changes in too short a time. Jerry's death too sudden. There was nothing left to do but sag into the armless rocker, her hands dangling down on each side, her head tilted toward the ceiling, seeing nothing.

Where had all of this come from? Something had to change before he brought back the estimate. But she knew she had never felt this way before. Not with Jerry. Not with Clay. A wave of humiliation swept through her. She felt pity for Jerry and a longing for him. He had already diminished, growing smaller and smaller, already moving away into the far reaches of her memory, if she were honest. Jerry's face had become shadowy, no longer clear.

Surely God had something to do with this. She had never been close to God, except when she called out to Him in desperate situations, of which there had been plenty.

If God was allowing Dave King to come into her life, He'd need to let her know somehow. Never devout, Hannah simply sat and stared, wondering how to pray, vaguely acknowledging a Higher Power, but without proper words to turn her thoughts into an actual prayer.

She tried, instead, to focus on her business. She hoped she'd have enough money to build the store and stock it with a decent amount of fabrics. She had no idea how to go about contacting the textile mills or a wholesale store. Surely there was one. If she could find Harold Rocher's address or telephone number, he could give her all sorts of useful information. But she would need a Baltimore, Maryland phone book. Getting his information would be like looking for the proverbial needle in a haystack.

Hannah sat and watched the rain, heard the musical patter and the gurgling of the downspout. She imagined the limp, withered green grass in the lawn taking in the droplets, the soil becoming moist. She envisioned happy little earthworms aerating the ground, tunneling through the mud and grass roots.

The leaves from the oak trees dripped with moisture. Green and velvety, as thick as a crocheted curtain, the leaves spoke of health and steady growth each year, the roots buried deep under the surface, taking in the nutrients and moisture that was supplied without fail.

She thought of the West, where there was little moisture. Rain failed. The brittle drought, the endless, searing days parched throats and left the cows searching endlessly for grass and water.

And still she had loved it.

Now, what to do with the rest of this day? She wondered how long Dave King would take to finish his estimate. She should have offered to help him with his dishes.

He did not return.

Two weeks. Hannah went to church with Manny. She worked in her house, arranging, cleaning. She baked bread and a pie. She helped a farmer pick cucumbers and green beans. For a half day of backbreaking labor, she received one dollar. It was enough. She returned the following day and picked bushels of lima beans and more green beans under a sultry, sweltering sun, the air thick and wet with humidity and portent.

Straightening her back, she scanned the thunderheads in the distance. They looked like piles of black sheep's wool, with gray, threatening sky stretched from one horizon to another, the sun erased by scudding clouds.

She didn't mind the approaching storm. She bent her back and continued grabbing the stubborn lima beans, ripping them from their stalks by the handfuls with her strong fingers. If she could finish this row, she'd likely make two dollars, enough to purchase the few groceries she'd need for the week.

As Bennie D. paid her, his eyes scanned the skies. He told her she'd better get on home.

Hannah knew she'd picked too long. She could smell the rain, sense the wind in the churning clouds. But she'd left her windows open so she'd risk the hike home. If she got soaked, it was better than her house getting soaked.

As soon as she was out of his sight, she ran, her arms pumping at her sides, her feet flying along the road. She could hear the oncoming wind like a freight train and feel the moisture being propelled by the wind.

The storm hit her about halfway home, the wind taking her breath away, the rain slashing its fury into her face. She winced at the brilliant lightning followed by a drumroll of thunder. Rain streamed down her face, pelleted the top of her head. In a few seconds, she was soaked through her cotton dress.

The trees above her bent and swayed, lashed by the strength of the wind and rain. Her breath came in gasps. She heard the crunch of gravel behind her. Headlights pierced the barrage of rain like giant cat's eyes.

She slowed, unable to catch her breath, the water streaming down her face. The truck pulled up alongside her. The driver yelled at her, some watery garble she couldn't absorb, so she shook her head.

There was a blinding flash of lightning. Electricity sizzled through the atmosphere, followed by a horrendous thunderclap. She didn't hear the slam of the truck door as she continued marching through the torrential downpour, determined to make it home to close those windows.

Suddenly she was hauled back by two arms as thick and powerful as hawsers. She tried to scream, but only a hoarse, wet sound gurgled from her mouth. She was stuffed unceremoniously into a slippery upholstered truck seat, floundering and spluttering like a half-dead fish.

She wiped water from her eyes with the backs of both hands. Him!

"What's wrong with you?" His way of greeting.

Angrily, she glared at him with all the power of her black eyes, her face glistening, her hair a sleek, black cap. "I would have made it home," she stated forcefully.

Another blinding flash and a deep, reverberating roll of thunder. The windshield wipers were almost useless. A gust of wind rocked the truck. The air in the cab was heavy with moisture, stuffy with lack of oxygen, the driver hunched over the steering wheel, gripping it with both hands, his eyes searching for her house.

Hannah was dripping water over everything. When they

turned into the driveway of her house, she nudged Dave King and told him she needed to get out. Her windows were open.

Her house was soaked. Water streamed through both kitchen windows, spraying through the screens as if someone held their thumb across the nozzle of a hose. She ran to the bathroom after yanking the windows shut, grabbed towels and proceeded to mop up the ever-widening puddles of water.

She yelped, remembered the upstairs, dashing up the stairs and clunking the windows shut, hard. Clattering back down for more towels, she saw him at the sink wringing out towels, twisting them with those arms like logs.

Between them, the house was wiped clean—windowsills, walls, and the floor. The bucket was emptied and the towels were placed in the wringer washer.

Dave King leaned against the kitchen counter, his straw hat pulled low over his eyes, his arms crossed, and told her that if she saw a storm coming out of the northwest, she should stay put. And keep her windows closed when she went away on a sultry summer day.

"You know, if your windows were open in your store, you'd have a bunch of ruined fabric," he finished.

That raised her ire. "I'm not that dumb. If the windows of my store were open, I'd be here," she said, loudly.

"Still, you need to respect these Lancaster County storms. They can come up pretty quick."

She scowled, thinking he had no idea what a real storm was, what kind of weather she had survived out West.

Outside, the rain had not let up. Sheets of wind-driven rain pummeled the window glass and pounded the roof. Rivers of water sluiced through the downspout, the gutters overflowing in a sloppy current that splashed along the front of the porch.

Lightning lit up the dark kitchen as jagged streaks snaked

through the air, followed by claps of thunder like rifle shots. The wind howled. When hail began to bounce against the window panes and leap in the yard as if it was alive, Hannah had to admit to herself that it was a legit storm.

She ran to the living room door to watch the icy balls hit the lawn, bounce up, and fall back down in the watery grass.

She was aware of his presence behind her. She winced as the blue-white lightning illuminated the darkened house and endured the hard crack of thunder without showing the weakness she felt. She shivered.

"You're wet. Go change your clothes," he ordered.

Hannah went.

"I'll put on the tea kettle."

When Hannah emerged from her bedroom, she'd toweled her hair dry and was wearing a clean navy-blue dress with no apron. Her feet were encased in warm, black slippers. She was carrying her hairbrush, her hair a tousled, glossy mane spilling down her back. Tilting her head to the left, she began the slow task of removing the tangles, unselfconscious, watching the rain through the living room windows.

Dave watched her from his stance beside the kitchen stove. When she turned to say something mundane about the weather, he couldn't take his eyes off that tangled thicket of glossy black hair. He thought he'd been over those kinds of feelings. The loss of Lena and the babies was a heavy weight he carried around with him no matter how hard he tried to discard it. Grief and sorrow were like that. It took you to the depths of black loneliness and longing you'd never forget. After a few years, he'd honestly thought he would never feel the attraction necessary to become friends with another woman.

But there was something different about Hannah. She had given him quite a jolt the first time he met her. Later he decided he would do well to forget his initial attraction, given that attitude of hers. She was an angry, ill-mannered, brusque young woman; he didn't need that kind of challenge in his life.

He was too old to be swept in by a woman's looks alone. His mother had always said, "Choose your wife by considering whether she would make a good mother to your children." Hannah was anything but motherly.

Born the youngest in a family of twelve, Dave had known plenty of teasing, plenty of rough and tumble with a line of older brothers above him. He'd grown up kicking and pounding and running away from them. Now, there was not one of them who dared lift a hand to his massive strength.

He'd simply kept on growing and building muscle after the others had reached their full growth. And he didn't take any nonsense from anyone. Never had. It was his method of survival in a tribe of rowdy siblings.

He had fallen hard for Lena. Petite, soft-spoken, her hair like spun wheat, she was everything his brothers were not. He'd worried and prayed and was afraid for her frail body. When he took her to the hospital, there was nothing they could do to spare her or the babies. Too much infection.

He had entered a deep, dark place of intense suffering for a longer time than he cared to admit. He became obsessed with his work, the drawing of plans, the endless hard labor that became his saving grace.

Angry and blaming God, he retreated into a hermit-like existence until the kindly, old bishop came to visit him, his wife bringing his favorite dish of *schnitz un knepp*. They explained Lena's loss as a chastening and a polishing of a clay vessel that needed refinement.

After they had left, he wept most of the night, waking to a new day with the anger and self-pity banished forever by the kindly, old bishop's healing words. The death of Jesus on the cross for his sins became brighter and more real than it had ever been before.

And now, here was Hannah, like a sultry temptress. He couldn't be sure.

She turned, grimacing, as the hairbrush hit an especially large snarl. "Does it often rain like this? You'd think anything unfastened would be washed away."

He wanted to answer, but he couldn't. Not right away. He wanted to take the hairbrush away from her and run his hands through that luxurious mane of heavy black hair. Her large dark eyes were on his, waiting.

So powerful was his attraction to her, he had to gulp for air and was afraid he'd have a heart attack right there in her kitchen. "Uh . . . no. Well, yes, sometimes. But only in summer."

She finished with the brushing and reached back to grasp her heavy hair, expertly wrapping some sort of elastic band around it.

Then he had to put up with her nearness, the scent of her hair like spring rain and some tropical flower he couldn't name. His senses swam as he took a piece of tablet paper out of his pocket, pointing a finger to some numbers.

"Yes, yes." She nodded her head, agreeing, and sending off a fresh wave of floral scent.

"We can start in about ten days, weather permitting." All business now.

"And, what if the weather doesn't cooperate? I mean . . ." She spread her hands to indicate the downpour outside.

"Then it'll be later."

"And I'll be picking lima beans longer."

He laughed. "And getting caught in storms."

She smiled. Their gazes held. Both wondered if there could be love without pain.

Soon after Dave King left, the sun sank in a blaze of glory, illuminating every drop that hovered on blades of grass or beaded a gentle flower. The corn produced great yellow ears, every kernel filled in by the aid of the moisture that seeped up through the sturdy green stalks.

Hannah walked among the wet flowers and eyed the fields of healthy corn that grew like a miniature forest. She thought of her father.

She felt a growing sympathy that edged out her irritation and blame. No doubt that he'd imagined this for the prairie. Verdant growth for acres on end, spreading to the edge of the horizon. Life-giving rains, fat cattle that ambled among lush prairie broom grass, timothy, and all the other nutritious native grasses that grew wild, feeding his cattle at no cost to him.

He had traveled all that distance in faith believing that God would provide. Believing until it turned into human determination, eventually pushing him over the edge. The sadness of it clung to her in a new, claustrophobic way, until she no longer experienced the beauty of the glistening world around her.

Her mother. How had she endured? Well, it was in the past. She needed to move on. But that was difficult. What if she was to begin a friendship with Dave King? Would her irritation, her dislike of people, eventually pull them apart?

To explain his amber gaze was not possible. She could memorize, easily, the roundness of his nose, his full cheeks, his thick beard, and the indentation of the thin line of his mouth. So different from Jerry's features. No dark hair, dark eyes, the face she had come to know as well as her own.

All that wooly, curly hair. Hannah stepped up on the porch and sat on the wooden rocking chair her grandfather had given her, tucking her feet under her skirts to dry them. She gazed across the green lawn.

What would have been the outcome on the plains with rain like this? The wheat. Her father's corn crop. The cattle. Well, it wasn't the way of it. Not in the West. That was likely the reason it was so sparsely settled, whereas here, in this blessed valley, the soil and the climate drew people from every imaginable corner of the world. Immigrants from Ireland, Poland, Germany, Switzerland, the Netherlands. All sought a better life or religious freedom. Often both. Her own ancestors had arrived on some creaking, storm-tossed vessel, persecuted Swiss brethren who made their homes in Pennsylvania.

No, their homesteads. Some of these farms, most of them actually, had already been handed down for generations, and would remain in families for many more. So, a homestead could be anywhere folks chose to live, to prosper, to raise their families, live their lives in harmony with the folks around them.

Hannah smiled and tucked her feet into her skirts. This was her homestead. This adorable house with the kitchen cabinets painted white, and the hardwood flooring that shone from much polishing.

She loved every little corner, every clever closet tucked away throughout the house. She loved the curve of the railing that followed the stairway to the second floor and the built-in medicine cabinet and green tile in the bathroom.

Without Jerry, this would not have been possible. She laid her head on her propped-up knees and whispered a thank-you to her deceased husband.

Remorse was a terrible thing. That was the main reason she would have to stop her idiotic pull toward the carpenter. She would only become testy, irritated beyond control, and then she would speak harshly and be determined to have her own way.

She could never be a proper wife.

But still, he'd persuaded her to build the store where he thought best. That was something, after all.

Chapter 20

He told her the price, which was far less than she antici-pated.

She hid her elation under lowered brows, pursed lips, and what she hoped was a professional look, the aura of a business woman. She asked, "Can't you do any better than that?"

"Hey, look here! I'm already scraping the bottom. Giving you discounts here and there, you being a widow and all."

The old irritation. "I'm not poor," she snapped.

"I didn't say you were. Just wanted to give you a good price."

"Well, I hate the label of 'poor widow.'"

He couldn't help wondering how she had any funds at all, having lived in North Dakota all that time. Her husband must have had some money, or else she certainly couldn't have afforded all this.

He wore a white, short-sleeved shirt, the muscles of his mas-sive arms bulging from the too-tight sleeves, his neck rising from the open collar like the trunk of an oak. Buttons missing, a hole torn in the back, his trousers ripped, safety pins serving as but-tons in more than one place.

She avoided his amber eyes, deciding she would not allow herself to drown in their unexplainable depths.

Hannah winced when the machine arrived and tore up her back yard like a scissors to cloth, digging the footer, leveling the ground, removing chunks of turf like slices of cake and tossing them aside. A truck wheezed in, a solid chunk of cement blocks was unloaded, and the concrete mixer put to work by the tug of a rope on the gasoline engine.

Dave King strode among the men and machines, clearly the lord of his own domain. Two Amish boys with clean-cut jaws, their straw hats tossed aside, bent their backs and laid block like pros, with quick, precise movements. Dave worked along with them, whistling and watching everything with a practiced eye.

Now, she needed to find a supplier of fabric, a wholesale company from which to order the goods she would need. She thought maybe the post office in New Holland might be the best place to begin, but she needed a ride there. She really needed a horse and buggy, but she wasn't sure she could afford one until the store was up and running.

Dave came to the back door. "I forgot to bring my water jug along. Mind if I get a drink?" he asked.

"Help yourself."

He drank like a camel and said he'd be back for more if it was all right with her. She nodded, then quickly blurted out her predicament. He listened, fastening his eyes on her face. "If you wait until Saturday morning, I'll come by and give you a lift."

She made the mistake of meeting his eyes, becoming consumed by the warm, golden light beneath the brim of his old, darkened straw hat with rawhide string tied around the crown.

The kitchen disappeared. She felt unanchored, thrust into a world without gravity, unsure of anything she had ever been or what she would ever be. Her self-assurance, the reliance on her armor of anger and irritation was dissolving like sugar in boiling water, leaving her stumbling for a foothold, grasping for something, anything to hold onto.

His voice broke the spell. "If you have nothing else planned."

"Planned? Planned?" She couldn't imagine what he meant.

"I'll take you to the post office. Didn't you need an address or a telephone number?"

"Oh, that. Yes. Yes, I do." She felt like a child caught stealing candy. Her face flamed with an unimaginable embarrassment like she had never felt before. Then, there was nothing else to do but save herself from feeling smaller and smaller, that hated inward cringing, the self-loathing that was like an uncomfortable burr in a woolen sock. She glared at his brown work shoes and told him gruffly that he had mud on his shoes. Couldn't he respect a woman's floor?

He let himself out but not without seeing her discomfort, a cynical smile playing around his mouth.

When the door closed behind him, she locked it. Then she sat on the brown davenport feeling so miserable she wanted to die. Not really die, but at least fall into a faint so she'd be temporarily free from these churning insecurities. He made her feel like a bumbling teenager, and when he left, she wanted him to come back immediately!

She was frightened by her lack of understanding. It couldn't be what folks described as falling in love. Or could it? She did not love Dave King. Didn't even like him. She had never been in love and had no plans to be.

Like a moth trapped in a spider web, she beat against the confines of her self-inflected prison, hurting herself in the process. Where to turn? Who to ask? Her mother? No, she couldn't ask her mother. She was, or had been, a married woman. How could she ever approach her own mother with such an unusual question?

She had, quite simply, no idea where to turn. Hannah had never had the kinds of friends who spoke of liking boys and how it felt to be in love. This could not be love. It was misery!

How would she ever be able to sit beside him in a buggy? Buggies were so narrow. You could barely keep six inches away from the person sitting beside you.

Hannah took a deep breath to steady herself. She tiptoed to the window to peer out, checking to see if he had gone back to work.

He wasn't there. Now where had he gone? How could he have disappeared so fast?

For the rest of the week, she considered calling a driver, walking all the way to the Jones residence to use their telephone to let him know she would not need to go to the post office.

She thought of hiding in a closet or in the basement so he'd think she wasn't at home. Or, she could always lock the door and crawl under her bed. He'd drive in, knock, and eventually leave again.

No, she was turning into a sniveling, wet dishrag, a person with no backbone. She'd just march right out to his buggy and ask him to leave. She had no need of his assistance.

She thumbed through the six dresses she owned. Red? Too showy. Purple? Oh, she couldn't wear either one. She was a widow, so if she was going to be seen in public, it had to be black. She was in mourning for the traditional year, the time allotted by the Amish *ordnung* to dress in black.

She washed and ironed her black dress, cape, and apron, then fell into an awful despair of indecision. Should she wear a cape, or not? He might think her too fancy if she went without it. If she wore one, she'd look as though she was dressed for church.

She washed and starched her best white covering, ironing it with utmost care, using a paring knife to pleat the gathers properly.

Picking lima beans was out of the question. All week, there was no sign of Dave King's carpenter crew, which drove Hannah to distraction until she remembered that he was building a dairy barn over close to Leola at the same time he had worked her addition into his schedule.

By Friday evening, she sat herself down calmly, hands folded in her lap, working on her resolve to remain aloof and in full control of all her senses. She'd speak primly like the sorrowful widow she was.

He would surely respect her. She would keep her eyes averted demurely, accepting his kindness for what it was, an offer to get her to the post office. After that was decided, the realization hit her like a sledgehammer. He had absolutely no interest in her. If he had any romantic inclinations he'd never be seen with her on the streets of New Holland.

Never. It would be breaking all the rules of tradition, of respect. Well.

Well, that was interesting. All this craziness of washing and ironing and starching and pleating for nothing.

A thin drizzle was falling Saturday morning, a mist with the sky a dome of milky gray. No trace of the sun. The air was humid, tainted with the smell of summer's end, aging beanstalks and wet, crumpled weeds hanging like scraggly fur by the roadside.

Hannah threw on an old navy blue dress, pinned her everyday apron around her waist without bothering to see if it was straight or if her *leblein*—the fold of cloth sewn on the waistline—was in the center. She didn't wash her hair and left the clean covering in the drawer for church. Instead, she wore the slightly yellowed one she wore most days. Now that she realized he had no romantic interest in her, she felt much freer. She'd get over her own nonsense soon enough. It was probably just exhaustion from grieving and all the excitement from buying the house and starting her business.

Untroubled, at ease, she met him at the stoop, smiled, and

said she'd get her purse. Then she climbed into the buggy and sat with her hands in her lap.

"Ready?" He looked at her. In the dreary light of the rainy day with the humidity like a tropical rain forest, her skin glowed luminous, an olive hue to her tanned face. Her eyes were large and dark, her lips parted softly.

There was no avoiding touching him—his large frame took up most of the seat, leaving no gap between them. Her shoulder rested comfortably against his. Her leg touched the coarse texture of his denim trousers, but that was all right. No different than being seated beside Manny or Elam. Like a brother.

But he kept looking at her, even after they had pulled out on the road, the horse traveling at a fast clip through the gloom. Rain misted the horse's back like a glistening dew.

"Did your husband ever tell you that you are beautiful?" he asked suddenly, his voice low and gravelly, as if he had a sore throat.

Shocked, Hannah stared straight ahead, blinking rapidly. "Yes, he did. I think."

"You think? You don't know?"

"Yes, he did."

"You are beautiful."

She said nothing. Her mind had gone blank, as if an invisible eraser had wiped away any ability to speak or think. Now, how was she supposed to handle a situation like this?

"You've never had children?"

Stiffly, she told him they hadn't been married very long.

"Tell me about the West."

"It would take a long time to tell you about my life in North Dakota."

"Good. Then I'll come over this evening and we can talk about it."

"That wouldn't be proper."

"Why not?"

"Why would you? You have no interest in me."

"What makes you say that?

"You are going to New Holland. To town. If you . . . well, nothing."

"What?"

"Drive your horse. He's pulling toward the middle."

No more conversation was forthcoming. Her lips were sealed, as if padlocked. They drove into the town, tall brick buildings lining both sides of the street, automobiles parked on each side. Teal, blue, red, and silver trucks with metal racks or trucks with no racks at all. One gleaming vehicle contained one passenger wearing a white fedora and smoking a fat cigar, eyes half-closed in his wealthy insolence.

Hannah thought of the rusted out, dusty trucks of the West, wheezing and gasping, black smoke from overheated oil pans rolling behind them, loose wooden racks flapping like crows.

It took her a long time at the post office. The post master was a grizzled, stooped, and bent old man, his spectacles sliding down his nose with alarming regularity. His rheumy eyes examined her face as if he doubted her sincerity.

"Ball-ti-mer?"

"Yes, Baltimore. In Maryland."

He shook his head. "Big city."

"I know."

Shuffling to a back door, he returned with a dog-eared copy of telephone numbers from various states. Humming to himself, he pushed his glasses back up on his nose with an arthritic index finger.

Hannah shifted her weight from one foot to the other. She drummed on the countertop with her fingertips. She read every poster on the wall.

"You said Rocher, right?"

"Yes. Harold Rocher."

The humming resumed.

"If you'll let me . . ." Hannah began.

"No, no. I'm getting there. Rogers. Richard. Hmmm." Satisfied, he thumped the cover of the book and said, "Nope. Ain't no Rocher livin' in Bal-ti-mer."

"May I have a try?"

The bell above the door tinkled. It was Dave. Hannah looked up. "I'm going down a few blocks to the feed store. I'll be right back."

Hannah nodded.

"Look, I seriously need to locate this man. If you'll allow me to try . . ."

Reluctantly, the old post master handed over the book. Hannah found the Rocher's address and telephone number in a few minutes. She asked to use the telephone.

"Pay phone."

"That's all right. I need to contact this man."

Hannah dialed zero, spoke to an operator, and dropped the required amount of coins in the slot, waiting breathlessly until the third ring. She felt an unexpected rush of emotion when she heard Harry Rocher's compassionate voice. "Hello. Rocher's."

"Hello." Hannah swallowed, blinked back the moisture that filled her eyes. In a thick voice she said, "This is Hannah. Hannah Detweiler."

A pause. Then, "Hannah!" His voice took her back to his general store. Back to the scent of fabric and tools, coils of rope and plowshares and shovels, the dust, the blowing wind, the horse waiting in the shed till day's end. Then there was the long ride home across the blighted prairie clutching the staples that would keep her family alive, a bag of cornmeal and one of flour.

She bit her lip, blinked furiously, sniffed, and concentrated on a war bonds poster that said B uy U.S. B onds.

"Hannah! Dear girl, how are you?"

"I'm fine. I'm living back in Lancaster County. I want to start up a dry goods store and I need information on wholesale companies," she said, her voice thick with unshed tears.

"You're back in Lancaster? That must have been hard. I know how much you loved that homestead. How's your mother?"

"She's good. She lives with her father, my grandfather."

"You know, we don't live so awfully far apart. My wife and I would love to come and look you up. Guess what I'm doing? Working in a restaurant as a chef!" His excitement rose above the static on the line. "I love it. Love it. In the evening, I walk down to the harbor, feed the gulls, and watch the water. It grows on you, Hannah. Human beings are resilient. We bounce back. Doris is a different person. Oh, you have no idea. She sings, the radio is always on, she dances and visits her parents every day. You know they're old. You know what I cook? Fish, scallops, shrimp in olive oil and garlic, lobster—all of the food that comes from the sea. I love it. I love it."

Hannah could barely get a word in edgewise to remind him about the information she needed.

"Oh yes, yes, of course. I'll send it to you. Still have it all. I'll put it in an envelope, one of those brown ones." And then he was on to more descriptions of his colorful life.

When Hannah finally placed the phone receiver back in its cradle, she had used up all of her dimes.

So, that was Harold Rocher's reward. He had given in, accepted his wife's unhappiness, and did something about it, even if it meant a huge sacrifice for him, leaving the place he truly loved.

She thanked the postmaster, who grunted in her general direction. Hannah thought he was too old to be a postmaster. Weren't there some kind of rules about that? Old grouch! He needed to go home, make himself a cup of tea, and cover his knees with a blanket.

She told Dave that the old guy at the post office had to be a hundred years old. He laughed, loosened the neck rope, and backed the carriage up by drawing gently on the reins and pushing against the shafts.

He asked if she was able to talk to the person she wanted to ask information from. Hannah nodded, watching the horse's ears.

He tried again to spark conversation. "The old guy not very efficient, huh?"

"Hmm-mm."

They rode back along Main Street, carefully avoiding parked cars and trucks as big as houses that bore down on them. The towering brick buildings were stacked together like bales of hay, wedged tight. Hannah fought the feeling of being smothered by too-tall buildings, an excess of motor vehicles and pedestrians, everyone moving, their faces expressionless, not making eye contact, as if actually meeting someone they knew would destroy their single-minded goal of keeping to their schedule.

She breathed deeply when the town slid away and open fields and forests met them in their natural state—green, brown, and a dull yellow.

Dave looked over at her. "You don't like the town?" he asked. "I heard you did not want to return to Pennsylvania."

A pinched, "You don't know."

He drove on whistling under his breath, watching the scenery to the right, wondering what had produced the bad mood of his passenger. He did want to stay for the evening and hear her story. He wanted to get to know her better, or at least try to understand her. There was no doubt, he was intrigued and captivated by her.

He did not try to keep a conversation going but merely drove his horse and ignored his glowering companion.

As they approached her house, she seemed to brighten a bit.

She sat up straight as if the black mood had been left in New Holland at the post office. Until they reached the driveway.

"You can let me off and then leave. No need to turn in the drive." Her words were brittle and caustic.

Where Jerry would have agreed and gone on down the road thinking everything was all right and he'd bide his time, Dave put up an argument.

"You can snap out of it, Hannah. You have a lot of nerve getting all riled up by an old man who was doing the best he knew how. I didn't cause your bad mood and you're not taking it out on me."

Her mouth dropped open in surprise. She was not used to anyone standing up to her when she was in one of her black moods. She controlled her family with them. And she'd easily handled Jerry with them. When she was out of sorts, he made excuses for her and did anything he could to appease her. Only on a few occasions had he ever stood up to her. And here was this man, someone she barely knew, accusing her of wrongdoing, when it was all his fault.

His yellow gaze was not golden or warm and certainly did not cause her to go spinning off into a warm and lovely place of confusion. It was like a spark to gasoline. A clear, burning distaste for her behavior flickered from his amber scrutiny. A black blaze began in the depths of her own dark eyes. Without thinking she shot back, "Of course it's your fault!"

No one ever spoke to Dave King in that manner. Without giving her the benefit of an answer, he hauled back on the reins, the horse obediently lowering its haunches as it leaned against the britchment and pushed the carriage backward. A loosening of the reins in Dave's hands, a call to go forward with a hard tug to the left rein, and Hannah was conveyed unceremoniously to the stoop at the side of her house.

"Get out!"

Hannah got out. Stumbled out to be exact. She watched helplessly as he drove past her. She wanted to stamp her feet and yell at him to come back here right now because they had things to discuss. But it looked as if that would only make everything worse.

She didn't know whether she wanted him to leave or tie his horse. When she saw him climb down and unhitch—unhitch!—she was at a loss. What in the world? He had unhitched his horse, which meant he planned on a lengthy stay and not only an hour or so. In broad daylight! What if someone came?

Frantic now, she felt her knees weaken. Should she be afraid of this man? Embarrassed to be standing as if she had grown permanent roots down through the gravel, she kept her gaze on her shoe tops.

"Is your door locked?"

"No."

"Then I'll let myself in."

There was nothing to do but follow him in. He threw his hat on the table (didn't he know what clothes hooks were for?) and walked into the bathroom. He turned on the spigot and began soaping up, splashing water all the while.

Hannah did not know what to do. This big galumph marching into her house and using her bathroom as if he owned the place. Well, at least he washed. No one should ever drive a horse without washing their hands afterward.

He returned to find her standing by the table as if her one hand was nailed down on top. Her face was pale in the dreary afternoon light.

He pulled out a chair and sat down. As wide as the table. "All right, now. How was that mood my fault?" he asked.

"You're so dumb."

"Oh really. If I'm so dumb, you're sure you want me to go on with this addition?"

Not friendly. Not one word was meant to appease her, to make her feel better. She whirled away from the table, stomped down the hallway and was halfway to her bedroom, when she heard his footsteps like cast-iron pans thumping after her. Grasped firmly by his oversized hands, she was effectively stopped, then turned back toward the table, and not very gently.

"Just go on home," she breathed.

"Not until you tell me how this is my fault and why I am evidently extremely dense."

"Let me go!"

His hands fell away and immediately she felt their absence.

Her face was an open map of misery. He appeared calm, curious, settling slowly into his chair while Hannah collapsed into hers, her hands shaking.

Finally, she spoke. "All right, you asked, and I'll tell you how it is. If you drove to New Holland in broad daylight without caring at all if other Amish people saw us, it's obvious you have no interest in . . . in being my friend. Young widowers do not go sporting about town with widows their own age. You know that."

She could see he was amazed. Delighted, even. A broad grin creased his golden eyes, crow's-feet like combs on each side of his face, his smile spreading as he absorbed her words.

"So, you're upset that I'm not interested in you?"

"No. I mean, yes. Well, no. I just don't want people to talk. You know . . ."

"Well, I don't care what people say. Not now, not ever. I haven't in the past and I have no intention of beginning that bad habit. I live my life in the sight of God, trying to do what's right, and that's it.

"Am I interested in you? Should I be?" he finished. His eyebrows raised and his eyes were on her face.

He really should do something with that hair, Hannah was thinking. She kept her eyes somewhere along the top of his head, then let her eyelids fall, turning her gaze to her knees, which was the safest place with that look in his eyes.

He laughed outright. Reaching out, he touched her hand, then took it in his own. Her hands were not small, for a woman, but his engulfed hers like a baseball glove.

"Hannah, look at me."

When she did, the dark watching of her eyes melded with the amber search of his, creating a nameless space filled with light. She felt a complete knowing of his intentions, the goodness and depth of this man, the harmonious chord with the earth and its creatures, and God, above all. He would never need to mention his faith, or his love. It was all the same, forever.

After that, there were no words. The tug on her hand became an embrace as Hannah found herself held against that wide, deep chest, his arms holding her delicately as if he was cradling a small child.

He sighed. She felt his chest move, felt his breath on her hair. "Hannah, I am interested in you. You intrigue me. I want to know what makes you happy and sad and angry. But you know as well as I do that we both hold pain and fear. And you, it would seem, have a problem with telling the truth."

CHAPTER 21

THE LIGHT IN THE HOUSE SHONE OUT THROUGH THE RAIN. DAVE'S horse waited patiently in the shed. His ears flicked when two hands pulled on the window in the main house, lowering it against the falling rain. When nothing happened after that, he dozed off, to be awakened by two mice racing along the top pine board, squeaking, then tumbling off behind a few cardboard boxes.

Hannah and Dave sat at the kitchen table. Dave listened to her speak about North Dakota from her cache of memories. He watched her face, felt her sorrow, her joy, her helpless rage, every disaster and every disappointment that had seeped into her soul, creating who she had become. The only thing that bothered him was her senseless determination, the power she wielded by her own anger and selfishness, her family as compliant as bread dough.

As was his way, he told her this. A long silence followed. Then, "But I hated the thought of returning to Lancaster County."

"I know. And you were young. It's just that you and I getting together could be a full-on disaster! No one bosses me around. Lena was so mild, so meek in her spirit. And you . . ."

Suddenly, he asked why she'd married Jerry when her family returned to Pennsylvania. "His money," she answered. "The homestead couldn't go on without funds to start over after the drought."

"You didn't love him?"

Hannah turned her face away and shrugged her shoulders.

"That wasn't fair to him. Hannah, you use other folks for your own advantage."

"He wanted me. He agreed to everything. And he won me over, in the end."

"You loved him then?"

"I guess. I don't know. How can a person tell if they love someone?"

Dave was flummoxed, completely at a loss. Red flags of warning waved in the air, so real he could almost feel the breeze. He changed the subject, realizing that he needed time.

Together, they made a pot of chili with red kidney beans, ground beef, green peppers, and yellow onion. He added a can of corn, said he didn't like chili without it. She made a face, but he told her to try it. She'd probably never had it that way before.

He used a tablespoon to eat his chili. Hannah became worried that she may have underestimated the amount in the pot. He emptied all the soda crackers and ate a large bowl of applesauce. Taking out a pound of Lebanon bologna, he ate slice after slice on bread with mustard. Then he asked if she had pie or cake.

They washed and dried the dishes, side by side, talking about his interest in the construction world, how he got his start, and his plans for the future. She could see his incredible energy, his passion for his craft as she tried to understand his lack of interest in farming.

They parted late at night, each feeling the amiability between them, as well as the danger, the lack of trust. Did it make sense to try again after the flaws in their past? They circled, wary, their spirits eyeing one another, then moving back, yet drawn to each other by an invisible cord.

Hannah watched the mailbox for Harold's package almost as much as she watched Dave and his men as they erected the addition. It was amazing to watch the plate being bolted to the concrete that had been poured into the cement blocks. From there on it was like children building a house with Tinkertoys, except this was life-sized. Hammers swung, driving nails as if they were merely straight pins.

The roof was being put on the day her wholesale catalogs arrived. She left the package in the mailbox, not wanting Dave to see it. She wasn't talking to him, had avoided him all week. Allowing him to sit in her house and eat with her with all his oversized familiarity was going at breakneck speed down a steep, slippery slope. It would not happen again.

It was nice to feel her heart speed up as she remembered the feel of those massive arms being so careful of her. But there was always the memory of Jerry and her blatant mistreatment of him. Above all there was the humiliating truth that she didn't know what love was, or if she had ever been in love, or fallen in love—however you wanted to say it.

Very likely, if she were to marry Dave, it would be the same story. So it was safer, much safer, to stay away. He'd never asked her for a date, just sat in her house as big as a furnace and made himself at home. The amount of food he ate was alarming!

She thought of the size of her garden and the canning she would have to do. At least a hundred quarts of applesauce; perhaps a hundred and fifty. Would he eat an entire quart of canned peaches in one sitting?

Hannah snorted.

She worked on ordering supplies for her store with the help of her mother, who knew what type of fabrics the housewives would buy. Her grandfather kindly offered to finance some of her purchases, but Hannah waved him away. She was an independent woman, capable of managing her own affairs.

Ben and Elam worked on the shed in the back, converting it to a small horse barn, complete with a hydrant and underground water pipes from the new addition. They donated their old courting buggy, without a top, an open-seated, rattily old thing that suited Hannah just fine.

John Esh came to see what the addition was for, the nosy old thing. But then, she figured word would have to get around if she wanted any business, so she'd better train her thoughts along a more hospitable line. People like John Esh irked her so badly. Swaggering up to the carpenters with half the manure from his cow stable stuck to his cracked leather shoes, at least a week's growth of stubble on his cheeks. She was certain that the bulge on one side of his face wasn't a toothache. She'd been around too many tobacco-chomping ranchers to miss that wad of brown, juice-producing plug.

"Well, Davey!" he had boomed that day, his voice bringing her to the window immediately. It was as if he was announcing a hurricane!

Dave stopped his work and came over to him, pushing his hat to the back of his head, a huge grin on his face.

Hannah stepped back from the window. He liked this man. Well, good for him. Dave knocked on the back door and told her John had a horse for sale, a brown standard bred he'd sell for a hundred dollars.

Hannah drew down her eyebrows and said nothing for a while. Then, "Not without seeing him."

Smiling, Dave said, "I'll ask him to bring the horse over. He lives a few miles from here." Hannah nodded. When there was no returning smile, Dave went back to John, wondering why Hannah still intrigued him with that terrible attitude of hers.

Hannah's words were clipped, almost nonexistent as she negotiated the sale of the horse, a small, brown gelding with a white star on his forehead and one white foot.

John Esh began by touting the merits of his wonderful horse, smiling too much with that lopsided, swollen cheek. She told him the horse looked like a camel and surely needed to be wormed.

"Aw, come on. Now you're just driving a hard bargain, lady." His grin widened, eyes sparkling.

"I won't pay a hundred dollars. He's not worth it."

Taken aback, John Esh's smile puckered like a released rubber band, his mouth becoming pinched as a pained expression crossed his face. He made the usual mistake most folks made when they came in contact with her cold glare.

He smiled, wheedled, bowed, scraped, did anything to get back into her good graces, which had never been present to begin with. "I'll throw a harness in for a hundred."

"No doubt it won't be worth it, the way your shoes look."

John looked down at his offending shoes with beginnings of a fiery blush creeping up his neck.

In the end, she got her way. A horse, a harness that was perfectly serviceable, all for the frugal cost of one hundred dollars. She also got the boiling disapproval of Dave King, coupled with a vow to make restitution to that poor man, John Esh. She was planning on being the proprietor of a store? Well, he was having a talk with her.

Which he did, arriving unexpectedly on Saturday morning, his day off. He caught her off guard, downstairs cleaning the basement, wearing an old *dichly* over her uncombed hair that had not been washed for the better part of a week.

Dust swirled around her as she plied the coarse straw broom. A horrendous pounding on the side door propelled her up the steps, her heart racing, certain there was some emergency or calamity in the neighborhood.

Dave King.

She stopped and glared. "What?"

"Don't you ever use a normal good morning or hello?" he asked, his eyes not friendly, the brim of his straw hat serving to enhance his hostility. Almost, she shivered.

"Depends on who it is."

"So, I don't merit a greeting? Obviously, that poor John Esh didn't either." He pushed past her, threw his hat on a peg, went up the steps like a steaming locomotive and put the kettle on. Hannah followed, completely at a loss for words.

How dare he? She hadn't even invited him in. She certainly had not offered him a cup of tea, or whatever he had in mind with that teakettle. And he was angry! About John Esh.

She sat down. Then she remembered the dust in the cellar and got up and closed the door. She stood hesitantly, like a truant scholar, unsure what the teacher was going to say.

"Sit down."

She sat.

"You know, Hannah, if you are going to be operating a store, this simply is not going to work."

"What?"

"You don't like people. If you treat one customer the way you treated John Esh, word will get around and you won't have one person coming to buy your fabric. I don't care how nice it is or how low it's priced. You were rude, ill-mannered, ignorant, and downright mean. It's uncalled for."

Hannah leaped to her feet. "Out! Get out! It is none of your business how I choose to treat people."

Coolly, he looked at her in the brilliant morning sunlight that slanted in through the kitchen window, the snarls in her uncombed hair, the crooked *dichly*, the dust that had collected at the edge of each flaring nostril, turning them black. He took in her heaving chest and her steaming anger.

"Yes. It is. I'm working for you. I'm building your store. You are going to be out of business before you even begin. Take my advice, Hannah. Otherwise, your store is a lost cause."

"Get out of my kitchen!"

"No. The water isn't boiling and I'd like a cup of tea."

Emotions crashed and collided in Hannah's mind. She knew he was right. He also made her so mad that she wanted to punch him. Physically pound him with her fists. Helplessness fought with her anger and spilled over to quench his attraction. The sheer muscular size of the man, his arms and shoulders, his eyes and oh, just everything. She couldn't go marching out of his sight the way she'd done that once because that would mean he'd come after her and . . .

What she did do was slide back down into her chair. Thrusting her legs under the table, she crossed her arms while leaning against the chair back, adjusting her famous glare, her lips pulled in and pinched tightly together.

He got down two cups and found the tin canister of tea. Hannah had always been able to control those around her. Her inability to dominate Dave, to conquer him, tilted her whole world toward the steep slope of confusion. Even now, she scrambled to understand her thoughts.

What if she tried his way of dealing with people? Wouldn't it be a sort of protection? If the store failed, it wouldn't be her fault—it would be his, for convincing her to behave differently. It would be a kind of barrier against failure and disappointment. Of course, it would all be fake. She'd have to pretend to like people, which she really didn't—especially men.

Dave poured the tea and brought it to the table. He asked if there was pie. "It's nine o'clock. My break time."

"It's your day off. And I don't take a break."

He chose to ignore the winds off her iceberg. Going into the pantry, he lifted tops off containers until he found half of an apple pie. Yodeling with appreciation, he brought it to the table, going to the cupboard to find plates, a knife, and forks.

"Got any cheese? Apple pie is twice as good with cheese."

"I don't know."

"You don't know if you have cheese? Or you don't know if you like it with apple pie?

"Oh, shut up!"

He laughed. She liked the sound of his laugh. Like gravel rolling over stones. "You don't like me, either. Well, we'll just have to work on that."

He ate the entire remains of that pie plus the slice he'd set out for her, which she refused to touch. He ate almost a pound of Swiss cheese, and drank his tea in three gulps.

It was scary, his capacity for food!

He pushed the dishes away and crossed his arms on the table. She wished he wouldn't do that, the way his muscles bulged and all those blue veins ran up over his hands like trails.

"So," Dave asked. "Why do you dislike people like John Esh? The poor man. It was worse than seeing a cat play with a mouse, torturing it before the kill."

"It wasn't that bad," Hannah shot back.

"It sure was."

Hannah had no reply.

"It's un-Christian. The Lord tells us to love our neighbors as ourselves and you sure don't hate yourself."

"There you go, getting all preachy."

"You need to be preached to. You need to go to church and learn the ways of a Christian. Your attitude toward others is worldly. You're all about yourself, just like the world."

"You know, you aren't really being a good Christian yourself, sitting here numbering my faults like some sort of self-righteous Pharisee."

"You think?" He laughed again, the sound she had to admit

she loved. "I guess you're right, Hannah. I'm just concerned about your business is all. Plus . . ." His voice became very deep, cross-grained with feeling. "I would love to spend the rest of my life with you. I'm not one to cover anything up for pride's sake. I say what I think and feel. You are so terribly attractive, but I'm afraid of your . . . well, Hannah, you're just not a nice person."

"Thanks!"

"I'm trying to figure out why."

Hannah took a deep breath. She avoided his eyes and shook her head. Then, "You try being shamed and humiliated, cast out of all you know at the tender age of twelve. Riding in an old spring wagon with a tarp thrown over its ribs, with two old worm-ridden horses, a *schputt*!

"People either made fun of us or pitied us. I had a ghost-like mother who floated above the wagon, never really present. A father who was crazy in the head. We were hungry, Dave. Hungry!"

For a long moment, he said nothing. The clock on the shelf ticked loudly. A drip from the faucet echoed through the silence.

Then he said, "Boo-hoo."

Thinking she hadn't heard right, she said, "What?!"

"I said, boo-hoo."

Furious, she spat out, "Now *you're* making fun of me!"

"Yes, I am. You're the shining example of someone who blames their parents for the not-so-nice person you are today. That was in the past. It's over. Get over it. Forgive and forget and move on. Live a life free from all that garbage. God allowed all that in your life, so evidently there is a purpose.

"You know, Hannah, did you ever think that all the cruel weather, hunger, drought, all that stuff you told me, could have been avoided if you would have obeyed your mother and come back home to Lancaster where she wanted you to be? Did you ever think about the children of Israel's wandering in the desert when they were led by Moses, a man of God? Same thing. God could have led them all in a straight shot to the Promised Land, but He led them through trials and awful crazy stuff to teach them lessons. If they refused to learn, they perished!

"If you never learn to move on and stop blaming that godly mother of yours, or your imperfect father, you'll never get any further than being in your own tight cocoon, spun by a web of your own making, a dark prison where you sit and glower at other people with hate-filled eyes like you did to John Esh."

She said nothing, running her forefinger around the rim of her teacup.

"It may be cruel to speak to you like this, but I have a strong hunch no one ever had the backbone to do it before. Am I right?"

"Jerry did, some."

"Bless Jerry's heart. He must have been a great guy."

"He was." What kept her from pouring her heart out, confessing her mistreatment of Jerry and her ongoing remorse? She knew Dave deserved to hear it from her. How did he know . . . ?

She blurted out, "How do you know my mother was godly? Still a saint?"

"I had a long talk with her at your husband's funeral. I wanted to marry her, except for her age."

Hannah's mouth dropped open. "My mother? But . . ."

"I would have, except for you."

She stared at him, uncomprehendingly. "What are you talking about?"

"I'm teasing." He reached across the table and draped his enormous hand over hers. "I wasn't interested in your mother the same way I am in you. But she did remind me of what Lena would have been like had she lived to your mother's age. Your mother's a good woman, Hannah. It wouldn't kill you to admit it."

Hannah pulled her hand away, returning it safely to her lap.

He had no idea what her family was like, no idea what she'd been through. He barely knew her, and it was probably better to keep it that way.

The weekend was spent alone, the last cloying heat of August making Hannah even more miserable than she already was. All Dave had told her banged around in her head, giving her a tremendous, pounding headache until she put her fingers on either side of her head and groaned with the pain. She shed her clothes and went to lie down on her bed. But there wasn't even the whisper of a breeze, the curtains hanging stiff and straight, the air sultry with humidity.

She should have gone to church at Levi Stoltzfus's. Her mother would be disappointed by her absence. Manny would be searching the rows of women, eager to spot her face among them. But she hadn't felt up to dressing in her heavy black garments, with all the turmoil going on in her head, not to mention the steady weeping of her heart.

What if Dave's words were true? All that suffering, and all her fault? No, he hadn't said it that way. He'd merely stated the obvious. Could she have avoided it all? Of course, but she wanted the homestead. She had been determined to keep it. The truth was her life had also been enriched. The wind, the wide-open spaces, her communion with earth and sky. She'd come to know the weather patterns intimately, all as diverse as human faces.

She'd found reserves of strength and courage she could never have imagined. She'd loved and lost and yes, she had also learned. And here, her face burned with shame.

She had risen to her former level of dictator-like cruelty with her *grosfeelich* treatment of John Esh. Right in front of Dave.

Well, Dave didn't understand. It was all that manure on John Esh's shoes. That wad of tobacco in his cheek. Let Dave go and marry her mother. Hannah was certainly never going to be like Lena, the "perfect wife," his little angel. If that's what he wanted, he better keep looking. The man had no social graces himself. Every word out of his mouth served to put her in her place. It was like herding a good milk cow into a stanchion.

She tried to picture herself running the store, acting like she enjoyed people. She imagined John Esh coming into her store as she smiled sweetly and asked him to please wipe his feet. She could put a spittoon in her fabric shop. She could do it. Couldn't she?

She got up, shrugged into her dress, squinted into the mirror, and decided she looked old and mad and ugly. She pulled her mouth back into the caricature of a smile but felt she looked a lot like the witch in *Grimms' Fairy Tales.*

Why did he have to say that about her mother? He had said he was teasing, but she wasn't sure. Why wouldn't a man want a sweet, submissive, pushover wife instead of a mean-spirited, stubborn woman like Hannah? When she imagined her mother and Dave together she was taken captive by a fierce jealousy, one that made her want to slap them both.

Finally, when the heat became too oppressive, her thoughts as heavy as rocks, she dressed in her black Sunday garments, hitched up the brown gelding, and drove. She drove out to the Old Philadelphia Pike and turned right toward Bird-in-Hand, the small village where she believed her friend Priscilla had moved after marrying Abner Beiler.

She waved at oncoming teams, practicing the friendly gestures she had never much cared for. It felt fake, like she were pretending to be another person entirely. She allowed her eyes to glass over, giving her a sense of anonymity, as if she were a wax figure or a see-through spirit.

The sun beat down on the black bonnet that covered her head. Her black clothes grabbed at the fierce sun and held its heat to her skin. The horse (she still had to name him), a gallant, willing animal, kept up an even trot, the white foam that sprang from his sweating hide a testimony to her lack of a good washing before she had thrown the harness on his back.

Everywhere she looked there were farms or houses, sheds, automobiles, people in buggies. A black car roared past with a young boy hanging out of the window, his nose pinched between a thumb and forefinger, gesticulating, mimicking the smell of her, the horse and buggy, or both.

Hannah longed for a handful of ripe horse manure to stuff in his face, until she remembered she was pretending to be nice.

Well, what of it? She was only who she was—no more and no less—and thoughts couldn't hurt someone anyway, right? Could she help it if little boys like that made her want to retaliate? She wasn't a saint. She wasn't her mother, either. And she certainly wasn't Lena. If she was smart, she'd never give that arrogant Dave King the opportunity to compare the two of them.

She rode through the village of Bird-in-Hand, eyeing houses, going under the train tracks that ran over the arch of cement and stone bolstered by sturdy iron and tons of concrete, she hoped. She pulled on the right rein, on a whim, thinking she'd take a side road and find some shade to allow her horse a rest. Perhaps there'd be a passerby from time to time and she could inquire about Priscilla Beiler's whereabouts.

The horse slowed to a walk, then stood obediently beneath a canopy of maple branches with leaves like a heavy, green cloak, stirring faintly as if afraid to disturb the heat. Hannah loosened the neck rein on the horse, then fanned her face with her apron, finally wiping it across her neck and cheeks to dry her streaming perspiration. She scanned the hot, metallic sky for signs of a cooling thundershower, but there was none, not the slightest indication of relief.

There were no passersby, no one walking, not a buggy or a

car in sight. She didn't want to knock on doors to make inquiries, so she drove home in the stifling heat, a strange melancholy settling over her shoulders.

It was odd, this being alone among so many people. She had always relished isolation, but that was different, in North Dakota. To be alone on a great and glorious prairie was to be one with nature and the earth and God—all the same thing.

Here, she was alone, while others walked or rode together, sat down together at mealtime, drinking and eating and sharing their lives.

She sighed and decided to name her horse Flapper for the way his loose haunches flapped when he ran. Flap for short. "I guess it's just you and me, Flap," she said, thinking she was glad for a companion who couldn't berate her, question her, tell her she was a bad Christian or how poorly she compared to other people.

CHAPTER 22

HANNAH'S STORE WAS OPEN FOR BUSINESS ON THE TWENTIETH OF September. She stood behind the counter, the green metal cash box below her on a shelf, a small, speckled composition book to tally the day's sales beside her.

The room was almost square with white painted shelves along every wall, and a wide counter down the center of the room. The windows along three sides allowed plenty of natural light to enter, illuminating the area where women would inspect the various bolds of plain and patterned *duchsach* with calculating eyes.

Buttons, thread, bias tape, rickrack, elastic, needles, straight pins, hooks, and eyes. The list was endless. Manny had made small wooden bins to hold the notions. He'd painted them blue and brought them one Friday evening, as a surprise.

Sarah donated her best pair of Wiss fabric-cutting scissors. Hannah refused, at first, saying, "No, no, Mam. Not your Wiss scissors." But she knew they would make her task easier.

She would sell scissors in the future, but stocking her shelves had taken almost the whole of her bank account. Harold Rocher had given her access to some of the best textile mills in the Northeastern United States, so she was set to make a profit.

Dave King had been paid in full, the check handed over to him without fanfare, her face a cold mask. She had spoken only what was absolutely necessary until his part of the deal was over. And that was how things stayed.

He went home shrugging his shoulders and telling himself she could take him the way he was or stay alone. She told herself she had had enough of being told off. He could wash his own dishes and live by himself. She'd never be sweet and submissive, and if she didn't like people, well, he wasn't going to dig up some deep psychological reason for it that would only make her feel worse.

She welcomed her first customer, Sadie Lapp, a thin-as-a-rail spinster with a nose like a parrot's beak and a squawk to match. She roamed the store with a condescending air, asked dozens of questions that Hannah answered politely, although with an air of stretched martyrdom. Sadie bought one yard of white covering organdy, holding on to every dollar as long as she possibly could, counting out her own change twice, then folding the coins in a tiny leather packet. She lifted her apron and rummaged in her pocket to make sure the purse was beneath the large men's handkerchief nestling there, which had been used and reused, if her horrendous, honking, nose-blowing was any indication.

The effort to stay amiable drained Hannah. She stood behind the counter, her arms feeling like dishrags as she took slow, easy breaths.

All forenoon, then, women arrived. Some were brought by their husbands. Others drove teams themselves. Babies were slung on hips, carried around by strong arms attached to muscular shoulders. Big women, some of them. Big and rangy and uglier than a mud fence. But friendly, openly excited about Hannah Riehl's store.

At first, the smile she plastered on her face felt awkward and every bit as fake as it was. But as customers commented on her nice selection and her cash box began to fill, a natural excitement lit up her countenance. Her cheeks turned pink, a rosy glow surrounding her as she dropped coins into the metal box and folded dollar bills carefully, laying them down neatly as she did so.

"Do you have quilting thread?"

"No snap buttons? The kind you sew on?"

"Where's the chambray?"

Each time, Hannah was able to help, showing them the item. If there was something she didn't have, she wrote it on a tablet, to be ordered immediately.

At the end of the day, she had a little over sixty dollars in her cash box. Sixty dollars was wealth far beyond her imagination. She needed to keep it stowed away. Most of the money would go back into buying inventory.

She was sweeping the floor when the door was pushed open barely wide enough to allow two small girls to enter the store. Wide-eyed, their cherubic faces were both frightened and adventurous. They slipped in like a soft breeze, then stood uncertainly, staring at her.

"Hello," Hannah said, setting her broom against a shelf.

"Good evening." They spoke in low, well-modulated voices, sounding much older than their size. Hannah was held in the grip of two pairs of very blue eyes.

"May I help you find something?" she asked.

"Our brother is sick with chicken pox." The oldest girl cleared her throat. "Our mam sent us to see if you have baking soda and Epsom salts." The words were spoken clearly, without the usual lisp of a child.

Hannah shook her head. "I'm sorry, but I don't have those things in my store. Only fabric and other things that are used for sewing clothes."

Hannah was pinned behind the counter with a clear blue gaze. "You should. Mothers need those things sometimes."

Hannah agreed quickly. What was it with these small children holding her directly responsible for her lack of wisdom? "I have both of those things in the house if your mother would like to borrow them."

"Yes, she would like to."

Hannah hurried to the medicine cabinet in the bathroom and came back with both items. The girls were rooted to the same spot, just inside the door, their feet as still as if someone had nailed them there.

"You can just take these containers. I have more. Then you can return them sometime later," she told them.

"I think that would not suit my mam. Please pour some in a small poke and we will pay for it with the money she gave us."

Feeling as if she was under some strict requirement from a judge to obey them, Hannah did as she was told, without argument. She charged them twenty-five cents, which the girl handed over without hesitation, staring up at Hannah with unwavering blue eyes.

"Thank you."

With that, the girls turned and left, leaving her with the distinct feeling that she had fallen short. What odd little girls.

Well, she had met all sorts of women today, starting with that first old maid, Sadie Lapp, and ending with the two little girls. She was bone-weary. Her shoulders ached with a deep dull throb and her neck was stiff. She leaned her head from side to side and worked her shoulders to loosen them, smiling at the ceiling.

Cash. She had all that cash. She would label her first day a success. What a turn her life had taken now.

She swept the floor, surveying her small store with a sense of satisfaction. She knew her job at the hardware store in Pine had been for a reason. She had never imagined that those days spent arranging shelves and cleaning for Doris were anything other than a necessity, a means of survival.

Like Harold, she, too, lived now in an area she had been fiercely opposed to, but she was learning that it was possible to become accustomed to another environment, another way of life entirely. Going to church, interacting with strangers—women of her own faith but strangers nevertheless—seeing her mother and siblings, living among a close-knit community held together by a patchwork of fields and crops, clusters of woods, ribbons of creeks, all crisscrossed with roads and dotted with towns. This area was a beehive of energy, swarming with all sorts of human beings, the exact opposite of the vast open land with only waving grasses and the wind for company, the air as clear and pure as she imagined Heaven's to be.

She shook her head to clear her thoughts, then let herself out the door to feed Flap. He nickered, welcoming her presence, shook his head up and down as if to remind her that it was high time for a feeding. She scratched his forehead and told him he was a faithful steed. Common looking as all get out, but faithful.

He needed a pasture, a small plot of grass to eat. A place to kick up his heels and get some exercise in between his jaunts on the road. She could do it. She would have to put in some posts, but she'd seen it done plenty of times. She'd watched the Jenkins boys dig holes and set posts. All she'd need were locust posts and a few rolls of barbed wire. That meant she needed to make a trip to the neighbors to use their telephone to call the sawmill and she'd need to go to Zimmerman's Hardware for the barbed wire. She wished she could talk to someone about the cost.

Would a hundred dollars be enough? She couldn't use the sixty she already had. That needed to be set aside for new inventory. For a moment, she wished for a partner to help with all these things, but then she stopped herself. All that bowing to someone else's will, negotiating every problem that presented itself . . . it simply wasn't worth it.

The cold winds of autumn were already rustling the brilliant fall foliage by the time Hannah began digging post holes. Her work at the store kept her from ordering the posts immediately and then the delivery took an abominably long time. She knew she could wait until spring, but in her own driven way, she began digging until her fingers were covered in painful blisters that popped, exposing the tender layer of skin beneath. Still, she kept digging, her fingers covered with white adhesive tape, setting posts with aching shoulders, tamping down the dirt around them with a heavy digging iron. Blood seeped from beneath the adhesive tape, mixing with dirt and perspiration, but she kept on working feverishly every evening as the daylight hours became less and less.

She fell into bed, exhausted. Her back and shoulders burned with fatigue, her fingers and the palms of her hands throbbed with pain. Far into the night she lay awake, turning miserably, trying her best to lay her hands in a comfortable position. She thought about the cash she had from her store and wished she had a dog. It would be extremely comforting to know that a good watchdog would alert her to any prowlers.

Every morning she turned her face into a smiling, friendly shine, washed the painful blisters, and applied fresh adhesive tape. She hid her pain and bit back the winces that came unbidden.

That evening, she stopped digging and stood surveying her accomplishments. She still had over half of them to go. The pain in her left hand was excruciating. The dull ache had turned into a biting, heated thumping that made her sit down, unwrap a strand of tape, and hold her hand up to the golden autumn sunset.

Her whole hand was grotesquely swollen now. Bewildered, she lowered it, clutching it with her right hand and trying to decide what she should do.

Slowly, she got to her feet, only to find a horse and buggy turning in her driveway. It stopped at the shed, the driver remaining seated. Hannah turned her back to pick up the shovel and digging iron, rolled the offending, bloodied adhesive tape into a clump of grass, and turned to make her way to the visitor. Was it someone needing something from the store?

When Dave King stepped out of the buggy, she thought he might turn it on its side with all his weight hanging on one side. Now what did he want?

Irritation did its best to quench her gladness at the sight of him. So, he had come. Her heart pounded. She willed her painful, swollen hand out of her thoughts and marched ahead, gamely carrying the digging iron and shovel.

"What are you trying to do?" Came right to the point, didn't he?

"What do you mean, trying? What does it look like?"

"Tell me you're not digging fence post holes!"

Closer now, setting her tools against the side of the shed, she faced him. She'd forgotten the warmth of his eyes and the line of wrinkles on the side of his face. Now what was she supposed to do as she was caught under the spell of his golden eyes?

"I am building a fence." She spoke firmly, expertly, hiding away any trace of quivering, her heart pounding in her throat.

"By yourself?" He flung this over his shoulder as he tied his horse to the steel ring on the side of the shed.

"Who else?"

"You should have asked me. I'd gladly help you."

"I can build a fence."

He walked over to the first post, grasped it with both hands, and shook it. It seemed fairly stable, or so it seemed to Hannah.

He said nothing and she asked no questions. They both let well enough alone. If he thought the fence posts inadequate, he kept it to himself. She was not about to ask what he thought, either.

"How have you been, Hannah?"

The wind played with the strands of loose hair, tossed the ends of her black scarf. She wore no coat although the air felt chilly now that the day was coming to an end. "All right."

"Store going well?"

"So far."

After that bit of mundane conversation, words eluded them. Both seemed unsure, stripped of their usual lack of inhibition. For one thing, Hannah felt weak with the pain of her hand, her head spinning as the throbbing worsened.

"I'm going inside."

"May I come with you?"

"Up to you." She stepped inside and sagged into a chair, hoping the shadowed kitchen would mask the extreme pain she was enduring. He stood awkwardly, unsure of his welcome.

Hannah knew it was not going to work. She was so close to tears that she blurted out, "My hand is infected, I think."

"Let me see."

She thrust out her painful hand, swollen and discolored. He moved away from the sink and took her hand in his. Turning it over he bent his head to examine it more closely. He emitted a low whistle.

"You know this could be dangerous, don't you?"

She nodded.

"Why did you keep on going with these blisters?"

"Because I wanted to finish the fence."

He shook his head and thought of pliant Lena, who would never have started such a project. She would have left all the physical labor to him while she sat down in the soft, sweet grass with the gold of autumn surrounding her. She would have admired him and he would have known he was deeply loved and respected for his masculine strength.

Here was another type of woman entirely. Should he help her

with her badly infected hand, then leave and never return? All this circled around in his thoughts as he held her hand. Gruffly, he released her hand and said, "Wood ashes."

She shook her head. "I don't have any."

"Kerosene?"

She nodded yes.

So he soaked her hand in a dish of smelly kerosene, washed it with a mixture of homemade lye soap and boric acid, followed by a liberal dose of drawing salve, black, oily, and vile.

Hannah wrinkled her nose. She was close to tears watching his huge fingers with their fingernails the size of a small spoon, spreading the salve, tearing strips of fabric, and then winding them round and round her painful hand with so much care and precision. The thick curly head of hair above the hulking shoulders with yet another discolored, torn shirt, the perpetual scent of new lumber and soap . . .

"Thank you," she whispered.

He drew back and looked at her with a depth in his gaze, changing his eyes from gold to a deep, murky green that churned with strong feelings of . . . of what? What, exactly, was this?

Neither one understood. For one thing, they barely liked one another. He disapproved of her flagrant determination, her undermining of a man's strength. Her uncanny ability to make him feel worthless, the opposite of his first wife's adoration.

She could not bend him to her will the way she manipulated everyone else most of the time. There was nothing ordinary, nothing normal, between them. Yet, there was this unexplained draw toward one another.

Why did she occupy his thoughts most of the time? He knew it was foolhardy, this hitching up of his horse and driving to her house with no clear purpose. No speech, no prepared words to make his intent clear. You simply did not ask Hannah for a date. She'd laugh in his face and tell him no while enjoying his discomfiture.

She drew back, both of their thoughts driving a wedge between them.

"You know you'll have to repeat that in the morning," he stated, gruffly.

"Not kerosene."

"I'll bring you wood ashes."

"Aren't you going to church?"

"You will obviously not be going."

She nodded. The silence settled between them. Darkness crept over the kitchen. She got up, intent on lighting kerosene lamps, but could not strike a match.

"Here, let me do it."

She stepped aside. The soft yellow glow of the lamplight surrounded them, creating a coziness, a space where home and togetherness joined to form remembered evenings spent with loved ones.

Suddenly, Hannah spoke. "I'll need a fire before long. I wasn't sure if I wanted to bother with wood. I thought maybe I'd try coal. The only thing that keeps me from buying a coal stove is the thought of the harmful gas that can poison the air at night."

"Well, you can't dump a whole bucket of coal on a low fire and turn the damper too low. That's what causes it."

She pondered this. "So, you think wood is best?"

"Not really. With wood, you have the chimney to keep clean and sometimes there's a creosote problem. I'm thinking you wouldn't attempt climbing onto the roof to clean the chimney."

"Why not?"

"Because you might fall and break a leg. Or your back. Or worse, fall on your head and die."

Hannah snorted. Would he care? But she didn't ask.

The evening was turning into a ridiculous word play that didn't sufficiently provide a base for any meaningful conversation.

Finally, after a few self-conscious attempts at repeating bits of daily news and gossip, Dave asked if she didn't drink coffee or tea, or if she had lost the practice of offering some to visitors.

"Get it yourself."

Without answering, he got up to put the kettle on. He sank back into his chair and decided it was now or never. They were getting nowhere and he was afraid of confrontation or of stating his purpose—a state he had never experienced until he met Hannah.

"All right. The reason I came over tonight was to ask what you would say to beginning a regular, every Sunday evening courtship."

"I hate that word," Hannah blurted out.

"Well, friendship then. Relationship. Dating. Getting to know each other better. I don't care what you call it."

When there was no response from her, he let well enough alone and got up to get a few cups, the milk and sugar. He began opening cupboard doors as he searched for tea.

"Left," she directed him.

They sat with their steaming cups on the table. Dave pressed on. "I wasn't planning this, Hannah. But I can't get you out of my mind. So I figure we'll keep going with each other's company so we can find out if we want to get married some day. Isn't that what courtship is? What's wrong with that word?"

Hannah shrugged. "I don't know." Then, "I had an uncle who sang a silly song about froggie went a-courtin', and every time I hear that song I imagine a long-legged, slimy bullfrog like what Manny used to catch and throw at me."

Dave's laughter broke the restraint around them both.

"You're a prairie girl."

"I am. But I can't live there. I had to let the homestead go."

Dave shook his head, his heart in his eyes.

"It was the hardest thing I've ever done. To give up, let go, admit defeat, that was excruciating. I'm not sure if I'll ever get over it. I tell myself this is home, this is where I belong. Anywhere you have a home is your own personal space and you can be happy there. The store is a challenge, and it's fun to see if I can make a profit. But you wouldn't believe how tired I am at the end of the day from being nice to people. Smiling, you know. Helping people. It wears me down. All of this artificial smiling when I'd love to tell that Sadie Lapp to go home, wash under her arms, and eat a piece of cake to sweeten her up. It doesn't matter how hard I try. I just don't enjoy people."

Suddenly, she looked at him with an almost beseeching expression. "Do I always have to live here? I mean, I enjoy being close to my family, but I feel so . . . well, caged in."

"I thought you liked it here."

She pondered his statement, swirling her tea with a teaspoon, biting her lower lip. He could tell she was trying to say what she felt, but could not come to grips with her pride.

"Well, I do, I guess. But if I think of being here until I'm like Sadie Lapp, old and thin and tight and mean, well, I won't do it. You say you want to start a friendship. Does that mean here? No hope of ever moving somewhere, anywhere, where there are wide-open spaces and fewer people but decent weather? I mean, out West the weather is unpredictable. You can't win. Jerry did his best and he could have made it if anyone could have. But those grasshoppers were the final straw. It was the worst time of my life. And yet, it turned me toward Jerry, to . . ." Her voice drifted off.

Dave watched her face and wondered what the truth about that marriage had been. He didn't want that kind of marriage for himself. He was a builder, a carpenter by trade. It was all he knew. He had always planned to do that until the day he died. A few sentences out of her mouth and he was questioning his own vocation.

"I saw in the newspaper at the post office that folks are raising turkeys in Illinois. Amish people started a colony there. What is Illinois like, I wonder?" She spoke tentatively, gauging his reaction.

Dave watched her face. He saw the desperation of a captive suddenly grasping at a glimmer of hope, a ray of light illuminating her dark existence.

"You're serious."

"Of course. If I continue to wait on customers I'll become physically ill from the effort. It's just not me. It's not who I am. Look, this is how it is. I'm a loner. I don't need people and they don't need me. Call it what you want, I don't care. Perhaps I'm not a born-again Christian the way other people are. Sometimes I wonder if I need some spiritual conversion, but I can't be who I'm not. I have no desire to put on a false front so people accept me."

She launched into a vivid account of the two strange little girls and how she scuttled off to supply the items they requested. It was so unlike herself. She should have told them she didn't sell health remedies in a fabric store and to go home and stop bossing her around.

She finished with, "So, it's up to you. If you want me, this is what you get. Life has often handed me a bunch of sour grapes and I like to think I'm improving, year after year. But one thing I know. God knows me and He knows my heart. He gave me this nature so He'll have to help me as I go along."

Dave sat quietly, watching her as she finished her impassioned speech. Then, he got to his feet, found her hands, and tugged her upright. He held her hands, then released them and reached for her with both arms. He held her against his chest in a vice-like grip that took her breath away.

Lifting her chin, he gazed into her eyes in the soft glow of the kerosene lamp. He kissed her, sealing their commitment with the soft pressure of his lips on hers. He drew her closer still until Hannah was filled with the golden light of his love, a sensation that felt new and unexplored, promising a vast, sun-filled land of happiness.

CHAPTER 23

THEY WERE MARRIED IN A SMALL CEREMONY ON THE HOMESTEAD, her grandfather's farm. The stone house rang with *hochzeit velssa*, the traditional wedding songs. The tables were loaded with *roasht*, stewed sweet and sour celery, mashed potatoes, and gravy.

Some said Dave King wasted no time after he met that strange widow, Hannah Riehl, and her husband not long gone. Youthful spinsters pursed their lips, conceding to the loss of yet another available widower.

The more generous in spirit rejoiced with Dave, recognizing the aura of happiness surrounding the couple. Everyone could tell that he had met his match, the brooding Hannah no one really knew. It was a mystery. Who knew what went on in that dark head behind those penetrating eyes.

Sarah had never seen such loveliness and she cried for Hannah. Manny sat with Marybelle and counted the months until next November when she would become his bride. When the strawberries bloomed in spring, he would place his hand on hers and ask her to be his wife.

A week after Manny's wedding, Dave and Hannah moved to Illinois. He built low turkey barns on a vast area of almost three hundred acres of rolling grassland, and raised turkeys by the hundreds.

The farm was located in Central Illinois, close to the town of Falling Springs, with no neighbors in sight. An established Amish settlement, each family had the pioneering spirit, but in an area that had a far more hospitable climate than Hannah had experienced out West.

They paid less for their three hundred acres then they would have for a much smaller plot back in Lancaster County, and Hannah was able to sell her own house quickly and for a good price. They moved into the small, clapboard house. The sun shone and the winds of winter whistled around the corners like good-natured ghosts. Hannah sang and twirled, whistled and hummed her way through the days, embracing her husband and kissing him soundly at every opportunity. She fell in love deeply and thoroughly.

Hannah missed him when he was gone and threw herself into his arms when he returned. She noticed the colors in the winter sky, the deep blue shadows of the snow drifts, and told her husband she loved him every evening and every morning.

They held heated discussions. Dave was like a boulder, rock-solid and immovable. He made the decisions about the turkey barns, no matter how she railed against the idea. She pouted like a spoiled child, so he whistled his way through his days and ignored her, until she knew her silence wasn't going to change anything.

The first shipment of turkey poults arrived late that spring. Hannah stood in the middle of the sweet-smelling wood shavings and released them from their cardboard prisons, murmuring as she held them to her cheeks. Poor, frightened little birds, having to crouch in those awful cardboard boxes without food or water. She spent all day teaching the frightened poults how to find water and feed. The way they pecked at the wood shavings alarmed her.

Dave stood in the doorway, one elbow propped against the frame, watching her. "Hannah, they'll find the food when they get hungry enough," he told her.

"But, they're so dumb! If they don't stop eating these shavings, they'll die. It doesn't matter how many times I show them where to eat and drink, they forget immediately."

"Just let them go. They'll be all right."

The following morning, eleven turkey chicks lay on their backs with their legs like spindly wax flowers, their eyes closed. Dead. Hannah cried, becoming so upset that she blamed Dave for saying they'd be all right, when they obviously weren't.

Patiently, he explained that some of them would always die. Turkeys were not smart like young chicks were, which couldn't be helped.

He bought a team of Belgians and grew corn and hay, enjoying his days immensely. He wondered why he had thought he didn't like to farm, when this was so much better than moving around crowded Lancaster building things for people who were often too tightfisted to pay the amount his work was worth.

Sarah was born in summer, when the hay lay drying beneath the blazing sun. The old doctor held her upside down and spanked her bottom, until she let out a lusty wail of resentment. "This one's like her mother," he chortled to himself.

For hadn't Hannah led him on a merry chase, the likes of which the poor doctor had never experienced? Unconcerned about any prenatal care and refusing the appointments he made for her, he often had to drive out to their farm and then leave without seeing her. Not that he really minded. He enjoyed driving out to their idyllic little farm tucked between two rolling hills, a windbreak of chestnut and oak trees, and a few white pines. The barn was hip-roofed and painted red. The house was a small, two-story, like a square box with windows, a green shingled roof and green trim around every door and window.

There was a row of hedges along the porch and everything was repaired, painted, and neat. There was a flower garden the size of most folk's truck patch!

Her mother came on the train, arriving on a sweltering August day. She smiled and cooed as she examined her namesake with glad, quiet eyes. She held her, unwrapped her, and said she was a beautiful child. That was high praise from Hannah's stoic mother.

Hannah refused to stay down. When Sarah was five days old, she swept the kitchen, dusted the furniture, and walked out to the turkey barns. She came back white-faced and limp, sat in the rocking chair, and didn't say much that whole afternoon.

Her mother brought news from home. Grandfather Stoltzfus was ailing. He was no longer able to do his everyday chores. Elam and Ben should both be looking for wives. She feared there was something wrong with them, the way they made no attempt to date or even appear interested. Hannah snorted and told her mother to get over it. They were bachelors!

After Sarah left, Hannah was relieved. Now she could do as she pleased, which was exactly what she proceeded to do. She could not stand the way her mother folded clothes, so she went to the baby's changing table and refolded every tiny article of clothing and all of the diapers.

Sarah was not an easy baby. Her stomach cramped. She bent double with spasms of pain, screaming and crying, her face as red as a beet, her eyes squeezed shut, her mouth like a foghorn emitting the most awful yells Hannah had ever heard. Surely there was some remedy, Dave asked, his face white with the sounds of his daughter screaming in pain.

Hadn't he had enough, going through the fear for Hannah and the unborn baby, remembering the agony of losing Lena and the twins? There was Hannah, waltzing through the months before Sarah was born, without a trace of concern. And now, this.

It was more than he could take. He stomped out of the house and stayed out. Hannah was furious! Well, if this was how he was going to be, there would be no more children.

Sarah screamed and yelled her way through the first three months of her life. Well-meaning visitors all recommended a different remedy.

Catnip tea. Chamomile. Comfrey. Massaging the baby's feet. Wrapping her around a table leg. Touch her elbows to her knees. Loosen those muscles. A bit of baking soda to sweeten her stomach. Hannah told Dave if she tried everything they recommended, the baby wouldn't survive.

Suddenly, Sarah stopped crying, looked around with her dark brown eyes, and noticed a ray of sunshine reflected from the colored leaves outside. She rolled over and played with her hands and that was it.

She sat by herself at five months, crawled at six months, and walked by herself at eight. If she was not allowed to have what she wanted, she threw herself on the floor and kicked with all her little might, yelling.

Hannah said she was a mess! Dave watched his wife's face, a small grin playing around his mouth, as he asked, "I wonder why?" Hannah smacked his arm as he reached out for her and pulled her onto his lap, kissing her. He loved her as never before.

Samuel was born the following year, a gentle child with Dave's curly hair already sprouting all over his head like a good stand of alfalfa. He was born at almost ten pounds, his wails normal, his naps long and undisturbed by any gastric churning of his tender digestive system.

A sturdy newborn, he was a quiet baby, content to lay on a blanket, his eyes watching the play of sunbeams through the window panes, waving his large hands in the air and kicking his chunky feet with toes like marbles.

For months, the parents could not decipher Samuel's eye color. Mud, Hannah said. The color of mud. Dave disagreed and said his eyes were the color of dark peppermint tea.

Sarah, who was pronouncing whole sentences by the time she was eighteen months old, kept peering over the side of the crib saying, "*Sayna mol. Sayna mol.* I want to see!"

Hannah kept house with strict discipline for herself. Wash on Monday and Thursday. Iron on Tuesday. Bake bread on Wednesday. Pies and cakes and more bread on Saturday. Clean all day Friday. Every day, morning and evening, she was in the turkey houses, checking the growing turkeys, cleaning waterers, making sure their feed was fresh and clean.

She didn't particularly like the fowl themselves. She often thought of them as stupid and dumb, without much sense, even for a bird. But to be among them, caring for them, was so much better than being among people. At least turkeys didn't judge her or expect her to be someone she wasn't.

She often wondered why she had even tried to be the owner of a dry goods store. She hoped Sadie Lapp was happy after her father purchased the house, the store—everything. So happy to be out of Lancaster County, she walked among the gentle hills of Illinois, a good ten miles to the closest Amish neighbor, adapting to the isolation so quickly that Dave told her he'd never met a person like her.

Hannah felt fulfilled in a way she had never thought possible. The anger still flared, the embers of that fire never quite extinguished. But her bitterness was gone. Its miserable grip on her past that had chafed like an open wound was healed, scabbed over until only a small, unsightly white scar remained.

She still struggled with feeling inadequate, that she was not good enough to pass the inspection of others. The first time they attended church services in the home of Abram and Edna Troyer was nothing short of a punishment.

She began the morning by snapping at Dave who was taking an inordinate amount of time in the bathroom. She slapped little Sarah's fingers when she reached into her oatmeal bowl with her hands, which only served to fill the house with her awful howls of self-pity, which set Samuel to crying.

Until they were seated in the buggy, Hannah was on edge, having rolled and re-rolled her hair so many times her scalp smarted. Her covering looked lopsided and smashed, the strings unable to be tied in a decent bow.

Sarah's dark hair had to be put into "bobbies," those fashionable little rolls of hair twisted around bendable pieces of lead that Dave had flattened with a hammer.

First, Hannah wetted Sarah's black hair, smoothing it down with both hands and plastering it against her scalp, which set up a round of indignant howls of protest. Hannah, already stressed beyond endurance by her inability to comb her own hair just right, reacted to her daughter's howls by a smart cuff on her shoulder. "Stop it, Sarah!" This only brought on more howls, which was the last straw.

"Dave!" He appeared from the bedroom door in his white shirt, buttoning it with his large fingers, an accomplishment Hannah never could figure out given the size of those thick appendages.

"Help me with this."

At her side, he asked what he should do. "Hold her chin so she can't move her head." Grimly, Dave did as he was instructed, gently holding Sarah's face in his giant palms, his daughter's howls increasing when she saw she was outnumbered. Hannah rolled her hair around the lead and doubled back. When he thought everything was finished and he was free to go, Hannah tilted the unhappy child's chin to bring her face close to her own as she focused on the two rolls of hair, unhooking one to start over.

"What in the world?" Dave erupted.

"Don't start, Dave," Hannah said in a low, threatening voice.

And so the morning continued, the ride to church strained with impatience and ill feelings. It was one thing to comb a child's hair in such nonsensical forms, quite another to think everything had to be perfect. At one point he'd asked her if she needed a carpenter's level!

At the Troyer's house, the women standing in a large circle in the kitchen where church services would be held were openly curious, kind-faced and offering to help with the baby. Little Sarah stood at her mother's side, eyeing the women with dark eyes.

Hannah managed to smile, shake hands, greet the women with respect, but mostly kept to herself, offering her friendship to no one.

A young mother named Sally Miller, short, rotund, and happy, spoke more to Hannah than any of the others. She invited Hannah to a quilting the following week, telling her to bring the children. Barbara, her oldest daughter, would love to watch them. Hannah smiled, said all the right things, and had absolutely no intention of going to any quilting. She'd rather swallow a tablespoon of vinegar!

A quilting was a stretched piece of fabric surrounded by a bunch of cackling biddies that all talked at once and no one listened. Hannah couldn't quilt, for one thing, pricking her fingers incessantly and knotting the thread until she had to cut the needle loose.

Sally felt as if she'd made a friend as she chattered happily to her husband about Hannah the whole way home. What a beautiful girl she was! Her little girl looked exactly like her. She remarked how nice Hannah was and how she looked forward to their friendship.

Hannah, on the other hand, slouched against the side of the

buggy and told Dave that if Sally Miller thought she was going to a quilting, she had another think coming.

Dave raised his eyebrows and asked her why not? It would do her good to be among other women.

"If I want to hear a bunch of chatter, I can go out to the turkey barns. Same thing."

Samuel had fallen asleep on her lap. Sarah stood at Hannah's knees taking in the sights, the warm breeze laced with loose horse hair stirring her little bonnet strings.

They drove for miles, the steel wheels crunching on gravel roads, the ditches filled with rain water, dandelion, new grass, bluebells, and columbine. The landscape could only be described as beautiful, Hannah often thought. Mostly level, the land was covered with verdant grass, but enough woods and thickets to create an illusion of patchwork, shades of green so deep and brilliant they hurt Hannah's senses. Windy days, calm days, rain in the form of scattered showers, or hard, week-long clouds that dripped rain as if God had changed His mind about allowing another flood. Sunshine and beauty after the rain filled the land with millions of dew drops like costly diamonds.

Hannah loved Illinois. Here was the isolation she craved, with a compromising land that loved them back in the form of corn and hay, which Dave harvested and stored in the barn. He built a corn crib and filled it to the brim. He bought a herd of ten sheep.

He built fences, fertilized the grass, bought a few Herefords, and the farm was up and running. He marveled at the changes in his life, the contentment. He'd never imagined he wouldn't miss the pace of his carpentry, the dealing with people and the challenge of pleasing each customer.

Dave knew, though, that his wife was his biggest challenge. For sure. Her garden was immense, enough potatoes to last for three years, row after row of green beans and corn. Tomatoes enough for a shipment to a cannery.

Samuel was raised in the garden, sitting among plants like a little rabbit, playing with the cucumbers and beans. Sarah ran among the rows, covered with dirt, pulling out beanstalks with both hands wrapped tightly around the stalks, her heels digging into the soil, her eyes squeezed shut as she bit down her tongue and heaved and tugged, until Hannah spied her and yelled.

Her mother's voice was no threat to Sarah once she was on a mission. She kept tugging mightily, until she felt her mother's presence beside her, the whoosh of her hand and a firm whack on her skinny little bottom. "Stop it, Sarah!" Hannah exclaimed. "Those are not weeds. They're beans!"

"Weeds."

"No, they're not."

"No beans on here."

"There will be later. Leave them alone." And Hannah went back to her weeding. Sarah went back to pulling out the beanstalks, determined to prove her mother wrong.

What to do with an *ungehorsam*, disobedient, child? They could administer all the discipline they wanted but Sarah went her own way, her eyes popping and snapping.

Dave smiled and said there wasn't much Hannah could do; she was her mother's daughter. He imagined Hannah had been the same, a real handful.

The harvest from the garden was a steady flow of vegetables, the blue agate canner on the top of the gas range in constant use, preserving beans, peas and corn, tomatoes, peppers and onions and squash, sliced and shredded into relishes and compotes so that Dave had to build more shelves in the cellar.

Hannah whitewashed the stone walls with a mixture of lime and water, swept the packed earth floor, lined the new shelves with folded paper, carried everything down cellar, and stood back to survey her horn of plenty.

Without being aware of it, the hunger from her past drove her like a slave master. Hannah worked with a ferocious intensity, cutting only the smallest amount from the red beet tops, shaking off the clinging soil from the smallest onions and braiding them together with the larger ones.

Every ear of corn was saved, down to the smallest nubbin, the tip of her paring knife gouging deep holes to extricate the fat worm that feasted on her corn.

The smallest potatoes were sorted, put in Mason jars, and cold-packed for fried potatoes. Late in the fall, she covered the celery and the carrots with mounds of garden soil, a layer of straw heaped around the cabbages that had not been shredded and packed in crocks for sauerkraut.

She hummed and whistled, talked to her children, moved around her kitchen with the speed of a small whirlwind. She grabbed her husband by his heavy shoulders and kissed him after eating an onion, breathing the tainted odor into his face. She laughed and ran for dear life when he growled and came after her, until Sarah shrieked, frightened by the thumping noise of her father's boots.

This was on a good day, when Dave counted his wife among the best women he had ever encountered. He loved her with a fierce passion and thanked God for directing their paths together, in spite of having endured pain and grief.

Sometimes the cloud would descend and cover Hannah like a gray shroud. All conversation would cease, her eyes turn dark, her face morose. He always tried to conjure up the past few days and what he had said or done to bring this on. But, more often than not, he came up empty-handed.

Then he'd go his way, avoiding her as much as possible, enduring the silent meals, the slamming of serving dishes containing half-cooked potatoes and lumpy gravy. She had to crawl out of her foul moods by herself, he soon learned.

And he did what he could to help. He'd take the children out to the barn to play while he did the chores. He made sure the wringer on the washing machine was oiled. He weeded the potatoes. From time to time, he lost his temper and told her she was acting worse than a sullen child and needed a good spanking. That only served to prolong the frigid silence, but he said it anyway.

He came to accept these times, but learned not to tiptoe around her, which was what she wanted. She wanted to control him. He knew that, somehow, he had failed her and this was her way of making his suffer for his shortcomings.

Mostly, however, the sun shone. There was laughter and love and plenty of hard work, a church and community surrounding them like a protective fence.

There was plenty of food. The skies turned gray and showered them with rain. The wind blew and dried the land. Bees hummed from plant to plant and butterflies winged their erratic way from one milkweed pod to the next. There were fat woodchucks in the fence rows, shy deer in the woods behind the barn.

Hannah often thought of the wolves and the coyotes, those lurking, shaggy enemies that had inhabited so many of her thoughts in those long winter months when the snow flew past the kitchen window, hurled by the endless, powerful prairie winds of winter. Sometimes she cringed, patted her full stomach, went down to the cellar and stood, breathing heavily to calm her remembered feelings of panic. The food was there and would stay there. She could always come here to this dank, moist, earthy place and find potatoes and turnips, carrots, and onions. Tears would push to the surface and spill over. Her hand would reach out to touch the smooth, glass jars, feeling the tops of the lids, checking to make sure they were sealed.

Then she would pick up a potato, run her fingers across the

dry, dusty surface of its skin, and replace it carefully before turning to make her way back to the kitchen, feeling reassured.

"Have you ever been hungry?" she asked Dave one evening, adjusting her head on his shoulder as they lay together in bed, the children both tucked in for the night.

"Of course."

"No, I mean, hungry hungry. When you knew there might not be enough to go around. When you went to bed with an empty stomach?"

Dave considered her question. "No, never," he responded. "I have always had enough to eat. Maybe not what I wanted, but something to fill my stomach."

"It's not funny."

"I'm sure it's not."

There was a soft, comfortable silence. Dave stroked his wife's hair, that sleek, heavy mane he loved so much.

"I still shiver when I think of those winters on the prairie. I'll never forget them if I live to be a hundred years old."

"I would be happy to turn a hundred years old with you."

Silence. Then, "I'm not always nice."

"Doesn't matter. I love you." And he was asleep.

Hannah sighed, turning on her side. But sleep would not come. She knew what love was now. She'd figured it out, in her own way. Love was wanting to be with Dave. It was looking forward to mealtimes with him, craving the closeness of him, loving everything about him. The way he walked, the way he brushed his teeth and drank a glass of water. The way he ate a slice of bread in two gigantic gulps.

She felt his magnetic power, the physical pull of his strength. She felt less than him, conquered by him. She also had an emotional need that only he could fill. But this was her own knowledge, hidden away, never to be revealed.

Dave was no-nonsense, abrupt and businesslike, often

leaving her scrambling for security, a sense of trust and belonging. When she felt her handhold on this safety crumble, the dark cloud would descend and she was far too proud to ask for the reassurance of his love.

Wasn't she Hannah? The proud, the powerful woman who didn't need a man to make her happy? And underneath that thin veneer, a week and needy person resided, longing for his time, his attention, his caring. He was her light, her cornerstone.

Well . . . God and Jesus Christ first, of course. That relationship was on better ground than it had ever been. But Hannah figured that Dave came a close second.

CHAPTER 24

Seasons came and went. They planted and harvested, lived in the cold of winter and the warmth of summer. The turkey poults grew and were sold for a good profit. They were fed on corn raised in the fertile, rolling earth. The sheep multiplied and were shorn by the traveling Scottish sheepshearers, the wool sold for another fair amount of cash. The cattle grew fat and lazy. The yearling calves were hauled off to the livestock auction, resulting in a good check that came in the mail a week later.

Hannah planted lilac bushes and forsythia in a long row along the north side of the yard. She planted tulips, irises, daffodils, climbing roses that made a bower along the porch posts on either side of the stone walkway. All spoke of her love of beauty, the appreciation of the finer things in life.

She mowed and trimmed her yard. She fretted about moles and dandelions. She raked every wisp of hay from the driveway after Dave had hauled in the day's work from the fields.

The barn grew. Dave built an annex to the simple framed structure, then added a silo to house corn silage for fattening the steers in winter. He built another corn crib and an implement shed.

Sarah and Samuel went to school when Sarah was seven and Samuel was almost six. Samuel brought home report cards that made Hannah proud. Sarah's were wrinkled and torn, streaked with mud or food stains, peppered with Bs and Cs. Notes from frustrated teachers almost always fluttered to the ground from between the fold of the report card.

Emma was born two years after Samuel, a winsome child with straight dark hair so much like her sister's. When Rudy arrived, they had their hands full once more, his screams and wails echoing through the house until Hannah thought she would surely lose her sanity. Unprepared, with Rudy still screeching at the top of his lungs, Suvilla was born less than a year later.

This was Hannah's personal North Dakota. Here was her biggest challenge. So, she took the bit in her mouth and rose to meet it with the same determination that she did everything else.

If loving Dave produced all of these little ones, then she guessed it was God's will, finally absorbing some of that spirituality for herself. If the baby cried and she got precious little sleep, well, then, so be it. She rose at five o'clock and drank cup after cup of scalding black coffee and did loads of laundry she hand-fed through the wringer she turned herself. She built a roaring fire to heat the *elsa kessle* of cold water to boiling, adding lye soap and stirring the whole load with a stick, after she filled the gasoline engine and yanked it to life with its cord.

She took pride in achieving the whitest whites, bed linens and underwear, socks and nighties as white as the pure winter snow. She washed diapers by the dozens, took pride in the way they hung straight, bringing them in to fold on the kitchen table and thinking how Abner Troyer's wife, Lydia, asked how she got her diapers to look like new. Hannah had cast a disgusted look at the stained, yellow diaper in Lydia's hand and told her flat out she didn't use enough soap or wash them long enough. And, her hot water was not hot enough.

Lydia pinned the diaper on her baby, blinked, and mumbled something about the soap she got from her mother-in-law. But

Hannah knew better. Lydia was fat and lazy. She'd rather make doughnuts and eat them then do her washing. *That's what happens, Lydia*, she thought and sniffed indignantly as she moved off.

In some ways, Hannah remained the same, even as the years rolled by. She went to church faithfully, crowding into the buggy with her growing family every two weeks, except when one of the children became ill. She visited with the women of her church group, even laughed and smiled at the affairs of their community, the idle news and the gossip. But no matter how hard the young women tried to include her in their quiltings and Sunday evening suppers, she never went.

Dave wanted to go sometimes and told Hannah so. "Then go," she'd say. "Go ahead. I don't care." Sometimes he did, especially when the supper was held at the home of his favorite friend, Emanuel Stutzman.

They were both sheep farmers. Both enjoyed prosperity after the years of the Great Depression. Both enjoyed cattle auctions and a good game of checkers. Hannah couldn't stand Emanuel's wife. Thin, simpering, and just plain dumb, she'd bet Sarah was smarter at seven years old. For one thing, whoever heard of a name like Fronie? Maybe it wasn't her fault that her parents named her that, but she could come up with a more suitable nickname. If you didn't have the blues when you met her, you would afterward, the way she complained about everything from her tail bone to her sore eyes, her grouchy baby and her husband's foot odor. It was enough to make Hannah want to run out the door.

Dave suggested that Hannah could help her, perhaps give her some kindhearted, understanding tips about all her troubles. "She needs a good kick on her bottom, that's what," Hannah snorted. "Maybe if she'd do her work and quit rubbing that Watkin's salve over everything—her sore shoulder, her nostrils. You can smell the camphor before you see her!"

Dave didn't think it was funny. He told Hannah that her lack of compassion was frightening. He was afraid she'd have to pay for it someday, that God is not mocked.

"I don't pity people, no. The women especially. They need to get to work and quit their whining. Life is never easy. Get over it." And she pounded her bread dough and set it to rise.

Dave sat in the kitchen and watched his wife's strong shoulders, her muscular arms, and he thought, no, sometimes marriage wasn't easy. She made him angry with her refusal to socialize. He'd love to have a normal wife who would look forward to spending an evening giggling and talking, sharing recipes, trading fabric and buttons the way they did back home when he was a small boy. His mother loved a good game of Parcheesi and a round of Rook, becoming boisterous when they spent another evening with Roman Yoders.

So, if he would give his life for his wife, loving her the way Christ loved the church, did that mean he would always have to stay home, with no social life at all? He told Hannah that they were still young and he didn't want to stay at home all the time. This was after Emanuel told him to bring his family after the first snowfall. They would make homemade ice cream.

If there was anything Dave loved, it was hand-churned peanut butter ice cream. Hannah listened from the armless rocker, peering up at him with bleary eyes that were swollen and sleep-deprived, the tip of a diaper strung with other laundry from a line above the stove tickling her head. Suvilla threw a stream of milk across her shoulder, then arched her back and howled like a hyena.

She laid Suvilla calmly on the floor, stretched to her full height, looked Dave in the eye, and told him if he didn't shut up about Emanuel Stutzman and his ice cream freezer, she'd leave him.

"If you can't see farther than your own nose, all right then, go!" Dave answered, so angry he couldn't see straight.

They didn't go to the Stutzmans'. Hannah walked around the house thumping her heels, her chin in the air, and didn't speak. That was fine with Dave, who had no intention of bringing any warmth to the arctic atmosphere pervading the house.

Guilty about their own lack of forgiveness, they paid extra attention to the little ones, reading them stories and drawing pictures with them, without a word passing between Hannah and Dave.

The snow fell, the wind blew, the temperature dropped to below zero. But Dave stayed in the barn, determined to worry Hannah. She'd feel sorry for being so bullheaded.

Hannah clattered dishes and hoped Dave's toes would freeze. It was time he stopped being so selfish. Couldn't he see that she wasn't getting her rest, with Suvilla awake every two hours and not settling down for another hour? No, of course he couldn't. He was sound asleep, snoring like a truck without a muffler.

How could he? And a whole new set of self-pitying feelings took hold of her.

Who broke the silence then? They were never quite sure. They missed each other eventually, so one of them would comment on the weather, the sick ewe, the baby's cough. And, if there was a response, they knew they were on the way out of the silence, which was a huge relief. Laughter and conversation were restored and the good life resumed with stolen kisses and cuffs on the shoulder, fond, smoldering glances and little whirls of heady joy that neither one understood.

From time to time, Dave stood his ground and thundered an obstinate refusal to Sarah's incompetent plans. Things that made no sense. No, he would not build rabbit hutches on the north side of the barn, regardless of what she'd promised Sarah. Rabbits needed sunshine, especially morning sun.

Sarah whined and begged and balled her little fists, pounding his pants leg, whereupon she got a few spanks from his enormous, calloused hand and was told to go sit on the couch until she straightened up.

Hannah was furious but she was well-taught. For a mother to take the disobedient child's part was calling for heartache and sorrow. To turn children against their father was a slippery slope leading to disrespect, which led to more blatant disobedience. So she said nothing, although she thought she'd die of heart failure right then and there from all the belligerence churning in her chest.

He hadn't even heard her out. Rabbits did well on the north side of a building in summer, when the nights were cool and they were shaded from the day's heat. What did he know about rabbits? Probably nothing. She cried that evening when he told her she needed to speak with him about something like rabbit hutches before making any promises to Sarah. It wasn't fair to their daughter to punish her for her reactions.

Why did a husband's words mean so much, though? When Dave said what he thought, the words were heavy and became uncomfortably embedded in her conscience and stuck in her thoughts regardless of how often she told herself she didn't care what he thought. She cared an awful lot, no matter if she brushed it off or not. So, Sarah had no rabbits that summer.

When Suvilla stopped her incessant crying, Hannah thanked God with a grateful heart. She resumed her work with her usual bursts of energy, painted the porch floor with gray enamel paint, so shiny it looked wet. Dave built a porch swing and added an extra two by four to the ceiling joist, hanging the swing with sturdy hooks.

With the profusion of purple lilacs, the irises, and roses, Hannah's porch swing was her evening paradise, a vacation from her hard work and the constant childcare that consumed each day. She would sit, idly pushing the swing with one foot, an arm slung across the back, listening to the sounds of the robins' frenzied chirping as they settled themselves for the night.

She always hoped that Dave would join her, and often he did. She loved these warm evenings when the children played in the yard and the swing would groan under his bulk. They would talk, share their day, and make future plans. Hannah would reach over to straighten his collar, to lift a piece of hay from his beard, hoping he would capture her hand and hold it.

For Hannah did love her husband with an adoration that bordered on worship. Most of the time. But submitting to someone's will other than her own was a monumental task, one that drained her energy, often taking away the sunshine from her existence.

She wished someone would have told her the inordinate amount of giving up that was included in the headiness of romance. How many young girls were swept off their feet by the good looks of an ardent suitor, courted politely under the strict eyes of their parents, married in a godly ceremony that promised days of sunshine and rain? The minister could have included tornadoes and hurricanes and flash floods, in their case!

But she knew she'd do it all over again. Have all these babies, work on the farm with Dave. It was the challenge of a lifetime and, increasingly, a deep contentment and peace she could never really figure out.

She loved the farm and she loved Illinois.

When church services were announced to be held at Dave King's, Hannah felt the same lurch of excitement she always felt. Here were two weeks of *rishting*, preparation for services to be held in their home on a lovely Sunday in May. At least she hoped it would be lovely. Hannah had long planned the display of her flowers, her yard mowed, raked, and trimmed, flower beds without one weed, the soil hoed and loosened with fresh petunias planted in small clumps. The women would walk along the stone pathway to the house, thinking how Hannah was a talented frau, everything so neat and presentable, the growth of flowers amazing.

She washed walls, yanked beds apart, and cleaned the frames and slats with strong-smelling soap. She poured baking soda on mattresses, wiped the steel bedspring coils, washed quilts and blankets, sheets and pillow cases, hanging them on her sturdy wash line. She thanked God for Dave's clothesline poles, thinking she'd be able to hang a ton of clothes on those lines and the poles wouldn't even bend.

She polished windows with vinegar water and clean muslin cloths. She yanked dressers away from walls, upended chairs and small stands, threw articles of clothing from the drawers, and wiped them with the same odorous soap. Not a corner of a closet or drawer went uncleaned. Not a ladybug or a spider remained safe.

Hannah cleaned all day every day and made cold sandwiches for Dave at lunch time. She slapped bean soup on the table for supper. The children were put to bed early so Hannah could collapse on the couch for a moment, her shoulders aching, her lower back on fire with pain.

Dave told her he'd rub it with horse liniment, which brought a snort of mammoth proportions. Everyone stayed out of Hannah's way, even the unruly Sarah, who took pity on Suvilla with her wet diaper and her runny nose, standing in the middle of the kitchen and howling to herself with her mother nowhere about when they got home from school.

Sarah wiped Suvilla's nose, laid her on the floor, and changed her diaper. Then she gave her saltine crackers to eat, all the while glaring at her mother for being so negligent.

They had a colossal argument. Dave wanted to hold services in the house, spring weather being unpredictable the way it was. Hannah insisted on the barn. Why not? It would save him so much work not having to clear out the furniture before setting the long wooden benches in place.

"All you have to do is spread clean straw, sweep cobwebs, and we're ready. The weather is unseasonably warm, Dave."

"It is this week. It's May, Hannah. Anything can happen, and usually does."

"I've never seen a pessimist like you."

"Why can't you give up, Hannah?"

"Because, it doesn't make any sense. It's warm enough to hold the service in the barn. The bays are almost empty. I can take the food and dishes out on Saturday and the house will stay untouched."

"What if it turns cold and rainy? No, we're going to hold services in the house."

With that certain look—his nostrils slightly flared, his amber eyes wide, his temper like a boiling cauldron beneath his compressed lips—Hannah knew there would be no budging.

She tried anyway. The children were in bed and they felt free to state their minds, which soon drifted from the subject at hand to other accusations, darts of demeaning epithets, genuine mud-slinging, resulting in Dave slamming the screen door, breaking the latch, and Hannah crying great bursts of tears, awash in self-pity and burning rebellion.

Neither one admitted their lack of sleep the following morning. They spoke in clipped tones at the breakfast table, asking only what was absolutely necessary, a half-strangled reply from the other.

She kept on cleaning, mowed the yard, washed the porch, and baked twenty-six snitz pies from the dried apples she'd stored in the pantry over winter. She mixed the peanut butter with molasses, made cup cheese from the crumbles she'd prepared beforehand, and opened ten quarts of sweet pickles and six quarts of spiced red beets.

And still Dave did not give in. Church services would be held in the house. It was so completely against her wishes that it was like taking a mouthful of warmed, slimy cod liver oil.

Grimly, she helped him move furniture. She couldn't stand the sight of his unruly mop of hair. Every time she gave him a bowl haircut, he looked like a tulip bulb. She still hadn't figured out why his face looked so out of proportion.

When had she ever thought this man handsome? Certainly not now as he tugged red-faced at yet another heavy piece of furniture that could have stayed exactly where it was if he'd listened to her.

On Sunday morning the temperature on the John Deere thermometer tacked to the porch post had the mercury somewhere between 30 and 40 degrees. Hannah had tumbled out of bed at four o'clock, shivering, the floor cold to her bare feet.

Wide-eyed and startled into speech, she told Dave perhaps they should start a fire in the living room. Before daylight, Hannah heard a roar, like distant rolling thunder, except there was no let up.

From the porch, she saw the cold rain that slanted in from the east, driven by a stiff wind. The dawn was gray and eerie, the moaning of the wind like a correctional ghost admonishing her to be grateful for once in her life, for her husband's good judgment.

The irises hung their soggy heads in the driving rain. The roses lost their red petals in the harsh wind. The lilacs waved and nodded, thoroughly soaked and battered by the cold rain.

Women scuttled up the stone walkway, their black bonnets pulled well past their faces, clutching babies and small baskets containing diapers and milk bottles, raisins and saltines for cranky little ones. Not one of them noticed the perfectly trimmed yard, the groomed flower beds, or the profusion of flowers planted according to Hannah's exact specifications. Every one that stepped from the buggy into the lashing torrent had one objective and that was to get to the house as swiftly as possible.

A warm fire burned in the cooking range, another one in the living room. Women held out their hands to the warmth, appreciating that the service would be held in the cozy house. Hannah smiled and nodded and kept her secret. No one would ever pry the fact out of her that she had tried to make the service be held in the barn.

Unbelievable, this weather. It was May. But she seated the women, sat erect with Suvilla on her lap, her face carefully arranged to appear caring and friendly. She was more than glad she had listened to Dave.

The minister droned on for an unspeakably long time. Hannah mostly worried about the coffee and whether the cheese would be too runny to spread on the bread. If the pie crust was hard or reasonably flaky.

Long after the last song had been sung, the tables set and re-set, everyone cleared out and Hannah sagged with relief into the armless rocker. Dave came in and stood in front of her, grinning. "So Hannah, weren't you glad you listened to me?"

"Go away. Just go and stop bothering me." But she had to smile in spite of herself.

And so the lives of Dave and Hannah King progressed through the years. A total of ten children joined their family by the time Hannah reached the age of forty-three, each one loved and cherished in her own way.

Samuel and Rudy followed their father's ways, but none of his boys ever grew to his size or stature. He remained the giant father figure, but a fair and level-headed one.

Daniel, Ezra, and Noah were in a line, all looking up to *Dat* with respect and even reverence. Noah had the same wild, untamed mop of hair as his father, his amber eyes and large hands and feet.

With Hannah's temperament, he was a genuine troublemaker

in school and in church, bloodying the nose of more than one boy older than himself. He swaggered, he spit, and went by the name of "Max." And yet, somehow, in spite of the thread of headstrong natures running between mother and father, they raised their brood in the Amish faith.

They all acted up as teenagers, bringing sleepless nights and humbling Hannah in a way that no horrific events of her lifetime ever had. The homestead in the West had been a constant chain of life's lessons, but not one of them served to smooth the rough edges of her personality the way her children did.

Sarah resisted all of her mother's advice. She pouted around the house and refused any form of discipline. She was quick to speak and quick to judge, the despair of Hannah's life until she decided, painfully, that we reap what we sow. It seemed her life was one constant flashback. Shot through with fiery remorse, Hannah begged forgiveness for her past and was rewarded with a spirit of humility, a sweetness in her nature of which she was quite unaware.

She went to quiltings and auctions, shook hands warmly and met people's gazes with friendly eyes and genuine caring. She stopped talking about innocent women who did not quite measure up to her standards.

Her hair turned gray. She threaded her hand through the crook of Dave's elbow as they stood by the woven wire fence, watching the baby lambs on a fine spring morning. All around them the earth bloomed. Dogwoods, redbuds, crab apple, cherry and apple blossoms opened and sang to God's glory. The woods were thick with new green leaves, burdock, plantain, dandelion, and thistle. Small creatures rattled the heavy plants and skittered away as the aging couple walked along the fence.

"Our homestead," Hannah whispered.

Dave patted the hand on his arm and turned his amber eyes

on her dark ones. "Yes, Hannah. Our homestead. Our place here on earth. I have never regretted a minute of our union."

Hannah snorted. "Oh, come on, Dave."

"I still love you. Even more now that we're older. I'm serious."

She held the gaze that still caused her knees to turn liquid, the unspoken language of love that had carried them through the rough times as well as the joyous ones.

The spring breeze sighed as he bent to kiss her, his wrinkled eyes filling with tears of gratitude and appreciation for his beloved.

The sun slid behind the thick, green forest, casting an ethereal light on the undulating farmland, bathing the white farmhouse and the red barn in a golden glow.

Hannah laid her head on her husband's shoulder, saw the perfect morning glow over the farm, and whispered again, "My homestead. My home where contentment and love reign."

THE END

GLOSSARY

an schöena ovat—a nice evening
an shauty soch—a sad thing
begräbniss—burial
Bisht die Hannah?—Are you Hannah?
Dat, doo kannsht net—Dad, you can't do that
demut—humility
demütich—humble
denke—thank you
dichly—kerchief
duchsach—fabric
eisa kessle—iron kettle
forehaltiss—future plans
freuheita—freedoms
gehorsam—obedient
gehorsamkeit—obedience
grosfeelich—proud
gute—good
hals schtark—determined
Herr saya—God's blessing
hochzeit velssa—wedding songs
Hott sie ken schema?—Has she no shame?
Iss eya net an bei kumma?—Is he not appearing?

ivva reck—overcoats

Kum yusht rei—Come on in

lied—song

Machets goot, Dat—Stay well, Dad

ordnung—Literally, "ordinary," or "discipline," it refers to an Amish community's agreed-upon rules for living, based on the Bible, particularly the New Testament. The *ordnung* can vary in small ways from community to community, reflecting the leaders' interpretations, local traditions, and historical practices.

rishting—preparing

roasht—a chicken and bread casserole

rumschpringa—Literally, "running around." A time of relative freedom for adolescents, beginning at about age sixteen. The period ends when a youth is baptized and joins the church, after which the youth can marry.

Sayna mol—I want to see

schnitz un knepp—dried apples cooked with chunks of home-cured ham and spices, with a covering of thick, floury dumplings called *knepp*

schputt—mockery

schtrāling—combing with a fine-toothed comb

smear kase—cup cheese

ungehorsam—disobedient

Vie bisht?—How are you?

vie ihr Dat—like her father

Vilt. See harriched net—Wild. She doesn't listen

Vos iss lets mit sie?—What is wrong with her?

OTHER BOOKS BY
LINDA BYLER

LIZZIE SEARCHES FOR LOVE SERIES

BOOK ONE

BOOK TWO

BOOK THREE

TRILOGY

COOKBOOK

SADIE'S MONTANA SERIES

BOOK ONE

BOOK TWO

BOOK THREE

TRILOGY

LANCASTER BURNING SERIES

BOOK ONE

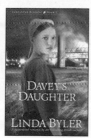

BOOK TWO

BOOK THREE

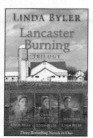

TRILOGY

HESTER'S HUNT FOR HOME SERIES

BOOK ONE

BOOK TWO

BOOK THREE

THE LITTLE AMISH
MATCHMAKER

THE CHRISTMAS
VISITOR

MARY'S CHRISTMAS
GOODBYE

BECKY MEETS HER
MATCH

A DOG FOR
CHRISTMAS

THE DAKOTA SERIES

BOOK ONE

BOOK TWO

BOOK THREE

ABOUT THE AUTHOR

LINDA BYLER WAS RAISED IN AN AMISH FAMILY AND IS AN ACTIVE member of the Amish church today. She writes all her novels by hand in a notebook. Linda is well-known within the Amish community as a columnist for a weekly Amish newspaper.

Linda is the author of five series of novels, all set among the Amish communities of North America: Lizzie Searches for Love, Sadie's Montana, Lancaster Burning, Hester's Hunt for Home, and the Dakota Series. Linda has also written five Christmas romances set among the Amish: *Mary's Christmas Goodbye, The Christmas Visitor, The Little Amish Matchmaker, Becky Meets Her Match*, and *A Dog for Christmas*. Linda has coauthored *Lizzie's Amish Cookbook: Favorite Recipes from Three Generations of Amish Cooks*!